This book belongs to

....

....

A Study in Scarlet
and other stories

A Study in Scarlet
and other stories

Arthur Conan Doyle

WORTH PRESS

SIGNATURE CLASSICS

First published in 2019 by Worth Press Ltd, Bath, England
Email: worthpress@btconnect.com

Concept, design, introduction, reset text and coloured images of this edition
© Worth Press Ltd, 2019

British Library Cataloguing in Publication Data
A catalogue record for this book is available from the British Library

ISBN: 978-1-84931-166-3

10 9 8 7 6 5 4 3 2 1

Publisher's Note   Every effort has been made to ensure the accuracy of the
information presented in this book. The publisher will not assume liability for damages
caused by inaccuracies in the data and makes no warranty whatsoever expressed or
implied. The publisher welcomes comments and corrections from readers, emailed
to worthpress@btconnect.com, which will be considered for incorporation in future
editions. Every effort has been made to trace copyright holders and seek permission
to use illustrative and other material. The publisher wishes to apologize for any
inadvertent errors or omissions and would be glad to rectify these in future editions.

The images used in this book come from either the public domain or from the public
commons unless otherwise stated.

Page Resetting: IDSUK Ltd
Images coloured by Chandra Creative and Content Solutions
Cover and Front Matter Design: Jess Moon

Printed and bound in China

Contents

Holmes and Watson: A Study in Friendship   vii

    MATTHEW BOOTH

Sherlock's London   xviii

    DAVID STUART DAVIS

A Study in Scarlet *Principal Characters*   xxviii

A Conan Doyle Timeline   xxxiv

London – The Setting of A Study in Scarlet   xxxviii

A STUDY IN SCARLET   1

THE SIGN OF THE FOUR   121

THE SPECKLED BAND   237

STORIES FROM *THE ADVENTURES OF SHERLOCK HOLMES*

    THE ADVENTURE OF THE ENGINEER'S THUMB   266

    THE ADVENTURE OF THE NOBLE BACHELOR   288

    THE ADVENTURE OF THE BERYL CORONET   311

    THE ADVENTURE OF THE COPPER BEECHES   337

STORIES FROM *MEMOIRS OF SHERLOCK HOLMES*

    THE ADVENTURE OF THE YELLOW FACE   364

    THE ADVENTURE OF THE STOCKBROKER'S CLERK   383

    THE ADVENTURE OF THE *GLORIA SCOTT*   402

Matthew Booth is the author of *Sherlock Holmes and the Giant's Hand*, published by Breese Books and the co-author of *The Further Exploits of Sherlock Holmes*, a collection of new stories, commissioned by Sparkling Books in 2016. He contributed two original Holmes stories to *The Game is Afoot*, a collection of Sherlock Holmes short stories published in 2008 by Wordsworth Editions and contributed a story to Wordsworth Editions' collection of original crime tales, *Crime Scenes*. Matthew is the creator of Anthony Rathe, a disgraced former barrister seeking redemption by solving those crimes which come his way. The character first appeared in a series of radio plays produced and syndicated by Imagination Theatre in America. Rathe now appears in *When Anthony Rathe Investigates* published by Sparkling Books. A lifelong devotee of crime and supernatural fiction, Matthew has provided a number of academic talks on such subjects as Sherlock Holmes, the works of Agatha Christie, crime fiction, Count Dracula, and the facts and theories concerning the crimes of Jack the Ripper. He is also a member of the Crime Writers' Association and a contributor to their monthly newsletter, *Red Herrings*.

David Stuart Davies is an author, playwright and editor. His fiction includes six novels featuring his wartime detective Johnny Hawke, Victorian puzzle solver Luther Darke, and nine Sherlock Holmes novels, the latest being *Sherlock Holmes and The Ripper Legacy*. *Sherlock Holmes and the Instrument of Death* is due to be published in 2020. His most recent novel is *Oliver Twist and The Mystery of Throate Manor*. His non-fiction work includes *Starring Sherlock Holmes*, detailing the film career of the Baker Street sleuth. David is regarded as an authority on Sherlock Holmes and is the author of three Holmes stage plays, *Sherlock Holmes: The Last Act, Sherlock Holmes: The Death and Life* and *Sherlock Holmes: The Last Testament*. David has also penned three dark gritty crime novels set in Yorkshire in the 1980s. He is a committee member of the Crime Writers' Association and edits their monthly publication *Red Herrings*. His collection of ghost and horror stories, *The Halloween Mask*, appeared in 2015, championed by Mark Gatiss who said they were 'pleasingly nasty'. David is General Editor of Wordsworth's Mystery & Supernatural series and also contributes a monthly blog on classic novels for the Wordsworth website. He is a past Fellow of the Royal Literary Fund and has appeared at many literary festivals and the Edinburgh Fringe performing his one-man presentation *The Game's Afoot – an evening with Sherlock Holmes and Arthur Conan Doyle*. David is also a member of the famed Detection Club.

Holmes and Watson:
A Study in Friendship
Matthew Booth

The fictional construct of the dominant hero and faithful sidekick is now so popular that it is almost impossible to imagine any form of entertainment where a variation of it does not appear. The examples are too numerous to list exhaustively, but one thinks of Poirot and Hastings, Morse and Lewis, Starsky and Hutch, even Batman and Robin. The tried and tested formula of a pair of opposites who complement each other in order to produce a formidable whole is so widely recognized today that it is almost taken for granted, so much so that it is easy to forget that the foundations for it were laid in the Sherlock Holmes stories of Sir Arthur Conan Doyle. There is perhaps no friendship in literature more enduring or more famous than the one between the detective and the doctor who shared those rooms at 221B Baker Street.

The relationship between Holmes and Watson does not appear fully formed in the stories. Like the characters themselves, it develops over the course of the four novels and 56 short stories which comprise what is known as the Sherlock Holmes canon. They first meet in the 1887 novella *A Study in Scarlet*, and in those initial stages of the relationship, they are wary of each other. The partnership is not formed instantaneously. Holmes interviews his various clients alone, having begged for the use of the sitting-room, forcing Watson to retire to the privacy of his own bedroom. He apologizes for Watson's inconvenience, explaining that: 'I have to use this room as a place of business, and these people are my clients.' Conversely, Watson feels unable to ask Holmes what his profession is and why these disparate visitors from all walks of life come to visit his new acquaintance. As Watson confesses, 'I had an opportunity of asking [Holmes] a point-blank question, and again my delicacy prevented me from forcing another man to confide in me.' This reticence on Watson's part and the similarly restrained attitude of Holmes thaw throughout the course of the stories, to the extent that in his introduction to one of their final cases together, 'The Creeping Man', Watson clearly states that their relationship has developed significantly from those early, hesitant times:

> 'The relations between us in those latter days were peculiar. He was a man of habits, narrow and concentrated habits, and I had become one of them. As an institution, I was like the violin, the shag tobacco, the old black pipe, the index books, and others perhaps less excusable. ... I was a whetstone for his mind. I stimulated him. He liked to think aloud in my presence. ... Such was my humble role in our alliance.'

Similarly, only a few years later, Holmes himself confesses that 'at this period of my life, the good Watson had passed almost beyond my ken. An occasional weekend visit was the most I ever saw of him.' ('The Lion's Mane'). These melancholy, almost elegiac, contemplations of the bond between them, told from respective points of view, are a far cry from the polite caution between Holmes and Watson in *A Study in Scarlet*. It is perhaps reflective of Conan Doyle's genius that he permitted the friendship between Holmes and Watson to change with the passing of time. Very few relationships remain constant and, despite Holmes calling Watson 'the one fixed point in a changing age', the friendship between these two characters is no different. It is a note of verisimilitude, an accurate portrait of a very human relationship, which elevates these stories above most, if not all, other crime fiction.

It is fair to say that not all of the Sherlock Holmes stories are ideal, either as detective stories or as tales of adventure. It has been said before that these are not detective fiction in the sense that Agatha Christie meant it; Holmes does not deal primarily with bodies in libraries of old retired colonels, or with murder in sleepy English villages, all solved with minimal fuss before afternoon tea in the vicarage garden. The Holmes stories have much more in common with the American 'hard-boiled' school of crime fiction, with murder committed for plausible human reasons and 'not just to provide a corpse', as Raymond Chandler once complained. Furthermore, they are stories set in Doyle's contemporary and recognizable world, instead of Christie's sanitized and fictional version of hers. And yet, the grind of having to produce plot after plot month after month took its toll on Doyle's imagination. Some of the stories falter in comparison with others but not one of them is without interest or satisfaction and that is due primarily to the interplay between the two main characters. Where the plots might stumble occasionally, the characters of Holmes and Watson do not, so that even if some of its parts may seem weaker than the others, the canon as a whole is bound together firmly by the relationship between the doctor and the detective. It is this growing comradeship which compels us to read and re-read the stories time and time again.

But what binds together Holmes and Watson?

On the face of it, neither of them appear to be sociable men. Newly arrived in London, having been invalided out of the army, Watson confesses to the reader in *A Study in Scarlet* that 'I had neither kith nor kin in England ... and I had no friends who would call upon me and break the monotony of my daily existence.' Similarly, when a client calls at 221B on a particularly dark and stormy night in 'The Five Orange Pips', Watson expresses surprise that someone should be calling so late. He suggests it might be some friend of Holmes, to which the detective replies, 'Except yourself, I have none. ... I do not encourage visitors.' And yet, these two seemingly unsociable and friendless men make an exception for each other. The question is, why?

For Watson, part of the attraction of his friendship with Holmes was the opportunity to witness genius first-hand: 'I had no keener pleasure than in following Holmes in his professional investigations and in admiring the rapid deductions, as swift as intuitions and yet always founded on a logical basis, with which he unravelled the problems which were submitted to him.' ('The Speckled Band'). On the other hand,

Holmes recognized the importance and benefit of having Watson by his side. In 'The Man with the Twisted Lip', Holmes confesses that 'a trusty comrade is always of use; and a chronicler still more so', before telling Watson that he has 'a grand gift of silence. It makes you quite invaluable as a companion.' Likewise, Holmes advises Sir Henry Baskerville that Watson's value as a companion cannot be underestimated: '...there is no man who is better worth having at your side when you are in a tight place. No one can say so more confidently than I.'

And yet, the relationship's success was due, as Holmes himself might have said, to something deeper and more subtle than this mutual appreciation of the other's superficial qualities. What is central to the enduring quality of the association between Holmes and Watson is their mutual dependency on each other, which in itself is a product of their disparate natures. There is an understanding between the two men, of each other, and of their respective needs. Like any successful partnership, Holmes and Watson tolerate the other's deficiencies as well as praising their strengths. The two of them do not always see eye to eye. An admiration of Holmes's talents does not prevent Watson from expressing displeasure or disagreement with some of Holmes's actions. Again, it is a note of authenticity injected into the relationship by Doyle perhaps to counteract some of the more outrageous and incredible plots.

Watson's initial assessment, in *A Study in Scarlet*, that Holmes was 'not a difficult man to live with' was soon dispelled by time. By the time of *The Sign of the Four*, Watson has discovered that Holmes was mercurial, that he could be 'bright, eager, and in excellent spirits, a mood which in his case alternated with fits of the blackest depression'. Watson had to learn to live with Holmes's intense egotism, which he confesses in 'The Copper Beeches' was not only a strong factor in Holmes's nature but one which Watson found repellent. His life with Holmes was, by his own admission, often tiresome and Watson discovered through it that he was perhaps a more patient man than he might otherwise have realized: 'I believe that I am one of the most long-suffering of mortals,' he stated in *The Valley of Fear* after Holmes has interrupted his own thoughts with a sardonic remark. That Holmes was a difficult man to tolerate is not an opinion solely applicable to Watson. Mrs Hudson, we are told in 'The Dying Detective', was just as long-suffering as Watson, coping as she did with 'the worst tenant in London'. It is not an unjustifiable accusation. In 'The Musgrave Ritual', Watson sets out some of Holmes's less salubrious tendencies, including keeping cigars in the coal-scuttle, tobacco in his Persian slipper, and unanswered correspondence skewered to the mantelpiece by a jack-knife. It is a testament to Watson's credibility and patience that he is able not only to confess that he is no saint insofar as tidiness is concerned but that he can be tolerant of these idiosyncrasies to a certain degree. On the subject of Holmes's untidy personal habits, Watson says: 'Not that I am in the least conventional in that respect myself. The rough-and-tumble work in Afghanistan...has made me rather more lax than befits a medical man. But with me there is a limit...' That limit is Holmes's insistence on indoor pistol practice. In a sardonic remark of his own, Watson condemns Holmes's patriotic adornment of the wall with a bullet-holed 'V.R.' by saying that 'neither the atmosphere nor the appearance of our room was improved by it.'

Perhaps Watson's greatest dispute with Holmes was the detective's use of cocaine during periods of inactivity, a habit to which the doctor objected vehemently. He confesses that he 'had learned to dread such periods of inaction, for I knew by experience that my companion's brain was so abnormally active that it was dangerous to leave it without material upon which to work' ('The Missing Three Quarter'). It is Watson who convinces Holmes to abandon the drug, as he notes in the same story: 'For years I had gradually weaned him from that drug mania which had once threatened to check his remarkable career... but I was well aware that the fiend was not dead, but sleeping; and I have known that the sleep was a light one.'

The cocaine habit is one of the most misunderstood aspects of the Holmes stories. Too often, filmmakers or pastiche writers seek to portray Holmes as a hopeless drug addict. The effect is to trivialize the dramatic importance of Holmes's use of cocaine, so that it becomes little more than a sensational gimmick or a cheap and unnecessary thrill. Doyle's use of the cocaine habit is much more subtle and effective. It is a weakness in an otherwise indestructible Holmes. Without it, Holmes is in danger of being entirely remote from his audience, too perfect and too in control. A hero without a flaw is an unsatisfying dramatic construct which allows no room for growth and the use of cocaine permits Doyle to show a crack in Holmes's marble, a human weakness in an otherwise calculating machine. To Holmes, cocaine is an uncontrollable urge which he seeks to justify as a means to escape lethargy, because he claims it is 'transcendently clarifying and stimulating to the mind that its secondary action is a matter of small moment'. It is left to Watson to voice the more pragmatic and scientific effect of the drug: 'It is a pathological and morbid process, which involves increased tissue-change and may at last leave a permanent weakness.' The use of cocaine is much more than a tawdry flouting of a social taboo. It is a literary device constructed by Doyle to demonstrate the difference between the two men: Holmes, with his rarefied and esoteric brain, approaching the drug as some sort of mental elixir against boredom; and Watson, with his sensible and medically trained brain providing a factual approach to the consequences and effects of the drug. In Doyle's hands, the cocaine becomes a metaphor for the characters of Holmes and Watson, a means to demonstrate not only the difference between the abstract thinker and the level-headed everyman but the balance which they bring to each other. For Doyle, no gimmicks need apply.

It is this difference of approach to the delicate matter of Holmes's drug use which perhaps offers the key to the most pertinent insight into the relationship between the two men and it is best illustrated in Watson's opening remarks to 'A Scandal in Bohemia'. Watson says that he has seen little of Holmes since Watson's marriage to Mary Morstan at the end of *The Sign of the Four*. Watson makes no secret of the fact that marriage has altered his perspective in life: 'My own complete happiness, and the home-centred interests which rise up around the man who first finds himself master of his own establishment, were sufficient to absorb all my attention.' This, again, is the practical man in the street accepting those social responsibilities which arise once he has assumed the mantle of husband and, no doubt, prospective father.

It is Watson fulfilling the role of the contemporary man in the street; it is Watson symbolizing what his readers would expect of such a man and which most of them would wish to think of as themselves. It is Watson as the epitome of the upright, respectable, and moral veneer of Victorian society.

Contrasting with that, we have Holmes, loathing every form of society, and who Watson tells us 'remained in our lodgings in Baker Street, buried among his old books, and alternating from week to week between cocaine and ambition, the drowsiness of the drug and the fierce energy of his own keen nature.' This is Holmes as the Bohemian aesthete, the direct contrast to the staunch and respectable Watson; it is the Holmes who is interested only in those 'narrow and concentrated habits' which Watson discussed in 'The Creeping Man'. When Watson looks up at the window of 221B, he sees Holmes pacing the room swiftly and eagerly, enabling him to draw only one conclusion: '[Holmes] was at work again. He had risen out of his drug-created dreams and was hot upon the scent of some new problem.' Drug-created dreams contrasting with home-centred interests: this is the juxtaposition which is at the heart of their friendship. Without Watson's guiding and steadying hand, Holmes would fall victim to his drug mania and those old books, to those impulses which he found irresistible in his search for constant stimulation. For Holmes, the presence of Watson was a calming influence, a means of curbing those efforts to keep his brain active. As he said himself in a typically back-handed compliment to the good doctor, 'Some people without possessing genius have a remarkable power of stimulating it. I confess, my dear fellow, that I am very much in your debt.'

But if Holmes needed Watson's calming influence, it is surely equally true to say that Watson needed Holmes's tempestuous one. He may well have cherished the home comforts which marriage brought with it, but it was the excitement of the chase which he craved above all else and it was Sherlock Holmes who could provide it. Having listened to Holmes's detailed account of his investigation into the murder of Colonel James Barclay in 'The Crooked Man', Watson talks of 'tingling with that half-sporting, half-intellectual pleasure which I invariably experienced when I associated myself with him in his investigations'. Again, after Holmes's unceremonious return from the dead after a three-year absence, we learn from 'The Empty House' that any indignation Watson may have felt by Holmes's deception over his supposed demise was soon far outweighed once Holmes had dragged the good doctor out on the trail of a murderer: 'It was indeed like old times when, at that hour, I found myself seated beside him in a hansom, my revolver in my pocket and the thrill of adventure in my heart.'

Therefore, it becomes clear that the basis of their relationship was that that they were essential to each other in order to manage their respective addictions. Holmes required Watson to curb his isolated nature and prevent a total dedication to those drug manias which plagued him; Watson needed Holmes to feed his love for adventure and to offer an opportunity to study and record those powers which so amazed him. They brought balance to each other. Individually, they were adrift and neither man was so egotistical as to refuse to recognize as much. In 'A Scandal in Bohemia', Holmes is outraged at Watson's suggestion that he should leave before the client arrives, stating, famously, 'I am lost without my Boswell'. But, once more, it is Watson who encapsulates best how lost they are when separated. Having been despatched by Holmes to act as sentry and bodyguard in *The Hound of the Baskervilles*, events seem to be taking over the doctor, leaving him out of his depth and bewildered. Feeling Holmes's absence more keenly than he might have anticipated, Watson ends his diary entry for 16 October with the simply worded but candid sentiment, 'I wish he were here.' It is a touching moment and its understated honesty perhaps illustrates the close bond between the two men and their mutual reliance on each other better than any other moment in the canon.

Despite these observations, however, it must not be forgotten that Doyle had created a very human and believable friendship when he paired Holmes with Watson. Their life together was not without its moments of humour and amiability. Upon hearing from Mr Jabez Wilson that the Red-Headed League had been dissolved without warning, Watson says that he and Holmes were so taken aback by the absurd development that they burst into laughter together. Watson himself could be the subject of Holmes's gentle ridicule and mischievous teasing. As Holmes says in *The Hound of the Baskervilles*: 'There is a delightful freshness about you, Watson, which makes it a pleasure to exercise any small powers which I possess at your expense.' Even in so dark a case as their investigation into Charles Augustus Milverton, the two men are not above poking fun at one another. In planning their campaign against the King of Blackmailers, Holmes explains his plot to burgle Milverton's house in order to retrieve some compromising letters on behalf of a client. Holmes asks Watson if he has some suitable attire for the criminal escapade:

' "Have you a pair of silent shoes?"
"I have rubber-soled tennis shoes."
"Excellent. And a mask?"
"I can make a couple out of black silk."
"I can see that you have a strong natural turn for this sort of thing." '

It is not difficult to imagine both Watson's eagerness and Holmes's gentle mockery of that eagerness in the exchange.

What Doyle managed to achieve with his creation of Holmes and Watson was a depiction of a friendship which was built on admiration, trust, fondness, and, above all, a recognition that the deficiencies of one were compensated for in the attributes of the other. Without Holmes, Watson would stagnate and, without Watson, Holmes would self-destruct; but this basis is supplemented by a close friendship and a mutual amiability. Individually, Holmes and Watson are incomplete; together, they are incomparable.

The relationship is far more complex and nuanced than those of most detective duos who followed in its wake and, to a large extent, the numerous film and TV adaptations of the Holmes canon cannot quite capture the magic of Doyle's original tales. The most famous incarnation of the duo, in the portrayals of Basil Rathbone and Nigel

Bruce, is perhaps as far away from Doyle's original conception as it is possible to get without falling into parody or satire. Rathbone's Holmes is suitably acerbic and arrogant, but his overall presentation of the detective is altogether too flawless to be entirely credible. His Holmes lacks the weaknesses and errors of judgment which Doyle knew were so important for the character. And Bruce's depiction of Watson is little more than a comic foil, a bumbling clown, whose stupidity is excused as a means of emphasizing Holmes's genius. So influential was this portrayal of Watson that it was copied, mimicked, and reiterated long after the Rathbone/Bruce series of films had ceased production. But what these filmmakers overlook is something which Doyle never did: undermining Watson's intelligence does not emphasize Holmes's genius. In fact, it does nothing more than dilute it, because if Holmes is presented properly, his genius does not need sharpening and, because of their natural balance to each other, Watson's intelligence likewise does not need to be blunted.

The later presentations of the Baker Street duo have done better. Jeremy Brett gave what is still largely regarded as the definitive portrayal of Sherlock Holmes in the Granada TV adaptations in the 1980s and 1990s. He was ably supported by two actors who strove to avoid the Brucian version of Watson, first David Burke and then Edward Hardwicke, both of whom understood that Watson was an intelligent man in his own right, whose apparent stupidity was only noticeable when exposed to the glare of Holmes's genius. Both Burke and Hardwicke were able to retain a wide-eyed wonder at Brett's Holmes without compromising Watson's own integrity or importance in the relationship. These adaptations remain one of the most faithful renditions of the original friendship and, arguably, they come closest to putting on screen what Doyle set down on paper.

The most recent screen versions of Sherlock Holmes and Dr Watson have been varied in their approach. Hollywood has given us a swashbuckling Holmes in the form of Robert Downey Jr, who presented a somewhat jaded and untidy Holmes rather too far removed from the source material. Much better is Jude Law's Watson, who is able to capture the doctor's admiration of his friend, as well as that sense of mild frustration with him which Doyle's Watson was not afraid to show. Law gives us a brave Watson, a man we can believe saw military action, and a man who is not afraid to stand his own ground. Similarly, in the BBC *Sherlock* series, Martin Freeman gives a keenly observed portrayal of a wounded man of action set adrift in a world of which he no longer feels part, until the moment he meets Benedict Cumberbatch's 'high-functioning sociopath' Holmes. The early episodes of this series particularly captured the essence of the relationship between Holmes and Watson, keenly observing that the everyman craves excitement and the genius demands a calming normality.

Whatever variation of the duo comes along next, its success or failure will depend on the core relationship between Sherlock Holmes and Dr Watson. The characters and the stories are strong enough to bear any amount of manipulation by other writers in other media, but those new approaches are more likely to fail than succeed if the particular connection and friendship between the two men is not captured correctly. In order to understand and appreciate that relationship completely, it is to Doyle's original stories that we must turn. It is in those sixty tales of murder, vengeance, treachery, and horror, that we will forever find the key to the enduring popularity of Sherlock Holmes and Dr Watson.

Sherlock's London
David Stuart Davies

When one thinks about the London of Sherlock Holmes, particularly the one presented in the many movies featuring the great detective, images of fog shrouded streets, dark alleys and ancient soot-besmirched old buildings come into our minds. Well, certainly these images were part of Victorian London at the time of Holmes's residence in the metropolis, but what is often forgotten is that during this period, the latter half of the nineteenth century, London was evolving as a city for modern times.

It is interesting to note that Sherlock Holmes's London is presented to us by his creator Arthur Conan Doyle, who grew up in Edinburgh and thus saw the greatly changing and evolving capital in Victorian times from an outsider's perspective. Indeed, when Doyle created Sherlock and wrote the first Holmes story, *A Study in Scarlet* (1887), he was living in Southsea and relied on his memories of various visits to London for background detail. Many of the locations in this particular story are more reminiscent of his native city than of London. In fact, Lauriston Gardens, the road in Brixton where the first murder victim is discovered in this novel, was named after a thoroughfare in Edinburgh near to where Conan Doyle grew up. By the time he penned the second novel, *The Sign of the Four* (1890), however, Doyle was living in the capital and more familiar with the locale.

London, the hub of the British Empire, was Sherlock Holmes's hunting ground, although of course he did venture into the nearby shires from time to time. This brilliant consulting detective was based in the heart of the city on Baker Street at the fictitious number 221B, where he shared rooms on the upper floor with Doctor John H. Watson. The pair first met when Watson had just returned from Afghanistan, invalided out of the army on a meagre pension. At this period of his life, Watson described London as, 'that great cesspool into which all idlers and loungers of the Empire are irresistibly drained'.

Watson was keen to share lodgings with someone in order to keep his expenses down. One lunch time in Criterion Bar in Piccadilly Circus he encountered Stamford, an old army friend who said he could solve Watson's problem. He took him to St Bartholomew's Hospital (Barts), in Farringdon, to a meet an unusual young man who was also in search of a co-lodger – a fellow by the name of Sherlock Holmes. He was carrying out research in the lab at the hospital: 'beating subjects in the dissecting room with a stick . . . to verify how far bruises may be produced after death'. Sherlock Holmes's first words to Watson – 'You have been in Afghanistan, I perceive' – established his remarkable deductive powers, and the rest is history.

When the stories were written, they were, of course, contemporary and therefore Doyle did not include conscious period dressing; this emerges in a subtle way, embedded in the text through casual references to locations, forms of transport, manners, dress, et al. It is forgotten by some readers that these were contemporary stories and not period tales. There was no need for the author to go into great descriptions concerning details of the time. They would be familiar to the readers. The scene setting was all done subtly – almost by osmosis. In this fashion the rich and complex variety of London emerges naturally in effective detail, providing a colourful but unobtrusive backdrop to the detective's investigations.

Doyle cunningly exploited the fascinating contrasts of the sprawling city in the stories. Therefore we have Holmes in 'The Man with the Twisted Lip' slumming it in the Bar of Gold, a seedy opium den in Upper Swandam Lane, 'a vile alley lurking behind the high wharves which line the north side of the river to the east of London Bridge'; and then visiting his brother Mycroft in the hallowed rooms of the Diogenes Club in Pall Mall, Whitehall. With this club, Doyle satirized all the exclusive gentlemen's clubs, which provided comfortable womblike environments for the higher echelons of London society. The Diogenes was described by Doyle as an establishment for 'the most unclubbable men in London'.

In the first recorded adventure, *A Study in Scarlet*, the major crime is committed in a deserted house in down-at-heel Brixton; while in 'The Second Stain' Holmes solves the case in the grand town house of Trelawney Hope, 'the European Secretary' – a kingpin of the British government.

It is popular to view Holmes's world as one of fog-bound cobbled streets, ghostly gas lamps that fail at 6 metres (20 feet) and dark old buildings. However, the facts present a different picture. During the years Sherlock Holmes spent in London – from approximately 1878 to 1904 – he lived through one of the greatest periods of change and development the city had ever known.

The Victorian age began with gas lamps, the telegram, and the musical box; it ended with electricity, the motor car, and the gramophone. Nothing remained constant. The change had actually started in earnest just after the young Queen Victoria ascended the throne in 1837. Even many locations referred to in the Holmes stories were relatively new. The Criterion Bar, for example, noted for its Byzantine ceiling, was only completed in 1873, a mere eight years before Watson's fateful meeting with Stamford. The following year Liverpool Street Station, serving the Great Eastern Railway, was opened. Holmes departed from this station on his way to Norfolk in the investigation Watson called 'The Dancing Men'; and Watson set off on his wild goose chase from here in 'The Retired Colourman'. All the major railway termini in London are mentioned in the Holmes stories and it must be remembered that rail travel was still relatively new then, the first railway station in London having been opened in 1837, within living memory of many readers of the Holmes tales.

Some other fairly new buildings mentioned in the stories include the House of Commons (1852), King's Cross Station (1852), St James's Hall (1858), and St Pancras Hotel (1873). The point is, of course, that what we may view through the golden fog of nostalgia as being quaint and historical was fresh and new to the young Holmes and Watson.

Here was a city, like the aspiring detective himself, contemporary, fast-moving and eager to make a special mark on the world.

Among the greatest changes Holmes observed during his residence in London was its altering façade. In the final twenty years of the nineteenth century London virtually renewed itself. Buildings were constantly springing up to present freshly minted vistas for the inhabitants of the metropolis. Included in this changing architectural canvas were Aldgate Station (1876), the easternmost on the Metropolitan Railway; and Hammersmith Bridge with its striking designs by Joseph Bazelgette, which is mentioned in 'The Six Napoleons.'

The streets of London during Holmes's time were clogged with vehicles: horse drawn cabs, carts, trams and hordes of pedestrians. A great boon to moving about the city was the introduction of the Underground. Londoners today take this swift and easy mode of transport for granted, but to the inhabitants of late Victorian times, the Underground was a great novelty. London was the first city to adopt an underground railway system with the opening of the Metropolitan Railway in 1863. Holmes and Watson travelled by Underground several times in their investigations. They used Aldersgate Station on their way to Saxe-Coburg Square in 'The Red Headed League' for example. In 'The Bruce Partington Plans', Doyle employed the mechanics of the underground system when creating his plot. The body of the murder victim, Cadogan West, was dumped on the roof of a carriage by the murderer but it was eventually dislodged and fell off due to the motion of the train travelling over the points near Aldersgate Station. Holmes made his way down the track and examined the body, making several pertinent deductions, which led him to the solution of the mystery.

There were also a great number of hotels built during this period to accommodate the increasing volume of visitors to London, including the big curve-fronted Grand Hotel by Trafalgar Square, which opened its doors in 1887. This is a candidate for the Northumberland Hotel where Sir Henry Baskerville stayed and lost his boots in *The Hound of the Baskervilles*. Further along Northumberland Avenue there was the Hotel Metropole (1885), probably disguised as the Hotel Cosmopolitan in 'The Blue Carbuncle' where the Countess of Morcar had her precious stone stolen.

Indeed, the city must have looked like one giant building site. In *The Sign of the Four*, Holmes was able to deduce that Watson had been to the Wigmore Street Post Office by making some deductions about road works:

> 'Observation tells me that you have a reddish mould adhering to your instep. Just opposite they have taken up the pavement and thrown up some earth, which lies in such a way that it is difficult to avoid treading in it in entering. The earth is of a peculiar reddish tint which is found, as far as I know, nowhere else in the neighbourhood.'

The building work here is a real boon to the detective.

One of the most important buildings to be erected during Holmes's Baker Street days was the headquarters for the Metropolitan Police. It was built on reclaimed land on the Victoria embankment. The architect, Norman Shaw, designed what A. P. Herbert described as 'a very constabulary kind of building'. It was faced with granite, appropriately quarried by convicts on Dartmoor. The police moved there in 1890 and the building was christened New Scotland Yard. No sooner had it opened than Holmes went to France on 'a matter of supreme importance to the French government' and then shortly afterwards had an encounter with a certain nefarious Professor Moriarty at the Reichenbach Falls. Presumed dead, consumed by the ferocious waters of the Falls, Holmes disappeared for three years, a period known to Sherlockians as 'The Great Hiatus'. Perhaps he thought that with the new, modernized headquarters, Inspectors Lestrade, Gregson, Hopkins and co. could manage without him. This turned out not to be the case. On returning to London in 1894, he found that they were still struggling with their investigations – on this occasion with the murder of the Honourable Ronald Adair who was shot with an airgun by a sniper (Colonel Sebastian Moran) while in his apartment in Park Lane. This avenue grew in popularity during the nineteenth century after improvements to Hyde Park Corner, which provided more affordable views of the park, attracting the nouveau riche to the street and led to it becoming one of the most fashionable roads to live in London. The events of the Adair murder case were recorded in 'The Empty House'.

It is interesting to note that a near neighbour of Sherlock Holmes until 1884 was Madame Tussaud's Waxwork Museum when it moved from 54–6 Baker Street round the corner to its present site on Marylebone Road, taking with it four hundred wax figures. One can imagine the detective visiting the exhibition so close to 221B as a *divertissement* when his business was slow. Perhaps it was on one of these visits that he conceived the possibility of using a wax dummy to aid him in some investigative subterfuge, which he did in the aforementioned 'The Empty House' and also 'The Mazarin Stone'. In both stories a life-like mannequin impersonated Holmes and fooled the villains.

During Holmes's detective career, new thoroughfares were grafted on to the old network of streets that patterned the city; the first really important new street was Victoria Street connecting Victoria Station with Westminster Abbey. Holmes used Victoria Station on many occasions; in particular when, disguised as a venerable Italian priest, he was escaping the clutches of Moriarty in 'The Final Problem'. This station provided the railway route to the coast and from there by ferry to the continent.

The fact that new roads were appearing regularly meant that Holmes's knowledge of the city would need to be constantly updated and amended. However, he was equal to the challenge as he demonstrated during the cab-ride in *The Sign of the Four*, which leads them from the West End to Wandsworth Road, which is described as 'the howling desert of South London'.

Watson observes:

'At first I had some idea as to the direction in which we were driving, but soon, what with our pace, the fog and my own limited knowledge of London, I lost my bearings and knew nothing, save that we seemed to be going a long way. Sherlock Holmes was never at fault, however, and he muttered the names as the cab rattled through squares and in and out by tortuous by-streets.'

While Watson's 'limited knowledge' suggests how difficult it was for an average fellow to keep up with the evolving geography of the city, Holmes's certainty of direction and location highlights his remarkable ability to keep abreast of the changing environment.

Most of the major institutions in London at the time are referred to in the stories and Holmes's investigations prompt him to visit Covent Garden market in search of a certain supplier of Christmas geese in 'The Blue Carbuncle'. The detective duo took relaxing walks in Hyde Park, notably in 'The Yellow Face'. Hyde Park, originally acquired by Henry VIII from the monks of Westminster Abbey, is the largest of four Royal Parks and is divided by the Serpentine and the Long Water. Both the Foreign Office ('The Second Stain') and the Admiralty (The Bruce Partington Plans') also feature in the Holmes canon.

When dining out, the detective duo favoured 'taking something nutritious' at Simpson's Dining Rooms, situated on the Strand. Simpson's still functions as a restaurant and it does not take too much imagination if you visit their dining room, built in 1828, to conjure up in your mind's eye two significant figures sitting at a window table overlooking the Strand, consuming traditional cuts of meat while discussing a case.

Although there is no record of Holmes visiting the Café Royal in Regent Street, it was outside this establishment that he was attacked by a hired thug in the case of 'The Dying Detective'.

Music played a large part in Holmes's life – he owned a Stradivarius and was an accomplished violinist. In several of the stories there are references to his visiting musical venues. For example both Holmes and Watson attended a Wagner recital at the Covent Garden Theatre in 'The Red Circle'. This theatre was rebuilt in 1858 after a disastrous fire had destroyed the earlier building and so was yet another comparatively new edifice in the heart of the city.

In 'The Red Headed League' Holmes attended a concert by the celebrated Spanish violinist Sarasate at St James's Hall, which had opened on 25 March 1858, designed by architect and artist Owen Jones, who had decorated the interior of the Crystal Palace. At the conclusion of *The Hound of the Baskervilles*, Holmes and Watson go to see the opera *Les Huguenots* by Giacomo Meyerbeer (1791 – 1864) – the actual venue isn't mentioned in the story but it is most likely to be the aforementioned Royal Opera House in Covent Garden.

London is dissected by the great River Thames which rises in central England and flows south-easterly across the city on its way to the North Sea. The city is some 100 kilometres (60 miles) inland from the mouth of the estuary. In *The Sign of the Four,* Holmes's agents, the juvenile Baker Street Irregulars, searched for the boat the *Aurora* up and down the Thames. The villain Jonathan Small had hired the vessel as a means of escape after stealing the Agra treasure. Once the *Aurora* had been located, Holmes was able to give chase down the river in a police launch from the Tower of London (built in 1078) to Barking Level. In 'The Five Orange Pips', John Openshaw is brutally murdered on the banks of the Thames and his body dumped in the river. Dead bodies floating in the river was not an uncommon phenomenon at this time and in 'The Red Headed League' it was feared that the eponymous character had met such a fate when some of his clothes were found in the water. Also Holmes had been working on a case near the river before falling ill in 'The Dying Detective'.

By the time Sherlock Holmes retired in the early days of the twentieth century, London, his base and operating headquarters for 23 years had become a different place from the one he had known when, after coming up from University, he had settled in lodgings in Montague Street, 'just around the corner from the British Museum', where he first set up as a consulting detective. At the end of his career, he had to a large extent become a fixed point in a changing age. While a young man he revelled in the whirligig of change but as late middle age beckoned he felt like a fish out of water. He describes his retirement in 'The Lion's Mane' as 'a withdrawal' to the Sussex Downs from 'the gloom of London'. How different from Watson's view of the younger Holmes in 'The Cardboard Box':

> 'He loved to lie in the very centre of five million people, with his filaments stretching out and running through them responsive to every little humour or suspicion of unsolved crime.'

What once inspired later depressed Sherlock Holmes. He felt the very human sensation that we all experience as we grow older: the pace of change becomes too fast and robs us of that sure ground that we thought we held. London with motor cars, cinemas, full electric lighting, and smooth tarmacadamed roads was a world in which Sherlock Holmes no longer felt at ease. He bade the city goodbye and retired to a cottage on the Sussex Downs where he kept bees. He is probably still there now.

Principal Characters

Sherlock Holmes is the well-known detective of 221B Baker Street and with his trademark pipe and deerstalker he is the personification of intellectual rigour and an analytical mind. Disdainful and egotistical, Holmes is renowned for his proficiency, logical reasoning, acute observation and precise attention to detail. His use of forensic science is way ahead of his time. Eccentric, brilliant and enigmatic, he is (apart from his association with Watson) generally solitary. Holmes is subject to mood swings and deep depression; he loses his appetite during times of intense intellectual activity, and he is a talented violin player.

He is also a chemist and has pertinent knowledge of geology and botany. Holmes describes himself as a 'consulting detective' with a wide variety of clients, including London's Scotland Yard. The tools Holmes uses include his famous magnifying glass; *A Study in Scarlet* was the first piece of detective fiction to describe this as an investigative tool.

Dr John Watson, born 1852, studied medicine at St Bartholomew's Hospital in London, gaining his degree from the University of London in 1878. His further training took place at Netley where he worked as an assistant surgeon in the British Army. Watson served in India with the 5th Northumberland Fusiliers and the 66th Berkshire Regiment of Foot. He was wounded during the second Anglo-Afghan war at the battle of Maiwand in 1880 and voyaged back on the troopship HMS *Orontes* to recover in London, where he is introduced to Sherlock Holmes. After some discussion, Holmes and Watson inspect the rooms at No. 221B, Baker Street and immediately decide to share this accommodation.

Watson is Sherlock Holmes's faithful friend, confidant, assistant and sometime flatmate. He is described as handsome, middle-sized, strongly built with a square jaw, thick neck, and a moustache. He is intelligent, rational, calm, modest and steadfast. He is astute, but conventional – a typical Victorian gentleman – and can never match Holmes's deductive skills and is ever amazed by the brilliance of his new detective friend. When the *A Study in Scarlet* case is solved, Watson is furious that the Press give Holmes no credit for his detection and so he endeavours to set the record straight. He is the story's narrator and establishes that the work to follow is a: 'Reprint from the Reminiscences of John H. Watson, MD, Late of the Army Medical Department.'

Stamford had been a dresser under Dr Watson at St Bartholomew's Hospital. They bump into each other in London's Criterion bar and Watson confides to Stamford that, due to his shoulder injury, he has been forced to leave the armed services and is now looking for a place to live. Stamford tells Watson that he is the second man the has met that day who us seeking lodgings; his friend Sherlock Holmes is hoping to share some rooms he has found but which cost too much for him alone. Stamford suggests that Watson should meet Holmes and takes him to St Bartholomew's where, in a laboratory, they find Holmes experimenting, seeking a test to detect human haemoglobin. A firm friendship ensues.

John Ferrier is a traveller heading west across the desert near Salt Lake City in the USA. He and his daughter Lucy are the only survivors of a small party of pioneers who have perished from dehydration and hunger. Brigham Young (who leads a Mormon group) rescues him and his adopted little girl, Lucy, from the desert. Ferrier eventually becomes aware of the dangerous attitudes of the Mormons and tries to escape Salt Lake City with Lucy and the man she loves, Jefferson Hope.

Jefferson Hope is a strong, young, and a very capable hunter. He falls in love with Lucy Ferrier and tries to help her and her father escape the clutches of the Mormon group. His bitter experiences turn Hope into a hard, vengeful man, obsessed with tracking down the two men (Drebber and Stangerson) responsible for the Ferriers' deaths. Eventually, after years of hunting for them, Hope works as a London cabby in order to help him narrow down the search even further. He discovers Drebber and Stangerson in London and murders both. After his capture, Jefferson Hope dies peacefully from an aortic aneurism the night before he is due to appear in court. He is regarded as manic but justified.

Lucy Ferrier is the adopted daughter of John Ferrier. She is beautiful, gentle and charming. Lucy falls in love with Jefferson Hope and they become engaged, but he is an outsider to the Mormon group and thus dubbed a Gentile and an enemy. The Mormons refuse to allow Lucy to marry a non-Mormon – so she, her father, and Jefferson Hope try to escape but are pursued and recaptured. Her father is killed and Lucy is eventually forced to marry one of the Elders' sons, Enoch Drebber. Tragically, within a month she dies of a broken heart. Drebber, who now inherits the Ferrier farm, seems indifferent to poor Lucy's death.

Enoch Drebber is the wealthy son of a Mormon Elder from Salt Lake City. He is a polygamist and uses his power among the Mormons to force Lucy Ferrier to become one of his wives. Throughout the story, Drebber is shown to be a drunken, lecherous lout. The body of an American traveller, subsequently revealed to be Enoch Drebber, is found in an abandoned house in London in 1881. This mysterious murder will become first joint case for Sherlock Holmes and Dr John Watson, as recounted in *A Study in Scarlet*.

He is pursued by Jefferson Hope who seeks revenge for the loss of his beloved Lucy; Hope will eventually murder Enoch.

Joseph Stangerson is the son of a Mormon Elder, and vies with Drebber for the hand of Lucy Ferrier. Stangerson is revealed to have been the one who murdered John Ferrier. He eventually becomes private secretary to Drebber and travels with him to Europe. He will also be murdered by the vengeful Jefferson Hope.

Brigham Young is Sherlock Holmes' first villain. Brutal and powerful – but charismatic – Brigham is the chief of the Mormons. He is a very capable but cold-hearted leader. Young leads the Mormons to Utah, declaring it to be their promised land. He turns Utah into an armed camp, with bands of men scouring the countryside to find young female brides. Claiming to speak for Joseph Smith and deemed a prophet, Young rules over the Elect with an iron fist. Some years before he had saved John and Lucy Ferrier when they were lost and at death's door in the desert. He refuses to let Lucy Ferrier marry a Gentile and forces the girl to choose between one of two Apostles, each of whom already have several wives. Young sends his Avenging Angels after the Ferriers when they escape from Utah. He is depicted as an evil tyrant and dictator but one with hypnotic allure.

Inspector G. Lestrade This Scotland Yard detective often consults Holmes and respects his abilities. He is kind to clients but impatient with Holmes. He is described as rat- or ferret-faced, short, sallow, dark-eyed, furtive and sly-looking, with fat, square hands. He dresses well and is expert in shorthand. His language is working-class but free of slang and coarseness; he does sometimes use archaic words.

Holmes regards him as quick and energetic but too conventional, lacking in imagination, and generally out of his depth. Holmes believes that Lestrade has reached his high rank in the CID purely through his bulldog tenacity. Lestrade is a bitter rival of Tobias Gregson, another Scotland Yard inspector – and one who publicly laughs at Lestrade's incorrect assumptions, even when he, too, is following the wrong trail!

An Arthur Conan Doyle Timeline

	1859	1876	1879	1887
Jules Verne	Arthur Conan Doyle born	Attends University of Edinburgh Medical School	*The Mystery of the Sasanna Valley* published	*A Study in Scarlet* published
UK and Ireland	*The Origin of the Species* published	First direct telegraph link between Britain and New Zealand	Zulu War begins	Golden Jubilee of Queen Victoria
Europe	Spain declares war on Morocco	Berlin Memorandum proposes armistice in Turkey	*A Doll's House* by Henrik Ibsen	Triple Alliance of Germany, Austria–Hungary and France ends
Rest of the World	Abolitionist leader John Brown hanged	Alexander Graham Bell patents the telephone	Thomas Edison demonstrates electric light	Japan annexes Iwo Jima

| 1859 | 1876 | 1879 | 1887 |

1890

The Sign of the Four published

Prince of Wales opens underground station at Stockwell

Vincent van Gogh shoots himself

Battle of Wounded Knee

1891

Gives up medical practice to write

Britain linked to continent by telephone

Paul Gauguin departs for Tahiti

Congress creates US Court of Appeal

1892

The Adventures of Sherlock Holmes published

Oscar Wilde's *Lady Windermere's Fan* premieres

Germany, Italy and Austria form Triple Alliance

General Electrical Company incorporated in New York

1893

The Adventure of the Final Problem published

Beatrix Potter first tells the story of Peter Rabbit

Russia signs military accord with France

Gandhi's first act of civil disobedience

1890   1891   1892   1893

	1894	1900	1901	1902
Jules Verne	*The Memoirs of Sherlock Holmes* published	Serves in Boer War	*The Hound of the Baskervilles* published	*The War in South Africa* published; Conan Doyle knighted
UK and Ireland	George Bernard Shaw's *The Arms and the Man* premieres	Hugo de Vries rediscovers Mendel's Laws of Genetics	Queen Victoria dies	Edward VII crowned
Europe	Olympic Committee founded in Paris	Lifting of the Siege of Mafeking	First Nobel Prize Ceremony in Stockholm	Denmark uses fingerprinting to identify criminals
Rest of the World	First Sino-Japanese war	Hawaii becomes US territory	Oil discovered in Texas	First motion picture theatre opens in Los Angeles

| | 1894 | 1900 | 1901 | 1902 |

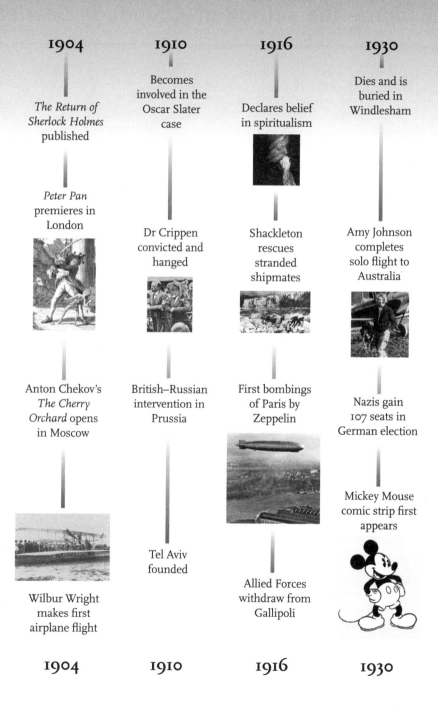

1904

The Return of
Sherlock Holmes
published

Peter Pan
premieres in
London

Anton Chekov's
The Cherry
Orchard opens
in Moscow

Wilbur Wright
makes first
airplane flight

1910

Becomes
involved in the
Oscar Slater
case

Dr Crippen
convicted and
hanged

British–Russian
intervention in
Prussia

Tel Aviv
founded

1916

Declares belief
in spiritualism

Shackleton
rescues
stranded
shipmates

First bombings
of Paris by
Zeppelin

Allied Forces
withdraw from
Gallipoli

1930

Dies and is
buried in
Windlesham

Amy Johnson
completes
solo flight to
Australia

Nazis gain
107 seats in
German election

Mickey Mouse
comic strip first
appears

1904

1910

1916

1930

London – the setting of *A Study in Scarlet*

221B Baker Street, where Holmes and Watson famously shared a flat

Barts Hospital, where Holmes and Watson first met

New Scotland Yard

Halliday's Private Hotel, where Stangerson was murdered, was in Little George Street

Lauriston Gardens off Brixton Road, where Drebber was found murdered

A Study in Scarlet

PART ONE

Being a reprint from the reminiscences of
John H. Watson MD
Late of the Army Medical Department

1

Mr Sherlock Holmes

In the year 1878 I took my degree of doctor of medicine of the University of London, and proceeded to Netley to go through the course prescribed for surgeons in the army. Having completed my studies there, I was duly attached to the Fifth Northumberland Fusiliers as assistant surgeon. The regiment was stationed in India at the time, and before I could join it the Second Afghan War had broken out. On landing at Bombay, I learned that my corps had advanced through the passes and was already deep in the enemy's country. I followed, however, with many other officers who were in the same situation as myself, and succeeded in reaching Kandahar in safety, where I found my regiment and at once entered upon my new duties.

The campaign brought honours and promotion to many, but for me it had nothing but misfortune and disaster. I was removed from my brigade and attached to the Berkshires, with whom I served at the fatal battle of Maiwand. There I was struck on the shoulder by a Jezail bullet, which shattered the bone and grazed the subclavian artery. I should have fallen into the hands of the murderous Ghazis had it not been for the devotion and courage shown by Murray, my orderly, who threw me across a packhorse and succeeded in bringing me safely to the British lines.

Worn with pain, and weak from the prolonged hardships which I had undergone, I was removed, with a great train of wounded sufferers, to the base hospital at Peshawar. Here I rallied, and had already improved so far as to be able to walk about the wards, and even to bask a little upon the verandah, when I was struck down by enteric fever, that curse of our Indian possessions. For months my life was despaired of, and when at last I came to myself and became convalescent, I was so weak and emaciated that a medical board determined that not a day should be lost in sending me back to England. I was despatched, accordingly, in the troopship *Orontes*, and landed a month later on Portsmouth jetty, with my health irretrievably ruined but with permission from a paternal government to spend the next nine months in attempting to improve it.

I had neither kith nor kin in England, and was therefore as free as air – or as free as an income of eleven shillings and sixpence a day will permit a man to be. Under such circumstances I naturally gravitated to London, that great cesspool into which all the loungers and idlers of the Empire are irresistibly drained. There I stayed for some time at a private hotel in the Strand, leading a comfortless, meaningless existence, and spending such money as I had considerably more freely than I ought. So alarming did the state of my finances become that I soon realised that I must either leave the metropolis and rusticate somewhere in the country, or that I must make a complete alteration in my style of living. Choosing the latter alternative, I began by making up my mind to leave the hotel and to take up my quarters in some less pretentious and less expensive domicile.

On the very day that I had come to this conclusion, I was standing at the Criterion Bar when someone tapped me on the shoulder and, turning round, I recognised young Stamford, who had been a dresser under me at Barts. The sight of a friendly face in the great wilderness of London is a pleasant thing indeed to a lonely man. In old days Stamford had never been a particular crony of mine, but now I hailed him with enthusiasm, and he, in his turn, appeared to be delighted to see me. In the exuberance of my joy, I asked him to lunch with me at the Holborn, and we started off together in a hansom.

'Whatever have you been doing with yourself, Watson?' he asked in undisguised wonder, as we rattled through the crowded London streets. 'You are as thin as a lath and as brown as a nut.'

I gave him a short sketch of my adventures, and had hardly concluded it by the time that we reached our destination.

'Poor devil!' he said commiseratingly, after he had listened to my misfortunes. 'What are you up to now?'

'Looking for lodgings,' I answered. 'Trying to solve the problem as to whether it is possible to get comfortable rooms at a reasonable price.'

'That's a strange thing,' remarked my companion, 'you are the second man today that has used that expression to me.'

'And who was the first?' I asked.

'A fellow who is working at the chemical laboratory up at the hospital. He was bemoaning himself this morning because he could not get someone to go halves with him in some nice rooms which he had found but which were too much for his purse.'

'By Jove!' I cried; 'if he really wants someone to share the rooms and the expense, I am the very man for him. I should prefer having a partner to being alone.'

Young Stamford looked rather strangely at me over his wine-glass. 'You don't know Sherlock Holmes yet,' he said; 'perhaps you would not care for him as a constant companion.'

'Why, what is there against him?'

'Oh, I didn't say there was anything against him. He is a little queer in his ideas – an enthusiast in some branches of science. As far as I know he is a decent fellow enough.'

'A medical student, I suppose,' said I.

'No – I have no idea what he intends to go in for. I believe he is well up in anatomy, and he is a first-class chemist, but as far as I know he has never taken out any systematic medical classes. His studies are very desultory and eccentric, but he has amassed a lot of out-of-the-way knowledge which would astonish his professors.'

'Did you never ask him what he was going in for?' I asked.

'No; he is not a man that it is easy to draw out, though he can be communicative enough when the fancy seizes him.'

'I should like to meet him,' I said. 'If I am to lodge with anyone, I should prefer a man of studious and quiet habits. I am not strong enough yet to stand much noise or excitement. I had enough of both in Afghanistan to last me for the remainder of my natural existence. How could I meet this friend of yours?'

'He is sure to be at the laboratory,' returned my companion. 'He either avoids the place for weeks, or else he works there from morning till night. If you like, we will drive round together after luncheon.'

'Certainly,' I answered, and the conversation drifted away into other channels.

As we made our way to the hospital after leaving the Holborn, Stamford gave me a few more particulars about the gentleman whom I proposed to take as a fellow-lodger.

'You mustn't blame me if you don't get on with him,' he said; 'I know nothing more of him than I have learned from meeting him occasionally in the laboratory. You proposed this arrangement, so you must not hold me responsible.'

'If we don't get on it will be easy to part company,' I answered. 'It seems to me, Stamford,' I added, looking hard at my companion, 'that you have some reason for washing your hands of the matter. Is this fellow's temper so formidable, or what is it? Don't be mealy-mouthed about it.'

'It is not easy to express the inexpressible,' he answered with a laugh. 'Holmes is a little too scientific for my tastes – it approaches to cold-bloodedness. I could imagine his giving a friend a little pinch of the latest vegetable alkaloid, not out of malevolence, you understand, but simply out of a spirit of enquiry in order to have an accurate idea of the effects. To do him justice, I think that he would take it himself with the same readiness. He appears to have a passion for definite and exact knowledge.'

'Very right too.'

'Yes, but it may be pushed to excess. When it comes to beating the subjects in the dissecting-rooms with a stick, it is certainly taking rather a bizarre shape.'

'Beating the subjects!'

'Yes, to verify how far bruises may be produced after death. I saw him at it with my own eyes.'

'And yet you say he is not a medical student?'

'No. Heaven knows what the objects of his studies are. But here we are, and you must form your own impressions about him.' As he spoke, we turned down a narrow lane and passed through a small side-door which opened into a wing of the great hospital. It was familiar ground to me, and I needed no guiding as we ascended the bleak stone staircase and made our way down the long corridor with its vista of whitewashed wall and dun-coloured doors. Near the farther end a low-arched passage branched away from it and led to the chemical laboratory.

This was a lofty chamber, lined and littered with countless bottles. Broad, low tables were scattered about, which bristled with retorts, test-tubes, and little Bunsen lamps, with their blue flickering flames. There was only one student in the room, who was bending over a distant table absorbed in his work. At the sound of our steps he glanced round and sprang to his feet with a cry of pleasure. 'I've found it! I've found it,' he shouted to my companion, running towards us with a test-tube in his hand. 'I have found a reagent which is precipitated by haemoglobin, and by nothing else.' Had he discovered a gold mine, greater delight could not have shone upon his features.

'Dr Watson, Mr Sherlock Holmes,' said Stamford, introducing us.

'How are you?' he said cordially, gripping my hand with a strength for which I should hardly have given him credit. 'You have been in Afghanistan, I perceive.'

'How on earth did you know that?' I asked in astonishment.

'Never mind,' said he, chuckling to himself. 'The question now is about haemoglobin. No doubt you see the significance of this discovery of mine?'

'It is interesting, chemically, no doubt,' I answered, 'but practically –'

'Why, man, it is the most practical medico-legal discovery for years. Don't you see that it gives us an infallible test for blood stains. Come over here now!' He seized me by the coat-sleeve in his eagerness, and drew me over to the table at which he had been working. 'Let us have some fresh blood,' he said, digging a long bodkin into his finger and drawing off the resulting drop of blood in a chemical pipette. 'Now, I add this small quantity of blood to a litre of water. You perceive that the resulting mixture has the appearance of pure water. The proportion of blood cannot be more than one in a million. I have no doubt, however, that we shall be able to obtain the characteristic reaction.' As he spoke, he threw into the vessel a few white crystals, and then added some drops of a transparent fluid. In an instant the contents assumed a dull mahogany colour and a brownish dust was precipitated to the bottom of the glass jar.

'Ha! ha!' he cried, clapping his hands, and looking as delighted as a child with a new toy. 'What do you think of that?'

'It seems to be a very delicate test,' I remarked.

'Beautiful! beautiful! The old guaiacum test was very clumsy and uncertain. So is the microscopic examination for blood corpuscles. The latter is valueless if the stains are a few hours old. Now, this appears to act as well whether the blood is old or new. Had this test been invented, there are hundreds of men now walking the earth who would long ago have paid the penalty of their crimes.'

'Indeed!' I murmured.

'Criminal cases are continually hinging upon that one point. A man is suspected of a crime months perhaps after it has been committed. His linen or clothes are examined and brownish stains discovered upon them. Are they blood stains, or mud stains, or rust stains, or fruit stains, or what are they? That is a question which has puzzled many an expert, and why? Because there was no reliable test.

Now we have the Sherlock Holmes test, and there will no longer be any difficulty.'

His eyes fairly glittered as he spoke, and he put his hand over his heart and bowed as if to some applauding crowd conjured up by his imagination.

'You are to be congratulated,' I remarked, considerably surprised at his enthusiasm.

'There was the case of Von Bischoff at Frankfurt last year. He would certainly have been hung had this test been in existence. Then there was Mason of Bradford, and the notorious Muller, and Lefevre of Montpellier, and Samson of New Orleans. I could name a score of cases in which it would have been decisive.'

'You seem to be a walking calendar of crime,' said Stamford with a laugh. 'You might start a paper on those lines. Call it the *Police News of the Past*.'

'Very interesting reading it might be made, too,' remarked Sherlock Holmes, sticking a small piece of plaster over the prick on his finger. 'I have to be careful,' he continued, turning to me with a smile, 'for I dabble with poisons a good deal.' He held out his hand as he spoke, and I noticed that it was all mottled over with similar pieces of plaster, and discoloured with strong acids.

'We came here on business,' said Stamford, sitting down on a high three-legged stool, and pushing another one in my direction with his foot. 'My friend here wants to take diggings; and as you were complaining that you could get no one to go halves with you, I thought that I had better bring you together.'

Sherlock Holmes seemed delighted at the idea of sharing his rooms with me. 'I have my eye on a suite in Baker Street,' he said, 'which would suit us down to the ground. You don't mind the smell of strong tobacco, I hope?'

'I always smoke "ship's" myself,' I answered.

'That's good enough. I generally have chemicals about, and occasionally do experiments. Would that annoy you?'

'By no means.'

'Let me see – what are my other shortcomings? I get in the dumps at times, and don't open my mouth for days on end. You must not think I am sulky when I do that. Just let me alone, and I'll soon be right. What have you to confess now? It's just as well for two fellows to know the worst of one another before they begin to live together.'

I laughed at this cross-examination. 'I keep a bull pup,' I said, 'and I object to row, because my nerves are shaken, and I get up at all sorts of ungodly hours, and I am extremely lazy. I have another set of vices when I'm well, but those are the principal ones at present.'

'Do you include violin playing in your category of rows?' he asked, anxiously.

'It depends on the player,' I answered. 'A well-played violin is a treat for the gods – a badly-played one . . . '

'Oh, that's all right,' he cried, with a merry laugh. 'I think we may consider the thing as settled – that is, if the rooms are agreeable to you.'

'When shall we see them?'

'Call for me here at noon tomorrow, and we'll go together and settle everything,' he answered.

'All right – noon exactly,' said I, shaking his hand.

We left him working among his chemicals, and we walked together towards my hotel.

'By the way,' I asked suddenly, stopping and turning upon Stamford, 'how the deuce did he know that I had come from Afghanistan?'

My companion smiled an enigmatical smile. 'That's just his little peculiarity,' he said. 'A good many people have wanted to know how he finds things out.'

'Oh! a mystery is it?' I cried, rubbing my hands. 'This is very piquant. I am much obliged to you for bringing us together. "The proper study of mankind is man," you know.'

'You must study him, then,' Stamford said, as he bade me goodbye. 'You'll find him a knotty problem, though. I'll wager he learns more about you than you about him. Goodbye.'

'Goodbye,' I answered, and strolled on to my hotel, considerably interested in my new acquaintance.

2

The Science of Deduction

We met next day, as he had arranged, and inspected the rooms at No. 221b, Baker Street, of which he had spoken at our meeting. They consisted of a couple of comfortable bedrooms and a single large airy sitting-room, cheerfully furnished and illuminated by two broad windows. So desirable in every way were the apartments, and so moderate did the terms seem when divided between us, that the bargain was concluded upon the spot, and we at once entered into possession. That very evening I moved my things round from the hotel, and on the following morning Sherlock Holmes followed me with several boxes and portmanteaus. For a day or two we were busily employed in unpacking and laying out our property to the best advantage. That done, we gradually began to settle down and to accommodate ourselves to our new surroundings.

Holmes was certainly not a difficult man to live with. He was quiet in his ways, and his habits were regular. It was rare for him to be up after ten at night, and he had invariably breakfasted and gone out before I rose in the morning. Sometimes he spent his day at the chemical laboratory, sometimes in the dissecting rooms, and occasionally in long walks, which appeared to take him into the lowest portions of the city. Nothing could exceed his energy when the working fit was upon him; but now and again a reaction would seize him, and for days on end he would lie upon the sofa in the sitting-room, hardly uttering a word or moving a muscle from morning to night. On these occasions I have noticed such a dreamy, vacant expression in his eyes that I might have suspected him of being addicted to the use of some narcotic had not the temperance and cleanliness of his whole life forbidden such a notion.

As the weeks went by, my interest in him and my curiosity as to his aims in life gradually deepened and increased. His very person and appearance were such as to strike the attention of the most casual observer. In height he was rather over six feet, and so excessively lean that he seemed to be considerably taller. His eyes were sharp and piercing, save during those intervals of torpor to which I have alluded; and his thin, hawklike nose gave his whole expression an air of alertness and decision. His chin, too, had the prominence and squareness which mark the man of determination. His hands were invariably blotted with ink and stained with chemicals, yet he was possessed of extraordinary delicacy of touch, as I frequently had occasion to observe when I watched him manipulating his fragile philosophical instruments.

The reader may set me down as a hopeless busy-body, when I confess how much this man stimulated my curiosity, and how often I endeavoured to break through the reticence which he showed on all that concerned himself. Before judgement is pronounced, however, be it remembered how objectless was my life and how little there was to engage my attention. My health forbade me from venturing out unless the weather was exceptionally genial, and I had no friends who would call upon me and break the monotony of my daily existence. Under these circumstances, I eagerly hailed the little mystery which hung around my companion, and spent much of my time in endeavouring to unravel it.

He was not studying medicine. He had himself, in reply to a question, confirmed Stamford's opinion upon that point. Neither did he appear to have pursued any course of reading which might fit him for a degree in science or any other recognised portal which would give him an entrance into the learned world. Yet his zeal for certain studies was remarkable, and within eccentric limits his knowledge was so extraordinarily ample and minute that his observations fairly astounded me. Surely no man would work so hard or attain such precise information unless he had some definite end in view. Desultory readers are seldom remarkable for the exactness of their learning. No man burdens his mind with small matters unless he has some very good reason for doing so.

His ignorance was as remarkable as his knowledge. Of contemporary literature, philosophy and politics he appeared to know next to nothing. Upon my quoting Thomas Carlyle, he enquired in the naïvest way who he might be and what he had done. My surprise reached a climax, however, when I found incidentally that he was ignorant of the Copernican Theory and of the composition of the Solar System. That any civilised human being in this nineteenth century should not be aware that the earth travelled round the sun appeared to be to me such an extraordinary fact that I could hardly realise it.

'You appear to be astonished,' he said, smiling at my expression of surprise. 'Now that I do know it I shall do my best to forget it.'

'To forget it!'

'You see,' he explained, 'I consider that a man's brain originally is like a little empty attic, and you have to stock it with such furniture as you choose. A fool takes in all the lumber of every sort that he comes across, so that the knowledge which might be useful to him gets crowded out, or at best is jumbled up with a lot of other things, so that he has a difficulty in laying his hands upon it. Now the skilled workman is very careful indeed as to what he takes into his brain-attic. He will have nothing but the tools which may help him in doing his work, but of these he has a large assortment, and all in the most perfect order. It is a mistake to think that that little room has elastic walls and can distend to any extent. Depend upon it there comes a time when for every addition of knowledge you forget something that you knew before. It is of the highest importance, therefore, not to have useless facts elbowing out the useful ones.'

'But the Solar System!' I protested.

'What the deuce is it to me?' he interrupted impatiently. 'You say that we go round the sun. If we went round the moon it would not make a pennyworth of difference to me or to my work.'

I was on the point of asking him what that work might be, but something in his manner showed me that the question would be an unwelcome one. I pondered over our short conversation, how-ever, and endeavoured to draw my deductions from it. He said that he would acquire no knowledge which did not bear upon his object. Therefore all the knowledge which he possessed was such as would be useful to him. I enumerated in my own mind all the various points upon which he had shown me that he was exceptionally well informed. I even took a pencil and jotted them down. I could not help smiling at the document when I had completed it. It ran in this way:

Sherlock Holmes – *his limits*

1 Knowledge of literature – nil
2 Knowledge of philosophy – nil
3 Knowledge of astronomy – nil
4 Knowledge of politics – feeble
5 Knowledge of botany – variable. Well up in belladonna, opium and poisons generally. Knows nothing of practical gardening.
6 Knowledge of geology – practical, but limited. Tells at a glance different soils from each other. After walks, has shown me splashes upon his trousers and told me by their colour and consistence in what part of London he had received them.
7 Knowledge of chemistry – profound
8 Knowledge of anatomy – accurate, but unsystematic
9 Knowledge of sensational literature – immense. He appears to know every detail of every horror perpetrated in the century.
10 Plays the violin well
11 Is an expert singlestick player, boxer, and swordsman
12 Has a good practical knowledge of British law

When I had got so far in my list I threw it into the fire in despair. 'If I can only find what the fellow is driving at by reconciling all these accomplishments and discovering a calling which needs them all,' I said to myself, 'I may as well give up the attempt at once.'

I see that I have alluded above to his powers upon the violin. These were very remarkable, but as eccentric as all his other accomplishments. That he could play pieces, and difficult pieces, I knew well, because at my request he had played me some of Mendelssohn's *Lieder*, and other favourites. When left to himself, however, he would seldom produce any music or attempt any recognised air. Leaning back in his armchair of an evening, he would close his eyes and scrape carelessly at the fiddle which was thrown across his knee. Sometimes the chords were sonorous and melancholy. Occasionally they were fantastic and cheerful. Clearly they reflected the thoughts which possessed him, but whether the music aided those thoughts, or whether the playing was simply the result of a whim or fancy, was more than I could determine. I might have rebelled against these exasperating solos had it not been that he usually terminated them by playing in quick succession a whole series of my favourite airs as a slight compensation for the trial upon my patience.

During the first week or so we had no callers, and I had begun to think that my companion was as friendless a man as I was myself. Presently, however, I found that he had many acquaintances, and those in the most different classes of society. There was one little sallow, rat-faced, dark-eyed fellow, who was introduced to me as Mr Lestrade, and who came three or four times in a single week. One morning a young girl called, fashionably dressed, and stayed for half an hour or more. The same afternoon brought a grey-headed seedy visitor, looking like a Jew pedlar, who appeared to me to be much excited, and who was closely followed by a slipshod elderly woman. On another occasion an old white-haired gentleman had an interview with my companion; and on another, a railway porter in his velveteen uniform. When any of these nondescript individuals put in an appearance Sherlock Holmes used to beg for the use of the sitting-room and I would retire to my bedroom. He always apologised to me for putting me to this inconvenience. 'I have to use this room as a place of business,' he said, 'and these people are my clients.' Again I had an opportunity of asking him a point-blank question, and again my delicacy prevented me from forcing another man to confide in me. I imagined at the time that he had some strong reason for not alluding to it, but he soon dispelled the idea by coming round to the subject of his own accord.

It was upon the 4th of March, as I have good reason to remember, that I rose somewhat earlier than usual, and found that Sherlock Holmes had not yet finished his breakfast. The landlady had become so accustomed to my late habits that my place had not been laid nor my coffee prepared. With the unreasonable petulance of mankind I rang the bell and gave a curt intimation that I was ready. Then I picked up a magazine from the table and attempted to while away the time with it, while my companion munched silently at his toast. One of the articles had a pencil mark at the heading, and I naturally began to run my eye through it.

Its somewhat ambitious title was 'The Book of Life', and it attempted to show how much an observant man might learn by an accurate and systematic examination of all that came in his way. It struck me as being a remarkable mixture of shrewdness and of absurdity. The reasoning was close and intense, but the deductions appeared to me to be far-fetched and exaggerated. The writer claimed by a momentary expression, a twitch of a muscle or a glance of an eye to fathom a man's inmost thoughts. Deceit, according to him, was an impossibility in the case of one trained to observation and analysis. His conclusions were as infallible as so many propositions of Euclid. So startling would his results appear to the uninitiated that until they learned the processes by which he had arrived at them they might well consider him as a necromancer.

From a drop of water [said the writer], a logician could infer the possibility of an Atlantic or a Niagara without having seen or heard of one or the other. So all life is a great chain, the nature of which is known wherever we are shown a single link of it. Like all other arts, the Science of Deduction and Analysis is one which can only be acquired by long and patient study, nor is life long enough to allow any mortal to attain the highest possible perfection in it. Before turning to those moral and mental aspects of the matter which present the greatest difficulties, let the enquirer begin by mastering more elementary problems. Let him, on meeting a fellow-mortal, learn at a glance to distinguish the history of the man and the trade or profession to which he belongs. Puerile as such an exercise may seem, it sharpens the faculties of observation, and teaches one where to look and what to look for. By a man's fingernails, by his coat-sleeve, by his boot, by his trouser-knees, by the callosities of his forefinger and thumb, by his expression, by his shirt—cuffs – by each of these things a man's calling is plainly revealed. That all united should fail to enlighten the competent enquirer in any case is almost inconceivable.

'What ineffable twaddle!' I cried, slapping the magazine down on the table; 'I never read such rubbish in my life.'

'What is it?' asked Sherlock Holmes.

'Why, this article,' I said, pointing at it with my egg-spoon as I sat down to my breakfast. 'I see that you have read it since you have marked it. I don't deny that it is smartly written. It irritates me though. It is evidently the theory of some armchair lounger who evolves all these neat little paradoxes in the seclusion of his own study. It is not practical. I should like to see him clapped down in a third-class carriage on the Underground, and asked to give the trades of all his fellow-travellers. I would lay a thousand to one against him.'

'You would lose your money,' Holmes remarked calmly. 'As for the article, I wrote it myself.'

'You!'

'Yes; I have a turn both for observation and for deduction. The theories which I have expressed there, and which appear to you to be so chimerical, are really extremely practical – so practical that I depend upon them for my bread and cheese.'

'And how?' I asked involuntarily.

'Well, I have a trade of my own. I suppose I am the only one in the world. I'm a consulting detective, if you can understand what that is. Here in London we have lots of government detectives and lots of private ones. When these fellows are at fault, they come to me, and I manage to put them on the right scent. They lay all the evidence before me, and I am generally able, by the help of my knowledge of the history of crime, to set them straight. There is a strong family resemblance about misdeeds, and if you have all the details of a thousand at your finger-ends, it is odd if you can't unravel the thousand and first. Lestrade is a well-known detective. He got himself into a fog recently over a forgery case, and that was what brought him here.'

'And these other people?'

'They are mostly sent on by private enquiry agencies. They are all people who are in trouble about something, and want a little enlightening. I listen to their story, they listen to my comments, and then I pocket my fee.'

'But do you mean to say,' I said, 'that without leaving your room you can unravel some knot which other men can make nothing of, although they have seen every detail for themselves?'

'Quite so. I have a kind of intuition that way. Now and again a case turns up which is a little more complex. Then I have to bustle about and see things with my own eyes. You see I have a lot of special knowledge which I apply to the problem, and which facilitates matters wonderfully. Those rules of deduction laid down in that article which aroused your scorn are invaluable to me in practical work. Observation with me is second nature. You appeared to be surprised when I told you, on our first meeting, that you had come from Afghanistan.'

'You were told, no doubt.'

'Nothing of the sort. I *knew* you came from Afghanistan. From long habit the train of thoughts ran so swiftly through my mind that I arrived at the conclusion without being conscious of intermediate steps. There were such steps, however. The train of reasoning ran, "Here is a gentleman of a medical type, but with the air of a military man. Clearly an army doctor, then. He has just come from the tropics, for his face is dark, and that is not the natural tint of his skin, for his wrists are fair. He has undergone hardship and sickness, as his haggard face says clearly. His left arm has been injured. He holds it in a stiff and unnatural manner. Where in the tropics could an English army doctor have seen much hardship and got his arm wounded? Clearly in Afghanistan." The whole train of thought did not occupy a second. I then remarked that you came from Afghanistan, and you were astonished.'

'It is simple enough as you explain it,' I said, smiling. 'You remind me of Edgar Allan Poe's Dupin. I had no idea that such individuals did exist outside of stories.'

Sherlock Holmes rose and lit his pipe. 'No doubt you think that you are complimenting me in comparing me to Dupin,' he observed. 'Now, in my opinion, Dupin was a very inferior fellow. That trick of his of breaking in on his friends' thoughts with an apropos remark after a quarter of an hour's silence is really very showy and superficial. He had some analytical genius, no doubt; but he was by no means such a phenomenon as Poe appeared to imagine.'

'Have you read Gaboriau's works?' I asked. 'Does Lecoq come up to your idea of a detective?'

Sherlock Holmes sniffed sardonically. 'Lecoq was a miserable bungler,' he said, in an angry voice; 'he had only one thing to recommend him, and that was his energy. That book made me positively ill. The question was how to identify an unknown prisoner. I could have done it in twenty-four hours. Lecoq took six months or so. It might be made a textbook for detectives to teach them what to avoid.'

I felt rather indignant at having two characters whom I had admired treated in this cavalier style. I walked over to the window, and stood looking out into the busy street. 'This fellow may be very clever,' I said to myself, 'but he is certainly very conceited.'

'There are no crimes and no criminals in these days,' he said, querulously. 'What is the use of having brains in our profession? I know well that I have it in me to make my name famous. No man lives or has ever lived who has brought the same amount of study and of natural talent to the detection of crime which I have done. And what is the result? There is no crime to detect, or, at most, some bungling villainy with a motive so transparent that even a Scotland Yard official can see through it.'

I was still annoyed at his bumptious style of conversation. I thought it best to change the topic.

'I wonder what that fellow is looking for?' I asked, pointing to a stalwart, plainly dressed individual who was walking slowly down the other side of the street, looking anxiously at the numbers. He had a large blue envelope in his hand and was evidently the bearer of a message.

'You mean the retired sergeant of marines,' said Sherlock Holmes.

'Brag and bounce!' thought I to myself. 'He knows that I cannot verify his guess.'

The thought had hardly passed through my mind when the man whom we were watching caught sight of the number on our door, and ran rapidly across the roadway. We heard a loud knock, a deep voice below, and heavy steps ascending the stair.

'For Mr Sherlock Holmes,' he said, stepping into the room and handing my friend the letter.

Here was an opportunity of taking the conceit out of him. He little thought of this when he made that random shot. 'May I ask, my lad,' I said, in the blandest voice, 'what your trade may be?'

'Commissionaire, sir,' he said, gruffly. 'Uniform away for repairs.'

'And you were?' I asked, with a slightly malicious glance at my companion.

'A sergeant, sir, Royal Marine Light Infantry, sir. No answer? Right, sir.'

He clicked his heels together, raised his hand in a salute, and was gone.

3

The Lauriston Gardens Mystery

I confess that I was considerably startled by this fresh proof of the practical nature of my companion's theories. My respect for his powers of analysis increased wondrously. There still remained some lurking suspicion in my mind, however, that the whole thing was a prearranged episode, intended to dazzle me, though what earthly object he could have in taking me in was past my comprehension. When I looked at him, he had finished reading the note, and his eyes had assumed the vacant, lack-lustre expression which showed mental abstraction.

'How in the world did you deduce that?' I asked.

'Deduce what?' said he petulantly.

'Why, that he was a retired sergeant of marines.'

'I have no time for trifles,' he answered, brusquely; then with a smile, 'Excuse my rudeness. You broke the thread of my thoughts; but perhaps it is as well. So you actually were not able to see that that man was a sergeant of marines?'

'No indeed.'

'It was easier to know it than to explain why I know it. If you were asked to prove that two and two made four, you might find some difficulty, and yet you are quite sure of the fact. Even across the street I could see a great blue anchor tattooed on the back of the fellow's hand. That smacked of the sea. He had a military carriage, however, and regulation side-whiskers. There we have the marine. He was a man with some amount of self-importance and a certain air of command. You must have observed the way in which he held his head and swung his cane. A steady, respectable, middle-aged man, too, on the face of him – all facts which led me to believe that he had been a sergeant.'

'Wonderful!' I ejaculated.

'Commonplace,' said Holmes, though I thought from his expression that he was pleased at my evident surprise and admiration. 'I said just now that there were no criminals. It appears that I am wrong – look at this!' He threw me over the note which the commissionaire had brought.

'Why,' I cried, as I cast my eye over it, 'this is terrible!'

'It does seem to be a little out of the common,' he remarked, calmly. 'Would you mind reading it to me aloud?'

This is the letter which I read to him:

My dear Mr Sherlock Holmes – There has been a bad business during the night at 3 Lauriston Gardens, off the Brixton Road. Our man on the beat saw a light there about two in the morning, and as the house was an empty one, suspected that something was amiss. He found the door open, and in the front room, which is bare of furniture, discovered the body of a gentleman, well dressed, and having cards in his pocket bearing the name of Enoch J. Drebber, Cleveland, Ohio, USA. There had been no robbery, nor is there any evidence as to how the man met his death. There are marks of blood in the room, but there is no wound upon his person. We are at a loss as to how he came into the empty house; indeed the whole affair is a puzzler. If you can come round to the house any time before twelve, you will find me there. I have left everything *in statu quo* until I hear from you. If you are unable to come, I shall give you fuller details, and would esteem it a great kindness if you would favour me with your opinion.

Yours faithfully,

TOBIAS GREGSON

'Gregson is the smartest of the Scotland Yarders,' my friend remarked; 'he and Lestrade are the pick of a bad lot. They are both quick and energetic, but conventional – shockingly so. They have their knives into one another, too. They are as jealous as a pair of professional beauties. There will be some fun over this case if they are both put upon the scent.'

I was amazed at the calm way in which he rippled on. 'Surely there is not a moment to be lost,' I cried; 'shall I go and order you a cab?'

'I'm not sure about whether I shall go. I am the most incurably lazy devil that ever stood in shoe leather – that is when the fit is on me, for I can be spry enough at times.'

'Why, it is just such a chance as you have been longing for.'

'My dear fellow, what does it matter to me? Supposing I unravel the whole matter, you may be sure that Gregson, Lestrade and Co. will pocket all the credit. That comes of being an unofficial personage.'

'But he begs you to help him.'

'Yes. He knows that I am his superior, and acknowledges it to me; but he would cut his tongue out before he would own it to any third person. However, we may as well go and have a look. I shall work it out on my own hook. I may have a laugh at them, if I have nothing else. Come on!'

He hustled on his overcoat, and bustled about in a way that showed that an energetic fit had superseded the apathetic one.

'Get your hat,' he said.

'You wish me to come?'

'Yes, if you have nothing better to do.'

A minute later we were both in a hansom, driving furiously for the Brixton Road. It was a foggy, cloudy morning, and a dun-coloured veil hung over the housetops, looking like the reflection of the mud-coloured streets beneath. My companion was in the best of spirits, and prattled away about Cremona fiddles and the difference between a Stradivarius and an Amati. As for myself, I was silent, for the dull weather and the melancholy business upon which we were engaged depressed my spirits.

'You don't seem to give much thought to the matter in hand,' I said at last, interrupting Holmes's musical disquisition.

'No data yet,' he answered. 'It is a capital mistake to theorise before you have all the evidence. It biases the judgement.'

'You will have your data soon,' I remarked, pointing with my finger; 'this is the Brixton Road, and that is the house, if I am not very much mistaken.'

'So it is. Stop, driver, stop!' We were still a hundred yards or so from it, but he insisted upon our alighting and we finished our journey upon foot.

Number 3, Lauriston Gardens, wore an ill-omened and minatory look. It was one of four houses which stood back some little way from the street, two being occupied and two empty. The latter looked out with three tiers of vacant melancholy windows, which were blank and dreary, save that here and there a 'To Let' card had developed like a cataract upon the bleared panes. A small garden sprinkled over with a scattered eruption of sickly plants separated each of these houses from the street and was traversed by a narrow pathway, yellowish in colour, and consisting apparently of a mixture of clay and of gravel. The whole place was very sloppy from the rain which had fallen through the night. The garden was bounded by a three-foot brick wall with a fringe of wood rails upon the top and against this wall was leaning a stalwart police constable, surrounded by a small knot of loafers, who craned their necks and strained their eyes in the vain hope of catching some glimpse of the proceedings within.

I had imagined that Sherlock Holmes would at once have hurried into the house and plunged into a study of the mystery. Nothing appeared to be further from his intention. With an air of nonchalance which, under the circumstances, seemed to me to border upon affectation, he lounged up and down the pavement, and gazed vacantly at the ground, the sky, the opposite houses and the line of railings. Having finished his scrutiny, he proceeded slowly down the path, or rather down the fringe of grass which flanked the path, keeping his eyes riveted upon the ground. Twice he stopped, and once I saw him smile, and heard him utter an exclamation of satisfaction. There were many marks of footsteps upon the wet clayey soil; but since the police had been coming and going over it, I was unable to see how my companion could hope to learn anything from it. Still I had had such extraordinary evidence of the quickness of his perceptive faculties that I had no doubt that he could see a great deal which was hidden from me.

At the door of the house we were met by a tall, white-faced, flaxen-haired man, with a notebook in his hand, who rushed forward and wrung my companion's hand with effusion. 'It is indeed kind of you to come,' he said. 'I have had everything left untouched.'

'Except that!' my friend answered, pointing at the pathway. 'If a herd of buffaloes had passed along there could not be a greater mess. No doubt, however, you had drawn your own conclusions, Gregson, before you permitted this.'

'I have had so much to do inside the house,' the detective said evasively. 'My colleague, Mr Lestrade, is here. I had relied upon him to look after this.'

Holmes glanced at me and raised his eyebrows sardonically. 'With two such men as yourself and Lestrade upon the ground there will not be much for a third party to find out,' he said.

Gregson rubbed his hands in a self-satisfied way. 'I think we have done all that can be done,' he answered; 'it's a queer case though, and I knew your taste for such things.'

'You did not come here in a cab?' asked Sherlock Holmes.

'No, sir.'

'Nor Lestrade?'

'No, sir.'

'Then let us go and look at the room.' With which inconsequent remark he strode on into the house, followed by Gregson, whose features expressed his astonishment.

A short passage, bare-planked and dusty, led to the kitchen and offices. Two doors opened out of it to the left and to the right. One of these had obviously been closed for many weeks. The other belonged to the dining-room, which was the apartment in which the mysterious affair had occurred. Holmes walked in, and I followed him with that subdued feeling at my heart which the presence of death inspires.

It was a large square room, looking all the larger from the absence of all furniture. A vulgar flaring paper adorned the walls, but it was blotched in places with mildew, and here and there great strips had become detached and hung down, exposing the yellow plaster beneath. Opposite the door was a showy fireplace, surmounted by a mantelpiece of imitation white marble. On one corner of this was stuck the stump of a red wax candle. The solitary window was so dirty that the light was hazy and uncertain, giving a dull grey tinge to everything, which was intensified by the thick layer of dust which coated the whole apartment.

All these details I observed afterwards. At present my attention was centred upon the single, grim, motionless figure which lay stretched upon the boards, with vacant, sightless eyes staring up at the discoloured ceiling. It was that of a man about forty-three or forty-four years of age, middle-sized, broad-shouldered, with crisp curling black hair and a short, stubbly beard. He was dressed in a heavy broadcloth frock-coat and waistcoat, with light-coloured trousers and immaculate collar and cuffs. A top hat, well brushed and trim, was placed upon the floor beside him. His hands were clenched and his arms thrown abroad, while his lower limbs were interlocked, as though his death struggle had been a grievous one. On his rigid face there stood an expression of horror, and, as it seemed to me, of hatred, such as I have never seen upon human features. This malignant and terrible contortion, combined with the low forehead, blunt nose and prognathous jaw, gave the dead man a singularly simous and apelike appearance, which was increased by his writhing, unnatural posture. I have seen death in many forms, but never has it appeared to me in a more fearsome aspect than in that dark, grimy apartment which looked out upon one of the main arteries of suburban London.

Lestrade, lean and ferret-like as ever, was standing by the doorway, and greeted my companion and myself.

'This case will make a stir, sir,' he remarked. 'It beats anything I have seen, and I am no chicken.'

'There is no clue,' said Gregson.

'None at all,' chimed in Lestrade.

Sherlock Holmes approached the body, and, kneeling down, examined it intently. 'You are sure that there is no wound?' he asked, pointing to numerous gouts and splashes of blood which lay all round.

'Positive!' cried both detectives.

'Then, of course, this blood belongs to a second individual – presumably the murderer, if murder has been committed. It reminds me of the circumstances attendant on the death of Van Jansen, in Utrecht, in the year '34. Do you remember the case, Gregson?'

'No, sir.'

'Read it up – you really should. There is nothing new under the sun. It has all been done before.' As he spoke, his nimble fingers were flying here, there and everywhere, feeling, pressing, unbuttoning, examining, while his eyes wore the same faraway expression which I have already remarked upon. So swiftly was the examination made that one would hardly have guessed the minuteness with which it was conducted. Finally, he sniffed the dead man's lips, and then glanced at the soles of his patent-leather boots.

'He has not been moved at all?' he asked.

'No more than was necessary for the purposes of our examination.'

'You can take him to the mortuary now,' he said. 'There is nothing more to be learned.'

Gregson had a stretcher and four men at hand. At his call they entered the room and the stranger was lifted and carried out. As they raised him, a ring tinkled down and rolled across the floor. Lestrade grabbed it up and stared at it with mystified eyes.

'There's been a woman here,' he cried. 'It's a woman's wedding-ring.'

He held it out, as he spoke, upon the palm of his hand. We all gathered round him and gazed at it. There could be no doubt that the circlet of plain gold had once adorned the finger of a bride.

'This complicates matters,' said Gregson. 'Heaven knows, they were complicated enough before.'

'You're sure it doesn't simplify them?' observed Holmes. 'There's nothing to be learned by staring at it. What did you find in his pockets?'

'We have it all here,' said Gregson, pointing to a litter of objects upon one of the bottom steps of the stairs. 'A gold watch, No. 97163 by Barraud of London. Gold Albert chain, very heavy and solid. Gold ring, with masonic device. Gold pin – bulldog's head, with rubies as eyes. Russian-leather card-case, with cards of Enoch J. Drebber of Cleveland, corresponding with the E. J. D. upon the linen. No purse, but loose money to the extent of seven pounds thirteen. Pocket edition of Boccaccio's *Decameron*, with name of Joseph Stangerson upon the flyleaf. Two letters – one addressed to E. J. Drebber and one to Joseph Stangerson.'

'At what address?'

'American Exchange, Strand – to be left till called for. They are both from the Guion Steamship Company, and refer to the sailing of their boats from Liverpool. It is clear that this unfortunate man was about to return to New York.'

'Have you made any enquiries as to this man Stangerson?'

'I did it at once, sir,' said Gregson. 'I have had advertisements sent to all the newspapers, and one of my men has gone to the American Exchange, but he has not returned yet.'

'Have you sent to Cleveland?'

'We telegraphed this morning.'

'How did you word your enquiries?'

'We simply detailed the circumstances, and said that we should be glad of any information which could help us.'

'You did not ask for particulars on any point which appeared to you to be crucial?'

'I asked about Stangerson.'

'Nothing else? Is there no circumstance on which this whole case appears to hinge? Will you not telegraph again?'

'I have said all I have to say,' said Gregson, in an offended voice.

Sherlock Holmes chuckled to himself, and appeared to be about to make some remark, when Lestrade, who had been in the front room while we were holding this conversation in the hall, reappeared upon the scene, rubbing his hands in a pompous and self-satisfied manner.

'Mr Gregson,' he said, 'I have just made a discovery of the highest importance, and one which would have been overlooked had I not made a careful examination of the walls.'

The little man's eyes sparkled as he spoke, and he was evidently in a state of suppressed exultation at having scored a point against his colleague.

'Come here,' he said, bustling back into the room, the atmosphere of which felt clearer since the removal of its ghastly inmate. 'Now, stand there!'

He struck a match on his boot and held it up against the wall.

'Look at that!' he said, triumphantly.

I have remarked that the paper had fallen away in parts. In this particular corner of the room a large piece had peeled off, leaving a yellow square of coarse plastering. Across this bare space there was scrawled in blood-red letters a single word –

RACHE

'What do you think of that?' cried the detective, with the air of a showman exhibiting his show. 'This was overlooked because it was in the darkest corner of the room and no one thought of looking there. The murderer has written it with his or her own blood. See this smear where it has trickled down the wall! That disposes of the idea of suicide anyhow. Why was that corner chosen to write it on? I will tell you. See that candle on the mantelpiece. It was lit at the time, and if it was lit this corner would be the brightest instead of the darkest portion of the wall.'

'And what does it mean now that you *have* found it?' asked Gregson in a depreciatory voice.

'Mean? Why, it means that the writer was going to put the female name Rachel, but was disturbed before he or she had time to finish. You mark my words, when this case comes to be cleared up, you will find that a woman named Rachel has something to do with it. It's all very well for you to laugh, Mr Sherlock Holmes. You may be very smart and clever, but the old hound is the best, when all is said and done.'

'I really beg your pardon!' said my companion, who had ruffled the little man's temper by bursting into an explosion of laughter. 'You certainly have the credit of being the first of us to find this out and, as you say, it bears every mark of having been written by the other participant in last night's mystery. I have not had time to examine this room yet, but with your permission I shall do so now.'

As he spoke, he whipped a tape measure and a large round magnifying glass from his pocket. With these two implements he trotted noiselessly about the room, sometimes stopping, occasionally kneeling, and once lying flat upon his face. So engrossed was he with his occupation that he appeared to have forgotten our presence, for he chattered away to himself under his breath the whole time, keeping up a running fire of exclamations, groans, whistles and little cries suggestive of encouragement and of hope. As I watched him I was irresistibly reminded of a pure-blooded, well-trained foxhound as it dashes backwards and forwards through the covert, whining in its eagerness, until it comes across the lost scent. For twenty minutes or more he continued his researches, measuring with the most exact care the distance between marks which were entirely invisible to me, and occasionally applying his tape to the walls in an equally incomprehensible manner. In one place he gathered up very carefully a little pile of grey dust from the floor and packed it away in an envelope. Finally he examined with his glass the word upon the wall, going over every letter of it with the most minute exactness. This done, he appeared to be satisfied, for he replaced his tape and his glass in his pocket.

'They say that genius is an infinite capacity for taking pains,' he remarked with a smile. 'It's a very bad definition, but it does apply to detective work.'

Gregson and Lestrade had watched the manoeuvres of their amateur companion with considerable curiosity and some contempt. They evidently failed to appreciate the fact, which I had begun to realise, that Sherlock Holmes's smallest actions were all directed towards some definite and practical end.

'What do you think of it, sir?' they both asked.

'It would be robbing you of the credit of the case if I were to presume to help you,' remarked my friend. 'You are doing so well now that it would be a pity for anyone to interfere.' There was a world of sarcasm in his voice as he spoke. 'If you will let me know how your investigations go,' he continued, 'I shall be happy to give you any help I can. In the meantime I should like to speak to the constable who found the body. Can you give me his name and address?'

Lestrade glanced at his notebook. 'John Rance,' he said. 'He is off duty now. You will find him at 46 Audley Court, Kennington Park Gate.'

Holmes took a note of the address.

'Come along, doctor,' he said; 'we shall go and look him up. I'll tell you one thing which may help you in the case,' he continued, turning to the two detectives. 'There has been murder done, and the murderer was a man. He was more than six feet high, was in the prime of life, had small feet for his height, wore coarse, square-toed boots and smoked a Trichinopoly cigar. He came here with his victim in a four-wheeled cab, which was drawn by a horse with three old shoes and one new one on his off foreleg. In all probability the murderer had a florid face, and the fingernails of his right hand were remarkably long. These are only a few indications, but they may assist you.'

Lestrade and Gregson glanced at each other with an incredulous smile.

'If this man was murdered, how was it done?' asked the former.

'Poison,' said Sherlock Holmes curtly, and strode off. 'One other thing, Lestrade,' he added, turning round at the door: ' "Rache" is the German for "revenge"; so don't lose your time looking for Miss Rachel.'

With which Parthian shot he walked away, leaving the two rivals open-mouthed behind him.

4

What John Rance Had to Tell

It was one o'clock when we left No. 3, Lauriston Gardens. Sherlock Holmes led me to the nearest telegraph-office, whence he dispatched a long telegram. He then hailed a cab and ordered the driver to take us to the address given us by Lestrade.

'There is nothing like first-hand evidence,' he remarked; 'as a matter of fact, my mind is entirely made up upon the case, but still we may as well learn all that is to be learned.'

'You amaze me, Holmes,' said I. 'Surely you are not as sure as you pretend to be of all those particulars which you gave.'

'There's no room for a mistake,' he answered. 'The very first thing which I observed on arriving there was that a cab had made two ruts with its wheels close to the kerb. Now, up to last night, we have had no rain for a week, so that those wheels which left such a deep impression must have been there during the night. There were the marks of the horse's hoofs, too, the outline of one of which was far more clearly cut than that of the other three, showing that that was a new shoe. Since the cab was there after the rain began, and was not there at any time during the morning – I have Gregson's word for that – it follows that it must have been there during the night, and, therefore, that it brought those two individuals to the house.'

'That seems simple enough,' said I; 'but how about the other man's height?'

'Why, the height of a man, in nine cases out of ten, can be told from the length of his stride. It is a simple calculation enough, though there is no use my boring you with figures. I had this fellow's stride both on the clay outside and on the dust within. Then I had a way of checking my calculation. When a man writes on a wall, his instinct leads him to write about the level of his own eyes. Now that writing was just over six feet from the ground. It was child's play.'

'And his age?' I asked.

'Well, if a man can stride four and a half feet without the smallest effort, he can't be quite in the sere and yellow. That was the breadth of a puddle on the garden walk which he had evidently walked across. Patent-leather boots had gone round and Square-toes had hopped over. There is no mystery about it at all. I am simply applying to ordinary life a few of those precepts of observation and deduction which I advocated in that article. Is there anything else that puzzles you?'

'The fingernails and the Trichinopoly,' I suggested.

'The writing on the wall was done with a man's forefinger dipped in blood. My glass allowed me to observe that the plaster was slightly scratched in doing it, which would not have been the case if the man's nail had been trimmed. I gathered up some scattered ash from the floor. It was dark in colour and flakey – such an ash as is only made by a Trichinopoly. I have made a special study of cigar ashes – in fact, I have written a monograph upon the subject. I flatter myself that I can distinguish at a glance the ash of any known brand either of cigar or of tobacco. It is just in such details that the skilled detective differs from the Gregson and Lestrade type.'

'And the florid face?' I asked.

'Ah, that was a more daring shot, though I have no doubt that I was right. You must not ask me that at the present state of the affair.'

I passed my hand over my brow. 'My head is in a whirl,' I remarked; 'the more one thinks of it the more mysterious it grows. How came these two men – if there were two men – into an empty house? What has become of the cabman who drove them? How could one man compel another to take poison? Where did the blood come from? What was the object of the murderer since robbery had no part in it? How came the woman's ring there? Above all, why should the second man write up the word RACHE before decamping? I confess that I cannot see any possible way of reconciling all these facts.'

My companion smiled approvingly.

'You sum up the difficulties of the situation succinctly and well,' he said. 'There is much that is still obscure, though I have quite made up my mind on the main facts. As to poor Lestrade's discovery, it was simply a blind intended to put the police upon a wrong track, by suggesting Socialism and secret societies. It was not done by a German. The A, if you noticed, was printed somewhat after the German fashion. Now, a real German invariably prints in the Latin character, so that we may safely say that this was not written by one, but by a clumsy imitator who overdid his part. It was simply a ruse to divert enquiry into a wrong channel. I'm not going to tell you much more of the case, doctor. You know a conjuror gets no credit when once he has explained his trick; and if I show you too much of my method of working, you will come to the conclusion that I am a very ordinary individual after all.'

'I shall never do that,' I answered; 'you have brought detection as near an exact science as it ever will be brought in this world.'

My companion flushed up with pleasure at my words, and the earnest way in which I uttered them. I had already observed that he was as sensitive to flattery on the score of his art as any girl could be on that of her beauty.

'I'll tell you one other thing,' he said. 'Patent-leathers and Square-toes came in the same cab, and they walked down the pathway together as friendly as possible – arm in arm, in all probability. When they got inside, they walked up and down the room – or rather, Patent-leathers stood still while Square-toes walked up and down. I could read all that in the dust; and I could read that as he walked he grew more and more excited. That is shown by the increased length of his strides. He was talking all the while, and working himself up, no doubt, into a fury. Then the tragedy occurred. I've told you all I know myself now, for the rest is mere surmise and conjecture. We have a good working basis, however, on which to start. We must hurry up, for I want to go to Hallè's concert to hear Norman-Neruda this afternoon.'

This conversation had occurred while our cab had been threading its way through a long succession of dingy streets and dreary byways. In the dingiest and dreariest of them our driver suddenly came to a stand. 'That's Audley Court in there,' he said, pointing to a narrow slit in the line of dead-coloured brick. 'You'll find me here when you come back.'

Audley Court was not an attractive locality. The narrow passage led us into a quadrangle paved with flags and lined by sordid dwellings. We picked our way among groups of dirty children, and through lines of discoloured linen, until we came to Number 46, the door of which was decorated with a small slip of brass on which the name Rance was engraved. On enquiry we found that the constable was in bed, and we were shown into a little front parlour to await his coming.

He appeared presently, looking a little irritable at being disturbed in his slumbers. 'I made my report at the office,' he said.

Holmes took a half-sovereign from his pocket and played with it pensively. 'We thought that we should like to hear it all from your own lips,' he said.

'I shall be most happy to tell you anything I can,' the constable answered, with his eyes upon the little golden disc.

'Just let us hear it all in your own way as it occurred.'

Rance sat down on the horsehair sofa, and knitted his brows as though determined not to omit anything from his narrative.

'I'll tell it ye from the beginning,' he said. 'My time is from ten at night to six in the morning. At eleven there was a fight at the White Hart; but bar that all was quiet enough on the beat. At one o'clock it began to rain, and I met Harry Murcher – him who has the Holland Grove beat – and we stood together at the corner of Henrietta Street a-talkin'. Presently – maybe about two or a little after – I thought I would take a look round and see that all was right down the Brixton Road. It was precious dirty and lonely. Not a soul did I meet all the way down, though a cab or two went past me. I was a-strollin' down, thinkin' between ourselves how uncommon handy a four of gin hot would be, when suddenly the glint of a light caught me eye in the window of that same house. Now, I knew that them two houses in Lauriston Gardens was empty on account of him that owns them who won't have the drains seed to, though the very last tenant what lived in one of them died o' typhoid fever. I was knocked all in a heap, therefore, at seeing a light in the window, and I suspected as something was wrong. When I got to the door –'

'You stopped, and then walked back to the garden gate,' my companion interrupted. 'What did you do that for?'

Rance gave a violent jump, and stared at Sherlock Holmes with the utmost amazement upon his features.

'Why, that's true, sir,' he said; 'though how you come to know it, heaven only knows. Ye see when I got up to the door, it was so still and so lonesome, that I thought I'd be none the worse for someone with me. I ain't afeard of anything on this side o' the grave; but I thought that maybe it was him that died o' the typhoid inspecting the drains what killed him. The thought gave me a kind o' turn, and I walked back to the gate to see if I could see Murcher's lantern, but there wasn't no sign of him nor of anyone else.'

'There was no one in the street?'

'Not a livin' soul, sir, nor as much as a dog. Then I pulled myself together and went back and pushed the door open. All was quiet inside, so I went into the room where the light was a-burnin'. There was a candle flickerin' on the mantelpiece – a red wax one – and by its light I saw –'

'Yes, I know all that you saw. You walked round the room several times and you knelt down by the body, and then you walked through and tried the kitchen door, and then –'

John Rance sprang to his feet with a frightened face and suspicion in his eyes. 'Where was you hid to see all that?' he cried. 'It seems to me that you knows a deal more than you should.'

Holmes laughed and threw his card across the table to the constable. 'Don't get arresting me for the murder,' he said. 'I am one of the hounds and not the wolf; Mr Gregson or Mr Lestrade will answer for that. Go on, though. What did you do next?'

Rance resumed his seat, without, however, losing his mystified expression. 'I went back to the gate and sounded my whistle. That brought Murcher and two more to the spot.'

'Was the street empty then?'

'Well, it was, as far as anybody that could be of any good goes.'

'What do you mean?'

The constable's features broadened into a grin. 'I've seen many a drunk chap in my time,' he said, 'but never anyone so cryin' drunk as that cove. He was at the gate when I came out, a-leanin' up ag'in the railings, and a-singin' at the pitch o' his lungs about Columbine's New-fangled Banner, or some such stuff. He couldn't stand, far less help.'

'What sort of a man was he?' asked Sherlock Holmes.

John Rance appeared to be somewhat irritated at this digression. 'He was an uncommon drunk sort o' man,' he said. 'He'd ha' found hisself in the station if we hadn't been so took up.'

'His face – his dress – didn't you notice them?' Holmes broke in impatiently.

'I should think I did notice them, seeing that I had to prop him up – me and Murcher between us. He was a long chap with a red face, the lower part muffled round –'

'That will do,' cried Holmes. 'What became of him?'

'We'd enough to do without lookin' after him,' the policeman said, in an aggrieved voice. 'I'll wager he found his way home all right.'

'How was he dressed?'

'A brown overcoat.'

'Had he a whip in his hand?'

'A whip – no.'

'He must have left it behind,' muttered my companion. 'You didn't happen to see or hear a cab after that?'

'No.'

'There's a half-sovereign for you,' my companion said, standing up and taking his hat. 'I am afraid, Rance, that you will never rise in the force. That head of yours should be for use as well as ornament. You might have gained your sergeant's stripes last night. The man whom you held in your hands is the man who holds the clue of this mystery, and whom we are seeking. There is no use arguing about it now; I tell you that it is so. Come along, doctor.'

We started off for the cab together, leaving our informant incredulous, but obviously uncomfortable.

'The blundering fool!' Holmes said, bitterly, as we drove back to our lodgings. 'Just to think of his having such an incomparable bit of good luck, and not taking advantage of it.'

'I am rather in the dark still. It is true that the description of this man tallies with your idea of the second party in this mystery. But why should he come back to the house after leaving it? That is not the way of criminals.'

'The ring, man, the ring: that was what he came back for. If we have no other way of catching him, we can always bait our line with the ring. I shall have him, doctor – I'll lay you two to one that I have him. I must thank you for it all. I might not have gone but for you, and so have missed the finest study I ever came across: a study in scarlet, eh? Why shouldn't we use a little art jargon. There's the scarlet thread of murder running through the colourless skein of life, and our duty is to unravel it, and isolate it, and expose every inch of it. And now for lunch, and then for Norman-Neruda. Her attack and her bowing are splendid. What's that little thing of Chopin's she plays so magnificently: Tra–la–la–lira–lira–lay.'

Leaning back in the cab, this amateur bloodhound carolled away like a lark while I meditated upon the manysidedness of the human mind.

5

Our Advertisement Brings a Visitor

Our morning's exertions had been too much for my weak health, and I was tired out in the afternoon. After Holmes's departure for the concert, I lay down upon the sofa and endeavoured to get a couple of hours' sleep. It was a useless attempt. My mind had been too much excited by all that had occurred, and the strangest fancies and surmises crowded into it. Every time that I closed my eyes I saw before me the distorted, baboon-like countenance of the murdered man. So sinister was the impression which that face had produced upon me that I found it difficult to feel anything but gratitude for him who had removed its owner from the world. If ever human features bespoke vice of the most malignant type they were certainly those of Enoch J. Drebber of Cleveland. Still I recognised that justice must be done and that the depravity of the victim was no condonement in the eyes of the law.

The more I thought of it the more extraordinary did my companion's hypothesis, that the man had been poisoned, appear. I remembered how he had sniffed his lips, and had no doubt that he had detected something which had given rise to the idea. Then, again, if not poison, what had caused the man's death, since there was neither wound nor marks of strangulation? But, on the other hand, whose blood was that which lay so thickly upon the floor? There were no signs of a struggle, nor had the victim any weapon with which he might have wounded an antagonist. As long as all these questions were unsolved, I felt that sleep would be no easy matter, either for Holmes or myself. His quiet, self-confident manner convinced me that he had already formed a theory which explained all the facts, though what it was I could not for an instant conjecture.

He was very late in returning – so late that I knew that the concert could not have detained him all the time. Dinner was on the table before he appeared.

'It was magnificent,' he said, as he took his seat. 'Do you remember what Darwin says about music? He claims that the power of producing and appreciating it existed among the human race long before the power of speech was arrived at. Perhaps that is why we are so subtly influenced by it. There are vague memories in our souls of those misty centuries when the world was in its childhood.'

'That's rather a broad idea,' I remarked.

'One's ideas must be as broad as nature if they are to interpret nature,' he answered. 'What's the matter? You're not looking quite yourself. This Brixton Road affair has upset you.'

'To tell the truth, it has,' I said. 'I ought to be more case-hardened after my Afghan experiences. I saw my own comrades hacked to pieces at Maiwand without losing my nerve.'

'I can understand. There is a mystery about this which stimulates the imagination; where there is no imagination there is no horror. Have you seen the evening paper?'

'No.'

'It gives a fairly good account of the affair. It does not mention the fact that when the man was raised up a woman's wedding ring fell upon the floor. It is just as well it does not.'

'Why?'

'Look at this advertisement,' he answered. 'I had one sent to every paper this morning immediately after the affair.'

He threw the paper across to me and I glanced at the place indicated. It was the first announcement in the 'Found' column. 'In Brixton Road, this morning,' it ran, 'a plain gold wedding ring, found in the roadway between the White Hart Tavern and Holland Grove. Apply Dr Watson, 221b Baker Street, between eight and nine this evening.'

'Excuse my using your name,' he said. 'If I used my own some of these dunderheads would recognise it and want to meddle in the affair.'

'That is all right,' I answered. 'But supposing anyone applies, I have no ring.'

'Oh yes, you have,' said he, handing me one. 'This will do very well. It is almost a facsimile.'

'And who do you expect will answer this advertisement?'

'Why, the man in the brown coat – our florid friend with the square toes. If he does not come himself, he will send an accomplice.'

'Would he not consider it as too dangerous?'

'Not at all. If my view of the case is correct, and I have every reason to believe that it is, this man would rather risk anything than lose the ring. According to my notion he dropped it while stooping over Drebber's body, and did not miss it at the time. After leaving the house he discovered his loss and hurried back, but found the police already in possession owing to his own folly in leaving the candle burning. He had to pretend to be drunk in order to allay the suspicions which might have been aroused by his appearance at the gate. Now put yourself in that man's place. On thinking the matter over, it must have occurred to him that it was possible that he had lost the ring in the road after leaving the house. What would he do then? He would eagerly look out for the evening papers in the hope of seeing it among the articles found. His eye, of course, would light upon this. He would be overjoyed. Why should he fear a trap? There would be no reason in his eyes why the finding of the ring should be connected with the murder. He would come. He will come. You shall see him within an hour!'

'And then?' I asked.

'Oh, you can leave me to deal with him then. Have you any arms?'

'I have my old service revolver and a few cartridges.'

'You had better clean it and load it. He will be a desperate man; and though I shall take him unawares, it is as well to be ready for anything.'

I went to my bedroom and followed his advice. When I returned with the pistol, the table had been cleared, and Holmes was engaged in his favourite occupation of scraping upon his violin.

'The plot thickens,' he said, as I entered; 'I have just had an answer to my American telegram. My view of the case is the correct one.'

'And that is?' I asked eagerly.

'My fiddle would be the better for new strings,' he remarked. 'Put your pistol in your pocket. When the fellow comes, speak to him in an ordinary way. Leave the rest to me. Don't frighten him by looking at him too hard.'

'It is eight o'clock now,' I said, glancing at my watch.

'Yes. He will probably be here in a few minutes. Open the door slightly. That will do. Now put the key on the inside. Thank you! This is a queer old book I picked up at a stall yesterday – *De Jure inter Gentes* – published in Latin at Liege in the Lowlands in 1642. Charles's head was still firm on his shoulders when this little brown-backed volume was struck off.'

'Who is the printer?'

'Philippe de Croy, whoever he may have been. On the flyleaf, in very faded ink, is written "Ex libris Gulielmi Whyte". I wonder who William Whyte was. Some pragmatical seventeenth-century lawyer, I suppose. His writing has a legal twist about it. Here comes our man, I think.'

As he spoke there was a sharp ring at the bell. Sherlock Holmes rose softly and moved his chair in the direction of the door. We heard the servant pass along the hall, and the sharp click of the latch as she opened it.

'Does Dr Watson live here?' asked a clear but rather harsh voice. We could not hear the servant's reply, but the door closed, and someone began to ascend the stairs. The footfall was an uncertain and shuffling one. A look of surprise passed over the face of my companion as he listened to it. It came slowly along the passage, and there was a feeble tap at the door.

'Come in,' I cried.

At my summons, instead of the man of violence whom we expected, a very old and wrinkled woman hobbled into the apartment. She appeared to be dazzled by the sudden blaze of light, and after dropping a curtsy, she stood blinking at us with her bleared eyes and fumbling in her pocket with nervous, shaky fingers. I glanced at my companion, and his face had assumed such a disconsolate expression that it was all I could do to keep my countenance.

The old crone drew out an evening paper, and pointed at our advertisement. 'It's this as has brought me, good gentlemen,' she said, dropping another curtsy, 'a gold wedding ring in the Brixton Road. It belongs to my girl Sally, as was married only this time twelve-month, which her husband is steward aboard a Union boat, and what he'd say if he come 'ome and found her without her ring is more than I can think, he being short enough at the best o' times, but more especially when he has the drink. If it please you, she went to the circus last night along with –'

'Is that her ring?' I asked.

'The Lord be thanked!' cried the old woman. 'Sally will be a glad woman this night. That's the ring.'

'And what may your address be?' I enquired, taking up a pencil.

'Number 13, Duncan Street, Houndsditch. A weary way from here.'

'The Brixton Road does not lie between any circus and Houndsditch,' said Sherlock Holmes sharply.

The old woman faced round and looked keenly at him from her little red-rimmed eyes. 'The gentleman asked me for *my* address,' she said. 'Sally lives in lodgings at 3 Mayfield Place, Peckham.'

'And your name is – ?'

'My name is Sawyer – hers is Dennis, which Tom Dennis married her – and a smart, clean lad, too, as long as he's at sea, and no steward in the company more thought of; but when on shore, what with the women and what with liquor shops –'

'Here is your ring, Mrs Sawyer,' I interrupted, in obedience to a sign from my companion; 'it clearly belongs to your daughter, and I am glad to be able to restore it to the rightful owner.'

With many mumbled blessings and protestations of gratitude the old crone packed it away in her pocket, and shuffled off down the stairs. Sherlock Holmes sprang to his feet the moment that she was gone and rushed into his room. He returned in a few seconds enveloped in an ulster and a cravat. 'I'll follow her,' he said, hurriedly; 'she

41

must be an accomplice and will lead me to him. Wait up for me.' The hall door had hardly slammed behind our visitor before Holmes had descended the stair. Looking through the window I could see her walking feebly along the other side, while her pursuer dogged her some little distance behind. 'Either his whole theory is incorrect,' I thought to myself, 'or else he will be led now to the heart of the mystery.' There was no need for him to ask me to wait up for him for I felt that sleep was impossible until I heard the result of his adventure.

It was close upon nine when he set out. I had no idea how long he might be, but I sat stolidly puffing at my pipe and skipping over the pages of Henri Murger's *Vie de Boh'me*. Ten o'clock passed, and I heard the footsteps of the maid as they pattered off to bed. Eleven, and the more stately tread of the landlady passed my door, bound for the same destination. It was close upon twelve before I heard the sharp sound of his latchkey. The instant he entered I saw by his face that he had not been successful. Amusement and chagrin seemed to be struggling for mastery, until the former suddenly carried the day, and he burst into a hearty laugh.

'I wouldn't have the Scotland Yarders know it for the world,' he cried, dropping into his chair; 'I have chaffed them so much that they would never have let me hear the end of it. I can afford to laugh, because I know that I will be even with them in the long run.'

'What is it then?' I asked.

'Oh, I don't mind telling a story against myself. That creature had gone a little way when she began to limp and show every sign of being footsore. Presently she came to a halt, and hailed a four-wheeler which was passing. I managed to be close to her so as to hear the address, but I need not have been so anxious, for she sang it out loud enough to be heard at the other side of the street, "Drive to 13 Duncan Street, Houndsditch," she cried. This begins to look genuine, I thought, and having seen her safely inside, I perched myself behind. That's an art which every detective should be an expert at. Well, away we rattled, and never drew rein until we reached the street in question. I hopped off before we came to the door, and strolled down the street in an easy lounging way. I saw the cab pull up. The driver jumped down, and I saw him open the door and stand expectantly. Nothing came out though. When I reached him, he was groping about frantically in the empty cab, and giving vent to the finest assorted collection of oaths that ever I listened to. There was no sign or trace of his passenger, and I fear it will be some time before he gets his fare. On enquiring at Number 13 we found that the house belonged to a respectable paper-hanger, named Keswick, and that no one of the name either of Sawyer or Dennis had ever been heard of there.'

'You don't mean to say,' I cried, in amazement, 'that that tottering, feeble old woman was able to get out of the cab while it was in motion, without either you or the driver seeing her?'

'Old woman be damned!' said Sherlock Holmes, sharply. 'We were the old women to be so taken in. It must have been a young man, and an active one, too, besides being an incomparable actor. The get-up was inimitable. He saw that he was followed, no doubt, and used this means of giving me the slip. It shows that the man we are after is not as lonely as I imagined he was, but has friends who are ready to risk something for him. Now, doctor, you are looking done-up. Take my advice and turn in.'

I was certainly feeling very weary, so I obeyed his injunction. I left Holmes seated in front of the smouldering fire, and long into the watches of the night I heard the low, melancholy wailings of his violin and knew that he was still pondering over the strange problem which he had set himself to unravel.

6

Tobias Gregson Shows
What He Can Do

The papers next day were full of the 'Brixton Mystery', as they termed it. Each had a long account of the affair, and some had leaders upon it in addition. There was some information in them which was new to me. I still retain in my scrapbook numerous clippings and extracts upon the case. Here is a condensation of a few of them.

The *Daily Telegraph* remarked that in the history of crime there had seldom been a tragedy which presented stranger features. The German name of the victim, the absence of all other motive, and the sinister inscription on the wall, all pointed to its perpetration by political refugees and revolutionists. The Socialists had many branches in America, and the deceased had, no doubt, infringed their unwritten laws and been tracked down by them. After alluding airily to the Vehmgericht, aqua tofana, Carbonari, the Marchioness de Brinvilliers, the Darwinian theory, the principles of Malthus and the Ratcliff Highway murders, the article concluded by admonishing the government and advocating a closer watch over foreigners in England.

The *Standard* commented upon the fact that lawless outrages of the sort usually occurred under a Liberal administration. They arose from the unsettling of the minds of the masses, and the consequent weakening of all authority. The deceased was an American gentleman who had been residing for some weeks in the metropolis. He had stayed at the boarding-house of Madame Charpentier, in Torquay Terrace, Camberwell. He was accompanied in his travels by his private secretary, Mr Joseph Stangerson. The two bade adieu to their landlady upon Tuesday, the 4th inst., and departed to Euston Station with the avowed intention of catching the Liverpool express. They were afterwards seen together upon the platform. Nothing more is known of them until Mr Drebber's body was, as recorded, discovered in an empty house in the Brixton Road, many miles from Euston. How he came there, or how he met his fate, are questions which are still involved in mystery. Nothing is known of the whereabouts of Stangerson. We are glad to learn that Mr Lestrade and Mr Gregson of Scotland Yard are both engaged upon the case, and it is confidently anticipated that these well-known officers will speedily throw light upon the matter.

The *Daily News* observed that there was no doubt as to the crime being a political one. The despotism and hatred of Liberalism which animated the Continental governments had had the effect of driving to our shores a number of men who might have made excellent citizens were they not soured by the recollection of all that they had undergone. Among these men there was a stringent code of honour, any infringement of which was punished by death. Every effort should be made to find the secretary, Stangerson, and to ascertain some particulars of the habits of the deceased. A great step had been gained by the discovery of the address of the house at which he had boarded – a result which was entirely due to the acuteness and energy of Mr Gregson of Scotland Yard.

Sherlock Holmes and I read these notices over together at breakfast, and they appeared to afford him considerable amusement.

'I told you that, whatever happened, Lestrade and Gregson would be sure to score.'

'That depends on how it turns out.'

'Oh, bless you, it doesn't matter in the least. If the man is caught, it will be *on account* of their exertions; if he escapes, it will be *in spite* of their exertions. It's heads I win and tails you lose. Whatever they do, they will have followers. *Un sot trouve toujours un plus sot qui l'admire.*'

'What on earth is this?' I cried, for at this moment there came the pattering of many steps in the hall and on the stairs, accompanied by audible expressions of disgust upon the part of our landlady.

'It's the Baker Street division of the detective police force,' said my companion gravely; and as he spoke there rushed into the room half a dozen of the dirtiest and most ragged street arabs that ever I clapped eyes on.

' 'Tention!' cried Holmes, in a sharp tone, and the six dirty little scoundrels stood in a line like so many disreputable statuettes. 'In future you shall send up Wiggins alone to report, and the rest of you must wait in the street. Have you found it, Wiggins?'

'No, sir, we hain't,' said one of the youths.

'I hardly expected you would. You must keep on until you do. Here are your wages.' He handed each of them a shilling. 'Now, off you go, and come back with a better report next time.'

He waved his hand, and they scampered away downstairs like so many rats, and we heard their shrill voices next moment in the street.

'There's more work to be got out of one of those little beggars than out of a dozen of the force,' Holmes remarked. 'The mere sight of an official-looking person seals men's lips. These youngsters, however, go everywhere, and hear everything. They are as sharp as needles, too; all they want is organisation.'

'Is it on this Brixton case that you are employing them?' I asked.

'Yes; there is a point which I wish to ascertain. It is merely a matter of time. Hallo! we are going to hear some news now with a vengeance! Here is Gregson coming down the road with beatitude written upon every feature of his face. Bound for us, I know. Yes, he is stopping. There he is!'

There was a violent peal at the bell, and in a few seconds the fair-haired detective came up the stairs, three steps at a time, and burst into our sitting-room.

'My dear fellow,' he cried, wringing Holmes's unresponsive hand, 'congratulate me! I have made the whole thing as clear as day.'

A shade of anxiety seemed to me to cross my companion's expressive face.

'Do you mean that you are on the right track?' he asked.

'The right track! Why, sir, we have the man under lock and key.'

'And his name is?'

'Arthur Charpentier, sub-lieutenant in Her Majesty's Navy,' cried Gregson pompously, rubbing his fat hands and inflating his chest.

Sherlock Holmes gave a sigh of relief and relaxed into a smile.

'Take a seat, and try one of these cigars,' he said. 'We are anxious to know how you managed it. Will you have some whisky and water?'

'I don't mind if I do,' the detective answered. 'The tremendous exertions which I have gone through during the last day or two have worn me out. Not so much bodily exertion, you understand, as the strain upon the mind. You will appreciate that, Mr Sherlock Holmes, for we are both brain-workers.'

'You do me too much honour,' said Holmes, gravely. 'Let us hear how you arrived at this most gratifying result.'

The detective seated himself in the armchair, and puffed complacently at his cigar. Then suddenly he slapped his thigh in a paroxysm of amusement.

'The fun of it is,' he cried, 'that that fool Lestrade, who thinks himself so smart, has gone off upon the wrong track altogether. He is after the secretary Stangerson, who had no more to do with the crime than the babe unborn. I have no doubt that he has caught him by this time.'

The idea tickled Gregson so much that he laughed until he choked.

'And how did you get your clue?'

'Ah, I'll tell you all about it. Of course, Dr Watson, this is strictly between ourselves. The first difficulty which we had to contend with was the finding of this American's antecedents. Some people would have waited until their advertisements were answered, or until parties came forward and volunteered information. That is not Tobias Gregson's way of going to work. You remember the hat beside the dead man?'

'Yes,' said Holmes; 'by John Underwood and Sons, 129 Camberwell Road.'

Gregson looked quite crestfallen. 'I had no idea that you noticed that,' he said. 'Have you been there?'

'No.'

'Ha!' cried Gregson, in a relieved voice; 'you should never neglect a chance, however small it may seem.'

'To a great mind, nothing is little,' remarked Holmes, sententiously.

'Well, I went to Underwood, and asked him if he had sold a hat of that size and description. He looked over his books, and came on it at once. He had sent the hat to a Mr Drebber, residing at Charpentier's Boarding Establishment, Torquay Terrace. Thus I got at his address.'

'Smart – very smart!' murmured Sherlock Holmes.

'I next called upon Madame Charpentier,' continued the detective. 'I found her very pale and distressed. Her daughter was in the room, too – an uncommonly fine girl she is, too; she was looking red about the eyes and her lips trembled as I spoke to her. That didn't escape my notice. I began to smell a rat. You know the feeling, Mr Sherlock Holmes, when you come upon the right scent – a kind of thrill in your nerves. "Have you heard of the mysterious death of your late boarder Mr Enoch J. Drebber, of Cleveland?" I asked.

'The mother nodded. She didn't seem able to get out a word. The daughter burst into tears. I felt more than ever that these people knew something of the matter.

'"At what o'clock did Mr Drebber leave your house for the train?" I asked.

'"At eight o'clock," she said, gulping in her throat to keep down her agitation. "His secretary, Mr Stangerson, said that there were two trains – one at nine-fifteen and one at eleven. He was to catch the first."

'"And was that the last which you saw of him?"

'A terrible change came over the woman's face as I asked the question. Her features turned perfectly livid. It was some seconds before she could get out the single word "Yes" – and when it did come it was in a husky, unnatural tone.

'There was silence for a moment, and then the daughter spoke in a calm, clear voice.

'"No good can ever come of falsehood, mother," she said. "Let us be frank with this gentleman. We *did* see Mr Drebber again."

'"God forgive you!" cried Madame Charpentier, throwing up her hands, and sinking back in her chair. "You have murdered your brother."

'"Arthur would rather that we spoke the truth," the girl answered firmly.

'"You had best tell me all about it now," I said. "Half confidences are worse than none. Besides, you do not know how much we know of it."

'"On your head be it, Alice!" cried her mother; and then turning to me, "I will tell you all, sir. Do not imagine that my agitation on behalf of my son arises from any fear lest he should have had a hand in this terrible affair. He is utterly innocent of it. My dread is, however, that in your eyes and in the eyes of others he may appear to be compromised. That, however, is surely impossible. His high character, his profession, his antecedents would all forbid it."

'"Your best way is to make a clean breast of the facts," I answered. "Depend upon it, if your son is innocent he will be none the worse."

'"Perhaps, Alice, you had better leave us together," she said, and her daughter withdrew. "Now, sir," she continued, "I had no intention of telling you all this, but since my poor daughter has disclosed it I have no alternative. Having once decided to speak, I will tell you all without omitting any particular."

'"It is your wisest course," said I.

'"Mr Drebber has been with us nearly three weeks. He and his secretary, Mr Stangerson, had been travelling on the Continent. I noticed a 'Copenhagen' label upon each of their trunks, showing that that had been their last stopping-place. Stangerson was a quiet, reserved man, but his employer, I am sorry to say, was far otherwise. He was coarse in his habits and brutish in his ways. The very night of his arrival he became very much the worse for drink, and, indeed, after twelve o'clock in the day he could hardly ever be said to be sober. His manners towards the maidservants were disgustingly free and familiar. Worst of all, he speedily assumed the same attitude towards my daughter, Alice, and spoke to her more than once in a way which, fortunately, she is too innocent to understand. On one occasion he actually seized her in his arms and embraced her – an outrage which caused his own secretary to reproach him for his unmanly conduct."

'"But why did you stand all this?" I asked. "I suppose that you can get rid of your boarders when you wish."

'Madame Charpentier blushed at my pertinent question. "Would to God that I had given him notice on the very day that he came," she said. "But it was a sore temptation. They were paying a pound a day each – fourteen pounds a week, and this is the slack season. I am a widow, and my boy in the navy has cost me much. I grudged to lose the money. I acted for the best. This last was too much, however, and I gave him notice to leave on account of it. That was the reason of his going."

'"Well?"

'"My heart grew light when I saw him drive away. My son is on leave just now, but I did not tell him anything of all this, for his temper is violent, and he is passionately fond of his sister. When I closed the door behind them a load seemed to be lifted from my mind. Alas, in less than an hour there was a ring at the bell, and I learned that Mr Drebber had returned. He was much excited, and evidently the worse for drink. He forced his way into the room, where I was sitting with my daughter, and made some incoherent remark about having missed his train. He then turned to Alice, and before my very face proposed to her that she should fly with him. 'You are of age,' he said, 'and there is no law to stop you. I have money enough and to spare. Never mind the old girl here, but come along with me now straight away. You shall live like a princess.' Poor Alice was so frightened that she shrank away from him, but he caught her by the wrist and endeavoured to draw her towards the door. I screamed, and at that moment my son Arthur came into the room. What happened then I do not know. I heard oaths and the confused sounds of a scuffle. I was too terrified to raise my head. When I did look up I saw Arthur standing in the doorway laughing, with a stick in his hand. 'I don't think that fine fellow will trouble us again,' he said. 'I will just go after him and see what he does with himself.' With those words he took his hat and started off down the street. The next morning we heard of Mr Drebber's mysterious death."

'This statement came from Madame Charpentier's lips with many gasps and pauses. At times she spoke so low that I could hardly catch the words. I made shorthand notes of all that she said, however, so that there should be no possibility of a mistake.'

'It's quite exciting,' said Sherlock Holmes, with a yawn. 'What happened next?'

'When Madame Charpentier paused,' the detective continued, 'I saw that the whole case hung upon one point. Fixing her with my eye in a way which I always find effective with women, I asked her at what hour her son returned.

'"I do not know," she answered.

'"Not know?"

'"No; he has a latchkey, and he let himself in."

'"After you went to bed?"

'"Yes."

'"When did you go to bed?"

'"About eleven."

'"So your son was gone at least two hours?"

'"Yes."

'"Possibly four or five."

'"Yes."

'"What was he doing during that time?"

'"I do not know," she answered, turning white to her very lips.

'Of course after that there was nothing more to be done. I found out where Lieutenant Charpentier was, took two officers with me, and arrested him. When I touched him on the shoulder and warned him to come quietly with us, he answered us as bold as brass, "I suppose you are arresting me for being concerned in the death of that scoundrel Drebber," he said. We had said nothing to him about it, so that his alluding to it had a most suspicious aspect.'

'Very,' said Holmes.

'He still carried the heavy stick which the mother described him as having when he followed Drebber. It was a stout oak cudgel.'

'What is your theory, then?'

'Well, my theory is that he followed Drebber as far as the Brixton Road. When there, a fresh altercation arose between them, in the course of which Drebber received a blow from the stick, in the pit of the stomach perhaps, which killed him without leaving any mark. The night was so wet that no one was about, so Charpentier dragged the body of his victim into the empty house. As to the candle, and the blood, and the writing on the wall, and the ring, they may all be so many tricks to throw the police on to the wrong scent.'

'Well done!' said Holmes in an encouraging voice. 'Really, Gregson, you are getting along. We shall make something of you yet.'

'I flatter myself that I have managed it rather neatly,' the detective answered proudly. 'The young man volunteered a statement, in which he said that after he had followed Drebber for some time the latter perceived him and took a cab in order to get away from him. On his way home he met an old shipmate, and took a long walk with him. On being asked where this old shipmate lived, he was unable to give any satisfactory reply. I think the whole case fits together uncommonly well. What amuses me is to think of Lestrade, who has started off upon the wrong scent. I am afraid he won't make much of it. Why, by Jove, here's the very man himself!'

It was indeed Lestrade, who had ascended the stairs while we were talking, and who now entered the room. The assurance and jauntiness which generally marked his demeanour and dress were, however, wanting. His face was disturbed and troubled, while his clothes were disarranged and untidy. He had evidently come with the intention of consulting with Sherlock Holmes, for on perceiving his colleague he appeared to be embarrassed and put out. He stood in the centre of the room, fumbling nervously with his hat and uncertain what to do. 'This is a most extraordinary case,' he said at last – 'a most incomprehensible affair.'

'Ah, you find it so, Mr Lestrade!' cried Gregson, triumphantly. 'I thought you would come to that conclusion. Have you managed to land the secretary, Mr Joseph Stangerson?'

'The secretary, Mr Joseph Stangerson,' said Lestrade, gravely, 'was murdered at Halliday's Private Hotel about six o'clock this morning.'

7

Light in the Darkness

The intelligence with which Lestrade greeted us was so momentous and so unexpected that we were all three fairly dumbfounded. Gregson sprang out of his chair and upset the remainder of his whisky and water. I stared in silence at Sherlock Holmes, whose lips were compressed and his brows drawn down over his eyes.

'Stangerson too!' he muttered. 'The plot thickens.'

'It was quite thick enough before,' grumbled Lestrade, taking a chair. 'I seem to have dropped into a sort of council of war.'

'Are you – are you sure of this piece of intelligence?' stammered Gregson.

'I have just come from his room,' said Lestrade. 'I was the first to discover what had occurred.'

'We have been hearing Gregson's view of the matter,' Holmes observed. 'Would you mind letting us know what you have seen and done?'

'I have no objection,' Lestrade answered, seating himself. 'I freely confess that I was of the opinion that Stangerson was concerned in the death of Drebber. This fresh development has shown me that I was completely mistaken. Full of the one idea, I set myself to find out what had become of the secretary. They had been seen together at Euston Station about half-past eight on the evening of the third. At two in the morning Drebber had been found in the Brixton Road. The question which confronted me was to find out how Stangerson had been employed between eight-thirty and the time of the crime, and what had become of him afterwards. I telegraphed to Liverpool, giving a description of the man, and warning them to keep a watch upon the American boats. I then set to work calling upon all the hotels and lodging-houses in the vicinity of Euston. You see, I argued that if Drebber and his companion had become separated, the natural course for the latter would be to put up somewhere in the vicinity for the night, and then to hang about the station again next morning.'

'They would be likely to agree on some meeting place beforehand,' remarked Holmes.

'So it proved. I spent the whole of yesterday evening in making enquiries entirely without avail. This morning I began very early, and at eight o'clock I reached Halliday's Private Hotel, in Little George Street. On my enquiry as to whether a Mr Stangerson was living there, they at once answered me in the affirmative.

'"No doubt you are the gentleman whom he was expecting," they said. "He has been waiting for a gentleman for two days."

'"Where is he now?" I asked.

'"He is upstairs in bed. He wished to be called at nine."

'"I will go up and see him at once," I said.

'It seemed to me that my sudden appearance might shake his nerves and lead him to say something unguarded. The boots volunteered to show me the room: it was on the second floor, and there was a small corridor leading up to it. The boots pointed out the door to me, and was about to go downstairs again when I saw something that made me feel sickish, in spite of my twenty years' experience. From under the door there curled a little red ribbon of blood which had meandered across the passage and formed a little pool along the skirting at the other side. I gave a cry, which brought the boots back. He nearly fainted when he saw it. The door was locked on the inside, but we put our shoulders to it and knocked it in. The window of the room was open, and beside the window, all huddled up, lay the body of a man in his nightdress. He was quite dead, and had been for some time, for his limbs were rigid and cold. When we turned him over the boots recognised him at once as being the same gentleman who had engaged the room under the name of Joseph Stangerson. The cause of death was a deep stab in the left side, which must have penetrated the heart. And now comes the strangest part of the affair. What do you suppose was above the murdered man?'

I felt a creeping of the flesh, and a presentiment of coming horror, even before Sherlock Holmes answered.

'The word RACHE, written in letters of blood,' he said.

'That was it,' said Lestrade, in an awestruck voice; and we were all silent awhile.

There was something so methodical and so incomprehensible about the deeds of this unknown assassin, that it imparted a fresh ghastliness to his crimes. My nerves, which were steady enough on the field of battle, tingled as I thought of it.

'The man was seen,' continued Lestrade. 'A milk boy, passing on his way to the dairy, happened to walk down the lane which leads from the mews at the back of the hotel. He noticed that a ladder, which usually lay there, was raised against one of the windows of the second floor, which was wide open. After passing, he looked back and saw a man descend the ladder. He came down so quietly and openly that the boy imagined him to be some carpenter or joiner at work in the hotel. He took no particular notice of him, beyond thinking in his own mind that it was early for him to be at work. He has an impression that the man was tall, had a reddish face, and was dressed in a long, brownish coat. He must have stayed in the room some little time after the murder, for we found blood-stained water in the basin, where he had washed his hands, and marks on the sheets where he had deliberately wiped his knife.'

I glanced at Holmes on hearing the description of the murderer which tallied so exactly with his own. There was, however, no trace of exultation or satisfaction upon his face.

'Did you find nothing in the room which could furnish a clue to the murderer?' he asked.

'Nothing. Stangerson had Drebber's purse in his pocket, but it seems that this was usual, as he did all the paying. There was eighty odd pounds in it, but nothing had been taken. Whatever the motives of these extraordinary crimes, robbery is certainly not one of them. There were no papers or memoranda in the murdered man's pocket except a single telegram, dated from Cleveland about a month ago and containing the words, "J. H. is in Europe". There was no name appended to this message.'

'And there was nothing else?' Holmes asked.

'Nothing of any importance. The man's novel, with which he had read himself to sleep, was lying upon the bed, and his pipe was on a chair beside him. There was a glass of water on the table, and on the windowsill a small chip ointment box containing a couple of pills.'

Sherlock Holmes sprang from his chair with an exclamation of delight.

'The last link,' he cried, exultantly. 'My case is complete.'

The two detectives stared at him in amazement.

'I have now in my hands,' my companion said, confidently, 'all the threads which have formed such a tangle. There are, of course, details to be filled in, but I am as certain of all the main facts, from the time that Drebber parted from Stangerson at the station, up to the discovery of the body of the latter, as if I had seen them with my own eyes. I will give you a proof of my knowledge. Could you lay your hand upon those pills?'

'I have them,' said Lestrade, producing a small white box; 'I took them and the purse and the telegram, intending to have them put in a place of safety at the police station. It was the merest chance my taking these pills, for I am bound to say that I do not attach any importance to them.'

'Give them here,' said Holmes. 'Now, doctor,' turning to me, 'are those ordinary pills?'

They certainly were not. They were of a pearly grey colour, small, round, and almost transparent against the light. 'From their lightness and transparency, I should imagine that they are soluble in water,' I remarked.

'Precisely so,' answered Holmes. 'Now would you mind going down and fetching that poor little devil of a terrier which has been bad so long, and which the landlady wanted you to put out of its pain yesterday.'

I went downstairs and carried the dog upstairs in my arms. Its laboured breathing and glazing eye showed that it was not far from its end. Indeed, its snow-white muzzle proclaimed that it had already exceeded the usual term of canine existence. I placed it upon a cushion on the rug.

'I will now cut one of these pills in two,' said Holmes, and drawing his penknife he suited the action to the word. 'One half we return into the box for future purposes. The other half I will place in this wine glass, in which is a teaspoonful of water. You perceive that our friend, the doctor, is right, and that it readily dissolves.'

'This may be very interesting,' said Lestrade, in the injured tone of one who suspects that he is being laughed at; 'I cannot see, however, what it has to do with the death of Mr Joseph Stangerson.'

'Patience, my friend, patience! You will find in time that it has everything to do with it. I shall now add a little milk to make the mixture palatable, and on presenting it to the dog we find that he laps it up readily enough.'

As he spoke he turned the contents of the wine glass into a saucer and placed it in front of the terrier, who speedily licked it dry. Sherlock Holmes's earnest demeanour had so far convinced us that we all sat in silence, watching the animal intently, and expecting some startling effect. None such appeared, however. The dog continued to lie stretched upon the cushion, breathing in a laboured way, but apparently neither the better nor the worse for its draught.

Holmes had taken out his watch, and as minute followed minute without result, an expression of the utmost chagrin and disappointment appeared upon his features. He gnawed his lip, drummed his fingers upon the table, and showed every other symptom of acute impatience. So great was his emotion that I felt sincerely sorry for him, while the two detectives smiled derisively, by no means displeased at this check which he had met.

'It can't be a coincidence,' he cried, at last springing from his chair and pacing wildly up and down the room; 'it is impossible that it should be a mere coincidence. The very pills which I suspected in the case of Drebber are actually found after the death of Stangerson. And yet they are inert. What can it mean? Surely my whole chain of reasoning cannot have been false. It is impossible! And yet this wretched dog is none the worse. Ah. I have it! I have it!' With a perfect shriek of delight he rushed to the box, cut the other pill in two, dissolved it, added milk, and presented it to the terrier. The unfortunate creature's tongue seemed hardly to have been moistened in it before it gave a convulsive shiver in every limb, and lay as rigid and lifeless as if it had been struck by lightning.

Sherlock Holmes drew a long breath, and wiped the perspiration from his forehead. 'I should have more faith,' he said; 'I ought to know by this time that when a fact appears to be opposed to a long train of deductions it invariably proves to be capable of bearing some other interpretation. Of the two pills in that box, one was of the most deadly poison, and the other was entirely harmless. I ought to have known that before ever I saw the box at all.'

This last statement appeared to me to be so startling that I could hardly believe that he was in his sober senses. There was the dead dog, however, to prove that his conjecture had been correct. It seemed to me that the mists in my own mind were gradually clearing away, and I began to have a dim, vague perception of the truth.

'All this seems strange to you,' continued Holmes, 'because you failed at the beginning of the enquiry to grasp the importance of the single real clue which was presented to you. I had the good fortune to seize upon that, and everything which has occurred since then has served to confirm my original supposition, and, indeed, was the logical sequence of it. Hence things which have perplexed you and made the case more obscure have served to enlighten me and to strengthen my conclusions. It is a mistake to confound strangeness with mystery. The most commonplace crime is often the most mysterious, because it presents no new or special features from which deductions may be drawn. This murder would have been infinitely more difficult to unravel had the body of the victim been simply found lying in the roadway without any of those *outrÈ* and sensational accompaniments which have rendered it remarkable. These strange details, far from making the case more difficult, have really had the effect of making it less so.'

Mr Gregson, who had listened to this address with considerable impatience, could contain himself no longer. 'Look here, Mr Sherlock Holmes,' he said, 'we are all ready to acknowledge that you are a smart man, and that you have your own methods of working. We want something more than mere theory and preaching now, though. It is a case of taking the man. I have made my case out, and it seems I was wrong. Young Charpentier could not have been engaged in this second affair. Lestrade went after his man, Stangerson, and it appears that he was wrong too. You have thrown out hints here, and hints there, and seem to know more than we do, but the time has come when we feel that we have a right to ask you straight how much you do know of the business. Can you name the man who did it?'

'I cannot help feeling that Gregson is right, sir,' remarked Lestrade. 'We have both tried, and we have both failed. You have remarked more than once since I have been in the room that you had all the evidence which you require. Surely you will not withhold it any longer.'

'Any delay in arresting the assassin,' I observed, 'might give him time to perpetrate some fresh atrocity.'

Thus pressed by us all, Holmes showed signs of irresolution. He continued to walk up and down the room with his head sunk on his chest and his brows drawn down, as was his habit when lost in thought.

'There will be no more murders,' he said at last, stopping abruptly and facing us. 'You can put that consideration out of the question. You have asked me if I know the name of the assassin. I do. The mere knowing of his name is a small thing, however, compared with the power of laying our hands upon him. This I expect very shortly to do. I have good hopes of managing it through my own arrangements; but it is a thing which needs delicate handling, for we have a shrewd and desperate man to deal with, who is supported, as I have had occasion to prove, by another who is as clever as himself. As long as this man has no idea that anyone can have a clue there is some chance of securing him; but if he had the slightest suspicion, he would change his name, and vanish in an instant among the four million inhabitants of this great city. Without meaning to hurt either of your feelings, I am bound to say that I consider these men to be more than a match for the official force, and that is why I have not asked your assistance. If I fail, I shall, of course, incur all the blame due to this omission; but that I am prepared for. At present I am ready to promise that the instant that I can communicate with you without endangering my own combinations, I shall do so.'

Gregson and Lestrade seemed to be far from satisfied by this assurance, or by the depreciating allusion to the detective police. The former had flushed up to the roots of his flaxen hair, while the other's beady eyes glistened with curiosity and resentment. Neither of them had time to speak, however, before there was a tap at the door, and the spokesman of the street arabs, young Wiggins, introduced his insignificant and unsavoury person.

'Please, sir,' he said, touching his forelock, 'I have the cab downstairs.'

'Good boy,' said Holmes, blandly. 'Why don't you introduce this pattern at Scotland Yard?' he continued, taking a pair of steel handcuffs from a drawer. 'See how beautifully the spring works. They fasten in an instant.'

'The old pattern is good enough,' remarked Lestrade, 'if we can only find the man to put them on.'

'Very good, very good,' said Holmes, smiling. 'The cabman may as well help me with my boxes. Just ask him to step up, Wiggins.'

I was surprised to find my companion speaking as though he were about to set out on a journey, since he had not said anything to me about it. There was a small portmanteau in the room, and this he pulled out and began to strap. He was busily engaged at it when the cabman entered the room.

'Just give me a help with this buckle, cabman,' he said, kneeling over his task, and never turning his head.

The fellow came forward with a somewhat sullen, defiant air, and put down his hands to assist. At that instant there was a sharp click, the jangling of metal, and Sherlock Holmes sprang to his feet again.

'Gentlemen,' he cried, with flashing eyes, 'let me introduce you to Mr Jefferson Hope, the murderer of Enoch Drebber and of Joseph Stangerson.'

The whole thing occurred in a moment – so quickly that I had no time to realise it. I have a vivid recollection of that instant, of Holmes's triumphant expression and the ring of his voice, of the cabman's dazed, savage face as he glared at the glittering handcuffs which had appeared as if by magic upon his wrists. For a second or two we might have been a group of statues. Then, with an inarticulate roar of fury, the prisoner wrenched himself free from Holmes's grasp and hurled himself through the window. Woodwork and glass gave way before him; but before he got quite through, Gregson, Lestrade and Holmes sprang upon him like so many staghounds. He was dragged back into the room, and then commenced a terrific conflict. So powerful and so fierce was he that the four of us were shaken off again and again. He appeared to have the convulsive strength of a man in an epileptic fit. His face and hands were terribly mangled by his passage through the glass, but the loss of blood had no effect in diminishing his resistance. It was not until Lestrade succeeded in getting his hand inside his neckcloth and half-strangling him that we made him realise that his struggles were of no avail; and even then we felt no security until we had pinioned his feet as well as his hands. That done, we rose to our feet breathless and panting.

'We have his cab,' said Sherlock Holmes. 'It will serve to take him to Scotland Yard. And now, gentlemen,' he continued, with a pleasant smile, 'we have reached the end of our little mystery. You are very welcome to put any questions that you like to me now, and there is no danger that I will refuse to answer them.'

PART TWO

The Country of the Saints

8

On the Great Alkali Plain

In the central portion of the great North American continent there lies an arid and repulsive desert, which for many a long year served as a barrier against the advance of civilisation. From the Sierra Nevada to Nebraska, and from the Yellowstone River in the north to the Colorado upon the south, is a region of desolation and silence. Nor is nature always in one mood throughout this grim district. It comprises snow-capped and lofty mountains, and dark and gloomy valleys. There are swift-flowing rivers which dash through jagged canyons; and there are enormous plains, which in winter are white with snow, and in summer are grey with the saline alkali dust. They all preserve, however, the common characteristics of barrenness, inhospitality and misery.

There are no inhabitants of this land of despair. A band of Pawnees or of Blackfeet may occasionally traverse it in order to reach other hunting-grounds, but the hardiest of the braves are glad to lose sight of those awesome plains, and to find themselves once more upon their prairies. The coyote skulks among the scrub, the buzzard flaps heavily through the air, and the clumsy grizzly bear lumbers through the dark ravines and picks up such sustenance as it can amongst the rocks. These are the sole dwellers in the wilderness.

In the whole world there can be no more dreary view than that from the northern slope of the Sierra Blanco. As far as the eye can reach stretches the great flat plain-land, all dusted over with patches of alkali and intersected by clumps of the dwarfish chaparral bushes. On the extreme verge of the horizon lies a long chain of mountain peaks with their rugged summits flecked with snow. In this great stretch of country there is no sign of life, nor of anything appertaining to life. There is no bird in the steel-blue heaven, no movement upon the dull, grey earth – above all, there is absolute silence. Listen as one may, there is no shadow of a sound in all that mighty wilderness; nothing but silence – complete and heart-subduing silence.

It has been said there is nothing appertaining to life upon the broad plain. That is hardly true. Looking down from the Sierra Blanco, one sees a pathway traced out across the desert, which winds away and is lost in the extreme distance. It is rutted with wheels and trodden down by the feet of many adventurers. Here and there are scattered white objects which glisten in the sun and stand out against the dull deposit of alkali. Approach, and examine them! They are bones: some large and coarse, others smaller and more delicate. The former have belonged to oxen, and the latter to men. For fifteen hundred miles one may trace this ghastly caravan route by these scattered remains of those who have fallen by the wayside.

Looking down on this very scene there stood, upon the fourth of May, 1847, a solitary traveller. His appearance was such that he might have been the very genius or demon of the region. An observer would have found it difficult to say whether he was nearer to forty or to sixty. His face was lean and haggard, and the brown parchment-like skin was drawn tightly over the projecting bones; his long, brown hair and beard were all flecked and dashed with white; his eyes were sunken in his head, and burned with an unnatural lustre, while the hand which grasped his rifle was hardly more fleshy than that of a skeleton. As he stood, he leaned upon his weapon for support, and yet his tall figure and the massive framework of his bones suggested a wiry and vigorous constitution. His gaunt face, however, and his clothes, which hung so baggily over his shrivelled limbs, proclaimed what it was that gave him that senile and decrepit appearance. The man was dying – dying from hunger and from thirst.

He had toiled painfully down the ravine and on to this little elevation in the vain hope of seeing some signs of water. Now the great salt plain stretched before his eyes to the distant belt of savage mountains, without a sign anywhere of plant or tree which might indicate the presence of moisture. In all that broad landscape there was no gleam of hope. North and east and west he looked with wild, questioning eyes, and then he realised that his wanderings had come to an end, and that there, on that barren crag, he was about to die. 'Why not here as well as in a feather bed, twenty years hence?' he muttered, as he seated himself in the shelter of a boulder.

Before sitting down, he had deposited upon the ground his useless rifle, and also a large bundle tied up in a grey shawl, which he had carried slung over his right shoulder. It appeared to be somewhat too heavy for his strength, for when he lowered it, it came down on the ground with some little violence. Instantly there broke from the grey parcel a little moaning cry, and from it there protruded a small, scared face, with very bright brown eyes, and two little speckled, dimpled fists.

'You've hurt me!' said a childish voice reproachfully.

'Have I, though,' the man answered penitently; 'I didn't go for to do it.' As he spoke he unwrapped the grey shawl and extricated a pretty little girl of about five years of age, whose dainty shoes and smart, pink frock with its little linen apron all bespoke a mother's care. The child was pale and wan, but her healthy arms and legs showed that she had suffered less than her companion.

'How is it now?' he answered anxiously, for she was still rubbing the towsy golden curls which covered the back of her head.

'Kiss it and make it well,' she said, with perfect gravity, showing the injured part up to him. 'That's what mother used to do. Where's mother?'

'Mother's gone. I guess you'll see her before long.'

'Gone, eh!' said the little girl. 'Funny, she didn't say goodbye; she 'most always did if she was just goin' over to auntie's for tea, and now she's been away three days. Say, it's awful dry, ain't it? Ain't there no water nor nothing to eat?'

'No, there ain't nothing, dearie. You'll just need to be patient awhile, and then you'll be all right. Put your head up ag'in me like that, and then you'll feel bullier. It ain't easy to talk when your lips is like leather, but I guess I'd best let you know how the cards lie. What's that you've got?'

'Pretty things! fine things!' cried the little girl enthusiastically, holding up two glittering fragments of mica. 'When we goes back to home I'll give them to brother Bob.'

'You'll see prettier things than them soon,' said the man confidently. 'You just wait a bit. I was going to tell you though – you remember when we left the river?'

'Oh, yes.'

'Well, we reckoned we'd strike another river soon, d'ye see. But there was somethin' wrong – compasses, or map, or somethin', and it didn't turn up. Water ran out. Just except a little drop for the likes of you, and – and –'

'And you couldn't wash yourself,' interrupted his companion gravely, staring up at his grimy visage.

'No, nor drink. And Mr Bender, he was the fust to go, and then Indian Pete, and then Mrs McGregor, and then Johnny Hones, and then, dearie, your mother.'

'Then mother's a deader too,' cried the little girl, dropping her face in her pinafore and sobbing bitterly.

'Yes, they all went except you and me. Then I thought there was some chance of water in this direction, so I heaved you over my shoulder and we tramped it together. It don't seem as though we've improved matters. There's an almighty small chance for us now!'

'Do you mean that we are going to die too?' asked the child, checking her sobs, and raising her tear-stained face.

'I guess that's about the size of it.'

'Why didn't you say so before?' she said, laughing gleefully. 'You gave me such a fright. Why, of course, now as long as we die we'll be with mother again.'

'Yes, you will, dearie.'

'And you too. I'll tell her how awful good you've been. I'll bet she meets us at the door of heaven with a big pitcher of water, and a lot of buckwheat cakes, hot, and toasted on both sides, like Bob and me was fond of. How long will it be first?'

'I don't know – not very long.' The man's eyes were fixed upon the northern horizon. In the blue vault of the heavens there had appeared three little specks which increased in size every moment, so rapidly did they approach. They speedily resolved themselves into three large brown birds, which circled over the heads of the two wanderers and then settled upon some rocks which overlooked them. They were buzzards, the vultures of the West, whose coming is the forerunner of death.

'Cocks and hens,' cried the little girl gleefully, pointing at their ill-omened forms, and clapping her hands to make them rise. 'Say, did God make this country?'

'Of course He did,' said her companion, rather startled by this unexpected question.

'He made the country down in Illinois, and He made the Missouri,' the little girl continued. 'I guess somebody else made the country in these parts. It's not nearly so well done. They forgot the water and the trees.'

'What would ye think of offering up some prayers?' the man asked diffidently.

'It ain't night yet,' she answered.

'It don't matter. It ain't quite regular, but He won't mind that, you bet. You say over them ones that you used to say every night in the wagon when we was on the plains.'

'Why don't you say some yourself?' the child asked with wondering eyes.

'I disremember them,' he answered. 'I hain't said none since I was half the height o' that gun. I guess it's never too late. You say them out, and I'll stand by and come in on the choruses.'

'Then you'll need to kneel down, and me too,' she said, laying the shawl out for that purpose. 'You've got to put your hands up like this. It makes you feel kind of good.'

It was a strange sight, had there been anything but the buzzards to see it. Side by side on the narrow shawl knelt the two wanderers, the little prattling child and the reckless, hardened adventurer. Her chubby face and his haggard, angular visage were both turned up to the cloudless heavens in heartfelt entreaty to that dread Being with whom they were face to face, while the two voices – the one thin and clear, the other deep and harsh – united in the entreaty for mercy and forgiveness. The prayers finished, they resumed their seat in the shadow of the boulder until the child fell asleep, nestling upon the broad breast of her protector. He watched over her slumber for some time, but nature proved to be too strong for him. For three days and three nights he had allowed himself neither rest nor repose. Slowly the eyelids drooped over the tired eyes, and the head sank lower and lower upon the breast, until the man's grizzled beard was mixed with the gold tresses of his companion, and both slept the same deep and dreamless slumber.

Had the wanderer remained awake for another half-hour a strange sight would have met his eyes. Far away on the extreme verge of the alkali plain there rose up a little spray of dust, very slight at first, and hardly to be distinguished from the mists of the distance, but gradually growing higher and broader until it formed a solid, well-defined cloud. This cloud continued to increase in size until it became evident that it could only be raised by a great multitude of moving creatures.

In more fertile spots the observer would have come to the conclusion that one of those great herds of bison which graze upon the prairie land was approaching him. This was obviously impossible in these arid wilds. As the whirl of dust drew nearer to the solitary bluff upon which the two castaways were reposing, the canvas-covered tilts of wagons and the figures of armed horsemen began to show up through the haze, and the apparition revealed itself as being a great caravan upon its journey for the West. But what a caravan! When the head of it had reached the base of the mountains, the rear was not yet visible on the horizon. Right across the enormous plain stretched the straggling array, wagons and carts, men on horseback and men on foot. Innumerable women who staggered along under burdens, and children who toddled beside the wagons or peeped out from under the white coverings. This was evidently no ordinary party of immigrants, but rather some nomad people who had been compelled from stress of circumstances to seek themselves a new country. There rose through the clear air a confused clattering and rumbling from this great mass of humanity, with the creaking of wheels and the neighing of horses. Loud as it was, it was not sufficient to rouse the two tired wayfarers above them.

At the head of the column there rode a score or more of grave, iron-faced men, clad in sombre, homespun garments and armed with rifles. On reaching the base of the bluff they halted, and held a short council among themselves.

'The wells are to the right, my brothers,' said one, a hard-lipped, clean-shaven man with grizzly hair.

'To the right of the Sierra Blanco – so we shall reach the Rio Grande,' said another.

'Fear not for water,' cried a third. 'He who could draw it from the rocks will not now abandon His chosen people.'

'Amen! amen!' responded the whole party.

They were about to resume their journey when one of the youngest and keenest-eyed uttered an exclamation and pointed up at the rugged crag above them. From its summit there fluttered a little wisp of pink, showing up hard and bright against the grey rocks behind. At the sight there was a general reining-in of horses and unslinging of guns, while fresh horsemen came galloping up to reinforce the vanguard. The word 'Redskins' was on every lip.

'There can't be any number of Injuns here,' said the elderly man who appeared to be in command. 'We have passed the Pawnees, and there are no other tribes until we cross the great mountains.'

'Shall I go forward and see, Brother Stangerson?' asked one of the band.

'And I,' 'And I,' cried a dozen voices.

'Leave your horses below and we will await you here,' the elder answered. In a moment the young fellows had dismounted, fastened their horses and were ascending the precipitous slope which led up to the object which had excited their curiosity. They advanced rapidly and noiselessly, with the confidence and dexterity of practised scouts. The watchers from the plain below could see them flit from rock to rock until their figures stood out against the skyline. The young man who had first given the alarm was leading them. Suddenly his followers saw him throw up his hands, as though overcome with astonishment, and on joining him they were affected in the same way by the sight which met their eyes.

On the little plateau which crowned the barren hills there stood a single giant boulder, and against this boulder there lay a tall man, long-bearded and hard-featured, but of an excessive thinness. His placid face and regular breathing showed that he was fast asleep. Beside him lay a little child, with her round, white arms encircling his brown, sinewy neck, and her golden-haired head resting upon the breast of his velveteen tunic. Her rosy lips were parted, showing the regular line of snow-white teeth within, and a faint smile played over her infantile features. Her plump little white legs, terminating in white socks and neat shoes with shining buckles, offered a strange contrast to the long, shrivelled members of her companion. On the ledge of rock above this strange couple there stood three solemn buzzards, who, at the sight of the newcomers, uttered raucous screams of disappointment and flapped sullenly away.

The cries of the foul birds awoke the two sleepers, who stared about them in bewilderment. The man staggered to his feet and looked down upon the plain which had been so desolate when sleep had overtaken him, and which was now traversed by this enormous body of men and of beasts. His face assumed an expression of incredulity as he gazed, and he passed his bony hand over his eyes. 'This is what they call delirium, I guess,' he muttered. The child stood beside him, holding on to the skirt of his coat, and said nothing, but looked all around her with the wondering, questioning gaze of childhood.

The rescuing party were speedily able to convince the two castaways that their appearance was no delusion. One of them seized the little girl and hoisted her upon his shoulder, while two others supported her gaunt companion, and assisted him towards the wagons.

'My name is John Ferrier,' the wanderer explained; 'me and that little un are all that's left o' twenty-one people. The rest is all dead o' thirst and hunger away down in the south.'

'Is she your child?' asked someone.

'I guess she is now,' the other cried, defiantly; 'she's mine 'cause I saved her. No man will take her from me. She's Lucy Ferrier from this day on. Who are you, though?' he continued, glancing with curiosity at his stalwart, sunburned rescuers; 'there seems to be a powerful lot of ye.'

'Nigh upon ten thousand,' said one of the young men; 'we are the persecuted children of God – the chosen of the Angel Merona.'

'I never heard tell on him,' said the wanderer. 'He appears to have chosen a fair crowd of ye.'

'Do not jest at that which is sacred,' said the other sternly. 'We are of those who believe in those sacred writings, drawn in Egyptian letters on plates of beaten gold, which were handed unto the holy Joseph Smith at Palmyra. We have come from Nauvoo, in the State of Illinois, where we had founded our temple. We have come to seek a refuge from the violent man and from the godless, even though it be the heart of the desert.'

The name of Nauvoo evidently recalled recollections to John Ferrier. 'I see,' he said; 'you are the Mormons.'

'We are the Mormons,' answered his companions with one voice.

'And where are you going?'

'We do not know. The hand of God is leading us under the person of our Prophet. You must come before him. He shall say what is to be done with you.'

They had reached the base of the hill by this time, and were surrounded by crowds of the pilgrims – pale-faced, meek-looking women; strong, laughing children; and anxious, earnest-eyed men. Many were the cries of astonishment and of commiseration which arose from them when they perceived the youth of one of the strangers and the destitution of the other. Their escort did not halt, however, but pushed on, followed by a great crowd of Mormons, until they reached a wagon which was conspicuous for its great size and for the gaudiness and smartness of its appearance. Six horses were yoked to it, whereas the others were furnished with two, or, at most, four apiece. Beside the driver there sat a man who could not have been more than thirty years of age, but whose massive head and resolute expression marked him as a leader. He was reading a brown-backed volume, but as the crowd approached he laid it aside, and listened attentively to an account of the episode. Then he turned to the two castaways.

'If we take you with us,' he said, in solemn words, 'it can only be as believers in our own creed. We shall have no wolves in our fold. Better far that your bones should bleach in this wilderness than that you should prove to be that little speck of decay which in time corrupts the whole fruit. Will you come with us on these terms?'

'Guess I'll come with you on any terms,' said Ferrier, with such emphasis that the grave elders could not restrain a smile. The leader alone retained his stern, impressive expression.

'Take him, Brother Stangerson,' he said, 'give him food and drink, and the child likewise. Let it be your task also to teach him our holy creed. We have delayed long enough. Forward! On, on to Zion!'

'On, on to Zion!' cried the crowd of Mormons, and the words rippled down the long caravan, passing from mouth to mouth until they died away in a dull murmur in the far distance. With a cracking of whips and a creaking of wheels the great wagons got into motion, and soon the whole caravan was winding along once more. The elder to whose care the two waifs had been committed led them to his wagon, where a meal was already awaiting them.

'You shall remain here,' he said. 'In a few days you will have recovered from your fatigues. In the meantime, remember that now and for ever you are of our religion. Brigham Young has said it, and he has spoken with the voice of Joseph Smith, which is the voice of God.'

9

The Flower of Utah

This is not the place to commemorate the trials and privations endured by the immigrant Mormons before they came to their final haven. From the shores of the Mississippi to the western slopes of the Rocky Mountains they had struggled on with a constancy almost unparalleled in history. The savage man and the savage beast, hunger, thirst, fatigue and disease – every impediment which nature could place in the way – had all been overcome with Anglo-Saxon tenacity. Yet the long journey and the accumulated terrors had shaken the hearts of the stoutest among them. There was not one who did not sink upon his knees in heartfelt prayer when they saw the broad valley of Utah bathed in the sunlight beneath them and learned from the lips of their leader that this was the promised land and that these virgin acres were to be theirs for evermore.

Young speedily proved himself to be a skilful administrator as well as a resolute chief. Maps were drawn and charts prepared, in which the future city was sketched out. All around farms were apportioned and allotted in proportion to the standing of each individual. The tradesman was put to his trade and the artisan to his calling. In the town streets and squares sprang up as if by magic. In the country there was draining and hedging, planting and clearing, until the next summer saw the whole country golden with the wheat crop. Everything prospered in the strange settlement. Above all, the great temple which they had erected in the centre of the city grew ever taller and larger. From the first blush of dawn until the closing of the twilight, the clatter of the hammer and the rasp of the saw were never absent from the monument which the immigrants erected to Him who had led them safe through many dangers.

The two castaways, John Ferrier and the little girl who had shared his fortunes and had been adopted as his daughter, accompanied the Mormons to the end of their great pilgrimage. Little Lucy Ferrier was borne along pleasantly enough in Elder Stangerson's wagon, a retreat which she shared with the Mormon's three wives and with his son, a headstrong, forward boy of twelve. Having rallied, with the elasticity of childhood, from the shock caused by her mother's death, she soon became a pet with the women, and reconciled herself to this new life in her moving canvas-covered home. In the meantime Ferrier, having recovered from his privations, distinguished himself as a useful guide and an indefatigable hunter. So rapidly did he gain the esteem of his new companions that when they reached the end of their wanderings it was unanimously agreed that he should be provided with as large and as fertile a tract of land as any of the settlers, with the exception of Young himself, and of Stangerson, Kemball, Johnston and Drebber, who were the four principal elders.

On the farm thus acquired John Ferrier built himself a substantial log house, which received so many additions in succeeding years that it grew into a roomy villa. He was a man of a practical turn of mind, keen in his dealings and skilful with his hands. His iron constitution enabled him to work morning and evening at improving and tilling his lands. Hence it came about that his farm and all that belonged to him prospered exceedingly. In three years he was better off than his neighbours, in six he was well-to-do, in nine he was rich, and in twelve there were not half a dozen men in the whole of Salt Lake City who could compare with him. From the great inland sea to the distant Wahsatch Mountains there was no name better known than that of John Ferrier.

There was one way and only one in which he offended the suscep-tibilities of his co-religionists. No argument or persuasion could ever induce him to set up a female establishment after the manner of his companions. He never gave reasons for this persistent refusal, but contented himself by resolutely and inflexibly adhering to his deter-mination. There were some who accused him of lukewarmness in his adopted religion, and others who put it down to greed of wealth and reluctance to incur expense. Others, again, spoke of some early love affair, and of a fair-haired girl who had pined away on the shores of the Atlantic. Whatever the reason, Ferrier remained strictly celi-bate. In every other respect he conformed to the religion of the young settlement, and gained the name of being an orthodox and straight-walking man.

Lucy Ferrier grew up within the log house, and assisted her adopted father in all his undertakings. The keen air of the mountains and the balsamic odour of the pine trees took the place of nurse and mother to the young girl. As year succeeded to year she grew taller and stronger, her cheek more ruddy and her step more elastic. Many a wayfarer upon the high road which ran by Ferrier's farm felt long-forgotten thoughts revive in their minds as they watched her lithe, girlish figure tripping through the wheatfields, or met her mounted upon her father's mustang, and managing it with all the ease and grace of a true child of the West. So the bud blossomed into a flower, and the year which saw her father the richest of the farmers left her as fair a specimen of American girlhood as could be found in the whole Pacific slope.

It was not the father, however, who first discovered that the child had developed into the woman. It seldom is in such cases. That mysterious change is too subtle and too gradual to be measured by dates. Least of all does the maiden herself know it until the tone of a voice or the touch of a hand sets her heart thrilling within her, and she learns, with a mixture of pride and of fear, that a new and a larger nature has awoke within her. There are few who cannot recall that day and remember the one little incident which heralded the dawn of a new life. In the case of Lucy Ferrier the occasion was serious enough in itself, apart from its future influence on her destiny and that of many besides.

It was a warm June morning, and the Latter Day Saints were as busy as the bees whose hive they have chosen for their emblem. In the fields and in the streets rose the same hum of human industry. Down the dusty high roads defiled long streams of heavily laden mules, all heading to the West, for the gold fever had broken out in California, and the overland route lay through the city of the Elect. There, too, were droves of sheep and bullocks coming in from the outlying pasturelands, and trains of tired immigrants, men and horses equally weary of their interminable journey. Through all this motley assemblage, threading her way with the skill of an accomplished rider, there galloped Lucy Ferrier, her fair face flushed with the exercise and her long chestnut hair floating out behind her. She had a commission from her father in the city, and was dashing in as she had done many a time before, with all the fearlessness of youth, thinking only of her task and how it was to be performed. The travel-stained adventurers gazed after her in astonishment, and even the unemotional Indians, journeying in with their pelties, relaxed their accustomed stoicism as they marvelled at the beauty of the pale-faced maiden.

She had reached the outskirts of the city when she found the road blocked by a great drove of cattle, driven by a half-dozen wild-looking herdsmen from the plains. In her impatience she endeavoured to pass this obstacle by pushing her horse into what appeared to be a gap. Scarcely had she got fairly into it, however, before the beasts closed in behind her, and she found herself completely embedded in the moving stream of fierce-eyed, long-horned bullocks. Accustomed as she was to deal with cattle, she was not alarmed at her situation, but took advantage of every opportunity to urge her horse on, in the hopes of pushing her way through the cavalcade. Unfortunately the horns of one of the creatures, either by accident or design, came in violent contact with the flank of the mustang and excited it to madness. In an instant it reared up upon its hind legs with a snort of rage, and pranced and tossed in a way that would have unseated any but a skilful rider. The situation was full of peril. Every plunge of the excited horse brought it against the horns again and goaded it to fresh madness. It was all that the girl could do to keep herself in the saddle, yet a slip would mean a terrible death under the hoofs of the unwieldy and terrified animals. Unaccustomed to sudden emergencies, her head began to swim, and her grip upon the bridle to relax. Choked by the rising cloud of dust and by the steam from the struggling creatures, she might have abandoned her efforts in despair but for a kindly voice at her elbow which assured her of assistance. At the same moment a sinewy, brown hand caught the frightened horse by the curb, and forcing a way through the drove, soon brought her to the outskirts.

'You're not hurt, I hope, miss,' said her preserver respectfully.

She looked up at his dark, fierce face, and laughed saucily. 'I'm awful frightened,' she said, naÔvely; 'whoever would have thought that Poncho would have been so scared by a lot of cows?'

'Thank God you kept your seat,' the other said earnestly. He was a tall, savage-looking young fellow, mounted on a powerful roan horse, and clad in the rough dress of a hunter, with a long rifle slung over his shoulders. 'I guess you are the daughter of John Ferrier,' he remarked; 'I saw you ride down from his house. When you see him, ask him if he remembers the Jefferson Hopes of St Louis. If he's the same Ferrier, my father and he were pretty thick.'

'Hadn't you better come and ask yourself?' she asked, demurely.

The young fellow seemed pleased at the suggestion, and his dark eyes sparkled with pleasure. 'I'll do so,' he said; 'we've. been in the mountains for two months, and are not over and above in visiting condition. He must take us as he finds us.'

'He has a good deal to thank you for, and so have I,' she answered, 'he's awful fond of me. If those cows had jumped on me he'd have never got over it.'

'Neither would I,' said her companion.

'You! Well, I don't see that it would make much matter to you, anyhow. You ain't even a friend of ours.'

The young hunter's dark face grew so gloomy over this remark that Lucy Ferrier laughed aloud.

'There, I didn't mean that,' she said; 'of course, you are a friend now. You must come and see us. Now I must push along, or father won't trust me with his business any more. Goodbye!'

'Goodbye,' he answered, raising his broad sombrero, and bending over her little hand. She wheeled her mustang round, gave it a cut with her riding-whip, and darted away down the broad road in a rolling cloud of dust.

Young Jefferson Hope rode on with his companions, gloomy and taciturn. He and they had been among the Nevada Mountains prospecting for silver and were returning to Salt Lake City in the hope of raising capital enough to work some lodes which they had discovered. He had been as keen as any of them upon the business until this sudden incident had drawn his thoughts into another channel. The sight of the fair young girl, as frank and wholesome as the Sierra breezes, had stirred his volcanic, untamed heart to its very depths. When she had vanished from his sight, he realised that a crisis had come in his life, and that neither silver speculations nor any other questions could ever be of such importance to him as this new and all-absorbing one. The love which had sprung up in his heart was not the sudden, changeable fancy of a boy, but rather the wild, fierce passion of a man of strong will and imperious temper. He had been accustomed to succeed in all that he undertook. He swore in his heart that he would not fail in this if human effort and human perseverance could render him successful.

He called on John Ferrier that night, and many times again, until his face was a familiar one at the farmhouse. John, cooped up in the valley, and absorbed in his work, had had little chance of learning the news of the outside world during the last twelve years. All this Jefferson Hope was able to tell him, and in a style which interested Lucy as well as her father. He had been a pioneer in California, and could narrate many a strange tale of fortunes made and fortunes lost in those wild, halcyon days. He had been a scout, too, and a trapper, a silver explorer and a ranchman. Wherever stirring adventures were to be had, Jefferson Hope had been there in search of them. He soon became a favourite with the old farmer, who spoke eloquently of his virtues. On such occasions, Lucy was silent, but her blushing cheek and her bright, happy eyes showed only too clearly that her young heart was no longer her own. Her honest father may not have observed these symptoms, but they were assuredly not thrown away upon the man who had won her affections.

One summer evening he came galloping down the road and pulled up at the gate. She was at the doorway, and came down to meet him. He threw the bridle over the fence and strode up the pathway.

'I am off, Lucy,' he said, taking her two hands in his, and gazing tenderly down into her face; 'I won't ask you to come with me now, but will you be ready to come when I am here again?'

'And when will that be?' she asked, blushing and laughing.

'A couple of months at the outside. I will come and claim you then, my darling. There's no one who can stand between us.'

'And how about father?' she asked.

'He has given his consent, provided we get these mines working all right. I have no fear on that head.'

'Oh, well; of course, if you and father have arranged it all, there's no more to be said,' she whispered, with her cheek against his broad breast.

'Thank God!' he said hoarsely, stooping and kissing her. 'It is settled, then. The longer I stay, the harder it will be to go. They are waiting for me at the canyon. Goodbye, my own darling – goodbye. In two months you shall see me.'

He tore himself from her as he spoke, and, flinging himself upon his horse, galloped furiously away, never even looking round, as though afraid that his resolution might fail him if he took one glance at what he was leaving. She stood at the gate, gazing after him until he vanished from her sight. Then she walked back into the house, the happiest girl in all Utah.

10

John Ferrier Talks with the Prophet

Three weeks had passed since Jefferson Hope and his comrades had departed from Salt Lake City. John Ferrier's heart was sore within him when he thought of the young man's return, and of the impending loss of his adopted child. Yet her bright and happy face reconciled him to the arrangement more than any argument could have done. He had always determined, deep down in his resolute heart, that nothing would ever induce him to allow his daughter to wed a Mormon. Such a marriage he regarded as no marriage at all, but as a shame and a disgrace. Whatever he might think of the Mormon doctrines, upon that one point he was inflexible. He had to seal his mouth on the subject, however, for to express an unorthodox opinion was a dangerous matter in those days in the Land of the Saints.

Yes, a dangerous matter – so dangerous that even the most saintly dared only whisper their religious opinions with bated breath, lest something which fell from their lips might be misconstrued, and bring down a swift retribution upon them. The victims of persecution had now turned persecutors on their own account, and persecutors of the most terrible description. Not the Inquisition of Seville, nor the German Vehmgericht, nor the Secret Societies of Italy, were ever able to put a more formidable machinery in motion than that which cast a cloud over the State of Utah.

Its invisibility, and the mystery which was attached to it, made this organisation doubly terrible. It appeared to be omniscient and omnipotent, and yet was neither seen nor heard. The man who held out against the Church vanished away, and none knew whither he had gone or what had befallen him. His wife and his children awaited him at home, but no father ever returned to tell them how he had fared at the hands of his secret judges. A rash word or a hasty act was followed by annihilation, and yet none knew what the nature might be of this terrible power which was suspended over them. No wonder that men went about in fear and trembling, and that even in the heart of the wilderness they dared not whisper the doubts which oppressed them.

At first this vague and terrible power was exercised only upon the recalcitrants who, having embraced the Mormon faith, wished afterwards to pervert or to abandon it. Soon, however, it took a wider range. The supply of adult women was running short, and polygamy without a female population on which to draw was a barren doctrine indeed. Strange rumours began to be bandied about – rumours of murdered immigrants and rifled camps in regions where Indians had never been seen. Fresh women appeared in the harems of the elders – women who pined and wept, and bore upon their faces the traces of an unextinguishable horror. Belated wanderers upon the mountains spoke of gangs of armed men, masked, stealthy and noiseless, who flitted by them in the darkness. These tales and rumours took substance and shape and were corroborated and recorroborated until they resolved themselves into a definite name. To this day, in the lonely ranches of the West, the name of the Danite Band, or the Avenging Angels, is a sinister and an ill-omened one.

Fuller knowledge of the organisation which produced such terrible results served to increase rather than to lessen the horror which it inspired in the minds of men. None knew who belonged to this ruthless society. The names of the participators in the deeds of blood and violence done under the name of religion were kept profoundly secret. The very friend to whom you communicated your misgivings as to the Prophet and his mission might be one of those who would come forth at night with fire and sword to exact a terrible reparation. Hence every man feared his neighbour, and none spoke of the things which were nearest his heart.

One fine morning John Ferrier was about to set out to his wheatfields, when he heard the click of the latch, and, looking through the window, saw a stout, sandy-haired middle-aged man coming up the pathway. His heart leapt to his mouth, for this was none other than the great Brigham Young himself. Full of trepidation – for he knew that such a visit boded him little good – Ferrier ran to the door to greet the Mormon chief. The latter, however, received his salutations coldly, and followed him with a stern face into the sitting-room.

'Brother Ferrier,' he said, taking a seat, and eyeing the farmer keenly from under his light-coloured eyelashes, 'the true believers have been good friends to you. We picked you up when you were starving in the desert, we shared our food with you, led you safe to the Chosen Valley, gave you a goodly share of land, and allowed you to wax rich under our protection. Is not this so?'

'It is so,' answered John Ferrier.

'In return for all this we asked but one condition: that was, that you should embrace the true faith, and conform in every way to its usages.

h

This you promised to do, and this, if common report says truly, you have neglected.'

'And how have I neglected it?' asked Ferrier, throwing out his hands in expostulation. 'Have I not given to the common fund? Have I not attended at the Temple? Have I not – ?'

'Where are your wives?' asked Young, looking round him. 'Call them in, that I may greet them.'

'It is true that I have not married,' Ferrier answered. 'But women were few, and there were many who had better claims than I. I was not a lonely man: I had my daughter to attend to my wants.'

'It is of that daughter that I would speak to you,' said the leader of the Mormons. 'She has grown to be the flower of Utah, and has found favour in the eyes of many who are high in the land.'

John Ferrier groaned internally.

'There are stories of her which I would fain disbelieve – stories that she is sealed to some Gentile. This must be the gossip of idle tongues.

'What is the thirteenth rule in the code of the sainted Joseph Smith? "Let every maiden of the true faith marry one of the elect; for if she wed a Gentile, she commits a grievous sin." This being so, it is impossible that you, who profess the holy creed, should suffer your daughter to violate it.'

John Ferrier made no answer, but he played nervously with his riding-whip.

'Upon this one point your whole faith shall be tested – so it has been decided in the Sacred Council of Four. The girl is young, and we would not have her wed grey hairs, neither would we deprive her of all choice. We elders have many heifers,* but our children must also be provided. Stangerson has a son and Drebber has a son and either of them would gladly welcome your daughter to their house. Let her choose between them. They are young and rich, and of the true faith. What say you to that?'

Ferrier remained silent for some little time with his brows knitted.

'You will give us time,' he said at last. 'My daughter is very young – she is scarce of an age to marry.'

'She shall have a month to choose,' said Young, rising from his seat. 'At the end of that time she shall give her answer.'

He was passing through the door when he turned, with flushed face and flashing eyes. 'It were better for you, John Ferrier,' he thundered, 'that you and she were now lying blanched skeletons upon the Sierra Blanco, than that you should pit your weak wills against the orders of the Holy Four!'

With a threatening gesture of his hand, he turned from the door, and Ferrier heard his heavy steps scrunching along the shingly path.

He was still sitting with his elbow upon his knee, considering how he should broach the matter to his daughter, when a soft hand was laid upon his, and looking up, he saw her standing beside him. One glance at her pale, frightened face showed him that she had heard what had passed.

'I could not help it,' she said, in answer to his look. 'His voice rang through the house. Oh, father, father, what shall we do?'

'Don't you scare yourself,' he answered, drawing her to him, and passing his broad, rough hand caressingly over her chestnut hair. 'We'll fix it up somehow or another. You don't find your fancy kind o' lessening for this chap, do you?'

A sob and a squeeze of his hand was her only answer.

'No; of course not. I shouldn't care to hear you say you did. He's a likely lad, and he's a Christian, which is more than these folk here, in spite o' all their praying and preaching. There's a party starting for Nevada tomorrow, and I'll manage to send him a message letting him know the hole we are in. If I know anything o' that young man, he'll be back here with a speed that would whip electro-telegraphs.'

Lucy laughed through her tears at her father's description. 'When he comes, he will advise us for the best. But it is for you that I am frightened, dear. One hears – one hears such dreadful stories about those who oppose the Prophet: something terrible always happens to them.'

'But we haven't opposed him yet,' her father answered. 'It will be time to look out for squalls when we do. We have a clear month before us; at the end of that, I guess we had best shin out of Utah.'

'Leave Utah!'

'That's about the size of it.'

'But the farm?'

'We will raise as much as we can in money, and let the rest go. To tell the truth, Lucy, it isn't the first time I have thought of doing it. I don't care about knuckling under to any man, as these folk do to their darned Prophet. I'm a freeborn American, and it's all new to me. Guess I'm too old to learn. If he comes browsing about this farm, he might chance to run up against a charge of buckshot travelling in the opposite direction.'

'But they won't let us leave,' his daughter objected.

'Wait till Jefferson comes, and we'll soon manage that. In the meantime, don't you fret yourself, my dearie, and don't get your eyes swelled up, else he'll be walking into me when he sees you. There's nothing to be afeard about, and there's no danger at all.'

John Ferrier uttered these consoling remarks in a very confident tone, but she could not help observing that he paid unusual care to the fastening of the doors that night, and that he carefully cleaned and loaded the rusty old shotgun which hung upon the wall of his bedroom.

11

A Flight for Life

On the morning which followed his interview with the Mormon Prophet, John Ferrier went into Salt Lake City, and having found his acquaintance who was bound for the Nevada Mountains, he entrusted him with his message to Jefferson Hope. In it he told the young man of the imminent danger which threatened them and how necessary it was that he should return. Having done thus he felt easier in his mind and returned home with a lighter heart.

As he approached his farm, he was surprised to see a horse hitched to each of the posts of the gate. Still more surprised was he on entering to find two young men in possession of his sitting-room. One, with a long, pale face, was leaning back in the rocking-chair, with his feet cocked up upon the stove. The other, a bull-necked youth with coarse, bloated features, was standing in front of the window with his hands in his pockets whistling a popular hymn. Both of them nodded to Ferrier as he entered, and the one in the rocking-chair commenced the conversation.

'Maybe you don't know us,' he said. 'This here is the son of Elder Drebber, and I'm Joseph Stangerson, who travelled with you in the desert when the Lord stretched out His hand and gathered you into the true fold.'

'As He will all the nations in His own good time,' said the other in a nasal voice; 'He grindeth slowly but exceeding small.'

John Ferrier bowed coldly. He had guessed who his visitors were.

'We have come,' continued Stangerson, 'at the advice of our fathers to solicit the hand of your daughter for whichever of us may seem good to you and to her. As I have but four wives and Brother Drebber here has seven, it appears to me that my claim is the stronger one.'

'Nay, nay, Brother Stangerson,' cried the other; 'the question is not how many wives we have, but how many we can keep. My father has now given over his mills to me, and I am the richer man.'

'But my prospects are better,' said the other, warmly. 'When the Lord removes my father, I shall have his tanning yard and his leather factory. Then I am your elder, and am higher in the Church.'

'It will be for the maiden to decide,' rejoined young Drebber, smirking at his own reflection in the glass. 'We will leave it all to her decision.'

During this dialogue John Ferrier had stood fuming in the doorway, hardly able to keep his riding-whip from the backs of his two visitors.

'Look here,' he said at last, striding up to them, 'when my daughter summons you, you can come, but until then I don't want to see your faces again.'

The two young Mormons stared at him in amazement. In their eyes this competition between them for the maiden's hand was the highest of honours both to her and her father.

'There are two ways out of the room,' cried Ferrier; 'there is the door, and there is the window. Which do you care to use?'

His brown face looked so savage, and his gaunt hands so threatening, that his visitors sprang to their feet and beat a hurried retreat. The old farmer followed them to the door.

'Let me know when you have settled which it is to be,' he said, sardonically.

'You shall smart for this!' Stangerson cried, white with rage. 'You have defied the Prophet and the Council of Four. You shall rue it to the end of your days.'

'The hand of the Lord shall be heavy upon you,' cried young Drebber; 'He will arise and smite you!'

'Then I'll start the smiting,' exclaimed Ferrier, furiously, and would have rushed upstairs for his gun had not Lucy seized him by the arm and restrained him. Before he could escape from her, the clatter of horses' hoofs told him that they were beyond his reach.

'The young canting rascals!' he exclaimed, wiping the perspiration from his forehead; 'I would sooner see you in your grave, my girl, than the wife of either of them.'

'And so should I, father,' she answered, with spirit; 'but Jefferson will soon be here.'

'Yes. It will not be long before he comes. The sooner the better, for we do not know what their next move may be.'

It was, indeed, high time that someone capable of giving advice and help should come to the aid of the sturdy old farmer and his adopted daughter. In the whole history of the settlement there had never been such a case of rank disobedience to the authority of the elders. If minor errors were punished so sternly, what would be the fate of this arch rebel? Ferrier knew that his wealth and position would be of no avail to him. Others as well known and as rich as himself had been spirited away before now, and their goods given over to the Church. He was a brave man, but he trembled at the vague, shadowy terrors which hung over him. Any known danger he could face with a firm lip, but this suspense was unnerving. He concealed his fears from his daughter, however, and affected to make light of the whole matter, though she, with the keen eye of love, saw plainly that he was ill at ease.

He expected that he would receive some message or remonstrance from Young as to his conduct, and he was not mistaken, though it came in an unlooked-for manner. Upon rising next morning he found, to his surprise, a small square of paper pinned on to the coverlet of his bed just over his chest. On it was printed in bold, straggling letters:

Twenty-nine days are given you for amendment, and then –

The dash was more fear-inspiring than any threat could have been. How this warning came into his room puzzled John Ferrier sorely, for his servants slept in an outhouse, and the doors and windows had all been secured. He crumpled the paper up and said nothing to his daughter, but the incident struck a chill into his heart. The twenty-nine

days were evidently the balance of the month which Young had promised. What strength or courage could avail against an enemy armed
with such mysterious powers? The hand which fastened that pin might
have struck him to the heart, and he could never have known who had
slain him.

Still more shaken was he next morning. They had sat down to their
breakfast, when Lucy with a cry of surprise pointed upwards. In the
centre of the ceiling was scrawled, with a burned stick apparently,
the number 28. To his daughter it was unintelligible, and he did not
enlighten her. That night he sat up with his gun and kept watch and
ward. He saw and he heard nothing, and yet in the morning a great 27
had been painted upon the outside of his door.

Thus day followed day; and as sure as morning came he found
that his unseen enemies had kept their register, and had marked up
in some conspicuous position how many days were still left to him
out of the month of grace. Sometimes the fatal numbers appeared
upon the walls, sometimes upon the floors, occasionally they were on
small placards stuck upon the garden gate or the railings. With all his
vigilance John Ferrier could not discover whence these daily warnings
proceeded. A horror which was almost superstitious came upon him
at the sight of them. He became haggard and restless, and his eyes had
the troubled look of some hunted creature. He had but one hope in
life now, and that was for the arrival of the young hunter from Nevada.

Twenty had changed to fifteen, and fifteen to ten, but there was no
news of the absentee. One by one the numbers dwindled down, and
still there came no sign of him. Whenever a horseman clattered down
the road, or a driver shouted at his team, the old farmer hurried to the
gate thinking that help had arrived at last. At last, when he saw five
give way to four and that again to three, he lost heart, and abandoned
all hope of escape. Single-handed, and with his limited knowledge
of the mountains which surrounded the settlement, he knew that he
was powerless. The more-frequented roads were strictly watched and
guarded, and none could pass along them without an order from the
council. Turn which way he would, there appeared to be no avoiding

the blow which hung over him. Yet the old man never wavered in his resolution to part with life itself before he consented to what he regarded as his daughter's dishonour.

He was sitting alone one evening pondering deeply over his troubles, and searching vainly for some way out of them. That morning had shown the figure 2 upon the wall of his house, and the next day would be the last of the allotted time. What was to happen then? All manner of vague and terrible fancies filled his imagination. And his daughter – what was to become of her after he was gone? Was there no escape from the invisible network which was drawn all round them? He sank his head upon the table and sobbed at the thought of his own impotence.

What was that? In the silence he heard a gentle scratching sound – low, but very distinct in the quiet of the night. It came from the door of the house. Ferrier crept out into the hall and listened intently. There was a pause for a few moments, and then the low, insidious sound was repeated. Someone was evidently tapping very gently upon one of the panels of the door. Was it some midnight assassin who had come to carry out the murderous orders of the secret tribunal? Or was it some agent who was marking up that the last day of grace had arrived? John Ferrier felt that instant death would be better than the suspense which shook his nerves and chilled his heart. Springing forward, he drew the bolt and threw the door open.

Outside all was calm and quiet. The night was fine, and the stars were twinkling brightly overhead. The little front garden lay before the farmer's eyes bounded by the fence and gate, but neither there nor on the road was any human being to be seen. With a sigh of relief Ferrier looked to right and to left, until, happening to glance straight down at his own feet, he saw to his astonishment a man lying flat upon his face upon the ground, with arms and legs all asprawl.

So unnerved was he at the sight that he leaned up against the wall with his hand to his throat to stifle his inclination to call out. His first thought was that the prostrate figure was that of some wounded or dying man, but as he watched it he saw it writhe along the ground and into the hall with the rapidity and noiselessness of a serpent. Once within the house the man sprang to his feet, closed the door, and revealed to the astonished farmer the fierce face and resolute expression of Jefferson Hope.

'Good God!' gasped John Ferrier. 'How you scared me. Whatever made you come in like that?'

'Give me food,' the other said, hoarsely. 'I have had no time for bite or sup for eight-and-forty hours.' He flung himself upon the cold meat and bread which were still lying upon the table from his host's supper, and devoured them voraciously. 'Does Lucy bear up well?' he asked, when he had satisfied his hunger.

'Yes. She does not know the danger,' her father answered.

'That is well. The house is watched on every side. That is why I crawled my way up to it. They may be darned sharp, but they're not quite sharp enough to catch a Washoe hunter.'

John Ferrier felt a different man now that he realised that he had a devoted ally. He seized the young man's leathery hand and wrung it cordially. 'You're a man to be proud of,' he said. 'There are not many who would come to share our danger and our troubles.'

'You've hit it there, pard,' the young hunter answered. 'I have a respect for you, but if you were alone in this business I'd think twice before I put my head into such a hornets' nest. It's Lucy that brings me here, and before harm comes on her I guess there will be one less o' the Hope family in Utah.'

'What are we to do?'

'Tomorrow is your last day and unless you act tonight you are lost. I have a mule and two horses waiting in the Eagle Ravine. How much money have you?'

'Two thousand dollars in gold and five in notes.'

'That will do. I have as much more to add to it. We must push for Carson City through the mountains. You had best wake Lucy. It is as well that the servants do not sleep in the house.'

While Ferrier was absent, preparing his daughter for the approaching journey, Jefferson Hope packed all the eatables that he could find into a small parcel, and filled a stoneware jar with water, for he knew by experience that the mountain wells were few and far between. He had hardly completed his arrangements before the farmer returned with his daughter all dressed and ready for a start. The greeting between the lovers was warm, but brief, for minutes were precious, and there was much to be done.

'We must make our start at once,' said Jefferson Hope, speaking in a low but resolute voice, like one who realises the greatness of the peril, but has steeled his heart to meet it. 'The front and back entrances are watched, but with caution we may get away through the side window and across the fields. Once on the road we are only two miles from the ravine where the horses are waiting. By daybreak we should be half-way through the mountains.'

'What if we are stopped?' asked Ferrier.

Hope slapped the revolver butt which protruded from the front of his tunic. 'If they are too many for us, we shall take two or three of them with us,' he said with a sinister smile.

The lights inside the house had all been extinguished, and from the darkened window Ferrier peered over the fields which had been his own, and which he was now about to abandon for ever. He had long nerved himself to the sacrifice, however, and the thought of the honour and happiness of his daughter outweighed any regret at his ruined fortunes. All looked so peaceful and happy, the rustling trees and the broad, silent stretch of grainland, that it was difficult to realise that the spirit of murder lurked through it all. Yet the white face and set expression of the young hunter showed that in his approach to the house he had seen enough to satisfy him upon that head.

Ferrier carried the bag of gold and notes, Jefferson Hope had the scanty provisions and water, while Lucy had a small bundle containing a few of her more valued possessions. Opening the window very slowly and carefully, they waited until a dark cloud had somewhat obscured the night, and then one by one passed through into the little garden. With bated breath and crouching low they stumbled across it and gained the shelter of the hedge, which they skirted until they came to the gap which opened into the cornfield. They had just reached this point when the young man seized his two companions and dragged them down into the shadow, where they lay silent and trembling.

It was as well that his prairie training had given Jefferson Hope the ears of a lynx. He and his friends had hardly crouched down before the melancholy hooting of a mountain owl was heard within a few yards of them and was immediately answered by another hoot at a small distance. At the same moment a vague, shadowy figure emerged from the gap for which they had been making, and uttered the plaintive signal cry again, on which a second man appeared out of the obscurity.

'Tomorrow at midnight,' said the first, who appeared to be in authority. 'When the whippoorwill calls three times.'

'It is well,' returned the other. 'Shall I tell Brother Drebber?'

'Pass it on to him, and from him to the others. Nine to seven!'

'Seven to five!' repeated the other; and the two figures flitted away in different directions. Their concluding words had evidently been some form of sign and countersign. The instant that their footsteps had died away in the distance, Jefferson Hope sprang to his feet, and helping his companions through the gap, led the way across the fields at the top of his speed, supporting and half-carrying the girl when her strength appeared to fail her.

'Hurry on! hurry on!' he gasped from time to time. 'We are through the line of sentinels. Everything depends on speed. Hurry on!'

Once on the high road, they made rapid progress. Only once did they meet anyone, and then they managed to slip into a field, and so avoid recognition. Before reaching the town the hunter branched away into a rugged and narrow footpath which led to the mountains. Two dark, jagged peaks loomed above them through the darkness, and the defile which led between them was the Eagle Canyon in which the horses were awaiting them. With unerring instinct Jefferson Hope picked his way among the great boulders and along the bed of a dried-up watercourse until he came to the retired corner, screened with rocks, where the faithful animals had been picketed. The girl was placed upon the mule, and old Ferrier upon one of the horses, with his money-bag, while Jefferson Hope led the other along the precipitous and dangerous path.

It was a bewildering route for anyone who was not accustomed to face nature in her wildest moods. On the one side a great crag towered up a thousand feet or more, black, stern and menacing, with long basaltic columns upon its rugged surface like the ribs of some petrified monster. On the other hand a wild chaos of boulders and debris made all advance impossible. Between the two ran the irregular track, so narrow in places that they had to travel in Indian file, and so rough that only practised riders could have traversed it at all. Yet, in spite of all dangers and difficulties, the hearts of the fugitives were light within them, for every step increased the distance between them and the terrible despotism from which they were flying.

They soon had a proof, however, that they were still within the jurisdiction of the Saints. They had reached the very wildest and most desolate portion of the pass when the girl gave a startled cry, and pointed upwards. On a rock which overlooked the track, showing out dark and plain against the sky, there stood a solitary sentinel. He saw them as soon as they perceived him, and his military challenge of 'Who goes there?' rang through the silent ravine.

'Travellers for Nevada,' said Jefferson Hope, with his hand upon the rifle which hung by his saddle.

They could see the lonely watcher fingering his gun and peering down at them, as if dissatisfied at their reply.

'By whose permission?' he asked.

'The Holy Four,' answered Ferrier. His Mormon experiences had taught him that that was the highest authority to which he could refer.

'Nine to seven,' cried the sentinel.

'Seven to five,' returned Jefferson Hope promptly, remembering the countersign which he had heard in the garden.

'Pass, and the Lord go with you,' said the voice from above. Beyond his post the path broadened out, and the horses were able to break into a trot. Looking back, they could see the solitary watcher leaning upon his gun, and knew that they had passed the outlying post of the Chosen People, and that freedom lay before them.

12

The Avenging Angels

All night their course lay through intricate defiles and over irregular and rock-strewn paths. More than once they lost their way, but Hope's intimate knowledge of the mountains enabled them to regain the track once more. When morning broke, a scene of marvellous though savage beauty lay before them. In every direction the great snow-capped peaks hemmed them in, peeping over each other's shoulders to the far horizon. So steep were the rocky banks on either side of them that the larch and the pine seemed to be suspended over their heads and to need only a gust of wind to come hurtling down upon them. Nor was the fear entirely an illusion, for the barren valley was thickly strewn with trees and boulders which had fallen in a similar manner. Even as they passed, a great rock came thundering down with a hoarse rattle which woke the echoes in the silent gorges and startled the weary horses into a gallop.

As the sun rose slowly above the eastern horizon the caps of the great mountains lit up one after the other, like lamps at a festival, until they were all ruddy and glowing. The magnificent spectacle cheered the hearts of the three fugitives and gave them fresh energy. At a wild torrent which swept out of a ravine they called a halt, and watered their horses while they partook of a hasty breakfast. Lucy and her father would fain have rested longer, but Jefferson Hope was inexorable. 'They will be upon our track by this time,' he said. 'Everything depends upon our speed. Once safe in Carson, we may rest for the remainder of our lives.'

During the whole of that day they struggled on through the defiles, and by evening they calculated that they were more than thirty miles from their enemies. At night-time they chose the base of a beetling crag, where the rocks offered some protection from the chill wind, and there, huddled together for warmth, they enjoyed a few hours' sleep. Before daybreak, however, they were up and on their way once more. They had seen no signs of any pursuers and Jefferson Hope began to think that they were fairly out of the reach of the terrible organisation whose enmity they had incurred. He little knew how far that iron grasp could reach, or how soon it was to close upon them and crush them.

About the middle of the second day of their flight their scanty store of provisions began to run out. This gave the hunter little uneasiness, however, for there was game to be had among the mountains, and he had frequently before had to depend upon his rifle for the needs of life. Choosing a sheltered nook, he piled together a few dried branches and made a blazing fire, at which his companions might warm themselves, for they were now nearly five thousand feet above the sea level, and the air was bitter and keen. Having tethered the horses, and bade Lucy adieu, he threw his gun over his shoulder, and set out in search of whatever chance might throw in his way. Looking back, he saw the old man and the young girl crouching over the blazing fire, while the three animals stood motionless in the background. Then the intervening rocks hid them from his view.

He walked for a couple of miles through one ravine after another without success, though, from the marks upon the bark of the trees, and other indications, he judged that there were numerous bears in the vicinity. At last, after two or three hours' fruitless search, he was thinking of turning back in despair when casting his eyes upwards he saw a sight which sent a thrill of pleasure through his heart. On the edge of a jutting pinnacle, three or four hundred feet above him,

95

there stood a creature somewhat resembling a sheep in appearance, but armed with a pair of gigantic horns. The bighorn – for so it is called – was acting, probably, as a guardian over a flock which was invisible to the hunter; but fortunately it was heading in the opposite direction and had not perceived him. Lying on his face, he rested his rifle upon a rock, and took a long and steady aim before drawing the trigger. The animal sprang into the air, tottered for a moment upon the edge of the precipice, and then came crashing down into the valley beneath.

The creature was too unwieldy to lift, so the hunter contented himself with cutting away one haunch and part of the flank. With this trophy over his shoulder, he hastened to retrace his steps, for the evening was already drawing in. He had hardly started, however, before he realised the difficulty which faced him. In his eagerness he had wandered far past the ravines which were known to him and it was no easy matter to pick out the path which he had taken. The valley in which he found himself divided and subdivided into many gorges, which were so like each other that it was impossible to distinguish one from the other. He followed one for a mile or more until he came to a mountain torrent which he was sure that he had never seen before. Convinced that he had taken the wrong turn, he tried another, but with the same result. Night was coming on rapidly, and it was almost dark before he at last found himself in a defile which was familiar to him. Even then it was no easy matter to keep to the right track, for the moon had not yet risen, and the high cliffs on either side made the obscurity more profound. Weighed down with his burden, and weary from his exertions, he stumbled along keeping up his heart by the reflection that every step brought him nearer to Lucy, and that he carried with him enough to ensure them food for the remainder of their journey.

He had now come to the mouth of the very defile in which he had left them. Even in the darkness he could recognise the outline of the cliffs which bounded it. They must, he reflected, be awaiting him anxiously, for he had been absent nearly five hours. In the gladness of his heart he put his hands to his mouth and made the glen re-echo to a loud halloo as a signal that he was coming. He paused and listened for an answer. None came save his own cry, which clattered up the dreary, silent ravines, and was borne back to his ears in countless repetitions. Again he shouted, even louder than before, and again no whisper came back from the friends whom he had left such a short time ago. A vague, nameless dread came over him, and he hurried onwards frantically, dropping the precious food in his agitation.

When he turned the corner, he came full in sight of the spot where the fire had been lit. There was still a glowing pile of wood ashes there, but it had evidently not been tended since his departure. The same dead silence still reigned all round. With his fears all changed to convictions, he hurried on. There was no living creature near the remains of the fire: animals, man, maiden, all were gone. It was only too clear that some sudden and terrible disaster had occurred during his absence – a disaster which had embraced them all, and yet had left no traces behind it.

Bewildered and stunned by this blow, Jefferson Hope felt his head spin round and had to lean upon his rifle to save himself from falling. He was essentially a man of action, however, and speedily recovered from his temporary impotence. Seizing a half-consumed piece of wood from the smouldering fire, he blew it into a flame, and proceeded with its help to examine the little camp. The ground was all stamped down by the feet of horses, showing that a large party of mounted men had overtaken the fugitives, and the direction of their tracks proved that they had afterwards turned back to Salt Lake City. Had they carried back both of his companions with them? Jefferson Hope had almost persuaded himself that they must have done so, when his eye fell upon an object which made every nerve of his body tingle within him. A little way on one side of the camp was a low-lying heap of reddish soil which had assuredly not been there before. There was no mistaking it for anything but a newly dug grave. As the young hunter approached it, he perceived that a stick had been planted on it, with a sheet of paper stuck in the cleft fork of it. The inscription upon the paper was brief, but to the point:

JOHN FERRIER

formerly of Salt Lake City

Died August 4th, 1860

The sturdy old man, whom he had left so short a time before, was gone, then, and this was all his epitaph. Jefferson Hope looked wildly round to see if there was a second grave, but there was no sign of one. Lucy had been carried back by their terrible pursuers to fulfil her original destiny, by becoming one of the harem of an elder's son. As the young fellow realised the certainty of her fate, and his own powerlessness to prevent it, he wished that he, too, was lying with the old farmer in his last silent resting-place.

Again, however, his active spirit shook off the lethargy which springs from despair. If there was nothing else left to him, he could at least devote his life to revenge. With indomitable patience and perseverance, Jefferson Hope possessed also a power of sustained vindictiveness, which he may have learned from the Indians amongst whom he had lived. As he stood by the desolate fire, he felt that the only one thing which could assuage his grief would be thorough and complete retribution, brought by his own hand upon his enemies. His strong will and untiring energy should, he determined, be devoted to that one end. With a grim, white face he retraced his steps to where he had dropped the food, and having stirred up the smouldering fire, he cooked enough to last him for a few days. This he made up into a bundle, and, tired as he was, he set himself to walk back through the mountains upon the track of the Avenging Angels.

For five days he toiled footsore and weary through the defiles which he had already traversed on horseback. At night he flung himself down among the rocks and snatched a few hours of sleep; but before daybreak he was always well on his way. On the sixth day, he reached the Eagle Canyon, from which they had commenced their ill-fated flight. Thence he could look down upon the home of the Saints. Worn and exhausted, he leaned upon his rifle and shook his gaunt hand fiercely at the silent, widespread city beneath him. As he looked at it, he observed that there were flags in some of the principal streets, and other signs of festivity. He was still speculating as to what this might mean when he heard the clatter of a horse's hoofs and saw a mounted man riding towards him. As he approached, he recognised him as a Mormon named Cowper, to whom he had rendered services at different times. He therefore accosted him when he got up to him, with the object of finding out what Lucy Ferrier's fate had been.

'I am Jefferson Hope,' he said. 'You remember me.'

The Mormon looked at him with undisguised astonishment – indeed, it was difficult to recognise in this tattered, unkempt wanderer, with ghastly white face and fierce, wild eyes, the spruce young hunter of former days. Having, however, at last satisfied himself as to his identity, the man's surprise changed to consternation.

'You are mad to come here,' he cried. 'It is as much as my own life is worth to be seen talking with you. There is a warrant against you from the Holy Four for assisting the Ferriers away.'

'I don't fear them, or their warrant,' Hope said, earnestly. 'You must know something of this matter, Cowper. I conjure you by everything you hold dear to answer a few questions. We have always been friends. For God's sake, don't refuse to answer me.'

'What is it?' the Mormon asked uneasily. 'Be quick. The very rocks have ears and the trees eyes.'

'What has become of Lucy Ferrier?'

'She was married yesterday to young Drebber. Hold up, man, hold up; you have no life left in you.'

'Don't mind me,' said Hope faintly. He was white to the very lips, and had sunk down on the stone against which he had been leaning. 'Married you say?'

'Married yesterday – that's what those flags are for on the Endowment House. There was some words between young Drebber and young Stangerson as to which was to have her. They'd both been in the party that followed them, and Stangerson had shot her father, which seemed to give him the best claim; but when they argued it out in council, Drebber's party was the stronger, so the Prophet gave her over to him. No one won't have her very long though, for I saw death in her face yesterday. She is more like a ghost than a woman. Are you off, then?'

'Yes, I am off,' said Jefferson Hope, who had risen from his seat. His face might have been chiselled out of marble, so hard and set was its expression, while its eyes glowed with a baleful light.

'Where are you going?'

'Never mind,' he answered; and, slinging his weapon over his shoulder, he strode off down the gorge and so away into the heart of the mountains to the haunts of the wild beasts. Amongst them all there was none so fierce and so dangerous as himself.

The prediction of the Mormon was only too well fulfilled. Whether it was the terrible death of her father or the effects of the hateful marriage into which she had been forced, poor Lucy never held up her head again, but pined away and died within a month. Her sottish husband, who had married her principally for the sake of John Ferrier's property, did not affect any great grief at his bereavement; but his other wives mourned over her, and sat up with her the night before the burial, as is the Mormon custom. They were grouped round the bier in the early hours of the morning, when, to their inexpressible fear and astonishment, the door was flung open, and a savage-looking, weather-beaten man in tattered garments strode into the room. Without a glance or a word to the cowering women, he walked up to the white, silent figure which had once contained the pure soul of Lucy Ferrier. Stooping over her, he pressed his lips reverently to her cold forehead, and then, snatching up her hand, he took the wedding-ring from her finger. 'She shall not be buried in that,' he cried, with a fierce snarl, and before an alarm could be raised sprang down the stairs and was gone. So strange and so brief was the episode that the watchers might have found it hard to believe it themselves, or persuade other people of it, had it not been for the undeniable fact that the circlet of gold which marked her as having been a bride had disappeared.

For some months Jefferson Hope lingered among the mountains, leading a strange, wild life, and nursing in his heart the fierce desire for vengeance which possessed him. Tales were told in the city of the weird figure which was seen prowling about the suburbs, and which haunted the lonely mountain gorges. Once a bullet whistled through Stangerson's window and flattened itself upon the wall within a foot of him. On another occasion, as Drebber passed under a cliff a great boulder crashed down on him, and he only escaped a terrible death by throwing himself upon his face. The two young Mormons were not long in discovering the reason of these attempts upon their lives and led repeated expeditions into the mountains in the hope of capturing or killing their enemy, but always without success. Then they adopted the precaution of never going out alone or after nightfall, and of having their houses guarded. After a time they were able to relax these measures, for nothing was either heard or seen of their opponent, and they hoped that time had cooled his vindictiveness.

Far from doing so, it had, if anything, augmented it. The hunter's mind was of a hard, unyielding nature, and the predominant idea of revenge had taken such complete possession of it that there was no room for any other emotion. He was, however, above all things, practical. He soon realised that even his iron constitution could not stand the incessant strain which he was putting upon it. Exposure and want of wholesome food were wearing him out. If he died like a dog among the mountains, what was to become of his revenge then? And yet such a death was sure to overtake him if he persisted. He felt that that was to play his enemy's game, so he reluctantly returned to the old Nevada mines, there to recruit his health and to amass money enough to allow him to pursue his object without privation.

His intention had been to be absent a year at the most, but a combination of unforeseen circumstances prevented his leaving the mines for nearly five. At the end of that time, however, his memory of his wrongs and his craving for revenge were quite as keen as on that memorable night when he had stood by John Ferrier's grave. Disguised, and under an assumed name, he returned to Salt Lake City, careless what became of his own life as long as he obtained what he knew to be justice. There he found evil tidings awaiting him. There had been a schism among the Chosen People a few months before, some of the younger members of the Church having rebelled against the authority of the elders, and the result had been the secession of a certain number of the malcontents, who had left Utah and become Gentiles. Among these had been Drebber and Stangerson; and no one knew whither they had gone. Rumour reported that Drebber had managed to convert a large part of his property into money, and that he had departed a wealthy man, while his companion, Stangerson, was comparatively poor. There was no clue at all, however, as to their whereabouts.

Many a man, however vindictive, would have abandoned all thought of revenge in the face of such a difficulty, but Jefferson Hope never faltered for a moment. With the small competence he possessed, eked out by such employment as he could pick up, he travelled from town to town through the United States in quest of his enemies. Year passed into year, his black hair turned grizzled, but still he wandered on, a human bloodhound, with his mind wholly set upon the one object to which he had devoted his life. At last his perseverance was rewarded. It was but a glance of a face in a window, but that one glance told him that Cleveland in Ohio possessed the men whom he was in pursuit of. He returned to his miserable lodgings with his plan of vengeance all arranged. It chanced, however, that Drebber, looking from his window, had recognised the vagrant in the street, and had read murder in his eyes. He hurried before a justice of the peace, accompanied by Stangerson, who had become his private secretary, and represented to him that they were in danger of their lives from the jealousy and hatred of an old rival. That evening Jefferson Hope was taken into custody, and not being able to find sureties, was detained for some weeks. When at last he was liberated it was only to find that Drebber's house was deserted, and that he and his secretary had departed for Europe.

Again the avenger had been foiled, and again his concentrated hatred urged him to continue the pursuit. Funds were wanting, however, and for some time he had to return to work, saving every dollar for his approaching journey. At last, having collected enough to keep life in him, he departed for Europe, and tracked his enemies from city to city, working his way in any menial capacity, but never overtaking the fugitives. When he reached St Petersburg, they had departed for Paris; and when he followed them there, he learned that they had just set off for Copenhagen. At the Danish capital he was again a few days late, for they had journeyed on to London, where he at last succeeded in running them to earth. As to what occurred there, we cannot do better than quote the old hunter's own account, as duly recorded in Dr Watson's journal, to which we are already under such obligations.

13

A Continuation of the Reminiscences of John Watson MD

Our prisoner's furious resistance did not apparently indicate any ferocity in his disposition towards ourselves, for on finding himself powerless, he smiled in an affable manner, and expressed his hopes that he had not hurt any of us in the scuffle. 'I guess you're going to take me to the police station,' he remarked to Sherlock Holmes. 'My cab's at the door. If you'll loose my legs I'll walk down to it. I'm not so light to lift as I used to be.'

Gregson and Lestrade exchanged glances, as if they thought this proposition rather a bold one; but Holmes at once took the prisoner at his word, and loosened the towel which we had bound round his ankles. He rose and stretched his legs, as though to assure himself that they were free once more. I remember that I thought to myself, as I eyed him, that I had seldom seen a more powerfully built man; and his dark, sunburned face bore an expression of determination and energy which was as formidable as his personal strength.

'If there's a vacant place for a chief of the police, I reckon you are the man for it,' he said, gazing with undisguised admiration at my fellow-lodger. 'The way you kept on my trail was a caution.'

'You had better come with me,' said Holmes to the two detectives.

'I can drive you,' said Lestrade.

'Good! and Gregson can come inside with me. You, too, doctor. You have taken an interest in the case, and may as well stick to us.'

I assented gladly, and we all descended together. Our prisoner made no attempt at escape, but stepped calmly into the cab which had been his, and we followed him. Lestrade mounted the box, whipped up the horse, and brought us in a very short time to our destination. We were ushered into a small chamber, where a police inspector noted down our prisoner's name and the names of the men with whose murder he had been charged. The official was a white-faced, unemotional man, who went through his duties in a dull, mechanical way. 'The prisoner will be put before the magistrates in the course of the week,' he said; 'in the meantime, Mr Jefferson Hope, have you anything that you wish to say? I must warn you that your words will be taken down, and may be used against you.'

'I've got a good deal to say,' our prisoner said slowly. 'I want to tell you gentlemen all about it.'

'Hadn't you better reserve that for your trial?' asked the inspector.

'I may never be tried,' he answered. 'You needn't look startled. It isn't suicide I am thinking of. Are you a doctor?' He turned his fierce, dark eyes upon me as he asked this last question.

'Yes, I am,' I answered.

'Then put your hand here,' he said, with a smile, motioning with his manacled wrists towards his chest.

I did so; and became at once conscious of an extraordinary throbbing and commotion which was going on inside. The walls of his chest seemed to thrill and quiver as a frail building would do inside when some powerful engine was at work. In the silence of the room I could hear a dull humming and buzzing noise which proceeded from the same source.

'Why,' I cried, 'you have an aortic aneurism!'

'That's what they call it,' he said, placidly. 'I went to a doctor last week about it, and he told me that it is bound to burst before many days have passed. It has been getting worse for years. I got it from over-exposure and under-feeding among the Salt Lake Mountains. I've done my work now, and I don't care how soon I go, but I should like to leave some account of the business behind me. I don't want to be remembered as a common cut-throat.'

The inspector and the two detectives had a hurried discussion as to the advisability of allowing him to tell his story.

105

'Do you consider, doctor, that there is immediate danger?' the former asked.

'Most certainly there is,' I answered.

'In that case it is clearly our duty, in the interests of justice, to take his statement,' said the inspector. 'You are at liberty, sir, to give your account, which I again warn you will be taken down.'

'I'll sit down, with your leave,' the prisoner said, suiting the action to the word. 'This aneurism of mine makes me easily tired, and the tussle we had half an hour ago has not mended matters. I'm on the brink of the grave, and I am not likely to lie to you. Every word I say is the absolute truth, and how you use it is a matter of no consequence to me.'

With these words, Jefferson Hope leaned back in his chair and began the following remarkable statement. He spoke in a calm and methodical manner, as though the events which he narrated were commonplace enough. I can vouch for the accuracy of the subjoined account, for I have had access to Lestrade's notebook, in which the prisoner's words were taken down exactly as they were uttered.

'It don't much matter to you why I hated these men,' he said; 'it's enough that they were guilty of the death of two human beings – a father and a daughter – and that they had, therefore, forfeited their own lives. After the lapse of time that had passed since their crime, it was impossible for me to secure a conviction against them in any court. I knew of their guilt, though, and I determined that I should be judge, jury and executioner all rolled into one. You'd have done the same if you have any manhood in you, if you had been in my place.

'That girl that I spoke of was to have married me twenty years ago. She was forced into marrying that same Drebber, and broke her heart over it. I took the marriage ring from her dead finger, and I vowed that his dying eyes should rest upon that very ring, and that his last thoughts should be of the crime for which he was punished. I have carried it about with me, and have followed him and his accomplice over two continents until I caught them. They thought to tire me out, but they could not do it. If I die tomorrow, as is likely enough, I die knowing that my work in this world is done, and well done. They have perished, and by my hand. There is nothing left for me to hope for, or to desire.

'They were rich and I was poor, so that it was no easy matter for me to follow them. When I got to London my pocket was about empty, and I found that I must turn my hand to something for my living. Driving and riding are as natural to me as walking, so I applied at a cab-owner's office, and soon got employment. I was to bring a certain sum a week to the owner, and whatever was over, that I might keep for myself. There was seldom much over, but I managed to scrape along somehow. The hardest job was to learn my way about, for I reckon that of all the mazes that ever were contrived, this city is the most confusing. I had a map beside me, though, and when once I had spotted the principal hotels and stations, I got on pretty well.

'It was some time before I found out where my two gentlemen were living; but I enquired and enquired until at last I dropped across them. They were at a boarding-house at Camberwell, over on the other side of the river. When once I found them out, I knew that I had them at my mercy. I had grown my beard, and there was no chance of their recognising me. I would dog them and follow them until I saw my opportunity. I was determined that they should not escape me again.

'They were very near doing it for all that. Go where they would about London, I was always at their heels. Sometimes I followed them on my cab, and sometimes on foot, but the former was the best, for then they could not get away from me. It was only early in the morning or late at night that I could earn anything, so that I began to get behindhand with my employer. I did not mind that, however, as long as I could lay my hand upon the men I wanted.

'They were very cunning, though. They must have thought that there was some chance of their being followed, for they would never go out alone, and never after nightfall. During two weeks I drove behind them every day, and never once saw them separate. Drebber himself was drunk half the time, but Stangerson was not to be caught napping. I watched them late and early, but never saw the ghost of a chance; but I was not discouraged, for something told me that the hour had almost come. My only fear was that this thing in my chest might burst a little too soon and leave my work undone.

'At last, one evening I was driving up and down Torquay Terrace, as the street was called in which they boarded, when I saw a cab drive up to their door. Presently some luggage was brought out and after a time Drebber and Stangerson followed it, and drove off. I whipped up my horse and kept within sight of them, feeling very ill at ease, for I feared that they were going to shift their quarters. At Euston Station they got out, and I left a boy to hold my horse and followed them on to the platform. I heard them ask for the Liverpool train, and the guard answer that one had just gone, and there would not be another for some hours. Stangerson seemed to be put out at that, but Drebber was rather pleased than otherwise. I got so close to them in the bustle that I could hear every word that passed between them. Drebber said that he had a little business of his own to do, and that if the other would wait for him he would soon rejoin him. His companion remonstrated with him, and reminded him that they had resolved to stick together. Drebber answered that the matter was a delicate one, and that he must go alone. I could not catch what Stangerson said to that, but the other burst out swearing, and reminded him that he was nothing more than his paid servant, and that he must not presume to dictate to him. On that the secretary gave it up as a bad job, and simply bargained with him that if he missed the last train he should rejoin him at Halliday's Private Hotel; to which Drebber answered that he would be back on the platform before eleven, and made his way out of the station.

'The moment for which I had waited so long had at last come. I had my enemies within my power. Together they could protect each other but singly they were at my mercy. I did not act, however, with undue precipitation. My plans were already formed. There is no satisfaction in vengeance unless the offender has time to realise who it is that strikes him, and why retribution has come upon him. I had my plans arranged by which I should have the opportunity of making the man who had wronged me understand that his old sin had found him out. It chanced that some days before a gentleman who had been engaged in looking over some houses in the Brixton Road had dropped the key of one of them in my carriage. It was claimed that same evening, and returned; but in the interval I had taken a moulding of it, and had a duplicate constructed. By means of this I had access to at least one spot in this great city where I could rely upon being free from interruption. How to get Drebber to that house was the difficult problem which I had now to solve.

'He walked down the road and went into one or two liquor shops, staying for nearly half an hour in the last of them. When he came out, he staggered in his walk, and was evidently pretty well on. There was a hansom just in front of me, and he hailed it. I followed it so close that the nose of my horse was within a yard of his driver the whole way. We rattled across Waterloo Bridge and through miles of streets, until, to my astonishment, we found ourselves back in the terrace in which he had boarded. I could not imagine what his intention was in returning there; but I went on and pulled up my cab a hundred yards or so from the house. He entered it, and his hansom drove away. Give me a glass of water, if you please. My mouth gets dry with the talking.'

I handed him the glass, and he drank it down.

'That's better,' he said. 'Well, I waited for a quarter of an hour, or more, when suddenly there came a noise like people struggling inside the house. Next moment the door was flung open and two men appeared, one of whom was Drebber, and the other was a young chap whom I had never seen before. This fellow had Drebber by the collar, and when they came to the head of the steps he gave him a shove and a kick which sent him half across the road. "You hound!" he cried, shaking his stick at him; "I'll teach you to insult an honest girl!" He was so hot that I think he would have thrashed Drebber with his cudgel, only that the cur staggered away down the road as fast as his legs would carry him. He ran as far as the corner and then, seeing my cab, he hailed me and jumped in. "Drive me to Halliday's Private Hotel," said he.

'When I had him fairly inside my cab, my heart jumped so with joy that I feared lest at this last moment my aneurism might go wrong. I drove along slowly, weighing in my own mind what it was best to do. I might take him right out into the country, and there in some deserted lane have my last interview with him. I had almost decided upon this, when he solved the problem for me. The craze for drink had seized him again, and he ordered me to pull up outside a gin palace. He went in, leaving word that I should wait for him. There he remained until closing time, and when he came out he was so far gone that I knew the game was in my own hands.

'Don't imagine that I intended to kill him in cold blood. It would only have been rigid justice if I had done so, but I could not bring myself to do it. I had long determined that he should have a show for his life if he chose to take advantage of it. Among the many billets which I have filled in America during my wandering life, I was once janitor and sweeper-out of the laboratory at York College. One day the professor was lecturing on poisons, and he showed his students some alkaloid, as he called it, which he had extracted from some South American arrow poison, and which was so powerful that the least grain meant instant death. I spotted the bottle in which this preparation was kept, and when they were all gone, I helped myself to a little of it. I was a fairly good dispenser, so I worked this alkaloid into small, soluble pills, and each pill I put in a box with a similar pill made without the poison. I determined at the time that when I had my chance my gentlemen should each have a draw out of one of these boxes, while I ate the pill that remained. It would be quite as deadly and a good deal less noisy than firing across a handkerchief. From that day I had always my pill boxes about with me, and the time had now come when I was to use them.

'It was nearer one than twelve, and a wild, bleak night, blowing hard and raining in torrents. Dismal as it was outside, I was glad within – so glad that I could have shouted out from pure exultation. If any of you gentlemen have ever pined for a thing, and longed for it during twenty long years, and then suddenly found it within your reach, you would understand my feelings. I lit a cigar, and puffed at it to steady my nerves, but my hands were trembling and my temples throbbing with excitement. As I drove, I could see old John Ferrier and sweet Lucy looking at me out of the darkness and smiling at me, just as plain as I see you all in this room. All the way they were ahead of me, one on each side of the horse, until I pulled up at the house in the Brixton Road.

'There was not a soul to be seen, nor a sound to be heard, except the dripping of the rain. When I looked in at the window, I found Drebber all huddled together in a drunken sleep. I shook him by the arm. "It's time to get out," I said.

'"All right, cabby," said he.

'I suppose he thought we had come to the hotel that he had mentioned, for he got out without another word, and followed me down the garden. I had to walk beside him to keep him steady, for he was still a little top-heavy. When we came to the door, I opened it, and led him into the front room. I give you my word that all the way the father and the daughter were walking in front of us.

'"It's infernally dark," said he, stamping about.

'"We'll soon have a light," I said, striking a match and putting it to a wax candle which I had brought with me. "Now, Enoch Drebber," I continued, turning to him, and holding the light to my own face, "who am I?"

'He gazed at me with bleared, drunken eyes for a moment, and then I saw horror spring up in them and convulse his whole features, which showed me that he knew me. He staggered back with a livid face, and I saw the perspiration break out upon his brow, while his teeth chattered in his head. At the sight I leaned my back against the door and laughed loud and long. I had always known that vengeance would be sweet, but I had never hoped for the contentment of soul which now possessed me.

'"You dog!" I said; "I have hunted you from Salt Lake City to St Petersburg, and you have always escaped me. Now, at last, your wanderings have come to an end, for either you or I shall never see tomorrow's

111

sun rise." He shrank still farther away as I spoke, and I could see on his face that he thought I was mad. So I was for the time. The pulses in my temples beat like sledgehammers, and I believe I would have had a fit of some sort if the blood had not gushed from my nose and relieved me.

'"What do you think of Lucy Ferrier now?" I cried, locking the door, and shaking the key in his face. "Punishment has been slow in coming, but it has overtaken you at last." I saw his coward lips tremble as I spoke. He would have begged for his life, but he knew well that it was useless.

'"Would you murder me?" he stammered.

'"There is no murder," I answered. "Who talks of murdering a mad dog? What mercy had you upon my poor darling, when you dragged her from her slaughtered father, and bore her away to your accursed and shameless harem?"

'"It was not I who killed her father," he cried.

'"But it was you who broke her innocent heart," I shrieked, thrusting the box before him. "Let the high God judge between us. Choose and eat. There is death in one and life in the other. I shall take what you leave. Let us see if there is justice upon the earth, or if we are ruled by chance."

'He cowered away with wild cries and prayers for mercy, but I drew my knife and held it to his throat until he had obeyed me. Then I swallowed the other, and we stood facing one another in silence for a minute or more, waiting to see which was to live and which was to die. Shall I ever forget the look which came over his face when the first warning pangs told him that the poison was in his system? I laughed as I saw it, and held Lucy's marriage ring in front of his eyes. It was but for a moment, for the action of the alkaloid is rapid. A spasm of pain contorted his features; he threw his hands out in front of him, staggered, and then, with a hoarse cry, fell heavily upon the floor. I turned him over with my foot, and placed my hand upon his heart. There was no movement. He was dead!

'The blood had been streaming from my nose, but I had taken no notice of it. I don't know what it was that put it into my head to write upon the wall with it. Perhaps it was some mischievous idea of setting the police upon a wrong track, for I felt light-hearted and cheerful. I remembered a German being found in New York with RACHE written up above him, and it was argued at the time in the newspapers that the secret societies must have done it. I guessed that what puzzled the New Yorkers would puzzle the Londoners, so I dipped my finger in my own blood and printed it on a convenient place on the wall. Then I walked down to my cab and found that there was nobody about, and that the night was still very wild. I had driven some distance when I put my hand into the pocket in which I usually kept Lucy's ring, and found that it was not there. I was thunderstruck at this, for it was the only memento that I had of her. Thinking that I might have dropped it when I stooped over Drebber's body, I drove back, and leaving my cab in a side street, I went boldly up to the house – for I was ready to dare anything rather than lose the ring. When I arrived there, I walked right into the arms of a police officer who was coming out, and only managed to disarm his suspicions by pretending to be hopelessly drunk.

'That was how Enoch Drebber came to his end. All I had to do then was to do as much for Stangerson, and so pay off John Ferrier's debt. I knew that he was staying at Halliday's Private Hotel, and I hung about all day, but he never came out. I fancy that he suspected something when Drebber failed to put in an appearance. He was cunning, was Stangerson, and always on his guard. If he thought he could keep me off by staying indoors he was very much mistaken. I soon found out which was the window of his bedroom, and early next morning I took advantage of some ladders which were lying in the lane behind the hotel, and so made my way into his room in the grey of the dawn. I woke him up and told him that the hour had come when he was to answer for the life he had taken so long before. I described Drebber's death to him, and I gave him the same choice of the poisoned pills. Instead of grasping at the chance of safety which that offered him, he sprang from his bed and flew at my throat. In self-defence I stabbed him to the heart. It would have been the same in any case, for Providence would never have allowed his guilty hand to pick out anything but the poison.

'I have little more to say, and it's as well, for I am about done up. I went on cabbing it for a day or so intending to keep at it until I could save enough to take me back to America. I was standing in the yard when a ragged youngster asked if there was a cabby there called Jefferson Hope, and said that his cab was wanted by a gentleman at 221b Baker Street. I went round suspecting no harm, and the next thing I knew, this young man here had the bracelets on my wrists, and as neatly shackled as ever I saw in my life. That's the whole of my story, gentlemen. You may consider me to be a murderer; but I hold that I am just as much an officer of justice as you are.'

So thrilling had the man's narrative been and his manner was so impressive that we had sat silent and absorbed. Even the professional detectives, blasÈ as they were in every detail of crime, appeared to be keenly interested in the man's story. When he had finished, we sat for some minutes in a stillness which was only broken by the scratching of Lestrade's pencil as he gave the finishing touches to his shorthand account.

'There is only one point on which I should like a little more information,' Sherlock Holmes said at last. 'Who was your accomplice who came for the ring which I advertised?'

The prisoner winked at my friend jocosely. 'I can tell my own secrets,' he said, 'but I don't get other people into trouble. I saw your advertisement, and I thought it might be a plant, or it might be the ring which I wanted. My friend volunteered to go and see. I think you'll own he did it smartly.'

'Not a doubt of that,' said Holmes, heartily.

'Now, gentlemen,' the inspector remarked, gravely, 'the forms of the law must be complied with. On Thursday the prisoner will be brought before the magistrates, and your attendance will be required. Until then I will be responsible for him.' He rang the bell as he spoke, and Jefferson Hope was led off by a couple of warders, while my friend and I made our way out of the station and took a cab back to Baker Street.

14

The Conclusion

We had all been warned to appear before the magistrates upon the Thursday; but when the Thursday came there was no occasion for our testimony. A higher judge had taken the matter in hand, and Jefferson Hope had been summoned before a tribunal where strict justice would be meted out to him. On the very night after his capture the aneurism burst, and he was found in the morning stretched upon the floor of the cell, with a placid smile upon his face, as though he had been able in his dying moments to look back upon a useful life, and on work well done.

'Gregson and Lestrade will be wild about his death,' Holmes remarked, as we chatted it over next evening. 'Where will their grand advertisement be now?'

'I don't see that they had very much to do with his capture,' I answered.

'What you do in this world is a matter of no consequence,' returned my companion, bitterly. 'The question is, what can you make people believe that you have done. Never mind,' he continued, more brightly, after a pause. 'I would not have missed the investigation for anything. There has been no better case within my recollection. Simple as it was, there were several most instructive points about it.'

'Simple!' I ejaculated.

'Well, really, it can hardly be described as otherwise,' said Sherlock Holmes, smiling at my surprise. 'The proof of its intrinsic simplicity is that without any help save a few very ordinary deductions I was able to lay my hand upon the criminal within three days.'

'That is true,' said I.

'I have already explained to you that what is out of the common is usually a guide rather than a hindrance. In solving a problem of this sort, the grand thing is to be able to reason backwards. That is a very useful accomplishment, and a very easy one, but people do not practise it much. In the everyday affairs of life it is more useful to reason forwards, and so the other comes to be neglected. There are fifty who can reason synthetically for one who can reason analytically.'

'I confess,' said I, 'that I do not quite follow you.'

'I hardly expected that you would. Let me see if I can make it clearer. Most people, if you describe a train of events to them, will tell you what the result would be. They can put those events together in their minds, and argue from them that something will come to pass. There are few people, however, who, if you told them a result, would be able to evolve from their own inner consciousness what the steps were which led up to that result. This power is what I mean when I talk of reasoning backwards, or analytically.'

'I understand,' said I.

'Now this was a case in which you were given the result and had to find everything else for yourself. Now let me endeavour to show you the different steps in my reasoning. To begin at the beginning. I approached the house, as you know, on foot, and with my mind entirely free from all impressions. I naturally began by examining the roadway, and there, as I have already explained to you, I saw clearly the marks of a cab, which, I ascertained by enquiry, must have been there during the night. I satisfied myself that it was a cab and not a private carriage by the narrow gauge of the wheels. The ordinary London growler is considerably less wide than a gentleman's brougham.

'This was the first point gained. I then walked slowly down the garden path, which happened to be composed of a clay soil, peculiarly suitable for taking impressions. No doubt it appeared to you to be a mere trampled line of slush, but to my trained eyes every mark upon its surface had a meaning. There is no branch of detective science which is so important and so much neglected as the art of tracing footsteps. Happily, I have always laid great stress upon it, and much practice has made it second nature to me. I saw the heavy footmarks of the constables, but I saw also the track of the two men who had first passed through the garden. It was easy to tell that they had been before the others, because in places their marks had been entirely obliterated by the others coming upon the top of them. In this way my second link was formed, which told me that the nocturnal visitors were two in number, one remarkable for his height (as I calculated from the length of his stride) and the other fashionably dressed, to judge from the small and elegant impression left by his boots.

'On entering the house this last inference was confirmed. My well-booted man lay before me. The tall one, then, had done the murder, if murder there was. There was no wound upon the dead man's person, but the agitated expression upon his face assured me that he had foreseen his fate before it came upon him. Men who die from heart disease, or any sudden natural cause, never by any chance exhibit agitation upon their features. Having sniffed the dead man's lips, I detected a slightly sour smell, and I came to the conclusion that he had had poison forced upon him. Again, I argued that it had been forced upon him from the hatred and fear expressed upon his face. By the method of exclusion, I had arrived at this result, for no other hypothesis would meet the facts. Do not imagine that it was a very unheard-of idea. The forcible administration of poison is by no means a new thing in criminal annals. The cases of Dolsky in Odessa and of Leturier in Montpellier will occur at once to any toxicologist.

'And now came the great question as to the reason why. Robbery had not been the object of the murder, for nothing was taken. Was it politics, then, or was it a woman? That was the question which confronted me. I was inclined from the first to the latter supposition. Political assassins are only too glad to do their work and to fly. This murder had, on the contrary, been done most deliberately, and the perpetrator had left his tracks all over the room, showing that he had been there all the time. It must have been a private wrong, and not a political one, which called for such a methodical revenge. When the inscription was discovered upon the wall, I was more inclined than ever to my opinion. The thing was too evidently a blind. When the ring was found, however, it settled the question. Clearly the murderer had used it to remind his victim of some dead or absent woman. It was at this point that I asked Gregson whether he had enquired in his telegram to Cleveland as to any particular point in Mr Drebber's former career. He answered, you remember, in the negative.

'I then proceeded to make a careful examination of the room, which confirmed me in my opinion as to the murderer's height, and furnished me with the additional details as to the Trichinopoly cigar and the length of his nails. I had already come to the conclusion, since there were no signs of a struggle, that the blood which covered the floor had burst from the murderer's nose in his excitement. I could perceive that the track of blood coincided with the track of his feet. It is seldom that any man, unless he is very full-blooded, breaks out in this way through emotion, so I hazarded the opinion that the criminal was probably a robust and ruddy-faced man. Events proved that I had judged correctly.

'Having left the house, I proceeded to do what Gregson had neglected. I telegraphed to the head of the police at Cleveland, limiting my enquiry to the circumstances connected with the marriage of Enoch Drebber. The answer was conclusive. It told me that Drebber had already applied for the protection of the law against an old rival in love, named Jefferson Hope, and that this same Hope was at present in Europe. I knew now that I held the clue to the mystery in my hand, and all that remained was to secure the murderer.

'I had already determined in my own mind that the man who had walked into the house with Drebber was none other than the man who had driven the cab. The marks in the road showed me that the horse had wandered on in a way which would have been impossible had there been anyone in charge of it. Where, then, could the driver be, unless he were inside the house? Again, it is absurd to suppose that any sane man would carry out a deliberate crime under the very eyes, as it were, of a third person, who was sure to betray him. Lastly, supposing one man wished to dog another through London, what better means could he adopt than to turn cab driver? All these considerations led me to the irresistible conclusion that Jefferson Hope was to be found among the jarveys of the metropolis.

'If he had been one, there was no reason to believe that he had ceased to be. On the contrary from his point of view, any sudden change would be likely to draw attention to himself. He would probably, for a time at least, continue to perform his duties. There was no reason to suppose that he was going under an assumed name. Why should he change his name in a country where no one knew his original one? I therefore organised my street-arab detective corps, and sent them systematically to every cab proprietor in London until they ferreted out the man that I wanted. How well they succeeded, and how quickly I took advantage of it, are still fresh in your recollection. The murder of Stangerson was an incident which was entirely unexpected, but which could hardly, in any case, have been prevented. Through it, as you know, I came into possession of the pills, the existence of which I had already surmised. You see, the whole thing is a chain of logical sequences without a break or flaw.'

'It is wonderful!' I cried. 'Your merits should be publicly recognised. You should publish an account of the case. If you won't, I will for you.'

'You may do what you like, doctor,' he answered. 'See here!' he continued, handing a paper over to me, 'look at this!'

It was the *Echo* for the day, and the paragraph to which he pointed was devoted to the case in question.

The public have lost a sensational treat through the sudden death of the man Hope, who was suspected of the murder of Mr Enoch Drebber and of Mr Joseph Stangerson. The details of the case will probably never be known now, though we are informed upon good authority that the crime was the result of an old-standing and romantic feud, in which love and Mormonism bore a part. It seems that both the victims belonged, in their younger days, to the Latter Day Saints, and Hope, the deceased prisoner, hails also from Salt

Lake City. If the case has had no other effect, it, at least, brings out in the most striking manner the efficiency of our detective police force, and will serve as a lesson to all foreigners that they will do wisely to settle their feuds at home, and not to carry them on to British soil. It is an open secret that the credit of this smart capture belongs entirely to the well-known Scotland Yard officials, Messrs Lestrade and Gregson. The man was apprehended, it appears, in the rooms of a certain Mr Sherlock Holmes, who has himself, as an amateur, shown some talent in the detective line, and who, with such instructors, may hope in time to attain to some degree of their skill. It is expected that a testimonial of some sort will be presented to the two officers as a fitting recognition of their services.

'Didn't I tell you so when we started?' cried Sherlock Holmes with a laugh. 'That's the result of all our Study in Scarlet: to get them a testimonial!'

'Never mind,' I answered; 'I have all the facts in my journal, and the public shall know them. In the meantime you must make yourself contented by the consciousness of success, like the Roman miser –

Populus me sibilat, at mihi plaudo
Ispe domi simul ac nummos contemplar in arca.'

The Sign of the Four

1

The Science of Deduction

Sherlock Holmes took his bottle from the corner of the mantelpiece and his hypodermic syringe from its neat morocco case. With his long, white, nervous fingers he adjusted the delicate needle and rolled back his left shirt-cuff. For some little time his eyes rested thoughtfully upon the sinewy forearm and wrist, all dotted and scarred with innumerable puncture-marks. Finally, he thrust the sharp point home, pressed down the tiny piston, and sank back into the velvet-lined armchair with a long sigh of satisfaction.

Three times a day for many months I had witnessed this performance, but custom had not reconciled my mind to it. On the contrary, from day to day I had become more irritable at the sight, and my conscience swelled nightly within me at the thought that I had lacked the courage to protest. Again and again I had registered a vow that I should deliver my soul upon the subject; but there was that in the cool, nonchalant air of my companion which made him the last man with whom one would care to take anything approaching to a liberty. His great powers, his masterly manner, and the experience which I had had of his many extraordinary qualities, all made me diffident and backward in crossing him.

Yet upon that afternoon, whether it was the Beaune which I had taken with my lunch, or the additional exasperation produced by the extreme deliberation of his manner, I suddenly felt that I could hold out no longer.

'Which is it today,' I asked, 'morphine or cocaine?'

He raised his eyes languidly from the old black-leather volume which he had opened.

'It is cocaine,' he said, 'a seven-per-cent solution. Would you care to try it?'

'No, indeed,' I answered, brusquely. 'My constitution has not got over the Afghan campaign yet. I cannot afford to throw any extra strain upon it.'

He smiled at my vehemence. 'Perhaps you are right, Watson,' he said. 'I suppose that its influence is physically a bad one. I find it, however, so transcendently stimulating and clarifying to the mind that its secondary action is a matter of small moment.'

'But consider!' I said, earnestly. 'Count the cost! Your brain may, as you say, be roused and excited, but it is a pathological and morbid process, which involves increased tissue-change, and may at last leave a permanent weakness. You know, too, what a black reaction comes upon you. Surely the game is hardly worth the candle. Why should you, for a mere passing pleasure, risk the loss of those great powers with which you have been endowed? Remember that I speak not only as one comrade to another, but as a medical man to one for whose constitution he is to some extent answerable.'

He did not seem offended. On the contrary, he put his fingertips together, and leaned his elbows on the arms of his chair, like one who has a relish for conversation.

'My mind,' he said, 'rebels at stagnation. Give me problems, give me work, give me the most abstruse cryptogram, or the most intricate analysis, and I am in my own proper atmosphere. I can dispense then with artificial stimulants. But I abhor the dull routine of existence. I crave for mental exaltation. That is why I have chosen my own particular profession, or rather created it, for I am the only one in the world.'

'The only unofficial detective?' I said, raising my eyebrows.

'The only unofficial consulting detective,' he answered. 'I am the last and highest court of appeal in detection. When Gregson or Lestrade or Athelney Jones are out of their depths – which, by the way, is their normal state – the matter is laid before me. I examine the data, as an expert, and pronounce a specialist's opinion. I claim no credit in such cases. My name figures in no newspaper. The work itself, the pleasure of finding a field for my peculiar powers, is my highest reward. But you have yourself had some experience of my methods of work in the Jefferson Hope case.'

'Yes, indeed,' said I, cordially. 'I was never so struck by anything in my life. I even embodied it in a small brochure, with the somewhat fantastic title of "A Study in Scarlet".'

He shook his head sadly.

'I glanced over it,' said he. 'Honestly, I cannot congratulate you upon it. Detection is, or ought to be, an exact science and should be treated in the same cold and unemotional manner. You have attempted to tinge it with romanticism, which produces much the same effect as if you worked a love story or an elopement into the fifth proposition of Euclid.'

'But the romance was there,' I remonstrated. 'I could not tamper with the facts.'

'Some facts should be suppressed, or, at least, a just sense of proportion should be observed in treating them. The only point in the case which deserved mention was the curious analytical reasoning from effects to causes by which I succeeded in unravelling it.'

I was annoyed at this criticism of a work which had been specially designed to please him. I confess, too, that I was irritated by the egotism which seemed to demand that every line of my pamphlet should be devoted to his own special doings. More than once during the years that I had lived with him in Baker Street I had observed that a small vanity underlay my companion's quiet and didactic manner. I made no remark, however, but sat nursing my wounded leg. I had had a Jezail bullet through it some time before, and, though it did not prevent me from walking, it ached wearily at every change of the weather.

'My practice has extended recently to the Continent,' said Holmes, after a while, filling up his old brier-root pipe. 'I was consulted last week by FranÁois le Villard, who, as you probably know, has come rather to the front lately in the French detective service. He has all the Celtic power of quick intuition, but he is deficient in the wide range of exact knowledge which is essential to the higher developments of his art. The case was concerned with a will, and possessed some features of interest. I was able to refer him to two parallel cases, the one at Riga in 1857 and the other at St Louis in 1871, which have suggested to him the true solution. Here is the letter which I had this morning acknowledging my assistance.'

He tossed over, as he spoke, a crumpled sheet of foreign notepaper. I glanced my eyes down it, catching a profusion of notes of admiration, with stray *'magnifiques'*, *'coup-de-maÓtres'* and *'tours-de-force'*, all testifying to the ardent admiration of the Frenchman.

'He speaks as a pupil to his master,' said I.

'Oh, he rates my assistance too highly,' said Sherlock Holmes, lightly. 'He has considerable gifts himself. He possesses two out of the three qualities necessary for the ideal detective. He has the power of observation and that of deduction. He is only wanting in knowledge, and that may come in time. He is now translating my small works into French.'

'Your works?'

'Oh, didn't you know?' he cried, laughing. 'Yes, I have been guilty of several monographs. They are all upon technical subjects. Here, for example, is one "Upon the Distinction Between the Ashes of the Various Tobaccos". In it I enumerate a hundred and forty forms of cigar, cigarette and pipe tobacco, with coloured plates illustrating the difference in the ash. It is a point which is continually turning up in criminal trials and which is sometimes of supreme importance as a clue. If you can say definitely, for example, that some murder had been done by a man who was smoking an Indian lunkah, it obviously narrows your field of search. To the trained eye there is as much difference between the black ash of a Trichinopoly and the white fluff of bird's-eye as there is between a cabbage and a potato.'

'You have an extraordinary genius for minutiae,' I remarked.

'I appreciate their importance. Here is my monograph upon the tracing of footsteps, with some remarks upon the uses of plaster of Paris as a preserver of impresses. Here, too, is a curious little work upon the influence of a trade upon the form of the hand, with lithotypes of the hands of slaters, sailors, cork-cutters, compositors, weavers and diamond-polishers. That is a matter of great practical interest to the scientific detective – especially in cases of unclaimed bodies, or in discovering the antecedents of criminals. But I weary you with my hobby.'

'Not at all,' I answered, earnestly. 'It is of the greatest interest to me, especially since I have had the opportunity of observing your practical application of it. But you spoke just now of observation and deduction. Surely the one to some extent implies the other.'

'Why, hardly,' he answered, leaning back luxuriously in his armchair and sending up thick blue wreaths from his pipe. 'For example, observation shows me that you have been to the Wigmore Street Post Office this morning, but deduction lets me know that when there you dispatched a telegram.'

'Right!' said I. 'Right on both points! But I confess that I don't see how you arrived at it. It was a sudden impulse upon my part, and I have mentioned it to no one.'

'It is simplicity itself,' he remarked, chuckling at my surprise – 'so absurdly simple that an explanation is superfluous; and yet it may serve to define the limits of observation and of deduction. Observation tells me that you have a little reddish mould adhering to your instep. Just opposite the Wigmore Street office they have taken up the pavement and thrown up some earth, which lies in such a way that it is difficult to avoid treading in it in entering. The earth is of this peculiar reddish tint which is found as far as I know nowhere else in the neighbourhood. So much is observation. The rest is deduction.'

'How, then, did you deduce the telegram?'

'Why, of course I knew that you had not written a letter, since I sat opposite to you all morning. I see also in your open desk there that you have a sheet of stamps and a thick bundle of postcards. What could you go into the post-office for, then, but to send a wire? Eliminate all other factors, and the one which remains must be the truth.'

'In this case it certainly is so,' I replied, after a little thought. 'The thing, however, is, as you say, of the simplest. Would you think me impertinent if I were to put your theories to a more severe test?'

'On the contrary,' he answered; 'it would prevent me from taking a second dose of cocaine. I should be delighted to look into any problem which you might submit to me.'

'I have heard you say that it is difficult for a man to have any object in daily use without leaving the impress of his individuality upon it in such a way that a trained observer might read it. Now, I have here a watch which has recently come into my possession. Would you have the kindness to let me have an opinion upon the character or habits of the late owner?'

I handed him over the watch with some slight feeling of amusement in my heart, for the test was, as I thought, an impossible one, and I intended it as a lesson against the somewhat dogmatic tone which he occasionally assumed. He balanced the watch in his hand, gazed hard at the dial, opened the back, and examined the works, first with his naked eyes and then with a powerful convex lens. I could hardly keep from smiling at his crestfallen face when he finally snapped the case to and handed it back.

'There are hardly any data,' he remarked. 'The watch has been recently cleaned, which robs me of my most suggestive facts.'

'You are right,' I answered. 'It was cleaned before being sent to me.'

In my heart I accused my companion of putting forward a most lame and impotent excuse to cover his failure. What data could he expect from an uncleaned watch?

'Though unsatisfactory, my research has not been entirely barren,' he observed, staring up at the ceiling with dreamy, lack-lustre eyes. 'Subject to your correction, I should judge that the watch belonged to your elder brother, who inherited it from your father.'

'That you gather, no doubt, from the H.W. upon the back?'

'Quite so. The W. suggests your own name. The date of the watch is nearly fifty years back and the initials are as old as the watch; so it was made for the last generation. Jewellery usually descends to the eldest son, and he is most likely to have the same name as the father. Your father has, if I remember right, been dead many years. It has, therefore, been in the hands of your eldest brother.'

'Right, so far,' said I. 'Anything else?'

'He was a man of untidy habits – very untidy and careless. He was left with good prospects, but he threw away his chances, lived for some time in poverty with occasional short intervals of prosperity, and, finally, taking to drink, he died. That is all I can gather.'

I sprang from my chair and limped impatiently about the room with considerable bitterness in my heart.

'This is unworthy of you, Holmes,' I said. 'I could not have believed that you would have descended to this. You have made enquiries into the history of my unhappy brother, and you now pretend to deduce this knowledge in some fanciful way. You cannot expect me to believe that you have read all this from his old watch! It is unkind, and, to speak plainly, has a touch of charlatanism in it.'

'My dear doctor,' said he, kindly, 'pray accept my apologies. Viewing the matter as an abstract problem, I had forgotten how personal and painful a thing it might be to you. I assure you, however, that I never even knew that you had a brother until you handed me the watch.'

'Then how in the name of all that is wonderful did you get these facts? They are absolutely correct in every particular.'

'Ah, that is good luck. I could only say what was the balance of probability. I did not at all expect to be accurate.'

'But it was not mere guesswork?'

'No, no: I never guess. It is a shocking habit – destructive to the logical faculty. What seems strange to you is only so because you do not follow my train of thought or observe the small facts upon which large inferences may depend. For example, I began by stating that your brother was careless. When you observe the lower part of that watch-case you notice that it is not only dinted in two places, but it is cut and marked all over from the habit of keeping other hard objects, such as coins or keys, in the same pocket. Surely it is no great feat to assume that a man who treats a fifty-guinea watch so cavalierly must be a careless man. Neither is it a very far-fetched inference that a man who inherits one article of such value is pretty well provided for in other respects.'

I nodded, to show that I followed his reasoning.

'It is very customary for pawnbrokers in England, when they take a watch, to scratch the number of the ticket with a pinpoint upon the inside of the case. It is more handy than a label, as there is no risk of the number being lost or transposed. There are no fewer than four such numbers visible to my lens on the inside of this case. Inference – that your brother was often at low water. Secondary inference – that he had occasional bursts of prosperity, or he could not have redeemed the pledge. Finally, I ask you to look at the inner plate, which contains the keyhole. Look at the thousands of scratches all round the hole – marks where the key has slipped. What sober man's key could have scored those grooves? But you will never see a drunkard's watch without them. He winds it at night, and he leaves these traces of his unsteady hand. Where is the mystery in all this?'

'It is as clear as daylight,' I answered. 'I regret the injustice which I did you. I should have had more faith in your marvellous faculty. May I ask whether you have any professional enquiry on foot at present?'

'None. Hence the cocaine. I cannot live without brainwork. What else is there to live for? Stand at the window here. Was ever such a dreary, dismal, unprofitable world? See how the yellow fog swirls down the street and drifts across the dun-coloured houses. What could be more hopelessly prosaic and material? What is the use of having powers, doctor, when one has no field upon which to exert them? Crime is commonplace, existence is commonplace, and no qualities save those which are commonplace have any function upon earth.'

I had opened my mouth to reply to this tirade, when, with a crisp knock, our landlady entered, bearing a card upon the brass salver.

'A young lady for you, sir,' she said, addressing my companion.

'Miss Mary Morstan,' he read. 'Hum! I have no recollection of the name. Ask the young lady to step up, Mrs Hudson. Don't go, doctor. I should prefer that you remain.'

2

The Statement of the Case

Miss Morstan entered the room with a firm step and an outward composure of manner. She was a blonde young lady, small, dainty, well gloved, and dressed in the most perfect taste. There was, however, a plainness and simplicity about her costume which bore with it a suggestion of limited means. The dress was a sombre greyish beige, untrimmed and unbraided, and she wore a small turban of the same dull hue, relieved only by a suspicion of white feather in the side. Her face had neither regularity of feature nor beauty of complexion, but her expression was sweet and amiable and her large blue eyes were singularly spiritual and sympathetic. In an experience of women which extends over many nations and three separate continents, I have never looked upon a face which gave a clearer promise of a refined and sensitive nature. I could not but observe that, as she took the seat which Sherlock Holmes placed for her, her lip trembled, her hand quivered and she showed every sign of intense inward agitation.

'I have come to you, Mr Holmes,' she said, 'because you once enabled my employer, Mrs Cecil Forrester, to unravel a little domestic complication. She was much impressed by your kindness and skill.'

'Mrs Cecil Forrester,' he repeated, thoughtfully. 'I believe that I was of some slight service to her. The case, however, as I remember it, was a very simple one.'

'She did not think so. But at least you cannot say the same of mine. I can hardly imagine anything more strange, more utterly inexplicable, than the situation in which I find myself.'

Holmes rubbed his hands and his eyes glistened. He leaned forward in his chair with an expression of extraordinary concentration upon his clear-cut, hawklike features.

'State your case,' said he, in brisk, business tones.

I felt that my position was an embarrassing one.

'You will, I am sure, excuse me,' I said, rising from my chair.

To my surprise, the young lady held up her gloved hand to detain me.

'If your friend,' she said, 'would be good enough to stop, he might be of inestimable service to me.'

I relapsed into my chair.

'Briefly,' she continued, 'the facts are these. My father was an officer in an Indian regiment, who sent me home when I was quite a child. My mother was dead, and I had no relative in England. I was placed, however, in a comfortable boarding establishment at Edinburgh, and there I remained until I was seventeen years of age. In the year 1878 my father, who was senior captain of his regiment, obtained twelve months' leave and came home. He telegraphed to me from London that he had arrived all safe, and directed me to come down at once, giving the Langham Hotel as his address. His message, as I remember, was full of kindness and love. On reaching London I drove to the Langham, and was informed that Captain Morstan was staying there, but that he had gone out the night before and had not returned. I waited all day without news of him. That night, on the advice of the manager of the hotel, I communicated with the police, and next morning we advertised in all the papers. Our enquiries led to no result; and from that day to this no word has ever been heard of my unfortunate father. He came home with his heart full of hope, to find some peace, some comfort, and instead –' She put her hand to her throat, and a choking sob cut short the sentence.

'The date?' asked Holmes, opening his notebook.

'He disappeared upon the 3rd of December 1878 – nearly ten years ago.'

'His luggage?'

'Remained at the hotel. There was nothing in it to suggest a clue – some clothes, some books and a considerable number of curiosities from the Andaman Islands. He had been one of the officers in charge of the convict guard there.'

'Had he any friends in town?'

'Only one that we know of – Major Sholto, of his own regiment, the 34th Bombay Infantry. The major had retired some little time before, and lived at Upper Norwood. We communicated with him, of course, but he did not even know that his brother officer was in England.'

'A singular case,' remarked Holmes.

'I have not yet described to you the most singular part. About six years ago – to be exact, upon the 4th of May 1882 – an advertisement appeared in *The Times* asking for the address of Miss Mary Morstan, and stating that it would be to her advantage to come forward. There was no name or address appended. I had at that time just entered the family of Mrs Cecil Forrester in the capacity of governess. By her advice I published my address in the advertisement column. The same day there arrived through the post a small cardboard box addressed to me, which I found to contain a very large and lustrous pearl. No word of writing was enclosed. Since then every year upon the same date there has always appeared a similar box, containing a similar pearl, without any clue as to the sender. They have been pronounced by an expert to be of a rare variety and of considerable value. You can see for yourselves that they are very handsome.'

She opened a flat box as she spoke, and showed me six of the finest pearls that I had ever seen.

'Your statement is most interesting,' said Sherlock Holmes. 'Has anything else occurred to you?'

'Yes, and no later than today. That is why I have come to you. This morning I received this letter, which you will perhaps read for yourself.'

'Thank you,' said Holmes. 'The envelope, too, please. Postmark, London, S.W. Date, July 7. Hum! Man's thumbmark on corner – probably postman. Best quality paper. Envelopes at sixpence a packet. Particular man in his stationery. No address. "Be at the third pillar from the left outside the Lyceum Theatre tonight at seven o'clock. If you are distrustful bring two friends. You are a wronged woman, and shall have justice. Do not bring police. If you do, all will be in vain. Your unknown friend." Well, really, this is a very pretty little mystery! What do you intend to do, Miss Morstan?'

'That is exactly what I want to ask you.'

'Then we shall most certainly go – you and I and – yes, why, Dr Watson is the very man. Your correspondent says two friends. He and I have worked together before.'

'But would he come?' she asked, with something appealing in her voice and expression.

'I shall be proud and happy,' said I, fervently, 'if I can be of any service.'

'You are both very kind,' she answered. 'I have led a retired life, and have no friends whom I could appeal to. If I am here at six it will do, I suppose?'

'You must not be later,' said Holmes. 'There is one other point, however. Is this handwriting the same as that upon the pearl-box addresses?'

'I have them here,' she answered, producing half a dozen pieces of paper.

'You are certainly a model client. You have the correct intuition. Let us see, now.' He spread out the papers upon the table, and gave little, darting glances from one to the other. 'They are disguised hands, except the letter,' he said, presently; 'but there can be no question as to the authorship. See how the irrepressible Greek *e* will break out, and see the twirl of the final *s*. They are undoubtedly by the same person. I should not like to suggest false hopes, Miss Morstan, but is there any resemblance between this hand and that of your father?'

'Nothing could be more unlike.'

'I expected to hear you say so. We shall look out for you, then, at six. Pray allow me to keep the papers. I may look into the matter before then. It is only half-past three. *Au revoir*, then.'

'*Au revoir*,' said our visitor; and with a bright, kindly glance from one to the other of us, she replaced her pearl-box in her bosom and hurried away.

Standing at the window, I watched her walking briskly down the street, until the grey turban and white feather were but a speck in the sombre crowd.

'What a very attractive woman!' I exclaimed, turning to my companion.

He had lit his pipe again, and was leaning back with drooping eye-lids. 'Is she?' he said, languidly; 'I did not observe.'

'You really are an automaton – a calculating machine,' I cried. 'There is something positively inhuman in you at times.'

He smiled gently.

'It is of the first importance,' he said, 'not to allow your judgement to be biased by personal qualities. A client is to me a mere unit, a factor in a problem. The emotional qualities are antagonistic to clear reasoning. I assure you that the most winning woman I ever knew was hanged for poisoning three little children for their insurance money, and the most repellent man of my acquaintance is a philanthropist who has spent nearly a quarter of a million upon the London poor.'

'In this case, however –'

'I never make exceptions. An exception disproves the rule. Have you ever had occasion to study character in handwriting? What do you make of this fellow's scribble?'

'It is legible and regular,' I answered. 'A man of business habits and some force of character.'

Holmes shook his head.

'Look at his long letters,' he said. 'They hardly rise above the common herd. That *d* might be an *a*, and that *l* an *e*. Men of character always differentiate their long letters, however illegibly they may write. There is vacillation in his *k*s and self-esteem in his capitals. I am going out now. I have some few references to make. Let me recommend this book – one of the most remarkable ever penned. It is Winwood Reade's *Martyrdom of Man*. I shall be back in an hour.'

I sat in the window with the volume in my hand, but my thoughts were far from the daring speculations of the writer. My mind ran upon our late visitor – her smiles, the deep, rich tones of her voice, the strange mystery which overhung her life. If she were seventeen at the time of her father's disappearance she must be seven-and-twenty now – a sweet age, when youth has lost its self-consciousness and become a little sobered by experience. So I sat and mused, until such dangerous thoughts came into my head that I hurried away to my desk and plunged furiously into the latest treatise upon pathology. What was I, an army surgeon with a weak leg and a weaker banking account, that I should dare to think of such things? She was a unit, a factor – nothing more. If my future were black, it was better surely to face it like a man than to attempt to brighten it by mere will-o'-the-wisps of the imagination.

3

In Quest of a Solution

It was half-past five before Holmes returned. He was bright, eager, and in excellent spirits, a mood which in his case alternated with fits of the blackest depression.

'There is no great mystery in this matter,' he said, taking the cup of tea which I had poured out for him; 'the facts appear to admit of only one explanation.'

'What! you have solved it already?'

'Well, that would be too much to say. I have discovered a suggestive fact, that is all. It is, however, *very* suggestive. The details are still to be added. I have just found, on consulting the back files of *The Times*, that Major Sholto, of Upper Norwood, late of the 34th Bombay Infantry, died upon the 28th of April 1882.'

'I may be very obtuse, Holmes, but I fail to see what this suggests.'

'No? You surprise me. Look at it in this way, then. Captain Morstan disappears. The only person in London whom he could have visited is Major Sholto. Major Sholto denies having heard that he was in London. Four years later Sholto dies. *Within a week of his death* Captain Morstan's daughter receives a valuable present, which is repeated from year to year, and now culminates in a letter which describes her as a wronged woman. What wrong can it refer to except this deprivation of her father? And why should the presents begin immediately after Sholto's death, unless it is that Sholto's heir knows something of the mystery and desires to make compensation? Have you any alternative theory which will meet the facts?'

'But what a strange compensation! And how strangely made! Why, too, should he write a letter now, rather than six years ago? Again, the letter speaks of giving her justice. What justice can she have? It is too much to suppose that her father is still alive. There is no other injustice in her case that you know of.'

'There are difficulties; there are certainly difficulties,' said Sherlock Holmes, pensively; 'but our expedition of tonight will solve them all. Ah, here is a four-wheeler, and Miss Morstan inside. Are you all ready? Then we had better go down, for it is a little past the hour.'

I picked up my hat and my heaviest stick, but I observed that Holmes took his revolver from his drawer and slipped it into his pocket. It was clear that he thought that our night's work might be a serious one.

Miss Morstan was muffled in a dark cloak, and her sensitive face was composed, but pale. She must have been more than woman if she did not feel some uneasiness at the strange enterprise upon which we were embarking, yet her self-control was perfect, and she readily answered the few additional questions which Sherlock Holmes put to her.

'Major Sholto was a very particular friend of papa's,' she said. 'His letters were full of allusions to the major. He and papa were in command of the troops at the Andaman Islands, so they were thrown a great deal together. By the way, a curious paper was found in papa's desk which no one could understand. I don't suppose that it is of the slightest importance, but I thought you might care to see it, so I brought it with me. It is here.'

Holmes unfolded the paper carefully and smoothed it out upon his knee. He then very methodically examined it all over with his double lens.

'It is paper of native Indian manufacture,' he remarked. 'It has at some time been pinned to a board. The diagram upon it appears to be a plan of part of a large building with numerous halls, corridors and passages. At one point is a small cross done in red ink, and above it is "3.37 from left" in faded pencil-writing. In the left-hand corner is a curious hieroglyphic like four crosses in a line with their arms touching. Beside it is written, in very rough and coarse characters, "The sign of the four – Jonathan Small, Mahomet Singh, Abdullah Khan, Dost Akbar". No, I confess that I do not see how this bears upon the matter. Yet it is evidently a document of importance. It has been kept carefully in a pocket-book, for the one side is as clean as the other.'

'It was in his pocket-book that we found it.'

'Preserve it carefully, then, Miss Morstan, for it may prove to be of use to us. I begin to suspect that this matter may turn out to be much deeper and more subtle than I at first supposed. I must reconsider my ideas.'

He leaned back in the cab, and I could see by his drawn brow and his vacant eye that he was thinking intently. Miss Morstan and I chatted in an undertone about our present expedition and its possible outcome, but our companion maintained his impenetrable reserve until the end of our journey.

It was a September evening, and not yet seven o'clock, but the day had been a dreary one, and a dense drizzly fog lay low upon the great city. Mud-coloured clouds drooped sadly over the muddy streets. Down the Strand the lamps were but misty splotches of diffused light, which threw a feeble circular glimmer upon the slimy pavement. The yellow glare from the shop-windows streamed out into the steamy, vaporous air and threw a murky, shifting radiance across the crowded thoroughfare. There was, to my mind, something eerie and ghostlike in the endless procession of faces which flitted across these narrow bars of light – sad faces and glad, haggard and merry. Like all human kind, they flitted from the gloom into the light, and so back into the gloom once more. I am not subject to impressions, but the dull, heavy evening, with the strange business upon which we were engaged, combined to make me nervous and depressed. I could see from Miss Morstan's manner that she was suffering from the same feeling. Holmes alone could rise superior to petty influences. He held his open notebook upon his knee, and from time to time he jotted down figures and memoranda in the light of his pocket-lantern.

At the Lyceum Theatre the crowds were already thick at the side-entrances. In front a continuous stream of hansoms and four-wheelers were rattling up, discharging their cargoes of shirt-fronted men and beshawled, bediamonded women. We had hardly reached the third pillar, which was our rendezvous, before a small, dark, brisk man in the dress of a coachman accosted us.

'Are you the parties who come with Miss Morstan?' he asked.

'I am Miss Morstan, and these two gentlemen are my friends,' said she.

He bent a pair of wonderfully penetrating and questioning eyes upon us.

'You will excuse me, miss,' he said, with a certain dogged manner, 'but I was to ask you to give me your word that neither of your companions is a police officer.'

'I give you my word on that,' she answered.

He gave a shrill whistle, on which a street arab led across a four-wheeler and opened the door. The man who had addressed us mounted to the box, while we took our places inside. We had hardly done so before the driver whipped up his horse, and we plunged away at a furious pace through the foggy streets.

The situation was a curious one. We were driving to an unknown place, on an unknown errand. Yet our invitation was either a complete hoax – which was an inconceivable hypothesis – or else we had good reason to think that important issues might hang upon our journey. Miss Morstan's demeanour was as resolute and collected as ever. I endeavoured to cheer and amuse her by reminiscences of my adventures in Afghanistan; but, to tell the truth, I was myself so excited at our situation, and so curious as to our destination, that my stories were slightly involved. To this day she declares that I told her one moving anecdote as to how a musket looked into my tent at the dead of night, and how I fired a double-barrelled tiger cub at it. At first I had some idea as to the direction in which we were driving; but soon, what with our pace, the fog, and my own limited knowledge of London, I lost my bearings, and knew nothing, save that we seemed to be going a very long way. Sherlock Holmes was never at fault, however, and he muttered the names as the cab rattled through squares and in and out by tortuous by-streets.

'Rochester Row,' said he. 'Now Vincent Square. Now we come out on the Vauxhall Bridge Road. We are making for the Surrey side, apparently. Yes. I thought so. Now we are on the bridge. You can catch glimpses of the river.'

We did indeed get a fleeting view of a stretch of the Thames, with the lamps shining upon the broad, silent water; but our cab dashed on, and was soon involved in a labyrinth of streets upon the other side.

'Wandsworth Road,' said my companion. 'Priory Road. Larkhall Lane. Stockwell Place. Robert Street. Coldharbour Lane. Our quest does not appear to take us to very fashionable regions.'

We had indeed reached a questionable and forbidding neighbourhood. Long lines of dull brick houses were only relieved by the coarse glare and tawdry brilliancy of public-houses at the corners. Then came rows of two-storeyed villas, each with a fronting of miniature garden, and then again interminable lines of new, staring brick buildings – the monster tentacles which the giant city was throwing out into the country. At last the cab drew up at the third house in a new terrace. None of the other houses were inhabited, and that at which we stopped was as dark as its neighbours, save for a single glimmer in the kitchen-window. On our knocking, however, the door was instantly thrown open by a Hindu servant, clad in a yellow turban, white, loose-fitting clothes, and a yellow sash. There was something strangely incongruous in this Oriental figure framed in the commonplace doorway of a third-rate suburban dwelling-house.

'The sahib awaits you,' said he, and even as he spoke there came a high, piping voice from some inner room.

'Show them in to me, khitmutgar,' it cried. 'Show them straight in to me.'

4

The Story of the Bald-Headed Man

We followed the Indian down a sordid and common passage, ill-lit and worse furnished, until he came to a door upon the right, which he threw open. A blaze of yellow light streamed out upon us, and in the centre of the glare there stood a small man with a very high head, a bristle of red hair all round the fringe of it, and a bald, shining scalp which shot out from among it like a mountain-peak from fir trees.

He writhed his hands together as he stood, and his features were in a perpetual jerk – now smiling, now scowling, but never for an instant in repose. Nature had given him a pendulous lip, and a too visible line of yellow and irregular teeth, which he strove feebly to conceal by constantly passing his hand over the lower part of his face. In spite of his obtrusive baldness, he gave the impression of youth. In point of fact, he had just turned his thirtieth year.

'Your servant, Miss Morstan,' he kept repeating, in a thin, high voice. 'Your servant, gentlemen. Pray step into my little sanctum. A small place, miss, but furnished to my own liking. An oasis of art in the howling desert of South London.'

We were all astonished by the appearance of the apartment into which he invited us. In that sorry house it looked as out-of-place as a diamond of the first water in a setting of brass. The richest and glossiest of curtains and tapestries draped the walls, looped back here and there to expose some richly mounted painting or Oriental vase. The carpet was of amber and black, so soft and so thick that the foot sank pleasantly into it, as into a bed of moss. Two great tiger-skins thrown athwart it increased the suggestion of Eastern luxury, as did a huge hookah which stood upon a mat in the corner. A lamp in the fashion of a silver dove was hung from an almost invisible golden wire in the centre of the room. As it burned it filled the air with a subtle and aromatic odour.

'Mr Thaddeus Sholto,' said the little man, still jerking and smiling. 'That is my name. You are Miss Morstan, of course. And these gentlemen –'

'This is Mr Sherlock Holmes, and this Dr Watson.'

'A doctor, eh?' cried he, much excited. 'Have you your stethoscope? Might I ask you – would you have the kindness? I have grave doubts as to my mitral valve, if you would be so very good. The aortic I may rely upon, but I should value your opinion upon the mitral.'

I listened to his heart, as requested, but was unable to find anything amiss, save, indeed, that he was in an ecstasy of fear, for he shivered from head to foot.

'It appears to be normal,' I said. 'You have no cause for uneasiness.'

'You will excuse my anxiety, Miss Morstan,' he remarked, airily. 'I am a great sufferer, and I have long had suspicions as to that valve. I am delighted to hear that they are unwarranted. Had your father, Miss Morstan, refrained from throwing a strain upon his heart, he might have been alive now.'

I could have struck the man across the face, so hot was I at this callous and offhand reference to so delicate a matter. Miss Morstan sat down, and her face grew white to the lips.

'I knew in my heart that he was dead,' said she.

'I can give you every information,' said he; 'and what is more, I can do you justice; and I will, too, whatever Brother Bartholomew may say. I am so glad to have your friends here, not only as an escort to you, but also as witnesses to what I am about to do and say. The three of us can show a bold front to Brother Bartholomew. But let us have no outsiders – no police or officials. We can settle everything satisfactorily among ourselves, without any interference. Nothing would annoy Brother Bartholomew more than any publicity.'

He sat down upon a low settee, and blinked at us enquiringly with his weak, watery blue eyes.

'For my part,' said Holmes, 'whatever you may choose to say will go no farther.'

I nodded to show my agreement.

'That is well! That is well!' said he. 'May I offer you a glass of Chianti, Miss Morstan? Or of Tokay? I keep no other wines. Shall I open a flask? No? Well, then, I trust that you have no objection to tobacco smoke, to the balsamic odour of the Eastern tobacco. I am a little nervous, and I find my hookah an invaluable sedative.'

He applied a taper to the great bowl, and the smoke bubbled merrily through the rosewater. We sat all three in a semi-circle, with our heads advanced and our chins upon our hands, while the strange, jerky little fellow, with his high, shining head, puffed uneasily in the centre.

'When I first determined to make this communication to you,' said he, 'I might have given you my address; but I feared that you might disregard my request and bring unpleasant people with you. I took the liberty, therefore, of making an appointment in such a way that my man Williams might be able to see you first. I have complete confidence in his discretion, and he had orders, if he were dissatisfied, to proceed no further in the matter. You will excuse these precautions, but I am a man of somewhat retiring, and I might even say refined, tastes, and there is nothing more unaesthetic than a policeman. I have a natural shrinking from all forms of rough materialism. I seldom come in contact with the rough crowd. I live, as you see, with some little atmosphere of elegance around me. I may call myself a patron of the arts. It is my weakness. The landscape is a genuine Corot, and, though a connoisseur might perhaps throw a doubt upon that Salvator Rosa, there cannot be the least question about the Bouguereau. I am partial to the modern French school.'

'You will excuse me, Mr Sholto,' said Miss Morstan, 'but I am here at your request to learn something which you desire to tell me. It is very late, and I should desire the interview to be as short as possible.'

'At the best, it must take some time,' he answered; 'for we shall certainly have to go to Norwood and see Brother Bartholomew. We shall all go and try if we can get the better of Brother Bartholomew. He is very angry with me for taking the course which has seemed right to me. I had quite high words with him last night. You cannot imagine what a terrible fellow he is when he is angry.'

'If we are to go to Norwood, it would perhaps be as well to start at once,' I ventured to remark.

He laughed until his ears were quite red.

'That would hardly do,' he cried. 'I don't know what he would say if I brought you in that sudden way. No, I must prepare you by showing you how we all stand to each other. In the first place, I must tell you that there are several points in the story of which I am myself ignorant. I can only lay the facts before you as far as I know them myself.

'My father was, as you may have guessed, Major John Sholto, once of the Indian Army. He retired some eleven years ago, and came to live at Pondicherry Lodge, in Upper Norwood. He had prospered in India, and brought back with him a considerable sum of money, a large collection of valuable curiosities and a staff of native servants. With these advantages he bought himself a house and lived in great luxury. My twin brother Bartholomew and I were the only children.

'I very well remember the sensation which was caused by the disappearance of Captain Morstan. We read the details in the papers, and knowing that he had been a friend of our father's, we discussed the case freely in his presence. He used to join in our speculations as to what could have happened. Never for an instant did we suspect that he had the whole secret hidden in his own breast, that of all men he alone knew the fate of Arthur Morstan.

'We did know, however, that some mystery, some positive danger, overhung our father. He was very fearful of going out alone, and he always employed two prizefighters to act as porters at Pondicherry Lodge. Williams, who drove you tonight, was one of them. He was once lightweight champion of England. Our father would never tell us what it was he feared, but he had a most marked aversion to men with wooden legs. On one occasion he actually fired his revolver at a wooden-legged man, who proved to be a harmless tradesman canvassing for orders. We had to pay a large sum to hush the matter up. My brother and I used to think this a mere whim of my father's; but events have since led us to change our opinion.

'Early in 1882 my father received a letter from India which was a great shock to him. He nearly fainted at the breakfast-table when he opened it, and from that day he sickened to his death. What was in the letter we could never discover, but I could see as he held it that it was short and written in a scrawling hand. He had suffered for years from an enlarged spleen, but he now became rapidly worse, and towards the end of April we were informed that he was beyond all hope, and that he wished to make a last communication to us.

'When we entered his room he was propped up with pillows and breathing heavily. He besought us to lock the door and to come upon either side of the bed. Then, grasping our hands, he made a remarkable statement to us, in a voice which was broken as much by emotion as by pain. I shall try and give it to you in his own very words.

'"I have only one thing," he said, "which weighs upon my mind at this supreme moment. It is my treatment of poor Morstan's orphan. The cursed greed which has been my besetting sin through life has withheld from her the treasure, half at least of which should have been hers. And yet I have made no use of it myself, so blind and foolish a thing is avarice. The mere feeling of possession has been so dear to me that I could not bear to share it with another. See that chaplet tipped with pearls beside the quinine-bottle? Even that I could not bear to part with, although I had got it out with the design of sending it to her. You, my sons, will give her a fair share of the Agra treasure. But send her nothing – not even the chaplet – until I am gone. After all, men have been as bad as this and have recovered.

'"I will tell you how Morstan died," he continued. "He had suffered for years from a weak heart, but he concealed it from everyone. I alone knew it. When in India, he and I, through a remarkable chain of circumstances, came into possession of a considerable treasure. I brought it over to England, and on the night of Morstan's arrival he came straight over here to claim his share. He walked over from the station, and was admitted by my faithful old Lal Chowdar, who is now dead. Morstan and I had a difference of opinion as to the division of the treasure, and we came to heated words. Morstan had sprung out of his chair in a paroxysm of anger, when he suddenly pressed his hand to his side, his face turned a dusky hue and he fell backwards, cutting his head against the corner of the treasure-chest. When I stooped over him I found, to my horror, that he was dead.

'"For a long time I sat half distracted, wondering what I should do. My first impulse was, of course, to call for assistance; but I could not but recognise that there was every chance that I would be accused of his murder. His death at the moment of a quarrel, and the gash in his

145

head, would be black against me. Again, an official enquiry could not be made without bringing out some facts about the treasure, which I was particularly anxious to keep secret. He had told me that no soul upon earth knew where he had gone. There seemed to be no necessity why any soul ever should know.

'"I was still pondering over the matter, when, looking up, I saw my servant, Lal Chowdar, in the doorway. He stole in and bolted the door behind him. 'Do not fear, sahib,' he said; 'no one need know that you have killed him. Let us hide him away, and who is the wiser?' 'I did not kill him,' said I. Lal Chowdar shook his head and smiled. 'I heard it all, sahib,' said he; 'I heard you quarrel, and I heard the blow. But my lips are sealed. All are asleep in the house. Let us put him away together.' That was enough to decide me. If my own servant could not believe my innocence, how could I hope to make it good before twelve foolish tradesmen in a jury-box? Lal Chowdar and I disposed of the body that night and within a few days the London papers were full of the mysterious disappearance of Captain Morstan. You will see from what I say that I can hardly be blamed in the matter. My fault lies in the fact that we concealed not only the body but also the treasure, and that I have clung to Morstan's share as well as to my own. I wish you, therefore, to make restitution. Put your ears down to my mouth. The treasure is hidden in –"

'At this instant a horrible change came over his expression; his eyes stared wildly, his jaw dropped, and he yelled, in a voice which I can never forget, "Keep him out! For Christ's sake, keep him out!" We both stared round at the window behind us upon which his gaze was fixed. A face was looking in at us out of the darkness. We could see the whitening of the nose where it was pressed against the glass. It was a bearded, hairy face, with wild, cruel eyes and an expression of concentrated malevolence. My brother and I rushed towards the window, but the man was gone. When we returned to my father, his head had dropped and his pulse had ceased to beat.

'We searched the garden that night, but found no sign of the intruder, save that just under the window a single footmark was visible in the flower-bed. But for that one trace, we might have thought that our imaginations had conjured up that wild, fierce face. We soon, however, had another and a more striking proof that there were secret agencies at work all round us. The window of my father's room was found open in the morning, his cupboards and boxes had been rifled, and upon his chest was fixed a torn piece of paper, with the words "The sign of the four" scrawled across it. What the phrase meant, or who our secret visitor may have been, we never knew. As far as we can judge, none of my father's property had been actually stolen, though everything had been turned out. My brother and I naturally associated this peculiar incident with the fear which haunted my father during his life; but it is still a complete mystery to us.'

The little man stopped to relight his hookah, and puffed thoughtfully for a few moments. We had all sat absorbed, listening to his extraordinary narrative. At the short account of her father's death Miss Morstan had turned deadly white, and for a moment I feared that she was about to faint. She rallied, however, on drinking a glass of water which I quietly poured out for her from a Venetian carafe upon the side-table. Sherlock Holmes leaned back in his chair with an abstracted expression and the lids drawn low over his glittering eyes. As I glanced at him I could not but think how, on that very day, he had complained bitterly of the commonplaceness of life. Here at least was a problem which would tax his sagacity to the utmost. Mr Thaddeus Sholto looked from one to the other of us with an obvious pride at the effect which his story had produced, and then continued, between the puffs of his overgrown pipe.

'My brother and I,' said he, 'were, as you may imagine, much excited as to the treasure which my father had spoken of. For weeks and for months we dug and delved in every part of the garden without discovering its whereabouts. It was maddening to think that the hiding-place was on his very lips at the moment that he died. We could judge the splendour of the missing riches by the chaplet which he had taken out. Over this chaplet Brother Bartholomew and I had some little discussion. The pearls were evidently of great value, and he was averse to parting with them, for, between friends, my brother was himself a little inclined to my father's fault. He thought, too, that if we parted with the chaplet it might give rise to gossip, and finally bring us into trouble. It was all that I could do to persuade him to let me find out Miss Morstan's address and send her a detached pearl at fixed intervals, so that at least she might never feel destitute.'

'It was a kindly thought,' said our companion, earnestly; 'it was extremely good of you.'

The little man waved his hand deprecatingly.

'We were your trustees,' he said; 'that was the view which I took of it, though Brother Bartholomew could not altogether see it in that light. We had plenty of money ourselves. I desired no more. Besides, it would have been such bad taste to have treated a young lady in so scurvy a fashion. *Le mauvais go°t m'ne au crime.* The French have a very neat way of putting these things. Our difference of opinion on this subject went so far that I thought it best to set up rooms for myself; so I left Pondicherry Lodge, taking the old khitmutgar and Williams with me. Yesterday, however, I learned that an event of extreme importance has occurred. The treasure has been discovered. I instantly communicated with Miss Morstan, and it only remains for us to drive out to Norwood and demand our share. I explained my views last night to Brother Bartholomew, so we shall be expected, if not welcome, visitors.'

Mr Thaddeus Sholto ceased, and sat twitching on his luxurious settee. We all remained silent, with our thoughts upon the new development which the mysterious business had taken. Holmes was the first to spring to his feet.

'You have done well, sir, from first to last,' said he. 'It is possible that we may be able to make you some small return by throwing some light upon that which is still dark to you. But, as Miss Morstan remarked just now, it is late, and we had best put the matter through without delay.'

Our new acquaintance very deliberately coiled up the tube of his hookah and produced from behind a curtain a very long, befrogged top-coat with astrakhan collar and cuffs. This he buttoned tightly up, in spite of the extreme closeness of the night, and finished his attire by putting on a rabbit-skin cap with hanging lappets which covered the ears, so that no part of him was visible save his mobile and peaky face.

'My health is somewhat fragile,' he remarked, as he led the way down the passage. 'I am compelled to be a valetudinarian.'

Our cab was awaiting us outside, and our programme was evidently prearranged, for the driver started off at once at a rapid pace. Thaddeus Sholto talked incessantly, in a voice which rose high above the rattle of the wheels.

'Bartholomew is a clever fellow,' said he. 'How do you think he found out where the treasure was? He had come to the conclusion that it was somewhere indoors: so he worked out all the cubic space of the house, and made measurements everywhere, so that not one inch should be unaccounted for. Among other things, he found that the height of the building was seventy-four feet, but on adding together the heights of all the separate rooms, and making every allowance for the space between, which he ascertained by borings, he could not bring the total to more than seventy feet. There were four feet unaccounted for. These could only be at the top of the building. He knocked a hole, therefore, in the lath and plaster ceiling of the highest room, and there, sure enough, he came upon another little garret above it, which had been sealed up and was known to no one. In the centre stood the treasure-chest, resting upon two rafters. He lowered it through the hole, and there it lies. He computes the value of the jewels at not less than half a million sterling.'

At the mention of this gigantic sum we all stared at one another open-eyed. Miss Morstan, could we secure her rights, would change from a needy governess to the richest heiress in England. Surely it was the place of a loyal friend to rejoice at such news; yet I am ashamed to say that selfishness took me by the soul, and that my heart turned as heavy as lead within me. I stammered out some few halting words of congratulation, and then sat downcast, with my head drooped, deaf to the babble of our new acquaintance. He was clearly a confirmed hypo-chondriac, and I was dreamily conscious that he was pouring forth interminable trains of symptoms, and imploring information as to the composition and action of innumerable quack nostrums, some of which he bore about in a leather case in his pocket. I trust that he may not remember any of the answers which I gave him that night. Holmes declares that he overheard me caution him against the great danger of taking more than two drops of castor-oil, while I recommended strychnine in large doses as a sedative. However that may be, I was certainly relieved when our cab pulled up with a jerk and the coachman sprang down to open the door.

'This, Miss Morstan, is Pondicherry Lodge,' said Mr Thaddeus Sholto, as he handed her out.

5

The Tragedy of Pondicherry Lodge

It was nearly eleven o'clock when we reached this final stage of our night's adventures. We had left the damp fog of the great city behind us, and the night was fairly fine. A warm wind blew from the westward, and heavy clouds moved slowly across the sky, with half a moon peeping occasionally through the rifts. It was clear enough to see for some distance, but Thaddeus Sholto took down one of the side-lamps from the carriage to give us a better light upon our way.

Pondicherry Lodge stood in its own grounds, and was girt round with a very high stone wall topped with broken glass. A single narrow iron-clamped door formed the only means of entrance. On this our guide knocked with a peculiar postman-like rat-tat.

'Who is there?' cried a gruff voice from within.

'It is I, McMurdo. You surely know my knock by this time.'

There was a grumbling sound and a clanking and jarring of keys. The door swung heavily back, and a short, deep-chested man stood in the opening, with the yellow light of the lantern shining upon his protruded face and twinkling, distrustful eyes.

'That you, Mr Thaddeus? But who are the others? I had no orders about them from the master.'

'No, McMurdo? You surprise me! I told my brother last night that I should bring some friends.'

'He hain't been out o' his room today, Mr Thaddeus, and I have no orders. You know very well that I must stick to regulations. I can let you in, but your friends they must just stop where they are.'

This was an unexpected obstacle. Thaddeus Sholto looked about him in a perplexed and helpless manner.

'This is too bad of you, McMurdo!' he said. 'If I guarantee them, that is enough for you. There is the young lady, too. She cannot wait on the public road at this hour.'

'Very sorry, Mr Thaddeus,' said the porter, inexorably. 'Folk may be friends o' yours, and yet no friends o' the master's. He pays me well to do my duty, and my duty I'll do. I don't know none o' your friends.'

'Oh, yes, you do, McMurdo,' cried Sherlock Holmes, genially. 'I don't think you can have forgotten me. Don't you remember the amateur who fought three rounds with you at Alison's rooms on the night of your benefit four years back?'

'Not Mr Sherlock Holmes!' roared the prizefighter. 'God's truth! how could I have mistook you? If instead o' standin' there so quiet you had just stepped up and given me that cross-hit of yours under the jaw, I'd ha' known you without a question. Ah, you're one that has wasted your gifts, you have! You might have aimed high, if you had joined the fancy.'

'You see, Watson, if all else fails me, I have still one of the scientific professions open to me,' said Holmes, laughing. 'Our friend won't keep us out in the cold now, I am sure.'

151

'In you come, sir, in you come – you and your friends,' he answered. 'Very sorry, Mr Thaddeus, but orders are very strict. Had to be certain of your friends before I let them in.'

Inside, a gravel path wound through desolate grounds to a huge clump of a house, square and prosaic, all plunged in shadow save where a moonbeam struck one corner and glimmered in a garret window. The vast size of the building, with its gloom and its deathly silence, struck a chill to the heart. Even Thaddeus Sholto seemed ill at ease, and the lantern quivered and rattled in his hand.

'I cannot understand it,' he said. 'There must be some mistake. I distinctly told Bartholomew that we should be here, and yet there is no light in his window. I do not know what to make of it.'

'Does he always guard the premises in this way?' asked Holmes.

'Yes, he has followed my father's custom. He was the favourite son, you know, and I sometimes think that my father may have told him more than he ever told me. That is Bartholomew's window up there where the moonshine strikes. It is quite bright, but there is no light from within, I think.'

'None,' said Holmes. 'But I see the glint of a light in that little window beside the door.'

'Ah, that is the housekeeper's room. That is where old Mrs Bernstone sits. She can tell us all about it. But perhaps you would not mind waiting here for a minute or two, for if we all go in together, and she has had no word of our coming, she may be alarmed. But, hush! what is that?'

He held up the lantern, and his hand shook until the circles of light flickered and wavered all round us. Miss Morstan seized my wrist, and we all stood, with thumping hearts, straining our ears. From the great black house there sounded through the silent night the saddest and most pitiful of sounds – the shrill, broken whimpering of a frightened woman.

'It is Mrs Bernstone,' said Sholto. 'She is the only woman in the house. Wait here. I shall be back in a moment.'

He hurried for the door, and knocked in his peculiar way. We could see a tall old woman admit him, and sway with pleasure at the very sight of him.

'Oh, Mr Thaddeus, sir, I am so glad you have come! I am so glad you have come, Mr Thaddeus, sir!'

We heard her reiterated rejoicings until the door was closed and her voice died away into a muffled monotone.

Our guide had left us the lantern. Holmes swung it slowly round, and peered keenly at the house, and at the great rubbish-heaps which cumbered the grounds. Miss Morstan and I stood together, and her hand was in mine. A wondrous subtle thing is love, for here were we two, who had never seen each other before that day, between whom no word or even look of affection had ever passed, and yet now in an hour of trouble our hands instinctively sought for each other. I have marvelled at it since, but at the time it seemed the most natural thing that I should go out to her so, and, as she has often told me, there was in her also the instinct to turn to me for comfort and protection. So we stood hand in hand, like two children, and there was peace in our hearts for all the dark things that surrounded us.

'What a strange place!' she said, looking round.

'It looks as though all the moles in England had been let loose in it. I have seen something of the sort on the side of a hill near Ballarat, where the prospectors had been at work.'

'And from the same cause,' said Holmes. 'These are the traces of the treasure-seekers. You must remember that they were six years looking for it. No wonder that the grounds look like a gravel-pit.'

At that moment the door of the house burst open, and Thaddeus Sholto came running out, with his hands thrown forward and terror in his eyes.

'There is something amiss with Bartholomew!' he cried. 'I am frightened! My nerves cannot stand it.'

He was, indeed, half blubbering with fear, and his twitching, feeble face peeping out from the great astrakhan collar had the helpless, appealing expression of a terrified child.

'Come into the house,' said Holmes, in his crisp, firm way.

'Yes, do!' pleaded Thaddeus Sholto. 'I really do not feel equal to giving directions.'

We all followed him into the housekeeper's room, which stood upon the left-hand side of the passage. The old woman was pacing up and down with a scared look and restless, picking fingers, but the sight of Miss Morstan appeared to have a soothing effect upon her.

'God bless your sweet, calm face!' she cried, with a hysterical sob. 'It does me good to see you. Oh, but I have been sorely tried this day!'

Our companion patted her thin, work-worn hand, and murmured some few words of kindly, womanly comfort, which brought the colour back into the other's bloodless cheeks.

'Master has locked himself in, and will not answer me,' she explained. 'All day I have waited to hear from him, for he often likes to be alone; but an hour ago I feared that something was amiss, so I went up and peeped through the keyhole. You must go up, Mr Thaddeus – you must go up and look for yourself. I have seen Mr Bartholomew Sholto in joy and in sorrow for ten long years, but I never saw him with such a face on him as that.'

Sherlock Holmes took the lamp and led the way, for Thaddeus Sholto's teeth were chattering in his head. So shaken was he that I had to pass my hand under his arm as we went up the stairs, for his knees were trembling under him. Twice as we ascended Holmes whipped his lens out of his pocket and carefully examined marks which appeared to me to be mere shapeless smudges of dust upon the coconut-matting which served as a stair-carpet. He walked slowly from step to step, holding the lamp low, and shooting keen glances to right and left. Miss Morstan had remained behind with the frightened housekeeper.

The third flight of stairs ended in a straight passage of some length, with a great picture in Indian tapestry upon the right of it and three doors upon the left. Holmes advanced along it in the same slow and methodical way, while we kept close at his heels, with our long, black shadows streaming backwards down the corridor. The third door was that which we were seeking. Holmes knocked without receiving any answer, and then tried to turn the handle and force it open. It was locked on the inside, however, and by a broad and powerful bolt, as we could see when we set our lamp up against it. The key being turned, however, the hole was not entirely closed. Sherlock Holmes bent down to it, and instantly rose again with a sharp intaking of the breath.

'There is something devilish in this, Watson,' said he, more moved than I had ever before seen him. 'What do you make of it?'

I stooped to the hole, and recoiled in horror. Moonlight was streaming into the room, and it was bright with a vague and shifty radiance. Looking straight at me, and suspended, as it were, in the air, for all beneath was in shadow, there hung a face – the very face of our companion Thaddeus. There was the same high, shining head, the same circular bristle of red hair, the same bloodless countenance. The features were set, however, in a horrible smile, a fixed and unnatural grin, which in that still and moonlit room was more jarring to the nerves than any scowl or contortion. So like was the face to that of our little friend that I looked round at him to make sure that he was indeed with us. Then I recalled to mind that he had mentioned to us that his brother and he were twins.

'This is terrible!' I said to Holmes. 'What is to be done?'

'The door must come down,' he answered, and, springing against it, he put all his weight upon the lock.

It creaked and groaned, but did not yield. Together we flung ourselves upon it once more, and this time it gave way with a sudden snap, and we found ourselves within Bartholomew Sholto's chamber.

It appeared to have been fitted up as a chemical laboratory. A double line of glass-stoppered bottles was drawn up upon the wall opposite the door, and the table was littered over with Bunsen burners, test-tubes and retorts. In the corners stood carboys of acid in wicker baskets. One of these appeared to leak or to have been broken, for a stream of dark-coloured liquid had trickled out from it, and the air was heavy with a peculiarly pungent, tar-like odour. A set of steps stood at one side of the room, in the midst of a litter of lath and plaster, and above them there was an opening in the ceiling large enough for a man to pass through. At the foot of the steps a long coil of rope was thrown carelessly together.

By the table, in a wooden armchair, the master of the house was seated all in a heap, with his head sunk upon his left shoulder, and that ghastly, inscrutable smile upon his face. He was stiff and cold and had clearly been dead many hours. It seemed to me that not only his features, but all his limbs, were twisted and turned in the most fantastic fashion. By his hand upon the table there lay a peculiar instrument – a brown, close-grained stick, with a stone head like a hammer, rudely lashed on with coarse twine. Beside it was a torn sheet of notepaper with some words scrawled upon it. Holmes glanced at it, and then handed it to me.

'You see,' he said, with a significant raising of the eyebrows.

In the light of the lantern I read, with a thrill of horror, 'The sign of the four.'

'In God's name, what does it all mean?' I asked.

'It means murder,' said he, stooping over the dead man. 'Ah! I expected it. Look here!'

He pointed to what looked like a long, dark thorn stuck in the skin just above the ear.

'It looks like a thorn,' said I.

'It is a thorn. You may pick it out. But be careful, for it is poisoned.'

I took it up between my finger and thumb. It came away from the skin so readily that hardly any mark was left behind. One tiny speck of blood showed where the puncture had been.

'This is all an insoluble mystery to me,' said I. 'It grows darker instead of clearer.'

'On the contrary,' he answered, 'it clears every instant. I only require a few missing links to have an entirely connected case.'

We had almost forgotten our companion's presence since we entered the chamber. He was still standing in the doorway, the very picture of terror, wringing his hands and moaning to himself. Suddenly, however, he broke out into a sharp, querulous cry.

'The treasure is gone!' he said. 'They have robbed him of the treasure! There is the hole through which we lowered it. I helped him to do it! I was the last person who saw him! I left him here last night, and I heard him lock the door as I came downstairs.'

'What time was that?'

'It was ten o'clock. And now he is dead, and the police will be called in, and I shall be suspected of having had a hand in it. Oh, yes, I am sure I shall. But you don't think so, gentlemen? Surely, you don't think that it was I? Is it likely that I would have brought you here if it were I? Oh, dear! oh, dear! I know that I shall go mad!'

He jerked his arms and stamped his feet in a kind of convulsive frenzy.

'You have no reason for fear, Mr Sholto,' said Holmes kindly, putting his hand upon his shoulder; 'take my advice and drive down to the station to report the matter to the police. Offer to assist them in every way. We shall wait here until your return.'

The little man obeyed in a half-stupefied fashion, and we heard him stumbling down the stairs in the dark.

6

Sherlock Holmes Gives a Demonstration

'Now, Watson,' said Holmes, rubbing his hands, 'we have half an hour to ourselves. Let us make good use of it. My case is, as I have told you, almost complete; but we must not err on the side of over-confidence. Simple as the case seems now, there may be something deeper underlying it.'

'Simple!' I ejaculated.

'Surely,' said he, with something of the air of a clinical professor expounding to his class. 'Just sit in the corner there, that your footprints may not complicate matters. Now to work! In the first place, how did these folk come, and how did they go? The door has not been opened since last night. What of the window?' He carried the lamp across to it, muttering his observations aloud the while, but addressing them to himself rather than to me. 'Window is snibbed on the inner side. Framework is solid. No hinges at the side. Let us open it. No water-pipe near. Roof quite out of reach. Yet a man has mounted by the window. It rained a little last night. Here is the print of a foot in mould upon the sill. And here is a circular muddy mark, and here again upon the floor, and here again by the table. See here, Watson! This is really a very pretty demonstration.'

I looked at the round, well-defined muddy discs.

'That is not a footmark,' said I.

'It is something much more valuable to us. It is the impression of a wooden stump. You see here on the sill is the boot-mark, a heavy boot with a broad metal heel, and beside it is the mark of the timber toe.'

'It is the wooden-legged man.'

'Quite so. But there has been someone else – a very able and efficient ally. Could you scale that wall, doctor?'

I looked out of the open window. The moon still shone brightly on that angle of the house. We were a good sixty feet from the ground, and, look where I would, I could see no foothold, nor as much as a crevice in the brickwork.

'It is absolutely impossible,' I answered.

'Without aid it is so. But suppose you had a friend up here who lowered you this good stout rope which I see in the corner, securing one end of it to this great hook in the wall. Then, I think, if you were an active man, you might swarm up, wooden leg and all. You would depart, of course, in the same fashion, and your ally would draw up the rope, untie it from the hook, shut the window, snib it on the inside, and get away in the way that he originally came. As a minor point, it may be noted,' he continued, fingering the rope, 'that our wooden-legged friend, though a fair climber, was not a professional sailor. His hands were far from horny. My lens discloses more than one blood-mark, especially towards the end of the rope, from which I gather that he slipped down with such velocity that he took the skin off his hand.'

'This is all very well,' said I; 'but the thing becomes more unintelligible than ever. How about this mysterious ally? How came he into the room?'

'Yes, the ally!' repeated Holmes, pensively. 'There are features of interest about this ally. He lifts the case from the regions of the commonplace. I fancy that this ally breaks fresh ground in the annals of crime in this country – though parallel cases suggest themselves from India, and, if my memory serves me, from Senegambia.'

'How came he, then?' I reiterated. 'The door is locked; the window is inaccessible. Was it through the chimney?'

'The grate is much too small,' he answered. 'I had already considered that possibility.'

'How, then?' I persisted.

'You will not apply my precept,' he said, shaking his head. 'How often have I said to you that when you have eliminated the impossible, whatever remains, *however improbable*, must be the truth? We know that he did not come through the door, the window, or the chimney. We also know that he could not have been concealed in the room, as there is no concealment possible. Whence, then, did he come?'

'He came through the hole in the roof!' I cried.

'Of course he did. He must have done so. If you will have the kindness to hold the lamp for me, we shall now extend our researches to the room above – the secret room in which the treasure was found.'

He mounted the steps, and, seizing a rafter with either hand, he swung himself up into the garret. Then, lying on his face, he reached down for the lamp, and held it while I followed him.

The chamber in which we found ourselves was about ten feet one way and six the other. The floor was formed by the rafters, with thin lath and plaster between, so that in walking one had to step from beam to beam. The roof ran up to an apex, and was evidently the inner shell of the true roof to the house. There was no furniture of any sort, and the accumulated dust of years lay thick upon the floor.

'Here you are, you see,' said Sherlock Holmes, putting his hand against the sloping wall. 'This is a trap-door which leads out on to the roof. I can press it back, and here is the roof itself, sloping at a gentle angle. This, then, is the way by which Number One entered. Let us see if we can find some other traces of his individuality.'

He held down the lamp to the floor, and as he did so I saw for the second time that night a startled, surprised look come over his face. For myself, as I followed his gaze, my skin was cold under my clothes. The floor was covered thickly with the prints of a naked foot – clear, well defined, perfectly formed, but scarce half the size of those of an ordinary man.

'Holmes,' I said, in a whisper, 'a child has done this horrid thing.'

He had recovered his self-possession in an instant.

'I was staggered for the moment,' he said, 'but the thing is quite natural. My memory failed me, or I should have been able to foretell it. There is nothing more to be learned here. Let us go down.'

'What is your theory, then, as to those footmarks?' I asked, eagerly, when we had regained the lower room once more.

'My dear Watson, try a little analysis yourself,' said he, with a touch of impatience. 'You know my methods. Apply them, and it will be instructive to compare results.'

'I cannot conceive anything which will cover the facts,' I answered.

'It will be clear enough to you soon,' he said, in an offhand way. 'I think that there is nothing else of importance here, but I will look.'

He whipped out his lens and a tape measure, and hurried about the room on his knees, measuring, comparing, examining, with his long, thin nose only a few inches from the planks, and his beady eyes gleaming and deep-set like those of a bird. So swift, silent and furtive were his movements, like those of a trained bloodhound picking out a scent, that I could not but think what a terrible criminal he would have made had he turned his energy and sagacity against the law instead of exerting them in its defence. As he hunted about he kept muttering to himself, and finally he broke out into a loud crow of delight.

'We are certainly in luck,' said he. 'We ought to have very little trouble now. Number One has had the misfortune to tread in the creosote. You can see the outline of the edge of his small foot here at the side of this evil-smelling mess. The carboy has been cracked, you see, and the stuff has leaked out.'

'What then?' I asked.

'Why, we have got him, that's all,' said he. 'I know a dog that would follow that scent to the world's end. If a pack can track a trailed herring across a shire, how far can a specially trained hound follow so pungent a smell as this? It sounds like a sum in the rule of three. The answer should give us the – But, halloa! here are the accredited representatives of the law.'

Heavy steps and the clamour of loud voices were audible from below, and the hall door shut with a loud crash.

'Before they come,' said Holmes, 'just put your hand here on this poor fellow's arm, and here on his leg. What do you feel?'

'The muscles are as hard as a board,' I answered.

'Quite so. They are in a state of extreme contraction, far exceeding the usual *rigor mortis*. Coupled with this distortion of the face, this Hippocratic smile, or *risus sardonicus*, as the old writers called it, what conclusion would it suggest to your mind?'

'Death from some powerful vegetable alkaloid,' I answered; 'some strychnine-like substance which would produce tetanus.'

'That was the idea which occurred to me the instant I saw the drawn muscles of the face. On getting into the room I at once looked for the means by which the poison had entered the system. As you saw, I discovered a thorn which had been driven or shot with no great force into the scalp. You observe that the part struck was that which would be turned towards the hole in the ceiling if the man were erect in his chair. Now examine this thorn.'

I took it up gingerly and held it in the light of the lantern. It was long, sharp and black, with a glazed look near the point as though some gummy substance had dried upon it. The blunt end had been trimmed and rounded off with a knife.

'Is that an English thorn?' he asked.

'No, it certainly is not.'

'With all these data you should be able to draw some just inference. But here are the regulars; so the auxiliary forces may beat a retreat.'

As he spoke, the steps which had been coming nearer sounded loudly in the passage, and a very stout, portly man in a grey suit strode heavily into the room. He was red-faced, burly and plethoric, with a pair of very small, twinkling eyes, which looked keenly out from between swollen and puffy pouches. He was closely followed by an inspector in uniform, and by the still palpitating Thaddeus Sholto.

'Here's a business!' he cried, in a muffled, husky voice. 'Here's a pretty business! But who are all these? Why, the house seems to be as full as a rabbit-warren!'

'I think you must recollect me, Mr Athelney Jones,' said Holmes, quietly.

'Why, of course I do!' he wheezed. 'It's Mr Sherlock Holmes, the theorist. Remember you! I'll never forget how you lectured us all on causes and inferences and effects in the Bishopgate jewel case. It's true you set us on the right track; but you'll own now that it was more by good luck than good guidance.'

'It was a piece of very simple reasoning.'

'Oh, come, now, come! Never be ashamed to own up. But what is all this? Bad business! Bad business! Stern facts here – no room for theories. How lucky that I happened to be out at Norwood over another case! I was at the station when the message arrived. What d'you think the man died of?'

'Oh, this is hardly a case for me to theorise over,' said Holmes, drily.

'No, no. Still, we can't deny that you hit the nail on the head sometimes. Dear me! Door locked, I understand. Jewels worth half a million missing. How was the window?'

'Fastened; but there are steps on the sill.'

'Well, well, if it was fastened the steps could have nothing to do with the matter. That's common sense. Man might have died in a fit; but then the jewels are missing. Ha! I have a theory. These flashes come upon me at times. Just step outside, sergeant, and you, Mr Sholto. Your friend can remain. What do you think of this, Holmes? Sholto was, on his own confession, with his brother last night. The brother died in a fit, on which Sholto walked off with the treasure! How's that?'

'On which the dead man very considerately got up and locked the door on the inside.'

'Hum! There's a flaw there. Let us apply common sense to the matter. This Thaddeus Sholto *was* with his brother; there *was* a quarrel: so much we know. The brother is dead and the jewels are gone. So much also we know. No one saw the brother from the time Thaddeus left him. His bed had not been slept in. Thaddeus is evidently in a most disturbed state of mind. His appearance is – well, not attractive. You see that I am weaving my web round Thaddeus. The net begins to close upon him.'

'You are not quite in possession of the facts yet,' said Holmes. 'This splinter of wood, which I have every reason to believe to be poisoned, was in the man's scalp where you still see the mark; this card, inscribed as you see it, was on the table, and beside it lay this rather curious stone-headed instrument. How does all that fit into your theory?'

'Confirms it in every respect,' said the fat detective, pompously. 'House is full of Indian curiosities. Thaddeus brought this up, and if this splinter be poisonous, Thaddeus may as well have made murderous use of it as any other man. The card is some hocus-pocus – a blind, as like as not. The only question is, how did he depart. Ah, of course, here is a hole in the roof.'

With great activity, considering his bulk, he sprang up the steps and squeezed through into the garret, and immediately afterwards we heard his exulting voice proclaiming that he had found the trap-door.

'He can find something,' remarked Holmes, shrugging his shoulders; 'he has occasional glimmerings of reason. *Il n'y a pas des sots si incommodes que ceux qui ont de l'esprit!*'

'You see!' said Athelney Jones, reappearing down the steps again; 'facts are better than theories, after all. My view of the case is confirmed. There is a trap-door communicating with the roof, and it is partly open.'

'It was I who opened it.'

'Oh, indeed! You did notice it, then?' He seemed a little crestfallen at the discovery. 'Well, whoever noticed it, it shows how our gentleman got away. Inspector!'

'Yes, sir,' from the passage.

'Ask Mr Sholto to step this way – Mr Sholto, it is my duty to inform you that anything which you may say will be used against you. I arrest you in the Queen's name as being concerned in the death of your brother.'

'There, now! Didn't I tell you?' cried the poor little man, throwing out his hands, and looking from one to the other of us.

'Don't trouble yourself about it, Mr Sholto,' said Holmes; 'I think that I can engage to clear you of the charge.'

'Don't promise too much, Mr Theorist, don't promise too much!' snapped the detective. 'You may find it a harder matter than you think.'

'Not only will I clear him, Mr Jones, but I will make you a free present of the name and description of one of the two people who were in this room last night. His name, I have every reason to believe, is Jonathan Small. He is a poorly educated man, small, active, with his right leg off, and wearing a wooden stump which is worn away upon the inner side. His left boot has a coarse, square-toed sole, with an iron band round the heel. He is a middle-aged man, much sunburned, and has been a convict. These few indications may be of some assistance to you, coupled with the fact that there is a good deal of skin missing from the palm of his hand. The other man –'

'Ah! the other man?' asked Athelney Jones, in a sneering voice, but impressed none the less, as I could easily see, by the precision of the other's manner.

'Is a rather curious person,' said Sherlock Holmes, turning upon his heel. 'I hope before very long to be able to introduce you to the pair of them. A word with you, Watson.'

He led me out to the head of the stair.

'This unexpected occurrence,' he said, 'has caused us rather to lose sight of the original purpose of our journey.'

'I have just been thinking so,' I answered; 'it is not right that Miss Morstan should remain in this stricken house.'

'No. You must escort her home. She lives with Mrs Cecil Forrester, in Lower Camberwell, so it is not very far. I will wait for you here if you will drive out again. Or perhaps you are too tired?'

'By no means. I don't think I could rest until I know more of this fantastic business. I have seen something of the rough side of life, but I give you my word that this quick succession of strange surprises tonight has shaken my nerve completely. I should like, however, to see the matter through with you, now that I have got so far.'

'Your presence will be of great service to me,' he answered. 'We shall work the case out independently, and leave this fellow Jones to exult over any mare's-nest which he may choose to construct. When you have dropped Miss Morstan, I wish you to go to No. 3, Pinchin Lane, down near the water's edge at Lambeth. The third house on the right-hand side is a bird-stuffer's; Sherman is the name. You will see a weasel holding a young rabbit in the window. Knock old Sherman up, and tell him, with my compliments, that I want Toby at once. You will bring Toby back in the cab with you.'

'A dog, I suppose?'

'Yes, a queer mongrel, with a most amazing power of scent. I would rather have Toby's help than that of the whole detective force of London.'

'I shall bring him then,' said I. 'It is one now. I ought to be back before three, if I can get a fresh horse.'

'And I,' said Holmes, 'shall see what I can learn from Mrs Bernstone, and from the Indian servant, who, Mr Thaddeus tells me, sleeps in the next garret. Then I shall study the great Jones's methods and listen to his not-too-delicate sarcasms. "*Wir sind gewohnt dass die Menschen verh^hnen was sie nicht verstehen.*" Goethe is always pithy.'

7

The Episode of the Barrel

The police had brought a cab with them, and in this I escorted Miss Morstan back to her home. After the angelic fashion of women, she had borne trouble with a calm face as long as there was someone weaker than herself to support, and I had found her bright and placid by the side of the frightened housekeeper. In the cab, however, she first turned faint, and then burst into a passion of weeping – so sorely had she been tried by the adventures of the night. She has told me since that she thought me cold and distant upon that journey. She little guessed the struggle within my breast, or the effort of self-restraint which held me back. My sympathies and my love went out to her, even as my hand had in the garden. I felt that years of the conventionalities of life could not teach me to know her sweet, brave nature as had this one day of strange experiences. Yet there were two thoughts which sealed the words of affection upon my lips. She was weak and helpless, shaken in mind and nerve. It was to take her at a disadvantage to obtrude love upon her at such a time. Worse still, she was rich. If Holmes's researches were successful, she would be an heiress. Was it fair, was it honourable, that a half-pay surgeon should take such advantage of an intimacy which chance had brought about? Might she not look upon me as a mere vulgar fortune-seeker? I could not bear to risk that such a thought should cross her mind. This Agra treasure intervened like an impassable barrier between us.

It was nearly two o'clock when we reached Mrs Cecil Forrester's. The servants had retired hours ago, but Mrs Forrester had been so interested by the strange message which Miss Morstan had received that she had sat up in the hope of her return. She opened the door herself, a middle-aged, graceful woman, and it gave me joy to see how tenderly her arm stole round the other's waist, and how motherly was the voice in which she greeted her. She was clearly no mere paid dependant but an honoured friend. I was introduced, and Mrs Forrester earnestly begged me to step in and to tell her our adventures. I explained, however, the importance of my errand, and promised faithfully to call and report any progress which we might make with the case. As we drove away I stole a glance back, and I still seem to see that little group on the step – the two graceful, clinging figures, the half-opened door, the hall light shining through stained glass, the barometer and the bright stair-rods. It was soothing to catch even that passing glimpse of a tranquil English home in the midst of the wild, dark business which had absorbed us.

And the more I thought of what had happened, the wilder and darker it grew. I reviewed the whole extraordinary sequence of events as I rattled on through the silent, gas-lit streets. There was the original problem: that, at least, was pretty clear now. The death of Captain Morstan, the sending of the pearls, the advertisement, the letter – we had had light upon all those events. They had only led us, however, to a deeper and far more tragic mystery. The Indian treasure, the curious plan found among Morstan's baggage, the strange scene at Major Sholto's death, the rediscovery of the treasure immediately followed by the murder of the discoverer, the very singular accompaniments to the crime, the footsteps, the remarkable weapons, the words upon the card, corresponding with those upon Captain Morstan's chart – here was, indeed, a labyrinth in which a man less singularly endowed than my fellow-lodger might well despair of ever finding the clue.

Pinchin Lane was a row of shabby, two-storeyed brick houses in the lower quarter of Lambeth. I had to knock for some time at No. 3 before I could make any impression. At last, however, there was the glint of a candle behind the blind, and a face looked out at the upper window.

'Go on, you drunken vagabond,' said the face. 'If you kick up any more row, I'll open the kennels and let out forty-three dogs upon you.'

'If you'll let one out, it's just what I have come for,' said I.

'Go on!' yelled the voice. 'So help me gracious, I have a wiper in this bag, an' I'll drop it on your 'ead if you don't hook it!'

'But I want a dog,' I cried.

'I won't be argued with!' shouted Mr Sherman. 'Now, stand clear; for when I say "Three", down goes the wiper.'

'Mr Sherlock Holmes –' I began; but the words had a most magical effect, for the window instantly slammed down, and within a minute the door was unbarred and open. Mr Sherman was a lanky, lean old man, with stooping shoulders, a stringy neck and blue-tinted glasses.

'A friend of Mr Sherlock is always welcome,' said he. 'Step in, sir. Keep clear of the badger, for he bites. Ah, naughty, naughty! would you take a nip at the gentleman?' This to a stoat, which thrust its wicked head and red eyes between the bars of its cage. 'Don't mind that, sir; it's only a slow-worm. It hain't got no fangs, so I gives it the run o' the room, for it keeps the beetles down. You must not mind my bein' just a little short wi' you at first, for I'm guyed at by the children, and there's many a one just comes down this lane to knock me up. What was it that Mr Sherlock Holmes wanted, sir?'

'He wanted a dog of yours.'

'Ah! that would be Toby.'

'Yes, "Toby" was the name.'

'Toby lives at No. 7 on the left here.'

He moved slowly forward with his candle among the queer animal family which he had gathered round him. In the uncertain, shadowy light I could see dimly that there were glancing, glimmering eyes peeping down at us from every cranny and corner. Even the rafters above our heads were lined by solemn fowls, who lazily shifted their weight from one leg to the other as our voices disturbed their slumbers.

Toby proved to be an ugly, long-haired, lop-eared creature, half spaniel and half lurcher, brown and white in colour, with a very clumsy, waddling gait. It accepted, after some hesitation, a lump of sugar which the old naturalist handed to me, and, having thus sealed an alliance, it followed me to the cab, and made no difficulties about accompanying me. It had just struck three on the Palace clock when I found myself back once more at Pondicherry Lodge. The ex-prizefighter McMurdo had, I found, been arrested as an accessory, and both he and Mr Sholto had been marched off to the station. Two constables guarded the narrow gate, but they allowed me to pass with the dog on my mentioning the detective's name.

Holmes was standing on the doorstep, with his hands in his pockets, smoking his pipe.

'Ah, you have him there!' said he. 'Good dog, then! Athelney Jones has gone. We have had an immense display of energy since you left. He has arrested not only friend Thaddeus, but the gatekeeper, the housekeeper and the Indian servant. We have the place to ourselves, but for a sergeant upstairs. Leave the dog here and come up.'

We tied Toby to the hall table, and reascended the stairs. The room was as we had left it, save that a sheet had been draped over the central figure. A weary-looking police sergeant reclined in the corner.

'Lend me your bull's-eye, sergeant,' said my companion. 'Now tie this bit of cord round my neck, so as to hang it in front of me. Thank you. Now I must kick off my boots and stockings. Just you carry them down with you, Watson. I am going to do a little climbing. And dip my handkerchief into the creosote. That will do. Now come up into the garret with me for a moment.'

We clambered up through the hole. Holmes turned his light once more upon the footsteps in the dust.

'I wish you particularly to notice these footmarks,' he said. 'Do you observe anything noteworthy about them?'

'They belong,' I said, 'to a child or a small woman.'

'Apart from their size, though. Is there nothing else?'

'They appear to be much as other footmarks.'

'Not at all. Look here! This is the print of a right foot in the dust. Now I make one with my naked foot beside it. What is the chief difference?'

'Your toes are all cramped together. The other print has each toe distinctly divided.'

'Quite so. That is the point. Bear that in mind. Now, would you kindly step over to that flap-window and smell the edge of the wood-work? I shall stay over here, as I have this handkerchief in my hand.'

I did as he directed, and was instantly conscious of a strong tarry smell.

'That is where he put his foot in getting out. If *you* can trace him, I should think that Toby will have no difficulty. Now run downstairs, loose the dog, and look out for Blondin.'

By the time that I got out into the grounds Sherlock Holmes was on the roof, and I could see him like an enormous glow-worm crawling very slowly along the ridge. I lost sight of him behind a stack of chimneys, but he presently reappeared, and then vanished once more upon the opposite side. When I made my way round there I found him seated at one of the corner eaves.

'That you, Watson?' he cried.

'Yes.'

'This is the place. What is that black thing down there?'

'A water-barrel.'

'Top on it?'

'Yes.'

'No sign of a ladder?'

'No.'

'Confound the fellow! It's a most breakneck place. I ought to be able to come down where he could climb up. The water-pipe feels pretty firm. Here goes, anyhow.'

There was a scuffling of feet, and the lantern began to come steadily down the side of the wall. Then with a light spring he came on to the barrel, and from there to the earth.

'It was easy to follow him,' he said, drawing on his stockings and boots. 'Tiles were loosened the whole way along, and in his hurry he had dropped this. It confirms my diagnosis, as you doctors express it.'

171

The object which he held up to me was a small pocket or pouch woven out of coloured grasses, and with a few tawdry beads strung round it. In shape and size it was not unlike a cigarette-case. Inside were half a dozen spines of dark wood, sharp at one end and rounded at the other, like that which had struck Bartholomew Sholto.

'They are hellish things,' said he. 'Look out that you don't prick yourself. I'm delighted to have them, for the chances are that they are all he has. There is the less fear of you or me finding one in our skin before long. I would sooner face a Martini bullet myself. Are you game for a six-mile trudge, Watson?'

'Certainly,' I answered.

'Your leg will stand it?'

'Oh, yes.'

'Here you are, doggy! Good old Toby! Smell it, Toby, smell it!' He pushed the creosote handkerchief under the dog's nose, while the creature stood with its fluffy legs separated, and with a most comical cock to its head, like a connoisseur sniffing the *bouquet* of a famous vintage. Holmes then threw the handkerchief to a distance, fastened a stout cord to the mongrel's collar, and led him to the foot of the water-barrel. The creature instantly broke into a succession of high, tremulous yelps, and, with his nose on the ground and his tail in the air, pattered off upon the trail at a pace which strained his leash and kept us at the top of our speed.

The east had been gradually whitening, and we could now see some distance in the cold, grey light. The square, massive house, with its black, empty windows and high, bare walls, towered up, sad and forlorn, behind us. Our course led right across the grounds, in and out among the trenches and pits with which they were scarred and inter-sected. The whole place, with its scattered dirt-heaps and ill-grown shrubs, had a blighted, ill-omened look which harmonised with the black tragedy which hung over it.

On reaching the boundary wall Toby ran along, whining eagerly, underneath its shadow, and stopped finally in a corner screened by a young beech. Where the two walls joined, several bricks had been loosened, and the crevices left were worn down and rounded upon the lower side, as though they had frequently been used as a ladder. Holmes clambered up, and, taking the dog from me, he dropped it over upon the other side.

'There's the print of wooden-leg's hand,' he remarked, as I mounted up beside him. 'You see the slight smudge of blood upon the white plaster. What a lucky thing it is that we have had no very heavy rain since yesterday! The scent will lie upon the road in spite of their eight-and-twenty hours' start.'

I confess that I had my doubts myself when I reflected upon the great traffic which had passed along the London road in the interval. My fears were soon appeased, however. Toby never hesitated or swerved, but waddled on in his peculiar rolling fashion. Clearly, the pungent smell of the creosote rose high above all other contending scents.

'Do not imagine,' said Holmes, 'that I depend for my success in this case upon the mere chance of one of these fellows having put his foot in the chemical. I have knowledge now which would enable me to trace them in many different ways. This, however, is the readiest, and, since fortune has put it into our hands, I should be culpable if I neglected it. It has, however, prevented the case from becoming the pretty little intellectual problem which it at one time promised to be. There might have been some credit to be gained out of it, but for this too palpable clue.'

'There is credit, and to spare,' said I. 'I assure you, Holmes, that I marvel at the means by which you obtain your results in this case, even more than I did in the Jefferson Hope murder. The thing seems to me to be deeper and more inexplicable. How, for example, could you describe with such confidence the wooden-legged man?'

'Pshaw, my dear boy! it was simplicity itself. I don't wish to be theatrical. It is all patent and above-board. Two officers who are in command of a convict guard learn an important secret as to buried treasure. A map is drawn for them by an Englishman named Jonathan Small. You remember that we saw the name upon the chart in Captain

Morstan's possession. He had signed it on behalf of himself and his associates – the sign of the four, as he somewhat dramatically called it. Aided by this chart, the officers – or one of them – gets the treasure and brings it to England, leaving, we will suppose, some condition under which he received it unfulfilled. Now, then, why did not Jonathan Small get the treasure himself? The answer is obvious. The chart is dated at a time when Morstan was brought into close association with convicts. Jonathan Small did not get the treasure because he and his associates were themselves convicts and could not get away.'

'But this is mere speculation,' said I.

'It is more than that. It is the only hypothesis which covers the facts. Let us see how it fits in with the sequel. Major Sholto remains at peace for some years, happy in the possession of his treasure. Then he receives a letter from India which gives him a great fright. What was that?'

'A letter to say that the men whom he had wronged had been set free.'

'Or had escaped. That is much more likely, for he would have known what their term of imprisonment was. It would not have been a surprise to him. What does he do then? He guards himself against a wooden-legged man – a white man, mark you, for he mistakes a white tradesman for him, and actually fires a pistol at him. Now, only one white man's name is on the chart. The others are Hindus or Mohammedans. There is no other white man. Therefore, we may say with confidence that the wooden-legged man is identical with Jonathan Small. Does the reasoning strike you as being faulty?'

'No: it is clear and concise.'

'Well, now, let us put ourselves in the place of Jonathan Small. Let us look at it from his point of view. He comes to England with the double idea of regaining what he would consider to be his rights, and of having his revenge upon the man who had wronged him. He found out where Sholto lived, and very possibly he established communications with someone inside the house. There is this butler, Lal Rao, whom we have not seen. Mrs Bernstone gives him a far from good character. Small could not find out, however, where the treasure was hid, for no one ever knew, save the major and one faithful servant who had died. Suddenly, Small learns that the major is on his deathbed. In a frenzy lest the secret of the treasure die with him, he runs the gauntlet of the guards, makes his way to the dying man's window, and is only deterred from entering by the presence of his two sons. Mad with hate, however, against the dead man, he enters the room that night, searches his private papers in the hope of discovering some memorandum relating to the treasure, and finally leaves a memento of his visit in the short inscription upon the card. He had doubtless planned beforehand that, should he slay the major, he would leave some such record upon the body as a sign that it was not a common murder, but, from the point of view of the four associates, something in the nature of an act of justice. Whimsical and bizarre conceits of this kind are common enough in the annals of crime, and usually afford valuable indications as to the criminal. Do you follow all this?'

'Very clearly.'

'Now, what could Jonathan Small do? He could only continue to keep a secret watch upon the efforts made to find the treasure. Possibly he leaves England and only comes back at intervals. Then comes the discovery of the garret, and he is instantly informed of it. We again trace the presence of some confederate in the household. Jonathan, with his wooden leg, is utterly unable to reach the lofty room of Bartholomew Sholto. He takes with him, however, a rather curious associate, who gets over this difficulty, but dips his naked foot into creosote, whence come Toby, and a six-mile limp for a half-pay officer with a damaged *tendo Achillis*.'

'But it was the associate, and not Jonathan, who committed the crime.'

'Quite so. And rather to Jonathan's disgust, to judge by the way he stamped about when he got into the room. He bore no grudge against Bartholomew Sholto, and would have preferred if he could have been simply bound and gagged. He did not wish to put his head in a halter. There was no help for it, however: the savage instincts of his companion had broken out, and the poison had done its work: so Jonathan Small left his record, lowered the treasure-box to the ground, and followed it himself. That was the train of events as far as I can decipher them. Of course, as to his personal appearance he must be middle-aged, and must be sunburned after serving his time in such an oven as the Andamans. His height is readily calculated from the length of his stride, and we know that he was bearded. His hairiness was the one point which impressed itself upon Thaddeus Sholto when he saw him at the window. I don't know that there is anything else.'

'The associate?'

'Ah, well, there is no great mystery in that. But you will know all about it soon enough. How sweet the morning air is! See how that one little cloud floats like a pink feather from some gigantic flamingo. Now the red rim of the sun pushes itself over the London cloud-bank. It shines on a good many folk, but on none, I dare bet, who are on a stranger errand than you and I. How small we feel, with our petty ambitions and strivings, in the presence of the great elemental forces of nature! Are you well up in your Jean Paul?'

'Fairly so. I worked back to him through Carlyle.'

'That was like following the brook to the parent lake. He makes one curious but profound remark. It is that the chief proof of man's real greatness lies in his perception of his own smallness. It argues, you see, a power of comparison and of appreciation which is in itself a proof of nobility. There is much food for thought in Richter. You have not a pistol, have you?'

'I have my stick.'

'It is just possible that we may need something of the sort if we get to their lair. Jonathan I shall leave to you, but if the other turns nasty I shall shoot him dead.'

He took out his revolver as he spoke, and having loaded two of the chambers, he put it back into the right-hand pocket of his jacket.

We had during this time been following the guidance of Toby down the half-rural villa-lined roads which lead to the metropolis. Now, however, we were beginning to come among continuous streets, where labourers and dockmen were already astir, and slatternly women were taking down shutters and brushing doorsteps. At the square-topped corner public-houses business was just beginning, and rough-looking men were emerging, rubbing their sleeves across their beards after their morning wet. Strange dogs sauntered up and stared wonderingly at us as we passed, but our inimitable Toby looked neither to the right nor to the left, but trotted onwards with his nose to the ground and an occasional eager whine which spoke of a hot scent.

We had traversed Streatham, Brixton, Camberwell, and now found ourselves in Kennington Lane, having borne away through the side-streets to the east of the Oval. The men whom we pursued seemed to have taken a curiously zig-zag road, with the idea probably of escaping observation. They had never kept to the main road if a parallel side-street would serve their turn. At the foot of Kennington Lane they had edged away to the left through Bond Street and Miles Street. Where the latter street turns into Knight's Place, Toby ceased to advance, but began to run backwards and forwards with one ear cocked and the other drooping, the very picture of canine indecision. Then he waddled round in circles, looking up to us from time to time, as if to ask for sympathy in his embarrassment.

'What the deuce is the matter with the dog?' growled Holmes. 'They surely would not take a cab, or go off in a balloon.'

'Perhaps they stood here for some time,' I suggested.

'Ah! it's all right. He's off again,' said my companion, in a tone of relief.

He was indeed off, for after sniffing round again he suddenly made up his mind, and darted away with an energy and determination such as he had not yet shown. The scent appeared to be much hotter than before, for he had not even to put his nose on the ground, but tugged at his leash and tried to break into a run. I could see by the gleam in Holmes's eyes that he thought we were nearing the end of our journey.

Our course now ran down Nine Elms until we came to Broderick and Nelson's large timber-yard, just past the White Eagle tavern. Here the dog, frantic with excitement, turned down through the side

THE SIGN OF THE FOUR

gate into the enclosure, where the sawyers were already at work. On the dog raced through sawdust and shavings, down an alley, round a passage, between two wood-piles, and finally, with a triumphant yelp, sprang upon a large barrel which still stood upon the hand-trolley on which it had been brought. With lolling tongue and blinking eyes, Toby stood upon the cask, looking from one to the other of us for some sign of appreciation. The staves of the barrel and the wheels of the trolley were smeared with a dark liquid, and the whole air was heavy with the smell of creosote.

Sherlock Holmes and I looked blankly at each other, and then burst simultaneously into an uncontrollable fit of laughter.

8

The Baker Street Irregulars

'What now?' I asked. 'Toby has lost his character for infallibility.'

'He acted according to his lights,' said Holmes, lifting him down from the barrel and walking him out of the timber-yard. 'If you consider how much creosote is carted about London in one day, it is no great wonder that our trail should have been crossed. It is much used now, especially for the seasoning of wood. Poor Toby is not to blame.'

'We must get on the main scent again, I suppose.'

'Yes. And, fortunately, we have no distance to go. Evidently what puzzled the dog at the corner of Knight's Place was that there were two different trails running in opposite directions. We took the wrong one. It only remains to follow the other.'

There was no difficulty about this. On being led to the place where he had committed his fault, Toby cast about in a wide circle and finally dashed off in a fresh direction.

'We must take care that he does not now bring us to the place where the creosote-barrel came from,' I observed.

'I had thought of that. But you notice that he keeps on the pavement, whereas the barrel passed down the roadway. No, we are on the true scent now.'

It tended down towards the riverside, running through Belmont Place and Prince's Street. At the end of Broad Street it ran right down to the water's edge, where there was a small wooden wharf. Toby led us to the very edge of this, and there stood whining, looking out on the dark current beyond.

'We are out of luck,' said Holmes. ' They have taken to a boat here.'

Several small punts and skiffs were lying about in the water and on the edge of the wharf. We took Toby round to each in turn, but though he sniffed earnestly, he made no sign.

Close to the rude landing-stage was a small brick house, with a wooden placard slung out through the second window. Mordecai Smith was printed across it in large letters, and underneath, *Boats to hire by the hour or day*. A second inscription above the door informed us that a steam launch was kept – a statement which was confirmed by a great pile of coke upon the jetty. Sherlock Holmes looked slowly round, and his face assumed an ominous expression.

'This looks bad,' said he. 'These fellows are sharper than I expected. They seem to have covered their tracks. There has, I fear, been preconcerted management here.'

He was approaching the door of the house, when it opened, and a little curly-headed lad of six came running out, followed by a stoutish, red-faced woman with a large sponge in her hand.

'You come back and be washed, Jack,' she shouted. 'Come back, you young imp; for if your father comes home and finds you like that, he'll let us hear of it.'

'Dear little chap!' cried Holmes, strategically. 'What a rosy-cheeked young rascal! Now, Jack, is there anything you would like?'

The youth pondered for a moment.

'I'd like a shillin',' said he.

'Nothing you would like better?'

'I'd like two shillin' better,' the prodigy answered, after some thought.

'Here you are, then! Catch! – A fine child, Mrs Smith!'

'Lor' bless you, sir, he is that, and forward. He gets almost too much for me to manage, 'specially when my man is away days at a time.'

'Away, is he?' said Holmes, in a disappointed voice. 'I am sorry for that, for I wanted to speak to Mr Smith.'

'He's been away since yesterday mornin', sir, and, truth to tell, I am beginning to feel frightened about him. But if it was about a boat, sir, maybe I could serve as well.'

'I wanted to hire his steam launch.'

'Why, bless you, sir, it is in the steam launch that he has gone. That's what puzzles me; for I know there ain't more coals in her than would take her to about Woolwich and back. If he'd been away in the barge I'd ha' thought nothin'; for many a time a job has taken him as far as Gravesend, and then if there was much doin' there he might ha' stayed over. But what good is a steam launch without coals?'

'He might have bought some at a wharf down the river.'

'He might, sir, but it weren't his way. Many a time I've heard him call out at the prices they charge for a few odd bags. Besides, I don't like that wooden-legged man, wi' his ugly face and outlandish talk. What did he want always knockin' about here for?'

'A wooden-legged man?' said Holmes, with bland surprise.

'Yes, sir, a brown, monkey-faced chap that's called more'n once for my old man. It was him that roused him up yesternight, and, what's more, my man knew he was comin', for he had steam up in the launch. I tell you straight, sir, I don't feel easy in my mind about it.'

'But, my dear Mrs Smith,' said Holmes, shrugging his shoulders, 'you are frightening yourself about nothing. How could you possibly tell that it was the wooden-legged man who came in the night? I don't quite understand how you can be so sure.'

'His voice, sir. I knew his voice, which is kind o' thick and foggy. He tapped at the winder – about three it would be. "Show a leg, matey," says he: "time to turn out guard." My old man woke up Jim – that's my eldest – and away they went, without so much as a word to me. I could hear the wooden leg clackin' on the stones.'

'And was this wooden-legged man alone?'

'Couldn't say, I am sure, sir. I didn't hear no one else.'

'I am sorry, Mrs Smith, for I wanted a steam launch, and I have heard good reports of the – Let me see, what is her name?'

'The *Aurora*, sir.'

'Ah! She's not that old green launch with a yellow line, very broad in the beam?'

'No, indeed. She's as trim a little thing as any on the river. She's been fresh painted, black with two red streaks.'

'Thanks. I hope that you will hear soon from Mr Smith. I am going down the river, and if I should see anything of the *Aurora* I shall let him know that you are uneasy. A black funnel, you say?'

'No, sir. Black with a white band.'

'Ah, of course. It was the sides which were black. Good-morning, Mrs Smith. There is a boatman here with a wherry, Watson. We shall take it and cross the river.'

'The main thing with people of that sort,' said Holmes, as we sat in the sheets of the wherry, 'is never to let them think that their information can be of the slightest importance to you. If you do, they will instantly shut up like an oyster. If you listen to them under protest, as it were, you are very likely to get what you want.'

'Our course now seems pretty clear,' said I.

'What would you do, then?'

'I would engage a launch and go down the river on the track of the *Aurora*.'

'My dear fellow, it would be a colossal task. She may have touched at any wharf on either side of the stream between here and Greenwich. Below the bridge there is a perfect labyrinth of landing-places for miles. It would take you days and days to exhaust them, if you set about it alone.'

'Employ the police, then.'

'No. I shall probably call Athelney Jones in at the last moment. He is not a bad fellow, and I should not like to do anything which would injure him professionally. But I have a fancy for working it out myself, now that we have gone so far.'

'Could we advertise, then, asking for information from wharfingers?'

'Worse and worse! Our men would know that the chase was hot at their heels, and they would be off out of the country. As it is, they are likely enough to leave, but as long as they think they are perfectly safe they will be in no hurry. Jones's energy will be of use to us there, for his view of the case is sure to push itself into the daily press, and the runaways will think that everyone is off on the wrong scent.'

'What are we to do, then?' I asked, as we landed near Millbank Penitentiary.

'Take this hansom, drive home, have some breakfast, and get an hour's sleep. It is quite on the cards that we may be afoot tonight again. Stop at a telegraph-office, cabby! We will keep Toby, for he may be of use to us yet.'

We pulled up at the Great Peter Street post-office, and Holmes dispatched his wire.

'Whom do you think that is to?' he asked, as we resumed our journey.

'I am sure I don't know.'

'You remember the Baker Street division of the detective police force whom I employed in the Jefferson Hope case?'

'Well?' said I, laughing.

'This is just the case where they might be invaluable. If they fail, I have other resources; but I shall try them first. That wire was to my dirty little lieutenant, Wiggins, and I expect that he and his gang will be with us before we have finished our breakfast.'

It was between eight and nine o'clock now, and I was conscious of a strong reaction after the successive excitements of the night. I was limp and weary, befogged in mind and fatigued in body. I had not the professional enthusiasm which carried my companion on, nor could I look at the matter as a mere abstract intellectual problem. As far as the death of Bartholomew Sholto went, I had heard little good of him, and could feel no intense antipathy to his murderers. The treasure, however, was a different matter. That, or part of it, belonged rightfully to Miss Morstan. While there was a chance of recovering it I was ready to devote my life to the one object. True, if I found it, it would probably put her for ever beyond my reach. Yet it would be a petty and selfish love which would be influenced by such a thought as that. If Holmes could work to find the criminals, I had a tenfold stronger reason to urge me on to find the treasure.

A bath at Baker Street and a complete change freshened me up wonderfully. When I came down to our room I found the breakfast laid and Holmes pouring out the coffee.

'Here it is,' said he, laughing and pointing to an open newspaper. 'The energetic Jones and the ubiquitous reporter have fixed it up between them. But you have had enough of the case. Better have your ham and eggs first.'

I took the paper from him and read the short notice, which was headed: Mysterious Business at Upper Norwood.

About twelve o'clock last night [said the *Standard*], Mr Bartholomew Sholto, of Pondicherry Lodge, Upper Norwood, was found dead in his room under circumstances which point to foul play. As far as we can learn, no actual traces of violence were found upon Mr Sholto's person, but a valuable collection of Indian gems which the deceased gentleman had inherited from his father has been carried off. The discovery was first made by Mr Sherlock Holmes and Dr Watson, who had called at the house with Mr Thaddeus Sholto, brother of the deceased. By a singular piece of good fortune, Mr Athelney Jones, the well-known member of

the detective police force, happened to be at the Norwood Police
Station, and was on the ground within half an hour of the first
alarm. His trained and experienced faculties were at once directed
towards the detection of the criminals, with the gratifying result
that the brother, Thaddeus Sholto, has already been arrested,
together with the housekeeper, Mrs Bernstone, an Indian butler
named Lal Rao, and a porter, or gatekeeper, named McMurdo. It
is quite certain that the thief or thieves were well acquainted with
the house, for Mr Jones's well-known technical knowledge and
his powers of minute observation have enabled him to prove conclusively that the miscreants could not have entered by the door
or by the window, but must have made their way across the roof
of the building, and so through a trap-door into a room which
communicated with that in which the body was found. This fact,
which has been very clearly made out, proves conclusively that
it was no mere haphazard burglary. The prompt and energetic
action of the officers of the law shows the great advantage of the
presence on such occasions of a single vigorous and masterful
mind. We cannot but think that it supplies an argument to those
who would wish to see our detectives more decentralised and so
brought into closer and more effective touch with the cases which
it is their duty to investigate.

'Isn't it gorgeous?' said Holmes, grinning over his coffee cup.
'What do you think of it?'

'I think that we have had a close shave ourselves of being arrested
for the crime.'

'So do I. I wouldn't answer for our safety now, if he should happen
to have another of his attacks of energy.'

At this moment there was a loud ring at the bell, and I could hear
Mrs Hudson, our landlady, raising her voice in a wail of expostulation
and dismay.

'By heavens, Holmes,' said I, half rising, 'I believe that they are
really after us.'

'No, it's not quite so bad as that. It is the unofficial force – the Baker Street irregulars.'

As he spoke, there came a swift pattering of naked feet upon the stairs, a clatter of high voices, and in rushed a dozen dirty and ragged little street arabs. There was some show of discipline among them, despite their tumultuous entry, for they instantly drew up in line and stood facing us with expectant faces. One of their number, taller and older than the others, stood forward with an air of lounging superiority which was very funny in such a disreputable little scarecrow.

'Got your message, sir,' said he, 'and brought 'em on sharp. Three bob and a tanner for tickets.'

'Here you are,' said Holmes, producing some silver. 'In future they can report to you, Wiggins, and you to me. I cannot have the house invaded in this way. However, it is just as well that you should all hear the instructions. I want to find the whereabouts of a steam launch called the *Aurora*, owner Mordecai Smith, black with two red streaks, funnel black with a white band. She is down the river somewhere. I want one boy to be at Mordecai Smith's landing-stage opposite Millbank to say if the boat comes back. You must divide it out among yourselves, and do both banks thoroughly. Let me know the moment you have news. Is that all clear?'

'Yes, guv'nor,' said Wiggins.

'The old scale of pay, and a guinea to the boy who finds the boat. Here's a day in advance. Now, off you go!'

He handed them a shilling each, and away they buzzed down the stairs, and I saw them a moment later streaming down the street.

'If the launch is above water they will find her,' said Holmes, as he rose from the table and lit his pipe. 'They can go everywhere, see everything, overhear everyone. I expect to hear before evening that they have spotted her. In the meanwhile, we can do nothing but await results. We cannot pick up the broken trail until we find either the *Aurora* or Mr Mordecai Smith.'

'Toby could eat these scraps, I dare say. Are you going to bed, Holmes?'

'No; I am not tired. I have a curious constitution. I never remember feeling tired by work, though idleness exhausts me completely. I am going to smoke and to think over this queer business to which my fair client has introduced us. If ever man had an easy task, this of ours ought to be. Wooden–legged men are not so common, but the other man must, I should think, be absolutely unique.'

'That other man again!'

'I have no wish to make a mystery of him to you, anyway. But you must have formed your own opinion. Now, do consider the data. Diminutive footmarks, toes never fettered by boots, naked feet, stone-headed wooden mace, great agility, small poisoned darts. What do you make of all this?'

'A savage!' I exclaimed. 'Perhaps one of those Indians who were the associates of Jonathan Small.'

'Hardly that,' said he. 'When first I saw signs of strange weapons, I was inclined to think so; but the remarkable character of the foot-marks caused me to reconsider my views. Some of the inhabitants of the Indian Peninsula are small men, but none could have left such marks as that. The Hindu proper has long and thin feet. The sandal-wearing Mohammedan has the great toe well separated from the others, because the thong is commonly passed between. These little darts, too, could only be shot in one way. They are from a blow-pipe. Now, then, where are we to find our savage?'

'South America,' I hazarded.

He stretched his hand up, and took down a bulky volume from the shelf.

'This is the first volume of a gazetteer which is now being published. It may be looked upon as the very latest authority. What have we here? "Andaman Islands, situated 340 miles to the north of Sumatra, in the Bay of Bengal." Hum! hum! What's all this? Moist climate, coral reefs, sharks, Port Blair, convict barracks, Rutland Island, cottonwoods – Ah, here we are! "The aborigines of the Andaman Islands may perhaps claim the distinction of being the smallest race upon this earth, though some anthropologists prefer the Bushmen of Africa, the Digger Indians of America, and the Tierra del Fuegians. The average height is rather below four feet, although many full-grown adults may be found who are very much smaller than this. They are a fierce, morose and intractable people, though capable of forming most devoted friendships when their confidence has once been gained." Mark that, Watson. Now, then, listen to this. "They are naturally hideous, having large, misshapen heads, small, fierce eyes and distorted features. Their feet and hands, however, are remarkably small. So intractable and fierce are they, that all the efforts of the British officials have failed to win them over in any degree. They have always been a terror to shipwrecked crews, braining the survivors with their stone-headed clubs or shooting them with their poisoned arrows. These massacres are invariably concluded by a cannibal feast." Nice, amiable people, Watson! If this fellow had been left to his own unaided devices, this affair might have taken an even more ghastly turn. I fancy that, even as it is, Jonathan Small would give a good deal not to have employed him.'

'But how came he to have so singular a companion?'

'Ah, that is more than I can tell. Since, however, we had already determined that Small had come from the Andamans, it is not so very wonderful that this islander should be with him. No doubt we shall know all about it in time. Look here, Watson; you look regularly done. Lie down there on the sofa, and see if I can put you to sleep.'

He took up his violin from the corner, and as I stretched myself out he began to play some low, dreamy, melodious air – his own, no doubt, for he had a remarkable gift for improvisation. I have a vague remembrance of his gaunt limbs, his earnest face, and the rise and fall of his bow. Then I seemed to be floated peacefully away upon a soft sea of sound, until I found myself in dreamland, with the sweet face of Mary Morstan looking down upon me.

9

A Break in the Chain

It was lte in the afternoon before I woke, strengthened and refreshed. Sherlock Holmes still sat exactly as I had left him, save that he had laid aside his violin and was deep in a book. He looked across at me as I stirred, and I noticed that his face was dark and troubled.

'You have slept soundly,' he said. 'I feared that our talk would wake you.'

'I heard nothing,' I answered. 'Have you had fresh news, then?'

'Unfortunately, no. I confess that I am surprised and disappointed. I expected something definite by this time. Wiggins has just been up to report. He says that no trace can be found of the launch. It is a provoking check, for every hour is of importance.'

'Can I do anything? I am perfectly fresh now, and quite ready for another night's outing.'

'No; we can do nothing. We can only wait. If we go ourselves, the message might come in our absence, and delay be caused. You can do what you will, but I must remain on guard.'

'Then I shall run over to Camberwell and call upon Mrs Cecil Forrester. She asked me to yesterday.'

'On Mrs Cecil Forrester?' asked Holmes with the twinkle of a smile in his eyes.

'Well, of course, on Miss Morstan too. They were to hear what happened.'

'I would not tell them too much,' said Holmes. 'Women are never to be entirely trusted – not the best of them.'

I did not pause to argue over this atrocious sentiment.

'I shall be back in an hour or two,' I remarked.

'All right! Good luck! But, I say, if you are crossing the water you may as well return Toby, for I don't think it is at all likely that we shall have any use for him now.'

I took our mongrel accordingly, and left him, together with a half-sovereign, at the old naturalist's in Pinchin Lane. At Camberwell I found Miss Morstan a little weary after her night's adventures, but very eager to hear the news. Mrs Forrester, too, was full of curiosity. I told them all that we had done, suppressing, however, the more dreadful parts of the tragedy. Thus, although I spoke of Mr Sholto's death, I said nothing of the exact manner and method of it. With all my omissions, however, there was enough to startle and amaze them.

'It is a romance!' cried Mrs Forrester. 'An injured lady, half a million in treasure, a black cannibal and a wooden-legged ruffian. They take the place of the conventional dragon or wicked earl.'

'And two knight-errants to the rescue,' added Miss Morstan, with a bright glance at me.

'Why, Mary, your fortune depends upon the issue of this search. I don't think that you are nearly excited enough. Just imagine what it must be to be so rich, and to have the world at your feet!'

It sent a little thrill of joy to my heart to notice that she showed no sign of elation at the prospect. On the contrary, she gave a toss of her proud head, as though the matter were one in which she took small interest.

'It is for Mr Thaddeus Sholto that I am anxious,' she said. 'Nothing else is of any consequence; but I think that he has behaved most kindly and honourably throughout. It is our duty to clear him of this dreadful and unfounded charge.'

It was evening before I left Camberwell, and quite dark by the time I reached home. My companion's book and pipe lay by his chair, but he had disappeared. I looked about in the hope of seeing a note, but there was none.

'I suppose that Mr Sherlock Holmes has gone out?' I said to Mrs Hudson as she came up to lower the blinds.

'No, sir. He has gone to his room, sir. Do you know, sir,' sinking her voice into an impressive whisper, 'I am afraid for his health.'

'Why so, Mrs Hudson?'

'Well, he's that strange, sir. After you was gone he walked and he walked, up and down and up and down, until I was weary of the sound of his footstep. Then I heard him talking to himself and muttering, and every time the bell rang out he came on the stairhead with, "What is that, Mrs Hudson?" And now he has slammed off to his room, but I can hear him walking away the same as ever. I hope he's not going to be ill, sir. I ventured to say something to him about cooling medicine, but he turned on me, sir, with such a look that I don't know however I got out of the room.'

'I don't think that you have any cause to be uneasy, Mrs Hudson,' I answered. 'I have seen him like this before. He has some small matter upon his mind which makes him restless.'

I tried to speak lightly to our worthy landlady, but I was myself somewhat uneasy when through the long night I still from time to time heard the dull sound of his tread, and knew how his keen spirit was chafing against this involuntary inaction.

At breakfast-time he looked worn and haggard, with a little fleck of feverish colour upon either cheek.

'You are knocking yourself up, old man,' I remarked. 'I heard you marching about in the night.'

'No, I could not sleep,' he answered. 'This infernal problem is consuming me. It is too much to be baulked by so petty an obstacle, when all else had been overcome. I know the men, the launch, everything; and yet I can get no news. I have set other agencies at work, and used every means at my disposal. The whole river has been searched on either side, but there is no news, nor has Mrs Smith heard of her husband. I shall come to the conclusion soon that they have scuttled the craft. But there are objections to that.'

'Or that Mrs Smith has put us on a wrong scent.'

'No, I think that may be dismissed. I had enquiries made and there is a launch of that description.'

'Could it have gone up the river?'

'I have considered that possibility too, and there is a search-party who will work up as far as Richmond. If no news comes today, I shall start off myself tomorrow, and go for the men rather than the boat. But surely, surely, we shall hear something.'

We did not, however. Not a word came to us either from Wiggins or from the other agencies. There were articles in most of the papers upon the Norwood tragedy. They all appeared to be rather hostile to the unfortunate Thaddeus Sholto. No fresh details were to be found, however, in any of them, save that an inquest was to be held upon the following day. I walked over to Camberwell in the evening to report our ill-success to the ladies, and on my return I found Holmes dejected and somewhat morose. He would hardly reply to my questions, and busied himself all the evening in an abstruse chemical analysis which involved much heating of retorts and distilling of vapours, ending at last in a smell which fairly drove me out of the apartment. Up to the small hours of the morning I could hear the clinking of his test-tubes, which told me that he was still engaged in his malodorous experiment.

In the early dawn I woke with a start, and was surprised to find him standing by my bedside, clad in a rude sailor dress with a pea-jacket and a coarse red scarf round his neck.

'I am off down the river, Watson,' said he. 'I have been turning it over in my mind, and I can see only one way out of it. It is worth trying, at all events.'

'Surely I can come with you, then?' said I.

'No; you can be much more useful if you will remain here as my representative. I am loath to go, for it is quite on the cards that some message may come during the day, though Wiggins was despondent about it last night. I want you to open all notes and telegrams, and to act on your own judgement if any news should come. Can I rely upon you?'

'Most certainly.'

'I am afraid that you will not be able to wire to me, for I can hardly tell yet where I may find myself. If I am in luck, however, I may not be gone so very long. I shall have news of some sort or other before I get back.'

I had heard nothing of him by breakfast-time. On opening the *Standard*, however, I found that there was a fresh allusion to the business.

With reference to the Upper Norwood tragedy [it remarked], we have reason to believe that the matter promises to be even more complex and mysterious than was originally supposed. Fresh evidence has shown that it is quite impossible that Mr Thaddeus Sholto could have been in any way concerned in the matter. He and the housekeeper, Mrs Bernstone, were both released yesterday evening. It is believed, however, that the police have a clue as to the real culprits, and that it is being prosecuted by Mr Athelney Jones, of Scotland Yard, with all his well-known energy and sagacity. Further arrests may be expected at any moment.

'That is satisfactory so far as it goes,' thought I. 'Friend Sholto is safe, at any rate. I wonder what the fresh clue may be, though it seems to be a stereotyped form whenever the police have made a blunder.'

I tossed the paper down upon the table, but at that moment my eye caught an advertisement in the agony column. It ran in this way:

Lost – Whereas Mordecai Smith, boatman, and his son Jim, left Smith's Wharf at or about three o'clock last Tuesday morning in the steam launch *Aurora*, black with two red stripes, funnel black with a white band, the sum of five pounds will be paid to anyone who can give information to Mrs Smith, at Smith's Wharf or at 221b Baker Street, as to the whereabouts of the said Mordecai Smith and the launch *Aurora*.

This was clearly Holmes's doing. The Baker Street address was enough to prove that. It struck me as rather ingenious, because it might be read by the fugitives without their seeing in it more than the natural anxiety of a wife for her missing husband.

It was a long day. Every time that a knock came to the door or a sharp step passed in the street, I imagined that it was either Holmes returning or an answer to his advertisement. I tried to read, but my thoughts would wander oft to our strange quest and to the ill-assorted and villainous pair whom we were pursuing. Could there be, I wondered, some radical flaw in my companion's reasoning? Might he not be suffering from some huge self-deception? Was it not possible that his nimble and speculative mind had built up this wild theory upon faulty premises? I had never known him to be wrong, and yet the keenest reasoner may occasionally be deceived. He was likely, I thought, to fall into error through the over-refinement of his logic – his preference for a subtle and bizarre explanation when a plainer and more commonplace one lay ready to his hand. Yet, on the other hand, I had myself seen the evidence, and I had heard the reasons for his deductions. When I looked back on the long chain of curious circumstances, many of them trivial in themselves, but all tending in the same direction, I could not disguise from myself that even if Holmes's explanation were incorrect the true theory must be equally outrÈ and startling.

At three o'clock in the afternoon there was a loud peal at the bell, an authoritative voice in the hall, and, to my surprise, no less a person than Mr Athelney Jones was shown up to me. Very different was he, however, from the brusque and masterful professor of common sense who had taken over the case so confidently at Upper Norwood. His expression was downcast, and his bearing meek and even apologetic.

'Good-day, sir; good-day,' said he. 'Mr Sherlock Holmes is out, I understand?'

'Yes, and I cannot be sure when he will be back. But perhaps you would care to wait. Take that chair and try one of these cigars.'

'Thank you; I don't mind if I do,' said he, mopping his face with a red bandanna handkerchief.

'And a whisky and soda?'

'Well, half a glass. It is very hot for the time of year; and I have had a good deal to worry and try me. You know my theory about this Norwood case?'

'I remember that you expressed one.'

'Well, I have been obliged to reconsider it. I had my net drawn tightly round Mr Sholto, sir, when pop he went through a hole in the middle of it. He was able to prove an alibi which could not be shaken. From the time that he left his brother's room he was never out of sight of someone or other. So it could not be he who climbed over roofs and through trap-doors. It's a very dark case, and my professional credit is at stake. I should be very glad of a little assistance.'

'We all need help sometimes,' said I.

'Your friend Mr Sherlock Holmes is a wonderful man, sir,' said he, in a husky and confidential voice. 'He's a man who is not to be beat. I have known that young man go into a good many cases, but I never saw the case yet that he could not throw a light upon. He is irregular in his methods, and a little quick perhaps in jumping at theories; but, on the whole, I think he would have made a most promising officer and I don't care who knows it. I have had a wire from him this morning, by which I understand that he has got some clue to this Sholto business. Here is his message.'

He took the telegram out of his pocket, and handed it to me. It was dated from Poplar at twelve o'clock. 'Go to Baker Street at once,' it said. 'If I have not returned, wait for me. I am close on the track of the Sholto gang. You can come with us tonight if you want to be in at the finish.'

'This sounds well. He has evidently picked up the scent again,' said I.

'Ah, then he has been at fault too,' exclaimed Jones, with evident satisfaction. 'Even the best of us are thrown off sometimes. Of course this may prove to be a false alarm; but it is my duty as an officer of the law to allow no chance to slip. But there is someone at the door. Perhaps this is he.'

A heavy step was heard ascending the stair, with a great wheezing and rattling as from a man who was sorely put to it for breath. Once or twice he stopped, as though the climb were too much for him, but at last he made his way to our door and entered. His appearance corresponded to the sounds which we had heard. He was an aged man, clad in seafaring garb, with an old pea-jacket buttoned up to his throat. His back was bowed, his knees were shaky, and his breathing was painfully asthmatic. As he leaned upon a thick oaken cudgel, his shoulders heaved in the effort to draw the air into his lungs. He had a coloured scarf round his chin, and I could see little of his face save a pair of keen dark eyes overhung by bushy white brows, and long grey side-whiskers. Altogether he gave me the impression of a respectable master mariner who had fallen into years and poverty.

'What is it, my man?' I asked.

He looked about him in the slow methodical fashion of old age.

'Is Mr Sherlock Holmes here?' said he.

'No; but I am acting for him. You can tell me any message you have for him.'

'It was to him himself I was to tell it,' said he.

'But I tell you I am acting for him. Was it about Mordecai Smith's boat?'

'Yes. I knows well where it is. An' I knows where the men he is after are. An' I knows where the treasure is. I knows all about it.'

'Then tell me, and I shall let him know.'

'It was to him I was to tell it,' he repeated, with the petulant obstinacy of a very old man.

'Well, you must wait for him.'

'No, no; I ain't goin' to lose a whole day to please no one. If Mr Holmes ain't here, then Mr Holmes must find it all out for himself. I don't care about the look of either of you, and I won't tell a word.'

He shuffled towards the door, but Athelney Jones got in front of him.

'Wait a bit, my friend,' said he. 'You have important information, and you must not walk off. We shall keep you, whether you like it or not, until our friend returns.'

The old man made a little run towards the door, but as Athelney Jones put his broad back up against it he recognised the uselessness of resistance.

'Pretty sort o' treatment this!' he cried, stamping his stick. 'I come here to see a gentleman, and you two, who I never saw in my life, seize me and treat me in this fashion!'

'You will be none the worse,' I said. 'We shall recompense you for the loss of your time. Sit over here on the sofa, and you will not have long to wait.'

He came across sullenly enough, and seated himself with his face resting on his hands. Jones and I resumed our cigars and our talk. Suddenly, however, Holmes's voice broke in upon us.

'I think that you might offer me a cigar too,' he said.

We both started in our chairs. There was Holmes sitting close to us with an air of quiet amusement.

'Holmes!' I exclaimed. 'You here! But where is the old man?'

'Here is the old man,' said he, holding out a heap of white hair. 'Here he is – wig, whiskers, eyebrows and all. I thought my disguise was pretty good, but I hardly expected that it would stand that test.'

'Ah, you rogue!' cried Jones, highly delighted. 'You would have made an actor, and a rare one. You had the proper workhouse cough, and those weak legs of yours are worth ten pounds a week. I thought I knew the glint of your eye, though. You didn't get away from us so easily, you see.'

'I have been working in that get-up all day,' said he, lighting his cigar. 'You see, a good many of the criminal classes begin to know me – especially since our friend here took to publishing some of my cases: so I can only go on the war-path under some simple disguise like this. You got my wire?'

'Yes; that was what brought me here.'

'How has your case prospered?'

'It has all come to nothing. I have had to release two of my prisoners, and there is no evidence against the other two.'

'Never mind. We shall give you two others in the place of them. But you must put yourself under my orders. You are welcome to all the official credit, but you must act on the lines that I point out. Is that agreed?'

'Entirely, if you will help me to the men.'

'Well, then, in the first place I shall want a fast police boat – a steam launch – to be at the Westminster Stairs at seven o'clock.'

'That is easily managed. There is always one about there; but I can step across the road and telephone to make sure.'

'Then I shall want two staunch men, in case of resistance.'

'There will be two or three in the boat. What else?'

'When we secure the men we shall get the treasure. I think that it would be a pleasure to my friend here to take the box round to the young lady to whom half of it rightfully belongs. Let her be the first to open it. Eh, Watson?'

'It would be a great pleasure to me.'

'Rather an irregular proceeding,' said Jones, shaking his head. 'However, the whole thing is irregular, and I suppose we must wink at it. The treasure must afterwards be handed over to the authorities until after the official investigation.'

'Certainly. That is easily managed. One other point. I should much like to have a few details about this matter from the lips of Jonathan Small himself. You know I like to work the details of my cases out. There is no objection to my having an unofficial interview with him, either here in my rooms or elsewhere, as long as he is efficiently guarded?'

'Well, you are master of the situation. I have had no proof yet of the existence of this Jonathan Small. However, if you can catch him, I don't see how I can refuse you an interview with him.'

'That is understood, then?'

'Perfectly. Is there anything else?'

'Only that I insist upon your dining with us. It will be ready in half an hour. I have oysters and a brace of grouse, with something a little choice in white wines. Watson, you have never yet recognised my merits as a housekeeper.'

10

The End of the Islander

Our meal was a merry one. Holmes could talk exceedingly well when he chose, and that night he did choose. He appeared to be in a state of nervous exaltation. I have never known him so brilliant. He spoke on a quick succession of subjects – on miracle plays, on medieval pottery, on Stradivarius violins, on the Buddhism of Ceylon, and on the warships of the future – handling each as though he had made a special study of it. His bright humour marked the reaction from his black depression of the preceding days. Athelney Jones proved to be a sociable soul in his hours of relaxation, and faced his dinner with the air of a *bon vivant*. For myself, I felt elated at the thought that we were nearing the end of our task, and I caught something of Holmes's gaiety. None of us alluded during dinner to the cause which had brought us together.

When the cloth was cleared, Holmes glanced at his watch, and filled up three glasses with port.

'One bumper,' said he, 'to the success of our little expedition. And now it is high time we were off. Have you a pistol, Watson?'

'I have my old service-revolver in my desk.'

'You had best take it, then. It is well to be prepared. I see that the cab is at the door. I ordered it for half-past six.'

It was a little past seven before we reached the Westminster Wharf, and found our launch awaiting us. Holmes eyed it critically.

'Is there anything to mark it as a police-boat?'

'Yes; that green lamp at the side.'

'Then take it off.'

The small change was made, we stepped on board, and the ropes were cast off. Jones, Holmes and I sat in the stern. There was one man at the rudder, one to tend the engines, and two burly police inspectors forward.

'Where to?' asked Jones.

'To the Tower. Tell them to stop opposite to Jacobson's Yard.'

Our craft was evidently a very fast one. We shot past the long lines of loaded barges as though they were stationary. Holmes smiled with satisfaction as we overhauled a river steamer and left her behind us.

'We ought to be able to catch anything on the river,' he said.

'Well, hardly that. But there are not many launches to beat us.'

'We shall have to catch the *Aurora*, and she has a name for being a clipper. I will tell you how the land lies, Watson. You recollect how annoyed I was at being baulked by so small a thing?'

'Yes.'

'Well, I gave my mind a thorough rest by plunging into a chemical analysis. One of our greatest statesmen has said that a change of work is the best rest. So it is. When I had succeeded in dissolving the hydrocarbon which I was at work at, I came back to the problem of the Sholtos, and thought the whole matter out again. My boys had been up the river and down the river without result. The launch was not at any landing-stage or wharf, nor had it returned. Yet it could hardly have been scuttled to hide their traces, though that always remained as a possible hypothesis if all else failed. I knew that this man Small had a certain degree of low cunning, but I did not think him capable of anything in the nature of delicate finesse. That is usually a product of higher education. I then reflected that since he had certainly been in London some time – as we had evidence that he maintained a continual watch over Pondicherry Lodge – he could hardly leave at a moment's notice, but would need some little time, if it were only a day, to arrange his affairs. That was the balance of probability, at any rate.'

'It seems to me to be a little weak,' said I: 'it is more probable that he had arranged his affairs before ever he set out upon his expedition.'

'No, I hardly think so. This lair of his would be too valuable a retreat in case of need for him to give it up until he was sure that he could do without it. But a second consideration struck me. Jonathan

Small must have felt that the peculiar appearance of his companion, however much he may have top-coated him, would give rise to gossip, and possibly be associated with this Norwood tragedy. He was quite sharp enough to see that. They had started from their headquarters under cover of darkness, and he would wish to get back before it was broad light. Now, it was past three o'clock, according to Mrs Smith, when they got the boat. It would be quite bright, and people would be about in an hour or so. Therefore, I argued, they did not go very far. They paid Smith well to hold his tongue, reserved his launch for the final escape and hurried to their lodgings with the treasure-box. In a couple of nights, when they had time to see what view the papers took, and whether there was any suspicion, they would make their way under cover of darkness to some ship at Gravesend or in the Downs, where no doubt they had already arranged for passages to America or the Colonies.'

'But the launch? They could not have taken that to their lodgings.'

'Quite so. I argued that the launch must be no great way off, in spite of its invisibility. I then put myself in the place of Small, and looked at it as a man of his capacity would. He would probably consider that to send back the launch or to keep it at a wharf would make pursuit easy if the police did happen to get on his track. How, then, could he conceal the launch and yet have her at hand when wanted? I wondered what I should do myself if I were in his shoes. I could only think of one way of doing it. I might hand the launch over to some boat-builder or repairer, with directions to make a trifling change in her. She would then be removed to his shed or yard, and so be effectually concealed, while at the same time I could have her at a few hours' notice.'

'That seems simple enough.'

'It is just these very simple things which are extremely liable to be overlooked. However, I determined to act on the idea. I started at once, in this harmless seaman's rig, and enquired at all the yards down the river. I drew blank at fifteen but at the sixteenth – Jacobson's – I learned that the *Aurora* had been handed over to them two days ago by a wooden-legged man, with some trivial directions as to her rudder.

"There ain't naught amiss with her rudder," said the foreman. "There she lies, with the red streaks." At that moment who should come down but Mordecai Smith, the missing owner! He was rather the worse for liquor. I should not, of course, have known him, but he bellowed out his name and the name of his launch. "I want her tonight at eight o'clock," said he – "eight o'clock sharp, mind, for I have two gentlemen who won't be kept waiting." They had evidently paid him well, for he was very flush of money, chucking shillings about to the men. I followed him some distance, but he subsided into an alehouse; so I went back to the yard, and happening to pick up one of my boys on the way, I stationed him as a sentry over the launch. He is to stand at the water's edge and wave his handkerchief to us when they start. We shall be lying off in the stream, and it will be a strange thing if we do not take men, treasure and all.'

'You have planned it all very neatly, whether they are the right men or not,' said Jones; 'but if the affair were in my hands I should have had a body of police in Jacobson's Yard, and arrested them when they came down.'

'Which would have been never. This man Small is a pretty shrewd fellow. He would send a scout on ahead, and if anything made him suspicious he would lie snug for another week.'

'But you might have stuck to Mordecai Smith, and so been led to their hiding-place,' said I.

'In that case I should have wasted my day. I think that it is a hundred to one against Smith knowing where they live. As long as he has liquor and good pay, why should he ask questions? They send him messages what to do. No, I thought over every possible course, and this is the best.'

While this conversation had been proceeding, we had been shooting the long series of bridges which span the Thames. As we passed the City the last rays of the sun were gilding the cross upon the summit of St Paul's. It was twilight before we reached the Tower.

'That is Jacobson's Yard,' said Holmes, pointing to a bristle of masts and rigging on the Surrey side. 'Cruise gently up and down here under cover of this string of lighters.' He took a pair of night-glasses from his pocket and gazed some time at the shore. 'I see my sentry at his post,' he remarked, 'but no sign of a handkerchief.'

'Suppose we go downstream a short way and lie in wait for them,' said Jones, eagerly.

We were all eager by this time, even the policemen and stokers, who had a very vague idea of what was going forward.

'We have no right to take anything for granted,' Holmes answered. 'It is certainly ten to one that they go downstream, but we cannot be certain. From this point we can see the entrance of the yard, and they can hardly see us. It will be a clear night with plenty of light. We must stay where we are. See how the folk swarm over yonder in the gas-light.'

'They are coming from work in the yard.'

'Dirty-looking rascals, but I suppose everyone has some little immortal spark concealed about him. You would not think it, to look at them. There is no *a priori* probability about it. A strange enigma is man!'

'Someone calls him a soul concealed in an animal,' I suggested.

'Winwood Reade is good upon the subject,' said Holmes. 'He remarks that, while the individual man is an insoluble puzzle, in the aggregate he becomes a mathematical certainty. You can, for example, never foretell what any one man will do, but you can say with precision what an average number will be up to. Individuals vary, but percentages remain constant. So says the statistician. But do I see a handkerchief? Surely there is a white flutter over yonder.'

'Yes, it is your boy,' I cried. 'I can see him plainly.'

'And there is the *Aurora*,' exclaimed Holmes, 'and going like the devil! Full speed ahead, engineer. Make after that launch with the yellow light. By heaven, I shall never forgive myself if she proves to have the heels of us!'

She had slipped unseen through the yard-entrance and passed behind two or three small craft, so that she had fairly got her speed up before we saw her. Now she was flying down the stream, near in to the shore, going at a tremendous rate. Jones looked gravely at her and shook his head.

'She is very fast,' he said. 'I doubt if we shall catch her.'

'We *must* catch her!' cried Holmes, between his teeth. 'Heap it on, stokers! Make her do all she can! If we burn the boat, we must have them!'

We were fairly after her now. The furnaces roared, and the powerful engines whizzed and clanked, like a great metallic heart. Her sharp, steep prow cut through the still river-water and sent two rolling waves to right and to left of us. With every throb of the engines we sprang and quivered like a living thing. One great yellow lantern in our bows threw a long, flickering funnel of light in front of us. Right ahead a dark blur upon the water showed where the *Aurora* lay, and the swirl of white foam behind her spoke of the pace at which she was going. We flashed past barges, steamers, merchant vessels, in and out, behind this one and round the other. Voices hailed us out of the darkness, but still the *Aurora* thundered on, and still we followed close upon her track.

'Pile it on, men, pile it on!' cried Holmes, looking down into the engine-room, while the fierce glow from below beat upon his eager, aquiline face. 'Get every pound of steam you can.'

'I think we gain a little,' said Jones, with his eyes on the *Aurora*.

'I am sure of it,' said I. 'We shall be up with her in a very few minutes.'

At that moment, however, as our evil fate would have it, a tug with three barges in tow blundered in between us. It was only by putting our helm hard down that we avoided a collision and before we could round them and recover our way the *Aurora* had gained a good two hundred yards. She was still, however, well in view, and the murky, uncertain twilight was settling into a clear starlit night. Our boilers were strained to their utmost, and the frail shell vibrated and creaked with the fierce energy which was driving us along. We had shot through the Pool, past the West India Docks, down the long Deptford Reach, and up again after rounding the Isle of Dogs. The dull blur in front of us resolved itself now clearly enough into the dainty *Aurora*. Jones turned our searchlight upon her, so that we could plainly see the figures upon her deck. One man sat by the stern, with something

203

black between his knees, over which he stooped. Beside him lay a
dark mass, which looked like a Newfoundland dog. The boy held the
tiller, while against the red glare of the furnace I could see old Smith,
stripped to the waist and shovelling coals for dear life. They may have
had some doubt at first as to whether we were really pursuing them,
but now as we followed every winding and turning which they took
there could no longer be any question about it. At Greenwich we were
about three hundred paces behind them. At Blackwall we could not
have been more than two hundred and fifty. I have coursed many creatures in many countries during my chequered career, but never did
sport give me such a wild thrill as this mad, flying manhunt down the
Thames. Steadily we drew in upon them, yard by yard. In the silence
of the night we could hear the panting and clanking of their machinery. The man in the stern still crouched upon the deck, and his arms
were moving as though he were busy, while every now and then he
would look up and measure with a glance the distance which still separated us. Nearer we came and nearer. Jones yelled to them to stop. We
were not more than four boat's-lengths behind them, both boats flying
at a tremendous pace. It was a clear reach of the river, with Barking
Level upon one side and the melancholy Plumstead Marshes upon the
other. At our hail the man in the stern sprang up from the deck and
shook his two clenched fists at us, cursing the while in a high, cracked
voice. He was a good-sized, powerful man, and as he stood poising
himself with legs astride, I could see that, from the thigh downwards,
there was but a wooden stump upon the right side. At the sound of
his strident, angry cries, there was a movement in the huddled bundle
upon the deck. It straightened itself into a little black man – the smallest I have ever seen – with a great, misshapen head and a shock of
tangled dishevelled hair. Holmes had already drawn his revolver, and
I whipped out mine at the sight of this savage, distorted creature. He
was wrapped in some sort of a dark ulster or blanket, which left only
his face exposed; but that face was enough to give a man a sleepless
night. Never have I seen features so deeply marked with all bestiality
and cruelty. His small eyes glowed and burned with a sombre light,

and his thick lips were writhed back from his teeth, which grinned and chattered at us with half-animal fury.

'Fire if he raises his hand,' said Holmes quietly.

We were within a boat's-length by this time, and almost within touch of our quarry. I can see the two of them now as they stood: the white man with his legs far apart, shrieking out curses, and the unhallowed dwarf with his hideous face, and his strong, yellow teeth gnashing at us in the light of our lantern.

It was well that we had so clear a view of him. Even as we looked he plucked out from under his covering a short, round piece of wood, like a school ruler, and clapped it to his lips. Our pistols rang out together. He whirled round, threw up his arms and, with a kind of choking cough, fell sideways into the stream. I caught one glimpse of his venomous, menacing eyes amid the white swirl of the waters. At the same moment the wooden-legged man threw himself upon the rudder and put it hard down, so that his boat made straight in for the southern bank, while we shot past her stern, only clearing her by a few feet. We were round after her in an instant, but she was already nearly at the bank. It was a wild and desolate place, where the moon glimmered upon a wide expanse of marshland, with pools of stagnant water and beds of decaying vegetation. The launch, with a dull thud, ran up upon the mud-bank, with her bow in the air and her stern flush with the water. The fugitive sprang out, but his stump instantly sank its whole length into the sodden soil. In vain he struggled and writhed. Not one step could he possibly take either forwards or backwards. He yelled in impotent rage, and kicked frantically into the mud with his other foot; but his struggles only bored his wooden pin the deeper into the sticky bank. When we brought our launch alongside he was so firmly anchored that it was only by throwing the end of a rope over his shoulder that we were able to haul him out and to drag him like some evil fish over our side. The two Smiths, father and son, sat sullenly in their launch, but came aboard meekly enough when commanded. The *Aurora* herself we hauled off and made fast to our stern. A solid iron chest of Indian workmanship stood upon the deck. This, there could be no question, was the same that had contained the ill-omened treasure of the Sholtos. There was no key, but it was of considerable weight, so we transferred it carefully to our own little cabin. As we steamed slowly upstream again we flashed our searchlight in every direction, but there was no sign of the Islander. Somewhere in the dark ooze at the bottom of the Thames lie the bones of that strange visitor to our shores.

'See here,' said Holmes, pointing to the wooden hatchway. 'We were hardly quick enough with our pistols.' There, sure enough, just behind where we had been standing, stuck one of those murderous darts which we knew so well. It must have whizzed between us at the instant we fired. Holmes smiled at it and shrugged his shoulders in his easy fashion, but I confess that it turned me sick to think of the horrible death which had passed so close to us that night.

11

The Great Agra Treasure

Our captive sat in the cabin opposite to the iron box which he had done so much and waited so long to gain. He was a sunburned reckless-eyed fellow, with a network of lines and wrinkles all over his mahogany features which told of a hard, open-air life. There was a singular prominence about his bearded chin which marked a man who was not to be easily turned from his purpose. His age may have been fifty or thereabouts, for his black, curly hair was thickly shot with grey. His face in repose was not an unpleasing one, though his heavy brows and aggressive chin gave him, as I had lately seen, a terrible expression when moved to anger. He sat now with his handcuffed hands upon his lap, and his head sunk upon his breast, while he looked with his keen, twinkling eyes at the box which had been the cause of his ill-doings. It seemed to me that there was more sorrow than anger in his rigid and contained countenance. Once he looked up at me with a gleam of something like humour in his eyes.

'Well, Jonathan Small,' said Holmes, lighting a cigar, 'I am sorry that it has come to this.'

'And so am I, sir,' he answered, frankly. 'I don't believe that I can swing over the job. I give you my word on the Book that I never raised hand against Mr Sholto. It was that little hellhound Tonga who shot one of his cursed darts into him. I had no part in it, sir. I was as grieved as if it had been my blood-relation. I welted the little devil with the slack end of the rope for it, but it was done and I could not undo it again.'

'Have a cigar,' said Holmes; 'and you had best take a pull out of my flask, for you are very wet. How could you expect so small and weak a man as this black fellow to overpower Mr Sholto and hold him while you were climbing the rope?'

'You seem to know as much about it as if you were there, sir. The truth is that I hoped to find the room clear. I knew the habits of the house pretty well, and it was the time when Mr Sholto usually went down to his supper. I shall make no secret of the business. The best defence that I can make is just the simple truth. Now, if it had been the old major I would have swung for him with a light heart. I would have thought no more of knifing him than of smoking this cigar. But it's cursed hard that I should be lagged over this young Sholto with whom I had no quarrel whatever.'

'You are under the charge of Mr Athelney Jones, of Scotland Yard. He is going to bring you up to my rooms, and I shall ask you for a true account of the matter. You must make a clean breast of it, for if you do I hope that I may be of use to you. I think I can prove that the poison acts so quickly that the man was dead before ever you reached the room.'

'That he was, sir. I never got such a turn in my life as when I saw him grinning at me with his head on his shoulder as I climbed through the window. It fairly shook me, sir. I'd have half killed Tonga for it if he had not scrambled off. That was how he came to leave his club, and some of his darts, too, as he tells me, which I dare say helped to put you on our track; though how you kept on it is more than I can tell. I don't feel no malice against you for it. But it does seem a queer thing,' he added, with a bitter smile, 'that I, who have a fair claim to half a million of money, should spend the first half of my life building a breakwater in the Andamans, and am like to spend the other half digging drains at Dartmoor. It was an evil day for me when first I clapped eyes upon the merchant Achmet and had to do with the Agra treasure, which never brought anything but a curse yet upon the man who owned it. To him it brought murder, to Major Sholto it brought fear and guilt, to me it has meant slavery for life.'

At this moment Athelney Jones thrust his face and shoulders into the tiny cabin.

'Quite a family party,' he remarked. 'I think I shall have a pull at that flask, Holmes. Well, I think we may all congratulate each other. Pity we didn't take the other alive: but there was no choice. I say, Holmes, you must confess that you cut it rather fine. It was all we could do to overhaul her.'

'All is well that ends well,' said Holmes. 'But I certainly did not know that the *Aurora* was such a clipper.'

'Smith says she is one of the fastest launches on the river, and that if he had had another man to help him with the engines we should never have caught her. He swears he knew nothing of this Norwood business.'

'Neither he did,' cried our prisoner – 'not a word. I chose his launch because I heard that she was a flier. We told him nothing; but we paid him well, and he was to get something handsome if we reached our vessel, the *Esmeralda*, at Gravesend, outward bound for the Brazils.'

'Well, if he has done no wrong we shall see that no wrong comes to him. If we are pretty quick in catching our men, we are not so quick in condemning them.' It was amusing to notice how the consequential Jones was already beginning to give himself airs on the strength of the capture. From the slight smile which played over Sherlock Holmes's face, I could see that the speech had not been lost upon him.

'We will be at Vauxhall Bridge presently,' said Jones, 'and shall land you, Dr Watson, with the treasure-box. I need hardly tell you that I am taking a very grave responsibility upon myself in doing this. It is most irregular; but of course an agreement is an agreement. I must, however, as a matter of duty, send an inspector with you, since you have so valuable a charge. You will drive, no doubt?'

'Yes, I shall drive.'

'It is a pity there is no key, that we may make an inventory first. You will have to break it open. Where is the key, my man?'

'At the bottom of the river,' said Small shortly.

'Hum! There was no use your giving this unnecessary trouble. We have had work enough already through you. However, doctor, I need not warn you to be careful. Bring the box back with you to the Baker Street rooms. You will find us there, on our way to the station.'

They landed me at Vauxhall, with my heavy iron box, and with a bluff, genial inspector as my companion. A quarter of an hour's drive brought us to Mrs Cecil Forrester's. The servant seemed surprised at so late a visitor. Mrs Cecil Forrester was out for the evening, she explained, and likely to be very late. Miss Morstan, however, was in the drawing room; so to the drawing-room I went, box in hand, leaving the obliging inspector in the cab.

She was seated by the open window, dressed in some sort of white diaphanous material, with a little touch of scarlet at the neck and waist. The soft light of a shaded lamp fell upon her as she leaned back in the basket chair, playing over her sweet, grave face, and tinting with a dull, metallic sparkle the rich coils of her luxuriant hair. One white arm and hand drooped over the side of the chair, and her whole pose and figure spoke of an absorbing melancholy. At the sound of my footfall she sprang to her feet, however, and a bright flush of surprise and of pleasure coloured her pale cheeks.

'I heard a cab drive up,' she said. 'I thought that Mrs Forrester had come back very early, but I never dreamed that it might be you. What news have you brought me?'

'I have brought something better than news,' said I, putting down the box upon the table and speaking jovially and boisterously, though my heart was heavy within me. 'I have brought you something which is worth all the news in the world. I have brought you a fortune.'

She glanced at the iron box.

'Is that the treasure, then?' she asked, coolly enough.

'Yes, this is the great Agra treasure. Half of it is yours and half is Thaddeus Sholto's. You will have a couple of hundred thousand each. Think of that! an annuity of ten thousand pounds. There will be few richer young ladies in England. Is it not glorious?'

I think that I must have been rather overacting my delight, and that she detected a hollow ring in my congratulations, for I saw her eyebrows rise a little, and she glanced at me curiously.

'If I have it,' said she, 'I owe it to you.'

'No, no,' I answered, 'not to me but to my friend Sherlock Holmes. With all the will in the world, I could never have followed up a clue which has taxed even his analytical genius. As it was, we very nearly lost it at the last moment.'

'Pray sit down and tell me all about it, Dr Watson,' said she.

I narrated briefly what had occurred since I had seen her last. Holmes's new method of search, the discovery of the *Aurora*, the appearance of Athelney Jones, our expedition in the evening and the wild chase down the Thames. She listened with parted lips and shining eyes to my recital of our adventures. When I spoke of the dart which had so narrowly missed us, she turned so white that I feared that she was about to faint.

'It is nothing,' she said, as I hastened to pour her out some water. 'I am all right again. It was a shock to me to hear that I had placed my friends in such horrible peril.'

'That is all over,' I answered. 'It was nothing. I will tell you no more gloomy details. Let us turn to something brighter. There is the treasure. What could be brighter than that? I got leave to bring it with me, thinking that it would interest you to be the first to see it.'

'It would be of the greatest interest to me,' she said. There was no eagerness in her voice, however. It had struck her, doubtless, that it might seem ungracious upon her part to be indifferent to a prize which had cost so much to win. 'What a pretty box!' she said, stooping over it. 'This is Indian work, I suppose?'

'Yes; it is Benares metalwork.'

'And so heavy!' she exclaimed, trying to raise it. 'The box alone must be of some value. Where is the key?'

'Small threw it into the Thames,' I answered. 'I must borrow Mrs Forrester's poker.'

There was in the front a thick and broad hasp, wrought in the image of a sitting Buddha. Under this I thrust the end of the poker and twisted it outward as a lever. The hasp sprang open with a loud snap. With trembling fingers I flung back the lid. We both stood gazing in astonishment. The box was empty!

No wonder that it was heavy. The ironwork was two-thirds of an inch thick all round. It was massive, well made and solid, like a chest constructed to carry things of great price, but not one shred or crumb of metal or jewellery lay within it. It was absolutely and completely empty.

'The treasure is lost,' said Miss Morstan, calmly.

As I listened to the words and realised what they meant, a great shadow seemed to pass from my soul. I did not know how this Agra treasure had weighed me down, until now that it was finally removed. It was selfish, no doubt, disloyal, wrong, but I could realise nothing save that the golden barrier was gone from between us.

'Thank God!' I ejaculated from my very heart.

She looked at me with a quick, questioning smile.

211

'Why do you say that?' she asked.

'Because you are within my reach again,' I said, taking her hand. She did not withdraw it. 'Because I love you, Mary, as truly as ever a man loved a woman. Because this treasure, these riches, sealed my lips. Now that they are gone I can tell you how I love you. That is why I said, "Thank God."'

'Then I say "Thank God," too,' she whispered, as I drew her to my side.

Whoever had lost a treasure, I knew that night that I had gained one.

12

The Strange Story of Jonathan Small

A very patient man was that inspector in the cab, for it was a weary time before I rejoined him. His face clouded over when I showed him the empty box.

'There goes the reward!' said he, gloomily. 'Where there is no money there is no pay. This night's work would have been worth a tenner each to Sam Brown and me if the treasure had been there.'

'Mr Thaddeus Sholto is a rich man,' I said; 'he will see that you are rewarded, treasure or no.'

The inspector shook his head despondently, however. 'It's a bad job,' he repeated; 'and so Mr Athelney Jones will think.'

His forecast proved to be correct, for the detective looked blank enough when I got to Baker Street and showed him the empty box. They had only just arrived, Holmes, the prisoner, and he, for they had changed their plans so far as to report themselves at a station upon the way. My companion lounged in his armchair with his usual listless expression, while Small sat stolidly opposite to him with his wooden leg cocked over his sound one. As I exhibited the empty box he leaned back in his chair and laughed aloud.

'This is your doing, Small,' said Athelney Jones, angrily.

'Yes, I have put it away where you shall never lay hand on it,' he cried, exultantly. 'It is my treasure, and if I can't have the loot I'll take darned good care that no one else does. I tell you that no living man has any right to it, unless it is three men who are in the Andaman convict-barracks and myself. I know now that I cannot have the use of it, and I know that they cannot. I have acted all through for them as much as for myself. It's been the sign of the four with us always. Well, I know that they would have had me do just what I have done, and throw the treasure into the Thames rather than let it go to kith or kin of Sholto or Morstan. It was not to make them rich that we did for Achmet. You'll find the treasure where the key is, and where little Tonga is. When I saw that your launch must catch us, I put the loot away in a safe place. There are no rupees for you this journey.'

'You are deceiving us, Small,' said Athelney Jones, sternly. 'If you had wished to throw the treasure into the Thames, it would have been easier for you to have thrown box and all.'

'Easier for me to throw, and easier for you to recover,' he answered, with a shrewd, sidelong look. 'The man that was clever enough to hunt me down is clever enough to pick an iron box from the bottom of a river. Now that they are scattered over five miles or so, it may be a harder job. It went to my heart to do it, though. I was half mad when you came up with us. However, there's no good grieving over it. I've had ups in my life, and I've had downs, but I've learned not to cry over spilled milk.'

'This is a very serious matter, Small,' said the detective. 'If you had helped justice, instead of thwarting it in this way, you would have had a better chance at your trial.'

'Justice!' snarled the ex-convict. 'A pretty justice! Whose loot is this, if it is not ours? Where is the justice that I should give it up to those who have never earned it? Look how I have earned it! Twenty long years in that fever-ridden swamp, all day at work under the mangrove tree, all night chained up in the filthy convict-huts, bitten by mosquitoes, racked with ague, bullied by every cursed black-faced policeman who loved to take it out of a white man. That was how I earned the Agra treasure, and you talk to me of justice because I cannot bear to feel that I have paid this price only that another may enjoy it! I would rather swing a score of times, or have one of Tonga's darts in my hide, than live in a convict's cell and feel that another man is at his ease in a palace with the money that should be mine.'

Small had dropped his mask of stoicism, and all this came out in a wild whirl of words, while his eyes blazed and the handcuffs clanked together with the impassioned movement of his hands. I could understand, as I saw the fury and the passion of the man, that it was no groundless or unnatural terror which had possessed Major Sholto when he first learned that the injured convict was upon his track.

'You forget that we know nothing of all this,' said Holmes, quietly. 'We have not heard your story, and we cannot tell how far justice may originally have been on your side.'

'Well, sir, you have been very fair-spoken to me, though I can see that I have you to thank that I have these bracelets upon my wrists. Still, I bear no grudge for that. It is all fair and above-board. If you want to hear my story, I have no wish to hold it back. What I say to you is God's truth, every word of it. Thank you, you can put the glass beside me here, and I'll put my lips to it if I am dry.

'I am a Worcestershire man myself, born near Pershore. I dare say you would find a heap of Smalls living there now if you were to look. I have often thought of taking a look round there, but the truth is that I was never much of a credit to the family, and I doubt if they would be so very glad to see me. They were all steady, chapel-going folk, small farmers, well known and respected over the countryside, while I was always a bit of a rover. At last, however, when I was about eighteen, I gave them no more trouble, for I got into a mess over a girl, and could only get out of it again by taking the Queen's shilling and joining the 3rd Buffs, which was just starting for India.

'I wasn't destined to do much soldiering, however. I had just got past the goose-step, and learned to handle my musket, when I was fool enough to go swimming in the Ganges. Luckily for me, my company sergeant, John Holder, was in the water at the same time, and he was one of the finest swimmers in the service. A crocodile took me, just as I was halfway across, and nipped off my right leg as clean as a surgeon could have done it, just above the knee. What with the shock and the loss of blood, I fainted, and should have been drowned if Holder had not caught hold of me and paddled for the bank. I was five months in hospital over it, and when at last I was able to limp out of it with this timber toe strapped to my stump I found myself invalided out of the army and unfitted for any active occupation.

'I was, as you can imagine, pretty down on my luck at this time, for I was a useless cripple, though not yet in my twentieth year. However, my misfortune soon proved to be a blessing in disguise. A man named Abel White, who had come out there as an indigo-planter, wanted an overseer to look after his coolies and keep them up to their work. He happened to be a friend of our colonel's who had taken an interest in me since the accident. To make a long story short, the colonel recommended me strongly for the post, and, as the work was mostly to be done on horseback, my leg was no great obstacle, for I had enough knee left to keep a good grip on the saddle. What I had to do was to ride over the plantation, to keep an eye on the men as they worked and to report the idlers. The pay was fair, I had comfortable quarters and altogether I was content to spend the remainder of my life in indigo-planting. Mr Abel White was a kind man, and he would often drop into my little shanty and smoke a pipe with me, for white folk out there feel their hearts warm to each other as they never do here at home.

'Well, I was never in luck's way long. Suddenly, without a note of warning, the great mutiny broke upon us. One month India lay as still and peaceful, to all appearance, as Surrey or Kent; the next there were two hundred thousand black devils let loose, and the country was a perfect hell. Of course you know all about it, gentlemen – a deal more than I do, very like, since reading is not in my line. I only know what I saw with my own eyes. Our plantation was at a place called Muttra, near the border of the North West Provinces. Night after night the whole sky was alight with the burning bungalows, and day after day we had small companies of Europeans passing through our estate with their wives and children, on their way to Agra, where were the nearest troops. Mr Abel White was an obstinate man. He had it in his head that the affair had been exaggerated, and that it would blow over as suddenly as it had sprung up. There he sat on his verandah, drinking whisky-pegs and smoking cheroots, while the country was in a blaze about him. Of course, we stuck by him, I and Dawson, who, with his wife, used to do the bookwork and the managing. Well, one fine day the crash came. I had been away on a distant plantation and was riding slowly home in the evening when my eye fell upon something all huddled together at the bottom of a steep nullah. I rode down to see what it was, and the cold struck through my heart when I found it was Dawson's wife, all cut into ribbons and half-eaten by jackals and native dogs. A little farther up the road Dawson himself was lying on his face, quite dead, with an empty revolver in his hand, and four sepoys lying across each other in front of him. I reined up my horse, wondering which way I should turn; but at that moment I saw thick smoke curling up from Abel White's bungalow, and the flames beginning to burst through the roof. I knew then that I could do my employer no good, but would only throw my own life away if I meddled in the matter. From where I stood I could see hundreds of the black fiends, with their red coats still on their backs, dancing and howling round the burning house. Some of them pointed at me, and a couple of bullets sang past my head: so I broke away across the paddy-fields, and found myself late at night safe within the walls at Agra.

'As it proved, however, there was no great safety here either. The whole country was up like a swarm of bees. Wherever the English could collect in little bands, they held just the ground that their guns commanded. Everywhere else they were helpless fugitives. It was a fight of the millions against the hundreds; and the cruellest part of it was that these men that we fought against, foot, horse and gunners, were our own picked troops, whom we had taught and trained, handling our own weapons and blowing our own bugle-calls. At Agra there were the 3rd Bengal Fusiliers, some Sikhs, two troops of horse and a battery of artillery. A volunteer corps of clerks and merchants had been formed, and this I joined, wooden leg and all. We went out to meet the rebels at Shahgunge early in July, and we beat them back for a time, but our powder gave out and we had to fall back upon the city.

'Nothing but the worst news came to us from every side – which is not to be wondered at, for if you look at the map you will see that we were right in the heart of it. Lucknow is rather better than a hundred miles to the east, and Cawnpore about as far to the south. From every point on the compass there was nothing but torture and murder and outrage.

'The city of Agra is a great place, swarming with fanatics and fierce devil-worshippers of all sorts. Our handful of men were lost among the narrow, winding streets. Our leader moved across the river, therefore, and took up his position in the old fort of Agra. I don't know if any of you gentlemen have ever read or heard anything of that old fort. It is a very queer place – the queerest that ever I was in, and I have been in some rum corners, too. First of all, it is enormous in size. I should think that the enclosure must be acres and acres. There is a modern part, which took all our garrison, women, children, stores and everything else, with plenty of room over. But the modern part is nothing like the size of the old quarter, where nobody goes, and which is given over to the scorpions and the centipedes. It is all full of great, deserted halls, and winding passages, and long corridors twisting in and out, so that it is easy enough for folk to get lost in it. For this reason it was seldom that anyone went into it, though now and again a party with torches might go exploring.

'The river washes along the front of the old fort, and so protects it, but on the sides and behind there are many doors, and these had to be guarded, of course, in the old quarter as well as in that which was actually held by our troops. We were short-handed, with hardly men enough to man the angles of the building and to serve the guns. It was impossible for us, therefore, to station a strong guard at every one of the innumerable gates. What we did was to organise a central guardhouse in the middle of the fort, and to leave each gate under the charge of one white man and two or three natives. I was selected to take charge during certain hours of the night of a small isolated door upon the south-west side of the building. Two Sikh troopers were placed under my command, and I was instructed if anything went wrong to fire my musket, when I might rely upon help coming at once from the central guard. As the guard was a good two hundred paces away, however, and as the space between was cut up into a labyrinth of passages and corridors, I had great doubts as to whether they could arrive in time to be of any use in case of an actual attack.

'Well, I was pretty proud at having this small command given me, since I was a raw recruit and a game-legged one at that. For two nights I kept the watch with my Punjabis. They were tall, fierce-looking chaps, Mahomet Singh and Abdullah Khan by name, both old fighting-men who had borne arms against us at Chilian Wallah. They could talk English pretty well, but I could get little out of them. They preferred to stand together and jabber all night in their queer Sikh lingo. For myself, I used to stand outside the gateway looking down on the broad, winding river and on the twinkling lights of the great city. The beating of drums, the rattle of tom-toms and the yells and howls of the rebels, drunk with opium and with bhang, were enough to remind us all night of our dangerous neighbours across the stream. Every two hours the officer of the night used to come round to all the posts, to make sure that all was well.

'The third night of my watch was dark and dirty, with a small, driving rain. It was dreary work standing in the gateway hour after hour in such weather. I tried again and again to make my Sikhs talk, but without much success. At two in the morning the rounds passed, and broke for a moment the weariness of the night. Finding that my companions would not be led into conversation, I took out my pipe and laid down my musket to strike a match. In an instant the two Sikhs were upon me. One of them snatched my firelock up and levelled it at my head, while the other held a great knife to my throat and swore between his teeth that he would plunge it into me if I moved a step.

'My first thought was that these fellows were in league with the rebels, and that this was the beginning of an assault. If our door were in the hands of the sepoys the place must fall, and the women and children be treated as they were in Cawnpore. Maybe you gentlemen think that I am just making out a case for myself, but I give you my word that when I thought of that, though I felt the point of the knife at my throat, I opened my mouth with the intention of giving a scream, if it was my last one, which might alarm the main guard. The man who held me seemed to know my thoughts for, even as I braced myself to it, he whispered: "Don't make a noise. The fort is safe enough. There are no rebel dogs on this side of the river." There was the ring of truth in what he said, and I knew that if I raised my voice I was a dead man. I could read it in the fellow's brown eyes. I waited, therefore, in silence, to see what it was that they wanted from me.

'"Listen to me, sahib," said the taller and fiercer of the pair, the one whom they called Abdullah Khan. "You must either be with us now, or you must be silenced for ever. The thing is too great a one for us to hesitate. Either you are heart and soul with us on your oath on the cross of the Christians, or your body this night shall be thrown into the ditch, and we shall pass over to our brothers in the rebel army. There is no middle way. Which is it to be – death or life? We can only give you three minutes to decide, for the time is passing, and all must be done before the rounds come again."

'"How can I decide?" said I. "You have not told me what you want of me. But I tell you now that if it is anything against the safety of the fort I will have no truck with it, so you can drive home your knife, and welcome."

'"It is nothing against the fort," said he. "We only ask you to do that which your countrymen come to this land for. We ask you to be rich. If you will be one of us this night, we will swear to you upon the naked knife, and by the threefold oath which no Sikh was ever known to break, that you shall have your fair share of the loot. A quarter of the treasure shall be yours. We can say no fairer."

'"But what is the treasure, then?" I asked. "I am as ready to be rich as you can be, if you will but show me how it can be done."

'"You will swear, then," said he, "by the bones of your father, by the honour of your mother, by the cross of your faith, to raise no hand and speak no word against us, either now or afterwards?"

'"I will swear it," I answered, "provided that the fort is not endangered."

'"Then, my comrade and I will swear that you shall have a quarter of the treasure, which shall be equally divided among the four of us."

'"There are but three," said I.

'"No; Dost Akbar must have his share. We can tell the tale to you while we await them. Do you stand at the gate, Mahomet Singh, and give notice of their coming. The thing stands thus, sahib, and I tell it to you because I know that an oath is binding upon a Feringhee, and that we may trust you. Had you been a lying Hindu, though you had sworn by all the gods in their false temples, your blood would have been upon the knife and your body in the water. But the Sikh knows the Englishman, and the Englishman knows the Sikh. Hearken, then, to what I have to say.

'"There is a rajah in the northern provinces who has much wealth, though his lands are small. Much has come to him from his father, and more still he has set by himself, for he is of a low nature, and hoards his gold rather than spend it. When the troubles broke out he would be friends both with the lion and the tiger – with the sepoy and with the Company's Raj. Soon, however, it seemed to him that the white men's day was come, for through all the land he could hear of nothing but of their death and their overthrow. Yet, being a careful man, he made such plans that, come what might, half at least of his treasure should be left to him. That which was in gold and silver he kept by him in the vaults of his palace; but the most precious stones and the choicest pearls that he had he put in an iron box and sent it by a trusty servant, who, under the guise of a merchant, should take it to the fort at Agra, there to lie until the land is at peace. Thus, if the rebels won he would have his money; but if the Company conquered, his jewels would be saved to him. Having thus divided his hoard, he threw himself into the cause of the sepoys, since they were strong upon his borders. By his doing this, mark you, sahib, his property becomes the due of those who have been true to their salt.

'"This pretended merchant, who travels under the name of Achmet, is now in the city of Agra, and desires to gain his way into the fort. He has with him as travelling-companion my foster-brother, Dost Akbar, who knows his secret. Dost Akbar has promised this night to lead him to a side-postern of the fort, and has chosen this one for his purpose. Here he will come presently and here he will find Mahomet Singh and myself awaiting him. The place is lonely, and none shall know of his coming. The world shall know of the merchant, Achmet, no more, but the great treasure of the rajah shall be divided among us. What say you to it, sahib?"

'In Worcestershire the life of a man seems a great and sacred thing; but it is very different when there is fire and blood all round you, and you have been used to meeting death at every turn. Whether Achmet the merchant lived or died was a thing as light as air to me, but at the talk about the treasure my heart turned to it, and I thought of what I might do in the old country with it, and how my folk would stare when they saw their ne'er-do-well coming back with his pockets full of gold moidores. I had, therefore, already made up my mind. Abdullah Khan, however, thinking that I hesitated, pressed the matter more closely.

'"Consider, sahib," said he, "that if this man is taken by the commandant he will be hung or shot, and his jewels taken by the government, so that no man will be a rupee the better for them. Now, since we do the taking of him, why should we not do the rest as well? The jewels will be as well with us as in the Company's coffers. There will be enough to make every one of us rich men and great chiefs. No one can know about the matter, for here we are cut off from all men. What could be better for the purpose? Say again, then, sahib, whether you are with us, or if we must look upon you as an enemy."

' "I am with you heart and soul," said I.

'"It is well," he answered, handing me back my firelock. "You see that we trust you, for your word, like ours, is not to be broken. We have now only to wait for my brother and the merchant."

'"Does your brother know, then, of what you will do?" I asked.

'"The plan is his. He has devised it. We will go to the gate and share the watch with Mahomet Singh."

'The rain was still falling steadily, for it was just the beginning of the wet season. Brown, heavy clouds were drifting across the sky, and it was hard to see more than a stone-cast. A deep moat lay in front of our door, but the water was in places nearly dried up, and it could easily be crossed. It was strange to me to be standing there with those two wild Punjabis waiting for the man who was coming to his death.

'Suddenly my eye caught the glint of a shaded lantern at the other side of the moat. It vanished among the mound-heaps, and then appeared again coming slowly in our direction.

'"Here they are!" I exclaimed.

'"You will challenge him, sahib, as usual," whispered Abdullah. "Give him no cause for fear. Send us in with him, and we shall do the rest while you stay here on guard. Have the lantern ready to uncover, that we may be sure that it is indeed the man."

'The light had flickered onwards, now stopping and now advancing, until I could see two dark figures upon the other side of the moat. I let them scramble down the sloping bank, splash through the mire, and climb halfway up to the gate, before I challenged them.

'"Who goes there?" said I, in a subdued voice.

'"Friends," came the answer. I uncovered my lantern and threw a flood of light upon them. The first was an enormous Sikh, with a black beard which swept nearly down to his cummerbund. Outside of a show I have never seen so tall a man. The other was a little, fat, round fellow, with a great yellow turban, and a bundle in his hand, done up in a shawl. He seemed to be all in a quiver with fear, for his hands twitched as if he had the ague, and his head kept turning to left and right with two bright little twinkling eyes, like a mouse when he ventures out from his hole. It gave me the chills to think of killing him, but I thought of the treasure, and my heart set as hard as a flint within me. When he saw my white face he gave a little chirrup of joy, and came running up towards me.

'"Your protection, sahib," he panted; "your protection for the unhappy merchant Achmet. I have travelled across Rajputana that I might seek the shelter of the fort at Agra. I have been robbed and beaten and abused because I have been the friend of the Company. It is a blessed night this when I am once more in safety – I and my poor possessions."

'"What have you in the bundle?" I asked.

'"An iron box," he answered, "which contains one or two little family matters which are of no value to others, but which I should be sorry to lose. Yet I am not a beggar; and I shall reward you, young sahib, and your governor also, if he will give me the shelter I ask."

'I could not trust myself to speak longer with the man. The more I looked at his fat, frightened face, the harder did it seem that we should slay him in cold blood. It was best to get it over.

'"Take him to the main guard," said I. The two Sikhs closed in upon him on each side, and the giant walked behind while they marched in through the dark gateway. Never was a man so compassed round with death. I remained at the gateway with the lantern.

'I could hear the measured tramp of their footsteps sounding through the lonely corridors. Suddenly it ceased, and I heard voices and a scuffle, with the sound of blows. A moment later there came, to my horror, a rush of footsteps coming in my direction, with the loud breathing of a running man. I turned my lantern down the long, straight passage, and there was the fat man, running like the wind, with a smear of blood across his face, and close at his heels, bounding like a tiger, the great, black-bearded Sikh, with a knife flashing in his hand. I have never seen a man run so fast as that little merchant. He was gaining on the Sikh, and I could see that if he once passed me and got to the open air he would save himself yet. My heart softened to him, but again the thought of his treasure turned me hard and bitter. I cast my firelock between his legs as he raced past, and he rolled twice over like a shot rabbit. Ere he could stagger to his feet the Sikh was upon him, and buried his knife twice in his side. The man never uttered moan nor moved muscle, but lay where he had fallen. I think myself that he may have broken his neck with the fall. You see, gentlemen, that I am keeping my promise. I am telling you every word of the business just exactly as it happened, whether it is in my favour or not.'

He stopped, and held out his manacled hands for the whisky and water which Holmes had brewed for him. For myself I confess that I had now conceived the utmost horror of the man, not only for this cold-blooded business in which he had been concerned but even more for the somewhat flippant and careless way in which he narrated it. Whatever punishment was in store for him, I felt that he might expect no sympathy from me. Sherlock Holmes and Jones sat with their hands upon their knees, deeply interested in the story, but with the same disgust written upon their faces. He may have observed it, for there was a touch of defiance in his voice and manner as he proceeded.

'It was all very bad, no doubt,' said he. 'I should like to know how many fellows in my shoes would have refused a share of this loot when they knew that they would have their throats cut for their pains. Besides, it was my life or his when once he was in the fort. If he had got out, the whole business would come to light, and I should have been court-martialled and shot as likely as not; for people were not very lenient at a time like that.'

'Go on with your story,' said Holmes, shortly.

'Well, we carried him in, Abdullah, Akbar and I. A fine weight he was, too, for all that he was so short. Mahomet Singh was left to guard the door. We took him to a place which the Sikhs had already prepared. It was some distance off, where a winding passage leads to a great empty hall, the brick walls of which were all crumbling to pieces. The earth floor had sunk in at one place, making a natural grave, so we left

Achmet the merchant there, having first covered him over with loose bricks. This done, we all went back to the treasure.

'It lay where he had dropped it when he was first attacked. The box was the same which now lies open upon your table. A key was hung by a silken cord to that carved handle upon the top. We opened it, and the light of the lantern gleamed upon a collection of gems such as I read of and thought about when I was a little lad at Pershore. It was blinding to look upon them. When we had feasted our eyes we took them all out and made a list of them. There were one hundred and forty-three diamonds of the first water, including one which has been called, I believe, "the Great Mogul", and is said to be the second largest stone in existence. Then there were ninety-seven very fine emeralds, and one hundred and seventy rubies, some of which, however, were small. There were forty carbuncles, two hundred and ten sapphires, sixty-one agates and a great quantity of beryls, onyxes, cat's-eyes, turquoises and other stones, the very names of which I did not know at the time though I have become more familiar with them since. Besides this, there were nearly three hundred very fine pearls, twelve of which were set in a gold coronet. By the way, these last had been taken out of the chest, and were not there when I recovered it.

'After we had counted our treasures we put them back into the chest and carried them to the gateway to show them to Mahomet Singh. Then we solemnly renewed our oath to stand by each other and be true to our secret. We agreed to conceal our loot in a safe place until the country should be at peace again, and then to divide it equally among ourselves. There was no use dividing it at present, for if gems of such value were found upon us it would cause suspicion, and there was no privacy in the fort nor any place where we could keep them. We carried the box, therefore, into the same hall where we had buried the body, and there, under certain bricks in the best-preserved wall, we made a hollow and put our treasure. We made careful note of the place, and next day I drew four plans, one for each of us, and put the sign of the four of us at the bottom, for we had sworn that we should each always act for all, so that none might take advantage.

That is an oath that I can put my hand to my heart and swear that I have never broken.

'Well, there's no use my telling you gentlemen what came of the Indian Mutiny. After Wilson took Delhi and Sir Colin relieved Lucknow the back of the business was broken. Fresh troops came pouring in, and Nana Sahib made himself scarce over the frontier. A flying column under Colonel Greathed came round to Agra and cleared the Pandies away from it. Peace seemed to be settling upon the country, and we four were beginning to hope that the time was at hand when we might safely go off with our share of the plunder. In a moment, however, our hopes were shattered by our being arrested as the murderers of Achmet.

'It came about in this way. When the rajah put his jewels into the hands of Achmet, he did it because he knew that he was a trusty man. They are suspicious folk in the East, however; so what does this rajah do but take a second even more trusty servant and set him to play the spy upon the first? The second man was ordered never to let Achmet out of his sight, and he followed him like his shadow. He went after him that night and saw him pass through the doorway. Of course, he thought he had taken refuge in the fort, and applied for admission there himself next day, but could find no trace of Achmet. This seemed to him so strange that he spoke about it to a sergeant of guides, who brought it to the ears of the commandant. A thorough search was quickly made and the body was discovered. Thus at the very moment that we thought that all was safe we were all four seized and brought to trial on a charge of murder – three of us because we had held the gate that night, and the fourth because he was known to have been in the company of the murdered man. Not a word about the jewels came out at the trial, for the rajah had been deposed and driven out of India; so no one had any particular interest in them. The murder, however, was clearly made out, and it was certain that we must all have been concerned in it. The three Sikhs got penal servitude for life, and I was condemned to death, though my sentence was afterwards commuted into the same as the others'.

'It was rather a queer position that we found ourselves in then. There we were all four tied by the leg and with precious little chance of ever getting out again, while we each held a secret which might have put each of us in a palace if we could only have made use of it. It was enough to make a man eat his heart out to have to stand the kick and the cuff of every petty jack-in-office, to have rice to eat and water to drink, when that gorgeous fortune was ready for him outside, just waiting to be picked up. It might have driven me mad; but I was always a pretty stubborn one, so I just held on and bided my time.

'At last it seemed to me to have come. I was changed from Agra to Madras, and from there to Blair Island in the Andamans. There are very few white convicts at this settlement and, as I had behaved well from the first, I soon found myself a sort of privileged person. I was given a hut in Hope Town, which is a small place on the slopes of Mount Harriet, and I was left pretty much to myself. It is a dreary, fever-stricken place, and all beyond our little clearings was infested with wild cannibal natives, who were ready enough to blow a poisoned dart at us if they saw a chance. There was digging and ditching and yam-planting, and a dozen other things to be done, so we were busy enough all day; though in the evening we had a little time to ourselves. Among other things I learned to dispense drugs for the surgeon, and picked up a smattering of his knowledge. All the time I was on the lookout for a chance of escape; but it is hundreds of miles from any other land, and there is little or no wind in those seas: so it was a terribly difficult job to get away.

'The surgeon, Dr Somerton, was a fast, sporting young chap, and the other young officers would meet in his rooms of an evening and play cards. The surgery, where I used to make up my drugs, was next to his sitting-room, with a small window between us. Often, if I felt lonesome, I used to turn out the lamp in the surgery, and then, standing there, I could hear their talk and watch their play. I am fond of a hand at cards myself, and it was almost as good as having one to watch the others. There was Major Sholto, Captain Morstan and Lieutenant Bromley Brown, who were in command of the native troops, and there was the surgeon himself, and two or three prison-officials, crafty old hands who played a nice, sly, safe game. A very snug little party they used to make.

'Well, there was one thing which very soon struck me, and that was that the soldiers used always to lose and the civilians to win. Mind, I don't say there was anything unfair, but so it was. These prison-chaps had done little else than play cards ever since they had been at the Andamans, and they knew each other's game to a point, while the others just played to pass the time and threw their cards down anyhow. Night after night the soldiers got up poorer men, and the poorer they got the more keen they were to play. Major Sholto was the hardest hit. He used to pay in notes and gold at first, but soon it came to notes of hand and for big sums. He sometimes would win for a few deals, just to give him heart, and then the luck would set in against him worse than ever. All day he would wander about as black as thunder, and he took to drinking a deal more than was good for him.

'One night he lost even more heavily than usual. I was sitting in my hut when he and Captain Morstan came stumbling along on the way to their quarters. They were bosom friends, those two, and never far apart. The major was raving about his losses.

'"It's all up, Morstan," he was saying, as they passed my hut. "I shall have to send in my papers. I am a ruined man."

'"Nonsense, old chap!" said the other, slapping him upon the shoulder. "I've had a nasty facer myself, but – " That was all I could hear, but it was enough to set me thinking.

'A couple of days later Major Sholto was strolling on the beach: so I took the chance of speaking to him.

'"I wish to have your advice, major," said I.

'"Well, Small, what is it?" he asked, taking his cheroot from his lips.

'"I wanted to ask you, sir," said I, "who is the proper person to whom hidden treasure should be handed over. I know where half a million's worth lies, and, as I cannot use it myself, I thought perhaps the best thing that I could do would be to hand it over to the proper authorities, and then perhaps they would get my sentence shortened for me."

'"Half a million, Small?" he gasped, looking hard at me to see if I was in earnest.

'"Quite that, sir – in jewels and pearls. It lies there ready for anyone. And the queer thing about it is that the real owner is outlawed and cannot hold property, so that it belongs to the first comer."

'"To government, Small," he stammered, "to government." But he said it in a halting fashion, and I knew in my heart that I had got him.

'"You think, then, sir, that I should give the information to the governor-general?" said I, quietly.

'"Well, well, you must not do anything rash, or that you might repent. Let me hear all about it, Small. Give me the facts."

'I told him the whole story, with small changes, so that he could not identify the places. When I had finished he stood stock-still and full of thought. I could see by the twitch of his lip that there was a struggle going on within him.

'"This is a very important matter, Small," he said at last. "You must not say a word to anyone about it, and I shall see you again soon."

'Two nights later he and his friend, Captain Morstan, came to my hut in the dead of the night with a lantern.

'"I want you just to let Captain Morstan hear that story from your own lips, Small," said he.

'I repeated it as I had told it before.

'"It rings true, eh?" said he. "It's good enough to act upon?"

'Captain Morstan nodded.

'"Look here, Small," said the major. "We have been talking it over, my friend here and I, and we have come to the conclusion that this secret of yours is hardly a government matter, after all, but is a private concern of your own, which, of course, you have the power of disposing of as you think best. Now the question is: What price would you ask for it? We might be inclined to take it up, and at least look into it, if we could agree as to terms." He tried to speak in a cool, careless way, but his eyes were shining with excitement and greed.

'"Why, as to that, gentlemen," I answered, trying also to be cool, but feeling as excited as he did, "there is only one bargain which a man in my position can make. I shall want you to help me to my freedom, and to help my three companions to theirs. We shall then take you into partnership, and give you a fifth share to divide between you."

'"Hum!" said he. "A fifth share! That is not very tempting."

'"It would come to fifty thousand apiece," said I.

'"But how can we gain your freedom? You know very well that you ask an impossibility."

' "Nothing of the sort," I answered. "I have thought it all out to the last detail. The only bar to our escape is that we can get no boat fit for the voyage, and no provisions to last us for so long a time. There are plenty of little yachts and yawls at Calcutta or Madras which would serve our turn well. Do you bring one over. We shall engage to get aboard her by night, and if you will drop us on any part of the Indian coast you will have done your part of the bargain."

'"If there were only one," he said.

'"None or all," I answered. "We have sworn it. The four of us must always act together."

'"You see, Morstan," said he, "Small is a man of his word. He does not flinch from his friends. I think we may very well trust him."

'"It's a dirty business," the other answered. "Yet, as you say, the money will save our commissions handsomely."

'"Well, Small," said the major, "we must, I suppose, try and meet you. We must first, of course, test the truth of your story. Tell me where the box is hid, and I shall get leave of absence and go back to India in the monthly relief-boat to enquire into the affair."

'"Not so fast," said I, growing colder as he got hot. "I must have the consent of my three comrades. I tell you that it is four or none with us."

'"Nonsense!" he broke in. "What have three black fellows to do with our agreement?"

'"Black or blue," said I, "they are in with me, and we all go together."

'Well, the matter ended by a second meeting, at which Mahomet Singh, Abdullah Khan and Dost Akbar were all present. We talked the matter over again, and at last we came to an arrangement. We were to provide both the officers with charts of the part of the Agra fort, and mark the place in the wall where the treasure was hid. Major Sholto was to go to India to test our story. If he found the box he was to leave it there, to send out a small yacht provisioned for a voyage, which was to lie off Rutland Island and to which we were to make our way, and finally to return to his duties. Captain Morstan was then to apply for leave of absence, to meet us at Agra, and there we were to have a final division of the treasure, he taking the major's share as well as his own. All this we sealed by the most solemn oaths that the mind could think or the lips utter. I sat up all night with paper and ink, and by the morning I had the two charts all ready, signed with the sign of the four – that is, of Abdullah, Akbar, Mahomet and myself.

'Well, gentlemen, I weary you with my long story, and I know that my friend Mr Jones is impatient to get me safely stowed in chokey. I'll make it as short as I can. The villain Sholto went off to India, but he never came back again. Captain Morstan showed me his name among a list of passengers in one of the mail-boats very shortly afterwards. His uncle had died, leaving him a fortune, and he had left the army; yet he could stoop to treat five men as he had treated us. Morstan went over to Agra shortly afterwards, and found, as we expected, that the treasure was indeed gone. The scoundrel had stolen it all, without carrying out one of the conditions on which we had sold him the secret. From that day I lived only for vengeance. I thought of it by day and I nursed it by night. It became an overpowering, absorbing passion with me. I cared nothing for the law – nothing for the gallows. To escape, to track down Sholto, to have my hand upon his throat – that was my one thought. Even the Agra treasure had come to be a smaller thing in my mind than the slaying of Sholto.

'Well, I have set my mind on many things in this life, and never one which I did not carry out. But it was weary years before my time came. I have told you that I had picked up something of medicine. One day when Dr Somerton was down with a fever a little Andaman Islander was picked up by a convict-gang in the woods. He was sick to death, and had gone to a lonely place to die. I took him in hand, though he was as venomous as a young snake, and after a couple of months I got him all right and able to walk. He took a kind of fancy to me then, and would hardly go back to his woods but was always hanging about my hut. I learned a little of his lingo from him, and this made him all the fonder of me.

'Tonga – for that was his name – was a fine boatman, and owned a big, roomy canoe of his own. When I found that he was devoted to me and would do anything to serve me, I saw my chance of escape. I talked it over with him. He was to bring his boat round on a certain night to an old wharf which was never guarded, and there he was to pick me up. I gave him directions to have several gourds of water and a lot of yams, coconuts and sweet potatoes.

'He was staunch and true, was little Tonga. No man ever had a more faithful mate. On the night named he had his boat at the wharf. As it chanced, however, there was one of the convict-guard down there – a vile Pathan who had never missed a chance of insulting and injuring me. I had always vowed vengeance, and now I had my chance. It was as if fate had placed him in my way that I might pay my debt before I left the island. He stood on the bank with his back to me and his carbine on his shoulder. I looked about for a stone to beat out his brains with, but none could I see.

'Then a queer thought came into my head, and showed me where I could lay my hand on a weapon. I sat down in the darkness and unstrapped my wooden leg. With three long hops I was on him. He put his carbine to his shoulder, but I struck him full, and knocked the whole front of his skull in. You can see the split in the wood now where I hit him. We both went down together, for I could not keep my balance; but when I got up I found him lying quiet enough. I made for the boat, and in an hour we were well out at sea. Tonga had brought all his earthly possessions with him, his arms and his gods. Among other things, he had a long bamboo spear and some Andaman coconut-matting, with which I made a sort of a sail. For ten days we were beating about, trusting to luck, and on the eleventh we were picked up by a trader which was going from Singapore to Jeddah with a cargo of Malay pilgrims. They were a rum crowd, and Tonga and I soon managed to settle down among them. They had one very good quality: they let you alone and asked no questions.

'Well, if I were to tell you all the adventures that my little chum and I went through, you would not thank me, for I would have you here until the sun was shining. Here and there we drifted about the world, something always turning up to keep us from London. All the time, however, I never lost sight of my purpose. I would dream of Sholto at night. A hundred times I have killed him in my sleep. At last, however, some three or four years ago, we found ourselves in England. I had no great difficulty in finding where Sholto lived, and I set to work to discover whether he had realised the treasure, or if he still had it. I made friends with someone who could help me – I name no names, for I don't want to get anyone else in a hole – and I soon found that he still had the jewels. Then I tried to get at him in many ways; but he was pretty sly, and had always two prizefighters, besides his sons and his khitmutgar, on guard over him.

'One day, however, I got word that he was dying. I hurried at once to the garden, mad that he should slip out of my clutches like that, and, looking through the window, I saw him lying in his bed, with his sons on each side of him. I'd have come through and taken my chance with the three of them, only even as I looked at him his jaw dropped and I knew that he was gone. I got into his room the same night, though, and I searched his papers to see if there was any record of where he had hidden our jewels. There was not a line, however, so I came away, bitter and savage as a man could be. Before I left I bethought me that if I ever met my Sikh friends again it would be a satisfaction to know that I had left some mark of our hatred; so I scrawled down the sign of the four of us, as it had been on the chart, and I pinned it on his bosom. It was too much that he should be taken to the grave without some token from the men whom he had robbed and befooled.

'We earned a living at this time by my exhibiting poor Tonga at fairs and other such places as the black cannibal. He would eat raw meat and dance his war-dance, so we always had a hatful of pennies after a day's work. I still heard all the news from Pondicherry Lodge, and for some years there was no news to hear, except that they were hunting for the treasure. At last, however, came what we had waited for so long. The treasure had been found. It was up at the top of the house, in Mr Bartholomew Sholto's chemical laboratory. I came at once and had a look at the place, but I could not see how, with my wooden leg, I was to make my way up to it. I learned, however, about a trap-door in the roof, and also about Mr Sholto's supper-hour. It seemed to me that I could manage the thing easily through Tonga. I brought him out with me with a long rope wound round his waist. He could climb like a cat, and he soon made his way through the roof, but, as ill-luck would have it, Bartholomew Sholto was still in the room, to his cost. Tonga thought he had done something very clever in killing him, for when I came up by the rope I found him strutting about as proud as a peacock. Very much surprised was he when I made at him with the rope's end and cursed him for a little bloodthirsty imp. I took the treasure box and let it down, and then slid down myself, having first left the sign of the four upon the table, to show that the jewels had come back at last to those who had most right to them. Tonga then pulled up the rope, closed the window and made off the way that he had come.

'I don't know that I have anything else to tell you. I had heard a waterman speak of the speed of Smith's launch, the *Aurora*, so I thought she would be a handy craft for our escape. I engaged with old Smith, and was to give him a big sum if he got us safe to our ship. He knew, no doubt, that there was some screw loose, but he was not in our secrets. All this is the truth, and if I tell it to you gentlemen, it is not to amuse you – for you have not done me a very good turn – but it is because I believe the best defence I can make is just to hold back nothing, but let all the world know how badly I have myself been served by Major Sholto, and how innocent I am of the death of his son.'

'A very remarkable account,' said Sherlock Holmes. 'A fitting wind-up to an extremely interesting case. There is nothing at all new to me in the latter part of your narrative except that you brought your own rope. That I did not know. By the way, I had hoped that Tonga had lost all his darts; yet he managed to shoot one at us in the boat.'

'He had lost them all, sir, except the one which was in his blow-pipe at the time.'

'Ah, of course,' said Holmes. 'I had not thought of that.'

'Is there any other point which you would like to ask about?' asked the convict, affably.

'I think not, thank you,' my companion answered.

'Well, Holmes,' said Athelney Jones, 'you are a man to be humoured, and we all know that you are a connoisseur of crime; but duty is duty, and I have gone rather far in doing what you and your friend asked me. I shall feel more at ease when we have our storyteller here safe under lock and key. The cab still waits, and there are two inspectors downstairs. I am much obliged to you both for your assistance. Of course, you will be wanted at the trial. Good-night to you.'

'Good-night, gentlemen both,' said Jonathan Small.

'You first, Small,' remarked the wary Jones as they left the room. 'I'll take particular care that you don't club me with your wooden leg, whatever you may have done to the gentleman at the Andaman Isles.'

'Well, and there is the end of our little drama,' I remarked, after we had sat some time smoking in silence. 'I fear that it may be the last investigation in which I shall have the chance of studying your methods. Miss Morstan has done me the honour to accept me as a husband in prospective.'

Holmes gave a most dismal groan. 'I feared as much,' said he. 'I really cannot congratulate you.'

I was a little hurt. 'Have you any reason to be dissatisfied with my choice?' I asked.

'Not at all. I think she is one of the most charming young ladies I ever met, and might have been most useful in such work as we have been doing. She had a decided genius that way; witness the way in which she preserved that Agra plan from all the other papers of her father. But love is an emotional thing, and whatever is emotional is opposed to that true, cold reason which I place above all things. I should never marry myself, lest I bias my judgement.'

'I trust,' said I, laughing, 'that my judgement may survive the ordeal. But you look weary.'

'Yes, the reaction is already upon me. I shall be as limp as a rag for a week.'

'Strange,' said I, 'how terms of what in another man I should call laziness alternate with your fits of splendid energy and vigour.'

'Yes,' he answered, 'there are in me the makings of a very fine loafer, and also of a pretty spry sort of a fellow. I often think of those lines of old Goethe:

Schade dass die Natur nur einen Mensch aus dir schuf
Den zum würdigen Mann war und zum Schelmen der Stoff

'By the way, apropos of this Norwood business, you see that they had, as I surmised, a confederate in the house, who could be none other than Lal Rao, the butler: so Jones actually has the undivided honour of having caught one fish in his great haul.'

'The division seems rather unfair,' I remarked. 'You have done all the work in this business. I get a wife out of it, Jones gets the credit; pray what remains for you?'

'For me,' said Sherlock Holmes, 'there still remains the cocaine bottle.' And he stretched his long, white hand up for it.

The Speckled Band

1

The Speckled Band

On glancing over my notes of the seventy-odd cases in which I have during the last eight years studied the methods of my friend Sherlock Holmes, I find many tragic, some comic, a large number merely strange, but none commonplace; for, working as he did rather for the love of his art than for the acquirement of wealth, he refused to associate himself with any investigation which did not tend towards the unusual, and even the fantastic. Of all these varied cases, however, I cannot recall any which presented more singular features than that which was associated with the well-known Surrey family of the Roylotts of Stoke Moran. The events in question occurred in the early days of my association with Holmes, when we were sharing rooms as bachelors in Baker Street. It is possible that I might have placed them upon record before, but a promise of secrecy was made at the time, from which I have only been freed during the last month by the untimely death of the lady to whom the pledge was given. It is perhaps as well that the facts should now come to light, for I have reasons to know that there are widespread rumours as to the death of Dr Grimesby Roylott which tend to make the matter even more terrible than the truth.

It was early in April in the year 1883 that I woke one morning to find Sherlock Holmes standing, fully dressed, by the side of my bed. He was a late riser, as a rule, and as the clock on the mantelpiece showed me that it was only a quarter-past seven, I blinked up at him in some surprise, and perhaps just a little resentment, for I was myself regular in my habits.

'Very sorry to knock you up, Watson,' said he, 'but it's the common lot this morning. Mrs Hudson has been knocked up, she retorted upon me, and I on you.'

'What is it, then – a fire?'

'No; a client. It seems that a young lady has arrived in a considerable state of excitement, who insists upon seeing me. She is waiting now in the sitting-room. Now, when young ladies wander about the metropolis at this hour of the morning, and knock sleepy people up out of their beds, I presume that it is something very pressing which they have to communicate. Should it prove to be an interesting case, you would, I am sure, wish to follow it from the outset. I thought, at any rate, that I should call you and give you the chance.'

'My dear fellow, I would not miss it for anything.'

I had no keener pleasure than in following Holmes in his professional investigations and in admiring the rapid deductions, as swift as intuitions and yet always founded on a logical basis, with which he unravelled the problems which were submitted to him. I rapidly threw on my clothes and was ready in a few minutes to accompany my friend down to the sitting-room. A lady dressed in black and heavily veiled, who had been sitting in the window, rose as we entered.

'Good-morning, madam,' said Holmes cheerily. 'My name is Sherlock Holmes. This is my intimate friend and associate, Dr Watson, before whom you can speak as freely as before myself. Ha! I am glad to see that Mrs Hudson has had the good sense to light the fire. Pray draw up to it, and I shall order you a cup of hot coffee, for I observe that you are shivering.'

'It is not cold which makes me shiver,' said the woman in a low voice, changing her seat as requested.

'What, then?'

'It is fear, Mr Holmes. It is terror.' She raised her veil as she spoke, and we could see that she was indeed in a pitiable state of agitation, her face all drawn and grey, with restless, frightened eyes, like those of some hunted animal. Her features and figure were those of a woman of thirty, but her hair was shot with premature grey, and her expression was weary and haggard. Sherlock Holmes ran her over with one of his quick, all-comprehensive glances.

'You must not fear,' said he soothingly, bending forward and patting her forearm. 'We shall soon set matters right, I have no doubt. You have come in by train this morning, I see.'

'You know me, then?'

'No, but I observe the second half of a return ticket in the palm of your left glove. You must have started early, and yet you had a good drive in a dogcart, along heavy roads, before you reached the station.'

The lady gave a violent start and stared in bewilderment at my companion.

'There is no mystery, my dear madam,' said he, smiling. 'The left arm of your jacket is spattered with mud in no less than seven places. The marks are perfectly fresh. There is no vehicle save a dogcart which throws up mud in that way, and then only when you sit on the left-hand side of the driver.'

'Whatever your reasons may be, you are perfectly correct,' said she. 'I started from home before six, reached Leatherhead at twenty past, and came in by the first train to Waterloo. Sir, I can stand this strain no longer; I shall go mad if it continues. I have no one to turn to – none, save only one, who cares for me, and he, poor fellow, can be of little aid. I have heard of you, Mr Holmes; I have heard of you from Mrs Farintosh, whom you helped in the hour of her sore need. It was from her that I had your address. Oh, sir, do you not think that you could help me, too, and at least throw a little light through the dense darkness which surrounds me? At present it is out of my power to reward you for your services, but in a month or six weeks I shall be married, with the control of my own income, and then at least you shall not find me ungrateful.'

Holmes turned to his desk, and unlocking it, drew out a small case-book, which he consulted.

'Farintosh,' said he. 'Ah yes, I recall the case; it was concerned with an opal tiara. I think it was before your time, Watson. I can only say, madam, that I shall be happy to devote the same care to your case as

I did to that of your friend. As to reward, my profession is its own reward; but you are at liberty to defray whatever expenses I may be put to, at the time which suits you best. And now I beg that you will lay before us everything that may help us in forming an opinion upon the matter.'

'Alas!' replied our visitor, 'the very horror of my situation lies in the fact that my fears are so vague, and my suspicions depend so entirely upon small points, which might seem trivial to another, that even he to whom of all others I have a right to look for help and advice looks upon all that I tell him about it as the fancies of a nervous woman. He does not say so, but I can read it from his soothing answers and averted eyes. But I have heard, Mr Holmes, that you can see deeply into the manifold wickedness of the human heart. You may advise me how to walk amid the dangers which encompass me.'

'I am all attention, madam.'

'My name is Helen Stoner, and I am living with my stepfather, who is the last survivor of one of the oldest Saxon families in England, the Roylotts of Stoke Moran, on the western border of Surrey.'

Holmes nodded his head. 'The name is familiar to me,' said he.

'The family was at one time among the richest in England, and the estates extended over the borders into Berkshire in the north and Hampshire in the west. In the last century, however, four successive heirs were of a dissolute and wasteful disposition, and the family ruin was eventually completed by a gambler in the days of the Regency. Nothing was left save a few acres of ground, and the two-hundred-year-old house, which is itself crushed under a heavy mortgage. The last squire dragged out his existence there, living the horrible life of an aristocratic pauper; but his only son, my stepfather, seeing that he must adapt himself to the new conditions, obtained an advance from a relative which enabled him to take a medical degree and went out to Calcutta, where, by his professional skill and his force of character, he established a large practice. In a fit of anger, however, caused by some robberies which had been perpetrated in the house, he beat his native butler to death and narrowly escaped a capital sentence. As it was, he suffered a long term of imprisonment and afterwards returned to England a morose and disappointed man.

'When Dr Roylott was in India he married my mother, Mrs Stoner, the young widow of Major-General Stoner of the Bengal Artillery. My sister Julia and I were twins, and we were only two years old at the time of my mother's remarriage. She had a considerable sum of money – not less than a thousand pounds a year – and this she bequeathed to Dr Roylott entirely while we resided with him, with a provision that a certain annual sum should be allowed to each of us in the event of our marriage. Shortly after our return to England my mother died – she was killed eight years ago in a railway accident near Crewe. Dr Roylott then abandoned his attempts to establish himself in practice in London and took us to live with him in the old ancestral house at Stoke Moran. The money which my mother had left was enough for all our wants, and there seemed to be no obstacle to our happiness.

'But a terrible change came over our stepfather about this time. Instead of making friends and exchanging visits with our neighbours, who had at first been overjoyed to see a Roylott of Stoke Moran back in the old family seat, he shut himself up in his house and seldom came out save to indulge in ferocious quarrels with whoever might cross his path. Violence of temper approaching to mania has been hereditary in the men of the family, and in my stepfather's case it had, I believe, been intensified by his long residence in the tropics. A series of disgraceful brawls took place, two of which ended in the police-court, until at last he became the terror of the village, and folk would fly at his approach, for he is a man of immense strength and absolutely uncontrollable in his anger.

'Last week he hurled the local blacksmith over a parapet into a stream, and it was only by paying over all the money which I could gather together that I was able to avert another public exposure. He has no friends at all save the wandering gypsies, and he gives these vagabonds leave to encamp upon the few acres of bramble-covered land which represent the family estate, and accepts in return the hospitality of their tents, wandering away with them sometimes for weeks on end. He has a passion also for Indian animals, which are sent over to him by a correspondent, and he has at this moment a cheetah and a baboon, which wander freely over his grounds and are feared by the villagers almost as much as their master.

'You can imagine from what I say that my poor sister Julia and I had no great pleasure in our lives. No servant would stay with us, and for a long time we did all the work of the house. She was but thirty at the time of her death, and yet her hair had already begun to whiten, even as mine has.'

'Your sister is dead, then?'

'She died just two years ago, and it is of her death that I wish to speak to you. You can understand that, living the life which I have described, we were little likely to see anyone of our own age and position. We had, however, an aunt, my mother's maiden sister, Miss Honoria Westphail, who lives near Harrow, and we were occasionally allowed to pay short visits at this lady's house. Julia went there at Christmas two years ago, and met there a half-pay major of marines, to whom she became engaged. My stepfather learned of the engagement when my sister returned, and offered no objection to the marriage; but within a fortnight of the day which had been fixed for the wedding, the terrible event occurred which has deprived me of my only companion.'

Sherlock Holmes had been leaning back in his chair with his eyes closed and his head sunk in a cushion, but he half opened his lids now and glanced across at his visitor.

'Pray be precise as to details,' said he.

'It is easy for me to be so, for every event of that dreadful time is seared into my memory. The manor-house is, as I have already said, very old, and only one wing is now inhabited. The bedrooms in this wing are on the ground floor, the sitting-rooms being in the central block of the buildings. Of these bedrooms the first is Dr Roylott's, the second my sister's and the third my own. There is no communication between them, but they all open out into the same corridor. Do I make myself plain?'

'Perfectly so.'

'The windows of the three rooms open out upon the lawn. That fatal night Dr Roylott had gone to his room early, though we knew that he had not retired to rest, for my sister was troubled by the smell of the strong Indian cigars which it was his custom to smoke. She left her room, therefore, and came into mine, where she sat for some time, chatting about her approaching wedding. At eleven o'clock she rose to leave me, but she paused at the door and looked back.

'"Tell me, Helen," said she, "have you ever heard anyone whistle in the dead of the night?"

'"Never," said I.

'"I suppose that you could not possibly whistle, yourself, in your sleep?"

'"Certainly not. But why?"

'"Because during the last few nights I have always, about three in the morning, heard a low, clear whistle. I am a light sleeper and it has awakened me. I cannot tell where it came from – perhaps from the next room, perhaps from the lawn. I thought that I would just ask you whether you had heard it."

'"No, I have not. It must be those wretched gypsies in the plantation."

'"Very likely. And yet if it were on the lawn, I wonder that you did not hear it also."

'"Ah, but I sleep more heavily than you."

'"Well, it is of no great consequence, at any rate." She smiled back at me, closed my door, and a few moments later I heard her key turn in the lock.'

'Indeed,' said Holmes. 'Was it your custom always to lock yourselves in at night?'

'Always.'

'And why?'

'I think that I mentioned to you that the doctor kept a cheetah and a baboon. We had no feeling of security unless our doors were locked.'

'Quite so. Pray proceed with your statement.'

'I could not sleep that night. A vague feeling of impending mis-fortune impressed me. My sister and I, you will recollect, were twins, and you know how subtle are the links which bind two souls which are so closely allied. It was a wild night. The wind was howling out-side, and the rain was beating and splashing against the windows. Suddenly, amid all the hubbub of the gale, there burst forth the wild scream of a terrified woman. I knew that it was my sister's voice. I sprang from my bed, wrapped a shawl round me, and rushed into the corridor. As I opened my door I seemed to hear a low whistle, such as my sister had described, and a few moments later a clanging sound, as if a mass of metal had fallen. As I ran down the passage, my sister's door was unlocked, and revolved slowly upon its hinges. I stared at it horror-stricken, not knowing what was about to issue from it. By the light of the corridor-lamp I saw my sister appear at the opening, her face blanched with terror, her hands groping for help, her whole fig-ure swaying to and fro like that of a drunkard. I ran to her and threw my arms round her, but at that moment her knees seemed to give way and she fell to the ground. She writhed as one who is in terrible pain, and her limbs were dreadfully convulsed. At first I thought that she had not recognised me, but as I bent over her she suddenly shrieked out in a voice which I shall never forget, "Oh, my God! Helen! It was the band! The speckled band!" There was something else which she would fain have said, and she stabbed with her finger into the air in the direction of the doctor's room, but a fresh convulsion seized her and choked her words. I rushed out, calling loudly for my stepfa-ther, and I met him hastening from his room in his dressing-gown. When he reached my sister's side she was unconscious, and though he poured brandy down her throat and sent for medical aid from the village, all efforts were in vain, for she slowly sank and died without having recovered consciousness. Such was the dreadful end of my beloved sister.'

'One moment,' said Holmes; 'are you sure about this whistle and metallic sound? Could you swear to it?'

245

'That was what the county coroner asked me at the inquiry. It is my strong impression that I heard it, and yet, among the crash of the gale and the creaking of an old house, I may possibly have been deceived.'

'Was your sister dressed?'

'No, she was in her nightdress. In her right hand was found the charred stump of a match, and in her left a matchbox.'

'Showing that she had struck a light and looked about her when the alarm took place. That is important. And what conclusions did the coroner come to?'

'He investigated the case with great care, for Dr Roylott's conduct had long been notorious in the county, but he was unable to find any satisfactory cause of death. My evidence showed that the door had been fastened upon the inner side, and the windows were blocked by old-fashioned shutters with broad iron bars, which were secured every night. The walls were carefully sounded, and were shown to be quite solid all round, and the flooring was also thoroughly examined, with the same result. The chimney is wide, but is barred up by four large staples. It is certain, therefore, that my sister was quite alone when she met her end. Besides, there were no marks of any violence upon her.'

'How about poison?'

'The doctors examined her for it, but without success.'

'What do you think this unfortunate lady died of, then?'

'It is my belief that she died of pure fear and nervous shock, though what it was that frightened her I cannot imagine.'

'Were there gypsies in the plantation at the time?'

'Yes, there are nearly always some there.'

'Ah, and what did you gather from this allusion to a band – a speckled band?'

'Sometimes I have thought that it was merely the wild talk of delirium, sometimes that it may have referred to some band of people, perhaps to these very gypsies in the plantation. I do not know whether the spotted handkerchiefs which so many of them wear over their heads might have suggested the strange adjective which she used.'

Holmes shook his head, like a man who is far from being satisfied.

'These are very deep waters,' said he; 'pray go on with your narrative.'

'Two years have passed since then, and my life has been until lately lonelier than ever. A month ago, however, a dear friend, whom I have known for many years, has done me the honour to ask my hand in marriage. His name is Armitage – Percy Armitage – the second son of Mr Armitage of Crane Water, near Reading. My stepfather has offered no opposition to the match, and we are to be married in the course of the spring. Two days ago some repairs were started in the west wing of the building, and my bedroom wall has been pierced, so that I have had to move into the chamber in which my sister died, and to sleep in the very bed in which she slept. Imagine, then, my thrill of terror when last night, as I lay awake, thinking over her terrible fate, I suddenly heard in the silence of the night the low whistle which had been the herald of her own death. I sprang up and lit the lamp, but nothing was to be seen in the room. I was too shaken to go to bed again, however, so I dressed and as soon as it was daylight I slipped down, got a dog-cart at the Crown Inn, which is opposite, and drove to Leatherhead, whence I have come on this morning with the one object of seeing you and asking your advice.'

'You have done wisely,' said my friend. 'But have you told me all?'

'Yes, all.'

'Miss Roylott, you have not. You are screening your stepfather.'

'Why, what do you mean?'

For answer Holmes pushed back the frill of black lace which fringed the hand that lay upon our visitor's knee. Five little livid spots, the marks of four fingers and a thumb, were printed upon the white wrist.

'You have been cruelly used,' said Holmes.

The lady coloured deeply and covered over her injured wrist. 'He is a hard man,' she said, 'and perhaps he hardly knows his own strength.'

There was a long silence, during which Holmes leaned his chin upon his hands and stared into the crackling fire.

'This is a very deep business,' he said at last. 'There are a thousand details which I should desire to know before I decide upon our course of action. Yet we have not a moment to lose. If we were to come to Stoke Moran today, would it be possible for us to see over these rooms without the knowledge of your stepfather?'

'As it happens, he spoke of coming into town today upon some most important business. It is probable that he will be away all day and that there would be nothing to disturb you. We have a housekeeper now, but she is old and foolish and I could easily get her out of the way.'

'Excellent. You are not averse to this trip, Watson?'

'By no means.'

'Then we shall both come. What are you going to do yourself?'

'I have one or two things which I would wish to do now that I am in town. But I shall return by the twelve o'clock train, so as to be there in time for your coming.'

'And you may expect us early in the afternoon. I have myself some small business matters to attend to. Will you not wait and breakfast?'

'No, I must go. My heart is lightened already since I have confided my trouble to you. I shall look forward to seeing you again this afternoon.' She dropped her thick black veil over her face and glided from the room.

'And what do you think of it all, Watson?' asked Sherlock Holmes, leaning back in his chair.

'It seems to me to be a most dark and sinister business.'

'Dark enough and sinister enough.'

'Yet if the lady is correct in saying that the flooring and walls are sound, and that the door, window and chimney are impassable, then her sister must have been undoubtedly alone when she met her mysterious end.'

'What becomes, then, of these nocturnal whistles, and what of the very peculiar words of the dying woman?'

'I cannot think.'

'When you combine the ideas of whistles at night, the presence of a band of gypsies who are on intimate terms with this old doctor, the fact that we have every reason to believe that the doctor has an interest in preventing his stepdaughter's marriage, the dying allusion to a band and, finally, the fact that Miss Helen Stoner heard a metallic clang, which might have been caused by one of those metal bars that secured the shutters falling back into its place, I think that there is good ground to think that the mystery may be cleared along those lines.'

'But what, then, did the gypsies do?'

'I cannot imagine.'

'I see many objections to any such theory.'

'And so do I. It is precisely for that reason that we are going to Stoke Moran this day. I want to see whether the objections are fatal or if they may be explained away. But what, in the name of the devil . . .?'

The ejaculation had been drawn from my companion by the fact that our door had been suddenly dashed open and a huge man had framed himself in the aperture. His costume was a peculiar mixture of the professional and of the agricultural, consisting of a black top-hat, a long frock-coat and a pair of high gaiters, and he had a hunting-crop swinging in his hand. So tall was he that his hat actually brushed the cross-bar of the doorway, and his breadth seemed to span it across from side to side. A large face, seared with a thousand wrinkles, burned yellow with the sun and marked with every evil passion, was turned from one to the other of us, while his deep-set, bile-shot eyes and his high, thin, fleshless nose gave him somewhat the resemblance to a fierce old bird of prey.

'Which of you is Holmes?' asked this apparition.

'My name, sir; but you have the advantage of me,' said my companion quietly.

'I am Dr Grimesby Roylott, of Stoke Moran.'

'Indeed, doctor,' said Holmes blandly. 'Pray take a seat.'

'I will do nothing of the kind. My stepdaughter has been here. I have traced her. What has she been saying to you?'

'It is a little cold for the time of the year,' said Holmes.

'What has she been saying to you?' screamed the old man furiously.

'But I have heard that the crocuses promise well,' continued my companion imperturbably.

'Ha! You put me off, do you?' said our new visitor, taking a step forward and shaking his hunting-crop. 'I know you, you scoundrel! I have heard of you before. You are Holmes, the meddler.'

My friend smiled.

'Holmes, the busybody!'

His smile broadened.

'Holmes, the Scotland Yard Jack-in-office!'

Holmes chuckled heartily. 'Your conversation is most entertaining,' said he. 'When you go out close the door, for there is a decided draught.'

'I will go when I have said my say. Don't you dare to meddle with my affairs. I know that Miss Stoner has been here. I traced her! I am a dangerous man to fall foul of! See here.' He stepped swiftly forward, seized the poker and bent it into a curve with his huge brown hands. 'See that you keep yourself out of my grip,' he snarled, and hurling the twisted poker into the fireplace, he strode out of the room.

'He seems a very amiable person,' said Holmes, laughing. 'I am not quite so bulky, but if he had remained I might have shown him that my grip was not much more feeble than his own.' As he spoke he picked up the steel poker and, with a sudden effort, straightened it out again.

'Fancy his having the insolence to confound me with the official detective force! This incident gives zest to our investigation, however, and I only trust that our little friend will not suffer from her imprudence in allowing this brute to trace her. And now, Watson, we shall order breakfast, and afterwards I shall walk down to Doctors' Commons, where I hope to get some data which may help us in this matter.'

It was nearly one o'clock when Sherlock Holmes returned from his excursion. He held in his hand a sheet of blue paper, scrawled over with notes and figures.

'I have seen the will of the deceased wife,' said he. 'To determine its exact meaning I have been obliged to work out the present prices of the investments with which it is concerned. The total income, which at the time of the wife's death was little short of £1,100, is now, through the fall in agricultural prices, not more than £750. Each daughter can claim an income of £250 in case of marriage. It is evident, therefore, that if both girls had married, this beauty would have had a mere pittance, while even one marriage would cripple him to a very serious extent. My morning's work has not been wasted, since it has proved that he has the very strongest motives for standing in the way of anything of the sort. And now, Watson, this is too serious for dawdling, especially as the old man is aware that we are interesting ourselves in his affairs; so if you are ready, we shall call a cab and drive to Waterloo. I should be very much obliged if you would slip your revolver into your pocket. An Eley's No. 2 is an excellent argument with gentlemen who can twist steel pokers into knots. That and a toothbrush are, I think, all that we need.'

At Waterloo we were fortunate in catching a train for Leatherhead, where we hired a trap at the station inn and drove for four or five miles through the lovely Surrey lanes. It was a perfect day, with a bright sun and a few fleecy clouds in the heavens. The trees and wayside hedges were just throwing out their first green shoots, and the air was full of the pleasant smell of the moist earth. To me at least there was a strange contrast between the sweet promise of the spring and this sinister quest upon which we were engaged. My companion sat in the front of the trap, his arms folded, his hat pulled down over his eyes and his chin sunk upon his breast, buried in the deepest thought. Suddenly, however, he started, tapped me on the shoulder and pointed over the meadows.

'Look there!' said he.

A heavily timbered park stretched up in a gentle slope, thickening into a grove at the highest point. From amid the branches there jutted out the grey gables and high roof-tree of a very old mansion.

'Stoke Moran?' said he.

'Yes, sir, that be the house of Dr Grimesby Roylott,' remarked the driver.

'There is some building going on there,' said Holmes; 'that is where we are going.'

'There's the village,' said the driver, pointing to a cluster of roofs some distance to the left; 'but if you want to get to the house, you'll find it shorter to get over this stile, and so by the footpath over the fields. There it is, where the lady is walking.'

'And the lady, I fancy, is Miss Stoner,' observed Holmes, shading his eyes. 'Yes, I think we had better do as you suggest.'

We got off, paid our fare, and the trap rattled back on its way to Leatherhead.

'I thought it as well,' said Holmes, as we climbed the stile, 'that this fellow should think we had come here as architects, or on some definite business. It may stop his gossip. Good-afternoon, Miss Stoner. You see that we have been as good as our word.'

Our client of the morning had hurried forward to meet us with a face which spoke her joy. 'I have been waiting so eagerly for you,' she cried, shaking hands with us warmly. 'All has turned out splendidly. Dr Roylott has gone to town, and it is unlikely that he will be back before evening.'

'We have had the pleasure of making the doctor's acquaintance,' said Holmes, and in a few words he sketched out what had occurred. Miss Stoner turned white to the lips as she listened.

'Good heavens!' she cried, 'he has followed me, then.'

'So it appears.'

'He is so cunning that I never know when I am safe from him. What will he say when he returns?'

'He must guard himself, for he may find that there is someone more cunning than himself upon his track. You must lock yourself from him tonight. If he is violent, we shall take you away to your aunt's at Harrow. Now, we must make the best use of our time, so kindly take us at once to the rooms which we are to examine.'

The building was of grey, lichen-blotched stone, with a high central portion and two curving wings, like the claws of a crab, thrown out on each side. In one of these wings the windows were broken and blocked with wooden boards, while the roof was partly caved in, a picture of ruin. The central portion was in little better repair, but the right-hand block was comparatively modern, and the blinds in the windows, with the blue smoke curling up from the chimneys, showed that this was where the family resided. Some scaffolding had been erected against the end wall, and the stonework had been broken into, but there were no signs of any workmen at the moment of our visit. Holmes walked slowly up and down the ill-trimmed lawn and examined with deep attention the outsides of the windows.

'This, I take it, belongs to the room in which you used to sleep, the centre one to your sister's, and the one next to the main building to Dr Roylott's chamber?'

'Exactly so. But I am now sleeping in the middle one.'

'Pending the alterations, as I understand. By the way, there does not seem to be any very pressing need for repairs at that end wall.'

'There were none. I believe that it was an excuse to move me from my room.'

'Ah! that is suggestive. Now, on the other side of this narrow wing runs the corridor from which these three rooms open. There are windows in it, of course?'

'Yes, but very small ones. Too narrow for anyone to pass through.'

'As you both locked your doors at night, your rooms were unapproachable from that side. Now, would you have the kindness to go into your room and bar your shutters?'

Miss Stoner did so, and Holmes, after a careful examination through the open window, endeavoured in every way to force the shutter open, but without success. There was no slit through which a knife could be passed to raise the bar. Then with his lens he tested the hinges, but they were of solid iron, built firmly into the massive masonry. 'Hum!' said he, scratching his chin in some perplexity, 'my theory certainly presents some difficulties. No one could pass these shutters if they were bolted. Well, we shall see if the inside throws any light upon the matter.'

A small side door led into the whitewashed corridor from which the three bedrooms opened. Holmes refused to examine the third chamber, so we passed at once to the second, that in which Miss Stoner was now sleeping and in which her sister had met with her fate. It was a homely little room, with a low ceiling and a gaping fireplace, after the fashion of old country-houses. A brown chest of drawers stood in one corner, a narrow white-counterpaned bed in another, and a dressing-table on the left-hand side of the window. These articles, with two small wickerwork chairs, made up all the furniture in the room save for a square of Wilton carpet in the centre. The boards round and the panelling of the walls were of brown, worm-eaten oak, so old and discoloured that it may have dated from the original building of the house. Holmes drew one of the chairs into a corner and sat silent, while his eyes travelled round and round and up and down, taking in every detail of the apartment.

'Where does that bell communicate with?' he asked at last pointing to a thick bell-rope which hung down beside the bed, the tassel actually lying upon the pillow.

'It goes to the housekeeper's room.'

'It looks newer than the other things?'

'Yes, it was only put there a couple of years ago.'

'Your sister asked for it, I suppose?'

'No, I never heard of her using it. We used always to get what we wanted for ourselves.'

'Indeed, it seemed unnecessary to put so nice a bell-pull there. You will excuse me for a few minutes while I satisfy myself as to this floor.' He threw himself down upon his face with his lens in his hand and crawled swiftly backward and forward, examining minutely the cracks between the boards. Then he did the same with the woodwork with which the chamber was panelled. Finally he walked over to the bed and spent some time in staring at it and in running his eye up and down the wall. Finally he took the bell-rope in his hand and gave it a brisk tug.

'Why, it's a dummy,' said he.

'Won't it ring?'

'No, it is not even attached to a wire. This is very interesting. You can see now that it is fastened to a hook just above where the little opening for the ventilator is.'

'How very absurd! I never noticed that before.'

'Very strange!' muttered Holmes, pulling at the rope. 'There are one or two very singular points about this room. For example, what a fool a builder must be to open a ventilator into another room, when, with the same trouble, he might have communicated with the outside air!'

'That is also quite modern,' said the lady.

'Done about the same time as the bell-rope?' remarked Holmes.

'Yes, there were several little changes carried out about that time.'

'They seem to have been of a most interesting character – dummy bell-ropes and ventilators which do not ventilate. With your permission, Miss Stoner, we shall now carry our researches into the inner apartment.'

Dr Grimesby Roylott's chamber was larger than that of his step-daughter, but was as plainly furnished. A camp-bed, a small wooden shelf full of books, mostly of a technical character, an armchair beside the bed, a plain wooden chair against the wall, a round table and a large iron safe were the principal things which met the eye. Holmes walked slowly round and examined each and all of them with the keenest interest.

'What's in here?' he asked, tapping the safe.

'My stepfather's business papers.'

'Oh! you have seen inside, then?'

'Only once, some years ago. I remember that it was full of papers.'

'There isn't a cat in it, for example?'

'No. What a strange idea!'

'Well, look at this!' He took up a small saucer of milk which stood on the top of it.

'No; we don't keep a cat. But there is a cheetah and a baboon.'

'Ah, yes, of course! Well, a cheetah is just a big cat, and yet a saucer of milk does not go very far in satisfying its wants, I dare say. There is one point which I should wish to determine.' He squatted down in front of the wooden chair and examined the seat of it with the greatest attention.

'Thank you. That is quite settled,' said he, rising and putting his lens in his pocket. 'Hallo! Here is something interesting!'

The object which had caught his eye was a small dog-leash hung on one corner of the bed. The leash, however, was curled upon itself and tied so as to make a loop of whipcord.

'What do you make of that, Watson?'

'It's a common enough leash. But I don't know why it should be tied.'

'That is not quite so common, is it? Ah, me! it's a wicked world, and when a clever man turns his brains to crime it is the worst of all. I think that I have seen enough now, Miss Stoner, and with your permission we shall walk out upon the lawn.'

I had never seen my friend's face so grim or his brow so dark as it was when we turned from the scene of this investigation. We had walked several times up and down the lawn, neither Miss Stoner nor myself liking to break in upon his thoughts before he roused himself from his reverie.

'It is very essential, Miss Stoner,' said he, 'that you should absolutely follow my advice in every respect.'

'I shall most certainly do so.'

'The matter is too serious for any hesitation. Your life may depend upon your compliance.'

'I assure you that I am in your hands.'

'In the first place, both my friend and I must spend the night in your room.'

Both Miss Stoner and I gazed at him in astonishment.

'Yes, it must be so. Let me explain. I believe that that is the village inn over there?'

'Yes, that is the Crown.'

'Very good. Your windows would be visible from there?'

'Certainly.'

'You must confine yourself to your room, on pretence of a headache, when your stepfather comes back. Then when you hear him retire for the night, you must open the shutters of your window, undo the hasp, put your lamp there as a signal to us, and then withdraw quietly with everything which you are likely to want into the room which you used to occupy. I have no doubt that, in spite of the repairs, you could manage there for one night.'

'Oh, yes, easily.'

'The rest you will leave in our hands.'

'But what will you do?'

'We shall spend the night in your room, and we shall investigate the cause of this noise which has disturbed you.'

'I believe, Mr Holmes, that you have already made up your mind,' said Miss Stoner, laying her hand upon my companion's sleeve.

'Perhaps I have.'

'Then, for pity's sake, tell me what was the cause of my sister's death.'

'I should prefer to have clearer proofs before I speak.'

'You can at least tell me whether my own thought is correct, that she died from some sudden fright.'

'No, I do not think so. I think that there was probably some more tangible cause. And now, Miss Stoner, we must leave you, for if Dr Roylott returned and saw us our journey would have been in vain. Goodbye, and be brave, for if you will do what I have told you, you may rest assured that we shall soon drive away the dangers that threaten you.'

Sherlock Holmes and I had no difficulty in engaging a bedroom and sitting-room at the Crown Inn. They were on the upper floor, and from our window we could command a view of the avenue gate, and of the inhabited wing of Stoke Moran Manor House. At dusk we saw Dr Grimesby Roylott drive past, his huge form looming up beside the little figure of the lad who drove him. The boy had some slight difficulty in undoing the heavy iron gates, and we heard the hoarse roar of the doctor's voice and saw the fury with which he shook his clenched fists at him. The trap drove on, and a few minutes later we saw a sudden light spring up among the trees as the lamp was lit in one of the sitting-rooms.

'Do you know, Watson,' said Holmes, as we sat together in the gathering darkness, 'I have really some scruples as to taking you tonight. There is a distinct element of danger.'

'Can I be of assistance?'

'Your presence might be invaluable.'

'Then I shall certainly come.'

'It is very kind of you.'

'You speak of danger. You have evidently seen more in these rooms than was visible to me.'

'No, but I fancy that I may have deduced a little more. I imagine that you saw all that I did.'

'I saw nothing remarkable save the bell-rope, and what purpose that could answer I confess is more than I can imagine.'

'You saw the ventilator, too?'

'Yes, but I do not think that it is such a very unusual thing to have a small opening between two rooms. It was so small that a rat could hardly pass through.'

'I knew that we should find a ventilator before ever we came to Stoke Moran.'

'My dear Holmes!'

'Oh, yes, I did. You remember in her statement she said that her sister could smell Dr Roylott's cigar. Now, of course that suggested at once that there must be a communication between the two rooms. It could only be a small one or it would have been remarked upon at the coroner's enquiry. I deduced a ventilator.'

'But what harm can there be in that?'

'Well, there is at least a curious coincidence of dates. A ventilator is made, a cord is hung, and a lady who sleeps in the bed dies. Does not that strike you?'

'I cannot as yet see any connection.'

'Did you observe anything very peculiar about that bed?'

'No.'

'It was clamped to the floor. Did you ever see a bed fastened like that before?'

'I cannot say that I have.'

'The lady could not move her bed. It must always be in the same relative position to the ventilator and to the rope – or so we may call it, since it was clearly never meant for a bell-pull.'

'Holmes,' I cried, 'I seem to see dimly what you are hinting at. We are only just in time to prevent some subtle and horrible crime.'

'Subtle enough and horrible enough. When a doctor does go wrong he is the first of criminals. He has nerve and he has knowledge. Palmer and Pritchard were among the heads of their profession. This man strikes even deeper, but I think, Watson, that we shall be able to strike deeper still. But we shall have horrors enough before the night is over; for goodness' sake let us have a quiet pipe and turn our minds for a few hours to something more cheerful.'

About nine o'clock the light among the trees was extinguished, and all was dark in the direction of the Manor House. Two hours passed slowly away, and then, suddenly, just at the stroke of eleven, a single bright light shone out right in front of us.

'That is our signal,' said Holmes, springing to his feet; 'it comes from the middle window.'

As we passed out he exchanged a few words with the landlord, explaining that we were going on a late visit to an acquaintance, and that it was possible that we might spend the night there. A moment later we were out on the dark road, a chill wind blowing in our faces, and one yellow light twinkling in front of us through the gloom to guide us on our sombre errand.

There was little difficulty in entering the grounds, for unrepaired breaches gaped in the old park wall. Making our way among the trees, we reached the lawn, crossed it, and were about to enter through the window when out from a clump of laurel bushes there darted what seemed to be a hideous and distorted child, who threw itself upon the grass with writhing limbs and then ran swiftly across the lawn into the darkness.

'My God!' I whispered; 'did you see it?'

Holmes was for the moment as startled as I. His hand closed like a vice upon my wrist in his agitation. Then he broke into a low laugh and put his lips to my ear. 'It is a nice household,' he murmured. 'That is the baboon.'

I had forgotten the strange pets which the doctor affected. There was a cheetah, too; perhaps we might find it upon our shoulders at any moment. I confess that I felt easier in my mind when, after following Holmes's example and slipping off my shoes, I found myself inside the bedroom. My companion noiselessly closed the shutters, moved the lamp on to the table, and cast his eyes round the room. All was as we had seen it in the daytime.

Then creeping up to me and making a trumpet of his hand, he whispered into my ear again so gently that it was all that I could do to distinguish the words: 'The least sound would be fatal to our plans.'

I nodded to show that I had heard.

'We must sit without light. He would see it through the ventilator.'

I nodded again.

'Do not go to sleep; your very life may depend upon it. Have your pistol ready in case we should need it. I will sit on the side of the bed, and you in that chair.'

I took out my revolver and laid it on the corner of the table.

Holmes had brought up a long thin cane, and this he placed upon the bed beside him. By it he laid the box of matches and the stump of a candle. Then he turned down the lamp, and we were left in darkness.

How shall I ever forget that dreadful vigil? I could not hear a sound, not even the drawing of a breath, and yet I knew that my companion sat open-eyed, within a few feet of me, in the same state of nervous tension in which I was myself. The shutters cut off the least ray of light, and we waited in absolute darkness.

From outside came the occasional cry of a night-bird, and once at our very window a long-drawn cat-like whine, which told us that the cheetah was indeed at liberty. Far away we could hear the deep tones of the parish clock, which boomed out every quarter of an hour. How long they seemed, those quarters! Twelve struck, and one, and two, and three, and still we sat waiting silently for whatever might befall.

Suddenly there was the momentary gleam of a light up in the direction of the ventilator, which vanished immediately, but was succeeded by a strong smell of burning oil and heated metal. Someone in the next room had lit a dark-lantern. I heard a gentle sound of movement, and then all was silent once more, though the smell grew stronger. For half an hour I sat with straining ears. Then suddenly another sound became audible – a very gentle, soothing sound, like that of a small jet of steam escaping continually from a kettle. The instant that we heard it, Holmes sprang from the bed, struck a match and lashed furiously with his cane at the bell-pull.

'You see it, Watson?' he yelled. 'You see it?'

But I saw nothing. At the moment when Holmes struck the light, I heard a low, clear whistle, but the sudden glare flashing into my weary eyes made it impossible for me to tell what it was at which my friend lashed so savagely. I could, however, see that his face was deadly pale and filled with horror and loathing. He had ceased to strike and was gazing up at the ventilator when suddenly there broke from the silence of the night the most horrible cry to which I have ever listened. It swelled up louder and louder, a hoarse yell of pain and fear and anger all mingled in the one dreadful shriek. They say that away down in the village, and even in the distant parsonage, that cry raised the sleepers from their beds. It struck cold to our hearts, and I stood gazing at Holmes, and he at me, until the last echoes of it had died away into the silence from which it had arisen.

'What can it mean?' I gasped.

'It means that it is all over,' Holmes answered. 'And perhaps, after all, it is for the best. Take your pistol, and we will enter Dr Roylott's room.'

With a grave face he lit the lamp and led the way down the corridor. Twice he struck at the chamber door without any reply from within.

Then he turned the handle and entered, I at his heels, with the cocked pistol in my hand.

It was a singular sight which met our eyes. On the table stood a dark-lantern, with the shutter half open, throwing a brilliant beam of light upon the iron safe, the door of which was ajar. Beside this table, on the wooden chair, sat Dr Grimesby Roylott clad in a long grey dressing-gown, his bare ankles protruding beneath and his feet thrust into red heel-less Turkish slippers. Across his lap lay the short stock with the long leash which we had noticed during the day. His chin was cocked upwards and his eyes were fixed in a dreadful, rigid stare at the corner of the ceiling. Round his brow he had a peculiar yellow band, with brownish speckles, which seemed to be bound tightly round his head. As we entered he made neither sound nor motion.

'The band! the speckled band!' whispered Holmes.

I took a step forward. In an instant his strange headgear began to move, and there reared itself from among his hair the squat diamond-shaped head and puffed neck of a loathsome serpent.

'It is a swamp adder!' cried Holmes; 'the deadliest snake in India. He has died within ten seconds of being bitten. Violence does, in truth, recoil upon the violent, and the schemer falls into the pit which he digs for another. Let us thrust this creature back into its den, and we can then remove Miss Stoner to some place of shelter and let the county police know what has happened.'

As he spoke he drew the dog-whip swiftly from the dead man's lap, and throwing the noose round the reptile's neck he drew it from its horrid perch and, carrying it at arm's length, threw it into the iron safe, which he closed upon it.

Such are the true facts of the death of Dr Grimesby Roylott of Stoke Moran. It is not necessary that I should prolong a narrative which has already run to too great a length by telling how we broke the sad news to the terrified girl, how we conveyed her by the morning train to the care of her good aunt at Harrow, of how the slow process of official enquiry came to the conclusion that the doctor met his fate while indiscreetly playing with a dangerous pet. The little which I had yet to learn of the case was told me by Sherlock Holmes as we travelled back next day.

'I had,' said he, 'come to an entirely erroneous conclusion which shows, my dear Watson, how dangerous it always is to reason from insufficient data. The presence of the gypsies, and the use of the word "band", which was used by the poor girl, no doubt, to explain the appearance which she had caught a hurried glimpse of by the light of her match, were sufficient to put me upon an entirely wrong scent. I can only claim the merit that I instantly reconsidered my position when, however, it became clear to me that whatever danger threatened an occupant of the room could not come either from the window or the door. My attention was speedily drawn, as I have already remarked to you, to this ventilator, and to the bell-rope which hung down to the bed. The discovery that this was a dummy, and that the bed was clamped to the floor, instantly gave rise to the suspicion that the rope was there as a bridge for something passing through the hole and coming to the bed. The idea of a snake instantly occurred to me, and when I coupled it with my knowledge that the doctor was furnished with a supply of creatures from India, I felt that I was probably on the right track. The idea of using a form of poison which could not possibly be discovered by any chemical test was just such a one as would occur to a clever and ruthless man who had had an Eastern training. The rapidity with which such a poison would take effect would also, from his point of view, be an advantage. It would be a sharp-eyed coroner, indeed, who could distinguish the two little dark punctures which would show where the poison fangs had done their work. Then I thought of the whistle. Of course he must recall the snake before the morning light revealed it to the victim. He had trained it, probably by the use of the milk which we saw, to return to him when summoned. He would put it through this ventilator at the hour that he thought best, with the certainty that it would crawl down the rope and land on the bed. It might or might not bite the occupant, perhaps she might escape every night for a week, but sooner or later she must fall a victim.

'I had come to these conclusions before ever I had entered his room. An inspection of his chair showed me that he had been in the habit of standing on it, which of course would be necessary in order that he should reach the ventilator. The sight of the safe, the saucer of milk and the loop of whipcord were enough finally to dispel any doubts which may have remained. The metallic clang heard by Miss Stoner was obviously caused by her stepfather hastily closing the door of his safe upon its terrible occupant. Having once made up my mind, you know the steps which I took in order to put the matter to the proof. I heard the creature hiss, as I have no doubt that you did also, and I instantly lit the light and attacked it.'

'With the result of driving it through the ventilator.'

'And also with the result of causing it to turn upon its master at the other side. Some of the blows of my cane came home and roused its snakish temper, so that it flew upon the first person it saw. In this way I am no doubt indirectly responsible for Dr Grimesby Roylott's death, but I cannot say that it is likely to weigh very heavily upon my conscience.'

Stories from
The Adventures of
Sherlock Holmes

The Adventure of the Engineer's Thumb

Of all the problems which have been submitted to my friend, Mr Sherlock Holmes, for solution during the years of our intimacy, there were only two which I was the means of introducing to his notice – that of Mr Hatherley's thumb and that of Colonel Warburton's madness. Of these the latter may have afforded a finer field for an acute and original observer but the other was so strange in its inception and so dramatic in its details that it may be the more worthy of being placed upon record, even if it gave my friend fewer openings for those deductive methods of reasoning by which he achieved such remarkable results. The story has, I believe, been told more than once in the newspapers, but, like all such narratives, its effect is much less striking when set forth *en bloc* in a single half-column of print than when the facts slowly evolve before your own eyes, and the mystery clears gradually away as each new discovery furnishes a step which leads on to the complete truth. At the time, the circumstances made a deep impression upon me, and the lapse of two years has hardly served to weaken the effect.

It was in the summer of 1889, not long after my marriage, that the events occurred which I am now about to summarise. I had returned to civil practice and had finally abandoned Holmes in his Baker Street rooms, although I continually visited him and occasionally even persuaded him to forgo his Bohemian habits so far as to come and visit us. My practice had steadily increased, and as I happened to live at no very great distance from Paddington Station, I got a few patients from among the officials. One of these, whom I had cured of a painful and lingering disease, was never weary of advertising my virtues and of endeavouring to send me on every sufferer over whom he might have any influence.

One morning, at a little before seven o'clock, I was awakened by the maid tapping at the door to announce that two men had come from Paddington and were waiting in the consulting-room. I dressed hurriedly, for I knew by experience that railway cases were seldom trivial, and hastened downstairs. As I descended, my old ally, the guard, came out of the room and closed the door tightly behind him.

'I've got him here,' he whispered, jerking his thumb over his shoulder; 'he's all right.'

'What is it, then?' I asked, for his manner suggested that it was some strange creature which he had caged up in my room.

'It's a new patient,' he whispered. 'I thought I'd bring him round myself; then he couldn't slip away. There he is, all safe and sound. I must go now, doctor; I have my dooties, just the same as you.' And off he went, this trusty tout, without even giving me time to thank him.

I entered my consulting-room and found a gentleman seated by the table. He was quietly dressed in a suit of heather tweed with a soft cloth cap which he had laid down upon my books. Round one of his hands he had a handkerchief wrapped, which was mottled all over with bloodstains. He was young, not more than five-and-twenty, I should say, with a strong, masculine face; but he was exceedingly pale and gave me the impression of a man who was suffering from some strong agitation, which it took all his strength of mind to control.

'I am sorry to knock you up so early, doctor,' said he, 'but I have had a very serious accident during the night. I came in by train this morning, and on enquiring at Paddington as to where I might find a doctor, a worthy fellow very kindly escorted me here. I gave the maid a card, but I see that she has left it upon the side-table.'

I took it up and glanced at it. 'Mr Victor Hatherley, hydraulic engineer, 16a Victoria Street (3rd floor)'. That was the name, style and abode of my morning visitor. 'I regret that I have kept you waiting,' said I, sitting down in my library-chair. 'You are fresh from a night journey, I understand, which is in itself a monotonous occupation.'

'Oh, my night could not be called monotonous,' said he, and laughed. He laughed very heartily, with a high, ringing note, leaning back in his chair and shaking his sides. All my medical instincts rose up against that laugh.

'Stop it!' I cried; 'pull yourself together!' and I poured out some water from a caraffe.

It was useless, however. He was off in one of those hysterical outbursts which come upon a strong nature when some great crisis is over and gone. Presently he came to himself once more, very weary and pale-looking.

'I have been making a fool of myself,' he gasped.

'Not at all. Drink this.' I dashed some brandy into the water, and the colour began to come back to his bloodless cheeks.

'That's better!' said he. 'And now, doctor, perhaps you would kindly attend to my thumb, or rather to the place where my thumb used to be.'

He unwound the handkerchief and held out his hand. It gave even my hardened nerves a shudder to look at it. There were four protruding fingers and a horrid red spongy surface where the thumb should have been. It had been hacked or torn right out from the roots.

'Good heavens!' I cried, 'this is a terrible injury. It must have bled considerably.'

'Yes, it did. I fainted when it was done, and I think that I must have been senseless for a long time. When I came to I found that it was still bleeding, so I tied one end of my handkerchief very tightly round the wrist and braced it up with a twig.'

'Excellent! You should have been a surgeon.'

'It is a question of hydraulics, you see, and came within my own province.'

'This has been done,' said I, examining the wound, 'by a very heavy and sharp instrument.'

'A thing like a cleaver,' said he.

'An accident, I presume?'

'By no means.'

'What! a murderous attack?'

'Very murderous indeed.'

'You horrify me.'

I sponged the wound, cleaned it, dressed it, and finally covered it over with cotton wadding and carbolised bandages. He lay back without wincing, though he bit his lip from time to time.

'How is that?' I asked when I had finished.

'Capital! Between your brandy and your bandage, I feel a new man. I was very weak, but I have had a good deal to go through.'

'Perhaps you had better not speak of the matter. It is evidently trying to your nerves.'

'Oh, no, not now. I shall have to tell my tale to the police; but, between ourselves, if it were not for the convincing evidence of this wound of mine, I should be surprised if they believed my statement, for it is a very extraordinary one, and I have not much in the way of proof with which to back it up; and, even if they believe me, the clues which I can give them are so vague that it is a question whether justice will be done.'

'Ha!' cried I, 'if it is anything in the nature of a problem which you desire to see solved, I should strongly recommend you to come to my friend, Mr Sherlock Holmes, before you go to the official police.'

'Oh, I have heard of that fellow,' answered my visitor, 'and I should be very glad if he would take the matter up, though of course I must use the official police as well. Would you give me an introduction to him?'

'I'll do better. I'll take you round to him myself.'

'I should be immensely obliged to you.'

'We'll call a cab and go together. We shall be just in time to have a little breakfast with him. Do you feel equal to it?'

'Yes; I shall not feel easy until I have told my story.'

'Then my servant will call a cab, and I shall be with you in an instant.' I rushed upstairs, explained the matter shortly to my wife, and in five minutes was inside a hansom, driving with my new acquaintance to Baker Street.

Sherlock Holmes was, as I expected, lounging about his sitting-room in his dressing-gown, reading the agony column of *The Times* and smoking his before-breakfast pipe, which was composed of all the plugs and dottles left from his smokes of the day before, all carefully dried and collected on the corner of the mantelpiece. He received us in his quietly genial fashion, ordered fresh rashers and eggs, and joined us in a hearty meal. When it was concluded he settled our new acquaintance upon the sofa, placed a pillow beneath his head and laid a glass of brandy and water within his reach.

'It is easy to see that your experience has been no common one, Mr Hatherley,' said he. 'Pray, lie down there and make yourself absolutely at home. Tell us what you can, but stop when you are tired and keep up your strength with a little stimulant.'

'Thank you,' said my patient, 'but I have felt another man since the doctor bandaged me, and I think that your breakfast has completed the cure. I shall take up as little of your valuable time as possible, so I shall start at once upon my peculiar experiences.'

Holmes sat in his big armchair with the weary, heavy-lidded expression which veiled his keen and eager nature, while I sat opposite to him, and we listened in silence to the strange story which our visitor detailed to us.

'You must know,' said he, 'that I am an orphan and a bachelor, residing alone in lodgings in London. By profession I am a hydraulic engineer, and I had considerable experience of my work during the seven years that I was apprenticed to Venner & Matheson, the well-known firm, of Greenwich. Two years ago, having served my time, and having also come into a fair sum of money through my poor father's death, I determined to start in business for myself and took professional chambers in Victoria Street.

'I suppose that everyone finds his first independent start in business a dreary experience. To me it has been exceptionally so. During two years I have had three consultations and one small job, and that is absolutely all that my profession has brought me. My gross takings amount to twenty-seven pounds ten. Every day, from nine in the morning until four in the afternoon, I waited in my little den, until at last my heart began to sink, and I came to believe that I should never have any practice at all.

'Yesterday, however, just as I was thinking of leaving the office, my clerk entered to say there was a gentleman waiting who wished to see me upon business. He brought up a card, too, with the name of Colonel Lysander Stark engraved upon it. Close at his heels came the colonel himself, a man rather over the middle size, but of an exceeding thinness. I do not think that I have ever seen so thin a man. His whole face sharpened away into nose and chin, and the skin of his cheeks was drawn quite tense over his outstanding bones. Yet this emaciation seemed to be his natural habit and due to no disease, for his eye was bright, his step brisk and his bearing assured. He was plainly but neatly dressed, and his age, I should judge, would be nearer forty than thirty.

'"Mr Hatherley?" said he, with something of a German accent. "You have been recommended to me, Mr Hatherley, as being a man who is not only proficient in his profession but is also discreet and capable of preserving a secret."

'I bowed, feeling as flattered as any young man would at such an address. "May I ask who it was who gave me so good a character?"

'"Well, perhaps it is better that I should not tell you that just at this moment. I have it from the same source that you are both an orphan and a bachelor and are residing alone in London."

'"That is quite correct," I answered; "but you will excuse me if I say that I cannot see how all this bears upon my professional qualifications. I understand that it was on a professional matter that you wished to speak to me?"

'"Undoubtedly so. But you will find that all I say is really to the point. I have a professional commission for you, but absolute secrecy is quite essential – *absolute* secrecy, you understand, and of course we may expect that more from a man who is alone than from one who lives in the bosom of his family."

'"If I promise to keep a secret," said I, "you may absolutely depend upon my doing so."

'He looked very hard at me as I spoke, and it seemed to me that I had never seen so suspicious and questioning an eye.

'"Do you promise, then?" said he at last.

'"Yes, I promise."

'"Absolute and complete silence before, during and after? No reference to the matter at all, either in word or writing?"

'"I have already given you my word."

'"Very good." He suddenly sprang up, and darting like lightning across the room, he flung open the door. The passage outside was empty.

'"That's all right," said he, coming back. "I know that clerks are sometimes curious as to their master's affairs. Now we can talk in safety." He drew up his chair very close to mine and began to stare at me again with the same questioning and thoughtful look.

'A feeling of repulsion and of something akin to fear had begun to rise within me at the strange antics of this fleshless man. Even my dread of losing a client could not restrain me from showing my impatience.

'"I beg that you will state your business, sir," said I; "my time is of value." Heaven forgive me for that last sentence, but the words came to my lips.

'"How would fifty guineas for a night's work suit you?" he asked.

'"Most admirably."

'"I say a night's work, but an hour's would be nearer the mark. I simply want your opinion about a hydraulic stamping machine which has got out of gear. If you show us what is wrong we shall soon set it right ourselves. What do you think of such a commission as that?"

'"The work appears to be light and the pay munificent."

'"Precisely so. We shall want you to come tonight by the last train."

'"Where to?"

'"To Eyford in Berkshire. It is a little place near the borders of Oxfordshire, and within seven miles of Reading. There is a train from Paddington which would bring you there at about 11.15."

'"Very good."

'"I shall come down in a carriage to meet you."

'"There is a drive, then?"

'"Yes, our little place is quite out in the country. It is a good seven miles from Eyford Station."

'"Then we can hardly get there before midnight. I suppose there would be no chance of a train back. I should be compelled to stop the night."

'"Yes, we could easily give you a shakedown."

'"That is very awkward. Could I not come at some more convenient hour?"

'"We have judged it best that you should come late. It is to recompense you for any inconvenience that we are paying to you, a young and unknown man, a fee which would buy an opinion from the very heads of your profession. Still, of course, if you would like to draw out of the business, there is plenty of time to do so."

'I thought of the fifty guineas, and of how very useful they would be to me. "Not at all," said I, "I shall be very happy to accommodate myself to your wishes. I should like, however, to understand a little more clearly what it is that you wish me to do."

'"Quite so. It is very natural that the pledge of secrecy which we have exacted from you should have aroused your curiosity. I have no wish to commit you to anything without your having it all laid before you. I suppose that we are absolutely safe from eavesdroppers?"

'"Entirely."

'"Then the matter stands thus. You are probably aware that fuller's-earth is a valuable product, and that it is only found in one or two places in England?"

'"I have heard so."

'"Some little time ago I bought a small place – a very small place – within ten miles of Reading. I was fortunate enough to discover that there was a deposit of fuller's-earth in one of my fields. On examining it, however, I found that this deposit was a comparatively small one, and that it formed a link between two very much larger ones upon the right and left – both of them, however, in the grounds of my neighbours. These good people were absolutely ignorant that their land contained that which was quite as valuable as a gold-mine. Naturally, it was to my interest to buy their land before they discovered its true value, but unfortunately I had no capital by which I could do this.

I took a few of my friends into the secret, however, and they suggested that we should quietly and secretly work our own little deposit and that in this way we should earn the money which would enable us to buy the neighbouring fields. This we have now been doing for some time, and in order to help us in our operations we erected a hydraulic press. This press, as I have already explained, has got out of order, and we wish your advice upon the subject. We guard our secret very jealously, however, and if it once became known that we had hydraulic engineers coming to our little house, it would soon rouse enquiry, and then, if the facts came out, it would be goodbye to any chance of getting these fields and carrying out our plans. That is why I have made you promise me that you will not tell a human being that you are going to Eyford tonight. I hope that I make it all plain?"

'"I quite follow you," said I. "The only point which I could not quite understand was what use you could make of a hydraulic press in excavating fuller's-earth, which, as I understand, is dug out like gravel from a pit."

'"Ah!" said he carelessly, "we have our own process. We compress the earth into bricks, so as to remove them without revealing what they are. But that is a mere detail. I have taken you fully into my confidence now, Mr Hatherley, and I have shown you how I trust you." He rose as he spoke. "I shall expect you, then, at Eyford at 11.15."

'"I shall certainly be there."

'"And not a word to a soul." He looked at me with a last long, questioning gaze, and then, pressing my hand in a cold, dank grasp, he hurried from the room.

'Well, when I came to think it all over in cool blood I was very much astonished, as you may both think, at this sudden commission which had been entrusted to me. On the one hand, of course, I was glad, for the fee was at least tenfold what I should have asked had I set a price upon my own services, and it was possible that this order might lead to other ones. On the other hand, the face and manner of my patron had made an unpleasant impression upon me, and I could not think that his explanation of the fuller's-earth was sufficient to explain the necessity for my coming at midnight and his extreme anxiety lest I should tell anyone of my errand. However, I threw all fears to the winds, ate a hearty supper, drove to Paddington, and started off, having obeyed to the letter the injunction as to holding my tongue.

'At Reading I had to change not only my carriage but my station. However, I was in time for the last train to Eyford, and I reached the little dim-lit station after eleven o'clock. I was the only passenger who got out there, and there was no one upon the platform save a single sleepy porter with a lantern. As I passed out through the wicket gate, however, I found my acquaintance of the morning waiting in the shadow upon the other side. Without a word he grasped my arm and hurried me into a carriage, the door of which was standing open. He drew up the windows on either side, tapped on the woodwork, and away we went as fast as the horse could go.'

'One horse?' interjected Holmes.

'Yes, only one.'

'Did you observe the colour?'

'Yes, I saw it by the sidelights when I was stepping into the carriage. It was a chestnut.'

'Tired-looking or fresh?'

'Oh, fresh and glossy.'

'Thank you. I am sorry to have interrupted you. Pray continue your most interesting statement.'

'Away we went then, and we drove for at least an hour. Colonel Lysander Stark had said that it was only seven miles, but I should think, from the rate that we seemed to go, and from the time that we took, that it must have been nearer twelve. He sat at my side in silence all the time, and I was aware, more than once when I glanced in his direction, that he was looking at me with great intensity. The country roads seem to be not very good in that part of the world, for we lurched and jolted terribly. I tried to look out of the windows to see something of where we were, but they were made of frosted glass and I could make out nothing save the occasional bright blur of a passing light. Now and then I hazarded some remark to break the monotony of the journey, but the colonel answered only in monosyllables, and the conversation soon flagged. At last, however, the bumping of the road was exchanged for the crisp smoothness of a gravel-drive, and the carriage came to a stand. Colonel Lysander Stark sprang out, and, as I followed after him, pulled me swiftly into a porch which gaped in front of us. We stepped, as it were, right out of the carriage and into the hall, so that I failed to catch the most fleeting glance of the front of the house. The instant that I had crossed the threshold the door slammed heavily behind us, and I heard faintly the rattle of the wheels as the carriage drove away.

'It was pitch dark inside the house, and the colonel fumbled about looking for matches and muttering under his breath. Suddenly a door opened at the other end of the passage and a long golden bar of light shot out in our direction. It grew broader, and a woman appeared with a lamp in her hand, which she held above her head, pushing her face forward and peering at us. I could see that she was pretty, and from the gloss with which the light shone upon her dark dress, I knew that it was a rich material. She spoke a few words in a foreign tongue in a tone as though asking a question, and when my companion answered in a gruff monosyllable she gave such a start that the lamp nearly fell from her hand. Colonel Stark went up to her, whispered something in her ear, and then, pushing her back into the room from whence she had come, he walked towards me again with the lamp in his hand.

'"Perhaps you will have the kindness to wait in this room for a few minutes," said he, throwing open another door. It was a quiet little plainly furnished room, with a round table in the centre, on which several German books were scattered. Colonel Stark laid down the lamp on the top of a harmonium beside the door. "I shall not keep you waiting an instant," said he, and vanished into the darkness.

'I glanced at the books upon the table, and in spite of my ignorance of German, I could see that two of them were treatises on science, the others being volumes of poetry. Then I walked across to the window, hoping that I might catch some glimpse of the countryside, but an oak shutter, heavily barred, was folded across it. It was a wonderfully silent house. There was an old clock ticking loudly somewhere in the passage, but otherwise everything was deadly still. A vague feeling of uneasiness began to steal over me. Who were these German people, and what were they doing living in this strange, out-of-the-way place? And where was the place? I was ten miles or so from Eyford, that was all I knew, but whether north, south, east or west, I had no idea. For that matter, Reading, and possibly other large towns, were within that radius, so the place might not be so secluded, after all. Yet it was quite certain, from the absolute stillness, that we were in the country. I paced up and down the room, humming a tune under my breath to keep up my spirits and feeling that I was thoroughly earning my fifty-guinea fee.

'Suddenly, without any preliminary sound in the midst of the utter stillness, the door of my room swung slowly open. The woman was standing in the aperture, the darkness of the hall behind her, the yellow light from my lamp beating upon her eager and beautiful face. I could see at a glance that she was sick with fear, and the sight sent a chill to my own heart. She held up one shaking finger to warn me to be silent, and she shot a few whispered words of broken English at me, her eyes glancing back, like those of a frightened horse, into the gloom behind her.

'"I would go," said she, trying hard, as it seemed to me, to speak calmly; "I would go. I should not stay here. There is no good for you to do."

'"But, madam," said I, "I have not yet done what I came for. I cannot possibly leave until I have seen the machine."

'"It is not worth your while to wait," she went on. "You can pass through the door; no one hinders." And then, seeing that I smiled and shook my head, she suddenly threw aside her constraint and made a step forward, with her hands wrung together. "For the love of heaven!" she whispered, "get away from here before it is too late!"

'But I am somewhat headstrong by nature, and the more ready to engage in an affair when there is some obstacle in the way. I thought of my fifty-guinea fee, of my wearisome journey and of the unpleasant night which seemed to be before me. Was it all to go for nothing? Why should I slink away without having carried out my commission, and without the payment which was my due? This woman might, for all I knew, be a monomaniac. With a stout bearing, therefore, though her manner had shaken me more than I cared to confess, I still shook my head and declared my intention of remaining where I was. She was about to renew her entreaties when a door slammed overhead, and the sound of several footsteps was heard upon the stairs. She listened for an instant, threw up her hands with a despairing gesture, and vanished as suddenly and as noiselessly as she had come.

'The newcomers were Colonel Lysander Stark and a short thick man with a chinchilla beard growing out of the creases of his double chin, who was introduced to me as Mr Ferguson.

'"This is my secretary and manager," said the colonel. "By the way, I was under the impression that I left this door shut just now. I fear that you have felt the draught."

'"On the contrary," said I, "I opened the door myself because I felt the room to be a little close."

'He shot one of his suspicious looks at me. "Perhaps we had better proceed to business, then," said he. "Mr Ferguson and I will take you up to see the machine."

'"I had better put my hat on, I suppose."

'"Oh, no, it is in the house."

'"What, you dig fuller's-earth in the house?"

'"No, no. This is only where we compress it. But never mind that. All we wish you to do is to examine the machine and to let us know what is wrong with it."

'We went upstairs together, the colonel first with the lamp, the fat manager and I behind him. It was a labyrinth of an old house, with corridors, passages, narrow winding staircases, and little low doors, the thresholds of which were hollowed out by the generations who had crossed them. There were no carpets and no signs of any furniture above the ground floor, while the plaster was peeling off the walls and the damp was breaking through in green, unhealthy blotches.

I tried to put on as unconcerned an air as possible, but I had not forgotten the warnings of the lady, even though I disregarded them, and I kept a keen eye upon my two companions. Ferguson appeared to be a morose and silent man, but I could see from the little that he said that he was at least a fellow-countryman.

'Colonel Lysander Stark stopped at last before a low door, which he unlocked. Within was a small, square room, in which the three of us could hardly get at one time. Ferguson remained outside, and the colonel ushered me in.

'"We are now," said he, "actually within the hydraulic press, and it would be a particularly unpleasant thing for us if anyone were to turn it on. The ceiling of this small chamber is really the end of the descending piston, and it comes down with the force of many tons upon this metal floor. There are small lateral columns of water outside which receive the force, and which transmit and multiply it in the manner which is familiar to you. The machine goes readily enough, but there is some stiffness in the working of it, and it has lost a little of its force. Perhaps you will have the goodness to look it over and to show us how we can set it right."

'I took the lamp from him, and I examined the machine very thoroughly. It was indeed a gigantic one, and capable of exercising enormous pressure. When I passed outside, however, and pressed down the levers which controlled it, I knew at once by the whishing sound that there was a slight leakage, which allowed a regurgitation of water through one of the side cylinders. An examination showed that one of the india-rubber bands which was round the head of a driving-rod had shrunk so as not quite to fill the socket along which it worked. This was clearly the cause of the loss of power, and I pointed it out to my companions, who followed my remarks very carefully and asked several practical questions as to how they should proceed to set it right. When I had made it clear to them, I returned to the main chamber of the machine and took a good look at it to satisfy my own curiosity. It was obvious at a glance that the story of the fuller's-earth was the merest fabrication, for it would be absurd to suppose that so powerful an engine could be designed for so inadequate a purpose. The walls were of wood, but the floor consisted of a large iron trough, and when I came to examine it I could see a crust of metallic deposit all over it. I had stooped and was scraping at this to see exactly what it was when I heard a muttered exclamation in German and saw the cadaverous face of the colonel looking down at me.

'"What are you doing there?" he asked.

'I felt angry at having been tricked by so elaborate a story as that which he had told me. "I was admiring your fuller's-earth," said I; "I think that I should be better able to advise you as to your machine if I knew what the exact purpose was for which it was used."

'The instant that I uttered the words I regretted the rashness of my speech. His face set hard, and a baleful light sprang up in his grey eyes.

'"Very well," said he, "you shall know all about the machine." He took a step backwards, slammed the little door, and turned the key in the lock. I rushed towards it and pulled at the handle, but it was quite secure, and did not give in the least to my kicks and shoves. "Hallo!" I yelled. "Hallo! Colonel! Let me out!"

'And then suddenly in the silence I heard a sound which sent my heart into my mouth. It was the clank of the levers and the swish of the leaking cylinder. He had set the engine at work. The lamp still stood upon the floor where I had placed it when examining the trough. By its light I saw that the black ceiling was coming down upon me, slowly, jerkily, but, as none knew better than myself, with a force which must within a minute grind me to a shapeless pulp. I threw myself, scream-ing, against the door, and dragged with my nails at the lock. I implored the colonel to let me out, but the remorseless clanking of the levers drowned my cries. The ceiling was only a foot or two above my head, and with my hand upraised I could feel its hard, rough surface. Then it flashed through my mind that the pain of my death would depend very much upon the position in which I met it. If I lay on my face the weight would come upon my spine, and I shuddered to think of that dreadful snap. Easier the other way, perhaps; and yet, had I the nerve to lie and look up at that deadly black shadow wavering down upon me? Already I was unable to stand erect, when my eye caught something which brought a gush of hope back to my heart.

'I have said that though the floor and ceiling were of iron, the walls were of wood. As I gave a last hurried glance around, I saw a thin line of yellow light between two of the boards, which broadened and broadened as a small panel was pushed backward. For an instant I could hardly believe that here was indeed a door which led away from death. The next instant I threw myself through, and lay half-fainting upon the other side. The panel had closed again behind me, but the crash of the lamp, and a few moments afterwards the clang of the two slabs of metal, told me how narrow had been my escape.

'I was recalled to myself by a frantic plucking at my wrist, and I found myself lying upon the stone floor of a narrow corridor, while a woman bent over me and tugged at me with her left hand, while she held a candle in her right. It was the same good friend whose warning I had so foolishly rejected.

'"Come! come!" she cried breathlessly. "They will be here in a moment. They will see that you are not there. Oh, do not waste the so-precious time, but come!"

'This time, at least, I did not scorn her advice. I staggered to my feet and ran with her along the corridor and down a winding stair. The latter led to another broad passage, and just as we reached it we heard the sound of running feet and the shouting of two voices, one answering the other from the floor on which we were and from the one beneath. My guide stopped and looked about her like one who is at her wit's end. Then she threw open a door which led into a bedroom, through the window of which the moon was shining brightly.

'"It is your only chance," said she. "It is high, but it may be that you can jump it."

'As she spoke a light sprang into view at the farther end of the passage, and I saw the lean figure of Colonel Lysander Stark rushing forward with a lantern in one hand and a weapon like a butcher's cleaver in the other. I rushed across the bedroom, flung open the window and looked out. How quiet and sweet and wholesome the garden looked in the moonlight, and it could not be more than thirty feet down. I clambered out upon the sill, but I hesitated to jump until I should have heard what passed between my saviour and the ruffian who pursued me. If she were ill-used, then at any risks I was determined to go back to her assistance. The thought had hardly flashed through my mind before he was at the door, pushing his way past her; but she threw her arms round him and tried to hold him back.

'"Fritz! Fritz!" she cried in English, "remember your promise after the last time. You said it should not be again. He will be silent! Oh, he will be silent!"

'"You are mad, Elise!" he shouted, struggling to break away from her. "You will be the ruin of us. He has seen too much. Let me pass, I say!" He dashed her to one side, and, rushing to the window, cut at me with his heavy weapon. I had let myself go, and was hanging by my hands to the sill when his blow fell. I was conscious of a dull pain, my grip loosened, and I fell into the garden below.

'I was shaken but not hurt by the fall; so I picked myself up and rushed off among the bushes as hard as I could run, for I understood that I was far from being out of danger yet. Suddenly, however, as I ran, a deadly dizziness and sickness came over me. I glanced down at my hand, which was throbbing painfully, and then, for the first time, saw that my thumb had been cut off and that blood was pouring from my wound. I endeavoured to tie my handkerchief round it, but there came a sudden buzzing in my ears and next moment I fell in a dead faint among the rose-bushes.

'How long I remained unconscious I cannot tell. It must have been a very long time, for the moon had sunk and a bright morning was breaking when I came to myself. My clothes were all sodden with dew and my coat-sleeve was drenched with blood from my wounded thumb. The smarting of it recalled in an instant all the particulars of my night's adventure and I sprang to my feet with the feeling that I might hardly yet be safe from my pursuers. But to my astonishment, when I came to look round me, neither house nor garden were to be seen. I had been lying in an angle of the hedge close by the highroad, and just a little lower down was a long building, which proved, upon my approaching it, to be the very station at which I had arrived upon the previous night. Were it not for the ugly wound upon my hand, all that had passed during those dreadful hours might have been an evil dream.

'Half dazed, I went into the station and asked about the morning train. There would be one to Reading in less than an hour. The same porter was on duty, I found, as had been there when I arrived. I enquired of him whether he had ever heard of Colonel Lysander Stark. The name was strange to him. Had he observed a carriage the night before waiting for me? No, he had not. Was there a police-station anywhere near? There was one about three miles off.

'It was too far for me to go, weak and ill as I was. I determined to wait until I got back to town before telling my story to the police. It was a little past six when I arrived, so I went first to have my wound dressed, and then the doctor was kind enough to bring me along here. I put the case into your hands and shall do exactly what you advise.'

We both sat in silence for some little time after listening to this extraordinary narrative. Then Sherlock Holmes pulled down from the shelf one of the ponderous commonplace books in which he placed his cuttings.

'Here is an advertisement which will interest you,' said he. 'It appeared in all the papers about a year ago. Listen to this: "Lost, on the 9th inst, Mr Jeremiah Hayling, aged twenty-six, a hydraulic engineer. Left his lodgings at ten o'clock at night and has not been heard of since. Was dressed in –' etc., etc. Ha! That represents the last time that the colonel needed to have his machine overhauled, I fancy.'

'Good heavens!' cried my patient. 'Then that explains what the girl said.'

'Undoubtedly. It is quite clear that the colonel was a cool and desperate man, who was absolutely determined that nothing should stand in the way of his little game, like those out-and-out pirates who will leave no survivor from a captured ship. Well, every moment now is precious, so if you feel equal to it we shall go down to Scotland Yard at once as a preliminary to starting for Eyford.'

Some three hours or so afterwards we were all in the train together, bound from Reading to the little Berkshire village. There were Sherlock Holmes, the hydraulic engineer, Inspector Bradstreet of Scotland Yard, a plain-clothes man and myself. Bradstreet had spread an ordnance map of the county out upon the seat and was busy with his compasses drawing a circle with Eyford for its centre.

'There you are,' said he. 'That circle is drawn at a radius of ten miles from the village. The place we want must be somewhere near that line. You said ten miles, I think, sir.'

'It was an hour's good drive.'

'And you think that they brought you back all that way when you were unconscious?'

'They must have done so. I have a confused memory, too, of having been lifted and conveyed somewhere.'

'What I cannot understand,' said I, 'is why they should have spared you when they found you lying fainting in the garden. Perhaps the villain was softened by the woman's entreaties.'

'I hardly think that likely. I never saw a more inexorable face in my life.'

'Oh, we shall soon clear up all that,' said Bradstreet. 'Well, I have drawn my circle, and I only wish I knew at what point upon it the folk that we are in search of are to be found.'

'I think I could lay my finger on it,' said Holmes quietly.

'Really, now!' cried the inspector, 'you have formed your opinion? Come, now, we shall see who agrees with you. I say it is south, for the country is more deserted there.'

'And I say east,' said my patient.

'I am for west,' remarked the plain-clothes man. 'There are several quiet little villages up there.'

'And I am for north,' said I, 'because there are no hills there, and our friend says that he did not notice the carriage go up any.'

'Come,' cried the inspector, laughing; 'it's a very pretty diversity of opinion. We have boxed the compass among us. Who do you give your casting vote to?'

'You are all wrong.'

'But we can't *all* be.'

'Oh, yes, you can. This is my point.' He placed his finger in the centre of the circle. 'This is where we shall find them.'

'But the ten-mile drive?' gasped Hatherley.

'Five out and five back. Nothing simpler. You say yourself that the horse was fresh and glossy when you got in. How could it be that if it had gone ten miles over heavy roads?'

'Indeed, it is a likely ruse enough,' observed Bradstreet thoughtfully. 'Of course there can be no doubt as to the nature of this gang.'

'None at all,' said Holmes. 'They are coiners on a large scale, and have used the machine to form the amalgam which has taken the place of silver.'

'We have known for some time that a clever gang was at work,' said the inspector. 'They have been turning out half-crowns by the thousand. We even traced them as far as Reading, but could get no farther, for they had covered their traces in a way that showed that they were very old hands. But now, thanks to this lucky chance, I think that we have got them right enough.'

But the inspector was mistaken, for those criminals were not destined to fall into the hands of justice. As we rolled into Eyford Station we saw a gigantic column of smoke which streamed up from behind a small clump of trees in the neighbourhood and hung like an immense ostrich feather over the landscape.

'A house on fire?' asked Bradstreet as the train steamed off again on its way.

'Yes, sir!' said the station-master.

'When did it break out?'

'I hear that it was during the night, sir, but it has got worse, and the whole place is in a blaze.'

'Whose house is it?'

285

'Dr Becher's.'

'Tell me,' broke in the engineer, 'is Dr Becher a German, very thin, with a long, sharp nose?'

The station-master laughed heartily. 'No, sir, Dr Becher is an Englishman, and there isn't a man in the parish who has a better-lined waistcoat. But he has a gentleman staying with him, a patient, as I understand, who is a foreigner, and he looks as if a little good Berkshire beef would do him no harm.'

The station-master had not finished his speech before we were all hastening in the direction of the fire. The road topped a low hill, and there was a great widespread whitewashed building in front of us, spouting fire at every chink and window, while in the garden in front three fire-engines were vainly striving to keep the flames under.

'That's it!' cried Hatherley, in intense excitement. 'There is the gravel-drive, and there are the rose-bushes where I lay. That second window is the one that I jumped from.'

'Well, at least,' said Holmes, 'you have had your revenge upon them. There can be no question that it was your oil-lamp which, when it was crushed in the press, set fire to the wooden walls, though no doubt they were too excited in the chase after you to observe it at the time. Now keep your eyes open in this crowd for your friends of last night, though I very much fear that they are a good hundred miles off by now.'

And Holmes's fears came to be realised, for from that day to this no word has ever been heard either of the beautiful woman, the sinister German or the morose Englishman. Early that morning a peasant had met a cart containing several people and some very bulky boxes driving rapidly in the direction of Reading, but there all traces of the fugitives disappeared, and even Holmes's ingenuity failed ever to discover the least clue as to their whereabouts.

The firemen had been much perturbed at the strange arrangements which they had found within, and still more so by discovering a newly severed human thumb upon a windowsill of the second floor. About sunset, however, their efforts were at last successful, and they subdued the flames, but not before the roof had fallen in and the whole place had been reduced to such absolute ruin that, save for some twisted cylinders and iron piping, not a trace remained of the machinery which had cost our unfortunate acquaintance so dearly. Large masses of nickel and of tin were discovered stored in an out-house, but no coins were to be found, which may have explained the presence of those bulky boxes which have been already referred to.

How our hydraulic engineer had been conveyed from the garden to the spot where he recovered his senses might have remained forever a mystery were it not for the soft mould, which told us a very plain tale. He had evidently been carried down by two persons, one of whom had remarkably small feet and the other unusually large ones. On the whole, it was most probable that the silent Englishman, being less bold or less murderous than his companion, had assisted the woman to bear the unconscious man out of the way of danger.

'Well,' said our engineer ruefully as we took our seats to return once more to London, 'it has been a pretty business for me! I have lost my thumb and I have lost a fifty-guinea fee, and what have I gained?'

'Experience,' said Holmes, laughing. 'Indirectly it may be of value, you know; you have only to put it into words to gain the reputation of being excellent company for the remainder of your existence.'

The Adventure of
the Noble Bachelor

The Lord St Simon marriage, and its curious termination, have long ceased to be a subject of interest in those exalted circles in which the unfortunate bridegroom moves. Fresh scandals have eclipsed it, and their more piquant details have drawn the gossips away from this four-year-old drama. As I have reason to believe, however, that the full facts have never been revealed to the general public, and as my friend Sherlock Holmes had a considerable share in clearing the matter up, I feel that no memoir of him would be complete without some little sketch of this remarkable episode.

It was a few weeks before my own marriage, during the days when I was still sharing rooms with Holmes in Baker Street, that he came home from an afternoon stroll to find a letter on the table waiting for him. I had remained indoors all day, for the weather had taken a sudden turn to rain, with high autumnal winds, and the Jezail bullet which I had brought back in one of my limbs as a relic of my Afghan campaign throbbed with dull persistence. With my body in one easy-chair and my legs upon another, I had surrounded myself with a cloud of newspapers until at last, saturated with the news of the day, I tossed them all aside and lay listless, watching the huge crest and monogram upon the envelope upon the table and wondering lazily who my friend's noble correspondent could be.

'Here is a very fashionable epistle,' I remarked as he entered. 'Your morning letters, if I remember right, were from a fishmonger and a tide-waiter.'

'Yes, my correspondence has certainly the charm of variety,' he answered, smiling, 'and the humbler are usually the more interesting. This looks like one of those unwelcome social summonses which call upon a man either to be bored or to lie.'

He broke the seal and glanced over the contents.

'Oh, come, it may prove to be something of interest, after all.'

'Not social, then?'

'No, distinctly professional.'

'And from a noble client?'

'One of the highest in England.'

'My dear fellow, I congratulate you.'

'I assure you, Watson, without affectation, that the status of my client is a matter of less moment to me than the interest of his case. It is just possible, however, that that also may not be wanting in this new investigation. You have been reading the papers diligently of late, have you not?'

'It looks like it,' said I ruefully, pointing to a huge bundle in the corner. 'I have had nothing else to do.'

'It is fortunate, for you will perhaps be able to post me up. I read nothing except the criminal news and the agony column. The latter is always instructive. But if you have followed recent events so closely you must have read about Lord St Simon and his wedding?'

'Oh, yes, with the deepest interest.'

'That is well. The letter which I hold in my hand is from Lord St Simon. I will read it to you, and in return you must turn over these papers and let me have whatever bears upon the matter. This is what he says:

'My dear Mr Sherlock Holmes – Lord Backwater tells me that I may place implicit reliance upon your judgement and discretion. I have determined, therefore, to call upon you and to consult you in reference to the very painful event which has occurred in connection with my wedding. Mr Lestrade, of Scotland Yard, is acting already in the matter, but he assures me that he sees no objection to your co-operation, and that he even thinks that it might be of some assistance. I will call at four o'clock in the afternoon, and should you have any other engagement at that time, I hope that you will postpone it, as this matter is of paramount importance. Yours faithfully,

ST SIMON.

'It is dated from Grosvenor Mansions, written with a quill pen, and the noble lord has had the misfortune to get a smear of ink upon the outer side of his right little finger,' remarked Holmes as he folded up the epistle.

'He says four o'clock. It is three now. He will be here in an hour.'

'Then I have just time, with your assistance, to get clear upon the subject. Turn over those papers and arrange the extracts in their order of time, while I take a glance as to who our client is.' He picked a red-covered volume from a line of books of reference beside the mantelpiece. 'Here he is,' said he, sitting down and flattening it out upon his knee. '"Lord Robert Walsingham de Vere St Simon, second son of the Duke of Balmoral." Hum! "Arms: Azure, three caltrops in chief over a fess sable. Born in 1846." He's forty-one years of age, which is mature for marriage. Was Under-Secretary for the Colonies in a late adminis-tration. The Duke, his father, was at one time Secretary for Foreign Affairs. They inherit Plantagenet blood by direct descent, and Tudor on the distaff side. Ha! Well, there is nothing very instructive in all this. I think that I must turn to you, Watson, for something more solid.'

'I have very little difficulty in finding what I want,' said I, 'for the facts are quite recent, and the matter struck me as remarkable. I feared to refer them to you, however, as I knew that you had an enquiry on hand and that you disliked the intrusion of other matters.'

'Oh, you mean the little problem of the Grosvenor Square furniture van. That is quite cleared up now – though, indeed, it was obvious from the first. Pray give me the results of your newspaper selections.'

'Here is the first notice which I can find. It is in the personal column of the *Morning Post*, and dates, as you see, from some weeks back: "A marriage has been arranged," it says, "and will, if rumour is correct, very shortly take place, between Lord Robert St Simon, second son of the Duke of Balmoral, and Miss Hatty Doran, the only daughter of Aloysius Doran, Esq., of San Francisco, California, USA." That is all.'

'Terse and to the point,' remarked Holmes, stretching his long, thin legs towards the fire.

'There was a paragraph amplifying this in one of the society papers of the same week. Ah, here it is: "There will soon be a call for protection in the marriage market, for the present free-trade principle appears to tell heavily against our home product. One by one the management of the noble houses of Great Britain is passing into the hands of our fair cousins from across the Atlantic. An important addition has been made during the last week to the list of the prizes which have been borne away by these charming invaders. Lord St Simon, who has shown himself for over twenty years proof against the little god's arrows, has now definitely announced his approaching marriage with Miss Hatty Doran, the fascinating daughter of a California millionaire. Miss Doran, whose graceful figure and striking face attracted much attention at the Westbury House festivities, is an only child, and it is currently reported that her dowry will run to considerably over the six figures, with expectancies for the future. As it is an open secret that the Duke of Balmoral has been compelled to sell his pictures within the last few years, and as Lord St Simon has no property of his own save the small estate of Birchmoor, it is obvious that the Californian heiress is not the only gainer by an alliance which will enable her to make the easy and common transition from a Republican lady to a British peeress."'

'Anything else?' asked Holmes, yawning.

'Oh, yes; plenty. Then there is another note in the *Morning Post* to say that the marriage would be an absolutely quiet one, that it would be at St George's, Hanover Square, that only half a dozen intimate friends would be invited, and that the party would return to the furnished house at Lancaster Gate which has been taken by Mr Aloysius Doran. Two days later – that is, on Wednesday last – there is a curt announcement that the wedding had taken place, and that the honeymoon would be passed at Lord Backwater's place, near Petersfield. Those are all the notices which appeared before the disappearance of the bride.'

'Before the what?' asked Holmes with a start.

'The vanishing of the lady.'

'When did she vanish, then?'

'At the wedding breakfast.'

'Indeed. This is more interesting than it promised to be; quite dramatic, in fact.'

'Yes; it struck me as being a little out of the common.'

'They often vanish before the ceremony, and occasionally during the honeymoon; but I cannot call to mind anything quite so prompt as this. Pray let me have the details.'

'I warn you that they are very incomplete.'

'Perhaps we may make them less so.'

'Such as they are, they are set forth in a single article of a morning paper of yesterday, which I will read to you. It is headed, "Singular Occurrence at a Fashionable Wedding":

'The family of Lord Robert St Simon has been thrown into the greatest consternation by the strange and painful episodes which have taken place in connection with his wedding. The ceremony, as shortly announced in the papers of yesterday, occurred on the previous morning; but it is only now that it has been possible to confirm the strange rumours which have been so persistently floating about. In spite of the attempts of the friends to hush the matter up, so much public attention has now been drawn to it that no good purpose can be served by affecting to disregard what is a common subject for conversation.

'The ceremony, which was performed at St George's, Hanover Square, was a very quiet one, no one being present save the father of the bride, Mr Aloysius Doran, the Duchess of Balmoral, Lord Backwater, Lord Eustace and Lady Clara St Simon (the younger brother and sister of the bridegroom) and Lady Alicia Whittington. The whole party proceeded afterwards to the house of Mr Aloysius Doran, at Lancaster Gate, where breakfast had been prepared. It appears that some little trouble was caused by a woman, whose name has not been ascertained, who endeavoured to force her way into the house after the bridal party, alleging that she had some claim upon Lord St Simon. It was only after a painful and prolonged scene that she was ejected by the butler and the footman. The bride, who had fortunately entered the house before this unpleasant interruption, had sat down to breakfast with the rest, when she complained of a sudden indisposition and retired to her room. Her prolonged absence having caused some comment, her father followed her, but learned from her maid that she had only come up to her chamber for an instant, caught up an ulster and bonnet, and hurried down to the passage. One of the footmen declared that he had seen a lady leave the house thus apparelled, but had refused to credit that it was his mistress, believing her to be with the company. On ascertaining that his daughter had disappeared, Mr Aloysius Doran, in conjunction with the bridegroom, instantly put themselves in communication with the police, and very energetic enquiries are being made, which will probably result in a speedy clearing up of this very singular business. Up to a late hour last night, however, nothing had transpired as to the whereabouts of the missing lady. There are rumours of foul play in the matter, and it is said that the police have caused the arrest of the woman who had caused the original disturbance, in the belief that, from jealousy or some other motive, she may have been concerned in the strange disappearance of the bride.'

'And is that all?'

'Only one little item in another of the morning papers, but it is a suggestive one.'

'And it is –'

'That Miss Flora Millar, the lady who had caused the disturbance, has actually been arrested. It appears that she was formerly a *danseuse* at the Allegro, and that she has known the bridegroom for some years. There are no further particulars, and the whole case is in your hands now – so far as it has been set forth in the public press.'

'And an exceedingly interesting case it appears to be. I would not have missed it for worlds. But there is a ring at the bell, Watson, and as the clock makes it a few minutes after four, I have no doubt that this will prove to be our noble client. Do not dream of going, Watson, for I very much prefer having a witness, if only as a check to my own memory.'

'Lord Robert St Simon,' announced our pageboy, throwing open the door. A gentleman entered, with a pleasant, cultured face, high-nosed and pale, with something perhaps of petulance about the mouth, and with the steady, well-opened eye of a man whose pleasant lot it had ever been to command and to be obeyed. His manner was brisk, and yet his general appearance gave an undue impression of age, for he had a slight forward stoop and a little bend of the knees as he walked. His hair, too, as he swept off his very curly-brimmed hat, was grizzled round the edges and thin upon the top. As to his dress, it was careful to the verge of foppishness, with high collar, black frock-coat, white waistcoat, yellow gloves, patent-leather shoes and light-coloured gaiters. He advanced slowly into the room, turning his head from left to right and swinging in his right hand the cord which held his golden eyeglasses.

'Good-day, Lord St Simon,' said Holmes, rising and bowing. 'Pray take the basket-chair. This is my friend and colleague, Dr Watson. Draw up a little to the fire, and we will talk this matter over.'

'A most painful matter to me, as you can most readily imagine, Mr Holmes. I have been cut to the quick. I understand that you have already managed several delicate cases of this sort, sir, though I presume that they were hardly from the same class of society.'

'No, I am descending.'

'I beg pardon.'

'My last client of the sort was a king.'

'Oh, really! I had no idea. And which king?'

'The King of Scandinavia.'

'What! Had he lost his wife?'

'You can understand,' said Holmes suavely, 'that I extend to the affairs of my other clients the same secrecy which I promise to you in yours.'

'Of course! Very right! very right! I'm sure I beg pardon. As to my own case, I am ready to give you any information which may assist you in forming an opinion.'

'Thank you. I have already learned all that is in the public prints, nothing more. I presume that I may take it as correct – this article, for example, as to the disappearance of the bride.'

Lord St Simon glanced over it. 'Yes, it is correct, as far as it goes.'

'But it needs a great deal of supplementing before anyone could offer an opinion. I think that I may arrive at my facts most directly by questioning you.'

'Pray do so.'

'When did you first meet Miss Hatty Doran?'

'In San Francisco, a year ago.'

'You were travelling in the States?'

'Yes.'

'Did you become engaged then?'

'No.'

'But you were on a friendly footing?'

'I was amused by her society, and she could see that I was amused.'

'Her father is very rich?'

'He is said to be the richest man on the Pacific slope.'

'And how did he make his money?'

'In mining. He had nothing a few years ago. Then he struck gold, invested it, and came up by leaps and bounds.'

'Now, what is your own impression as to the young lady's – your wife's character?'

The nobleman swung his glasses a little faster and stared down into the fire. 'You see, Mr Holmes,' said he, 'my wife was twenty before her father became a rich man. During that time she ran free in a mining camp and wandered through woods or mountains, so that her education has come from Nature rather than from the schoolmaster. She is what we call in England a tomboy, with a strong nature, wild and free, unfettered by any sort of traditions. She is impetuous – volcanic, I was about to say. She is swift in making up her mind and fearless in carrying out her resolutions. On the other hand, I would not have given her the name which I have the honour to bear' – he gave a little stately cough – 'had I not thought her to be at bottom a noble woman. I believe that she is capable of heroic self-sacrifice and that anything dishonourable would be repugnant to her.'

'Have you her photograph?'

'I brought this with me.' He opened a locket and showed us the full face of a very lovely woman. It was not a photograph but an ivory miniature, and the artist had brought out the full effect of the lustrous black hair, the large dark eyes, and the exquisite mouth. Holmes gazed long and earnestly at it. Then he closed the locket and handed it back to Lord St Simon.

'The young lady came to London, then, and you renewed your acquaintance?'

'Yes, her father brought her over for this last London season. I met her several times, became engaged to her, and have now married her.'

'She brought, I understand, a considerable dowry?'

'A fair dowry. Not more than is usual in my family.'

'And this, of course, remains to you, since the marriage is a *fait accompli*?'

'I really have made no enquiries on the subject.'

'Very naturally not. Did you see Miss Doran on the day before the wedding?'

'Yes.'

'Was she in good spirits?'

'Never better. She kept talking of what we should do in our future lives.'

'Indeed! That is very interesting. And on the morning of the wedding?'

'She was as bright as possible – at least until after the ceremony.'

'And did you observe any change in her then?'

'Well, to tell the truth, I saw then the first signs that I had ever seen that her temper was just a little sharp. The incident, however, was too trivial to relate and can have no possible bearing upon the case.'

'Pray let us have it, for all that.'

'Oh, it is childish. She dropped her bouquet as we went towards the vestry. She was passing the front pew at the time, and it fell over into the pew. There was a moment's delay, but the gentleman in the pew handed it up to her again, and it did not appear to be the worse for the fall. Yet when I spoke to her of the matter, she answered me abruptly; and in the carriage, on our way home, she seemed absurdly agitated over this trifling cause.'

'Indeed! You say that there was a gentleman in the pew. Some of the general public were present, then?'

'Oh, yes. It is impossible to exclude them when the church is open.'

'This gentleman was not one of your wife's friends?'

'No, no; I call him a gentleman by courtesy, but he was quite a common-looking person. I hardly noticed his appearance. But really I think that we are wandering rather far from the point.'

'Lady St Simon, then, returned from the wedding in a less cheerful frame of mind than she had gone to it. What did she do on re-entering her father's house?'

'I saw her in conversation with her maid.'

'And who is her maid?'

'Alice is her name. She is an American and came from California with her.'

'A confidential servant?'

'A little too much so. It seemed to me that her mistress allowed her to take great liberties. Still, of course, in America they look upon these things in a different way.'

'How long did she speak to this Alice?'

'Oh, a few minutes. I had something else to think of.'

'You did not overhear what they said?'

'Lady St Simon said something about "jumping a claim". She was accustomed to use slang of the kind. I have no idea what she meant.'

'American slang is very expressive sometimes. And what did your wife do when she finished speaking to her maid?'

'She walked into the breakfast-room.'

'On your arm?'

'No, alone. She was very independent in little matters like that. Then, after we had sat down for ten minutes or so, she rose hurriedly, muttered some words of apology, and left the room. She never came back.'

'But this maid, Alice, as I understand, deposes that she went to her room, covered her bride's dress with a long ulster, put on a bonnet, and went out.'

'Quite so. And she was afterwards seen walking into Hyde Park in company with Flora Millar, a woman who is now in custody, and who had already made a disturbance at Mr Doran's house that morning.'

'Ah, yes. I should like a few particulars as to this young lady, and your relations to her.'

Lord St Simon shrugged his shoulders and raised his eyebrows. 'We have been on a friendly footing for some years – I may say on a *very* friendly footing. She used to be at the Allegro. I have not treated her ungenerously, and she had no just cause of complaint against me, but you know what women are, Mr Holmes. Flora was a dear little thing, but exceedingly hot headed and devotedly attached to me. She wrote me dreadful letters when she heard that I was about to be married, and, to tell the truth, the reason why I had the marriage celebrated so quietly was that I feared lest there might be a scandal in the church. She came to Mr Doran's door just after we returned, and she endeavoured to push her way in, uttering very abusive expressions towards my wife, and even threatening her, but I had foreseen the possibility of something of the sort, and I had two police fellows there in private clothes, who soon pushed her out again. She was quiet when she saw that there was no good in making a row.'

'Did your wife hear all this?'

'No, thank goodness, she did not.'

'And she was seen walking with this very woman afterwards?'

'Yes. That is what Mr Lestrade, of Scotland Yard, looks upon as so serious. It is thought that Flora decoyed my wife out and laid some terrible trap for her.'

'Well, it is a possible supposition.'

'You think so, too?'

'I did not say a probable one. But you do not yourself look upon this as likely?'

'I do not think Flora would hurt a fly.'

'Still, jealousy is a strange transformer of characters. Pray what is your own theory as to what took place?'

'Well, really, I came to seek a theory, not to propound one. I have given you all the facts. Since you ask me, however, I may say that it has occurred to me as possible that the excitement of this affair, the consciousness that she had made so immense a social stride, had the effect of causing some little nervous disturbance in my wife.'

'In short, that she had become suddenly deranged?'

'Well, really, when I consider that she has turned her back – I will not say upon me, but upon so much that many have aspired to without success – I can hardly explain it in any other fashion.'

'Well, certainly that is also a conceivable hypothesis,' said Holmes, smiling. 'And now, Lord St Simon, I think that I have nearly all my data. May I ask whether you were seated at the breakfast-table so that you could see out of the window?'

'We could see the other side of the road and the park.'

'Quite so. Then I do not think that I need to detain you longer. I shall communicate with you.'

'Should you be fortunate enough to solve this problem –' said our client, rising.

'I have solved it.'

'Eh? What was that?'

'I say that I have solved it.'

'Where, then, is my wife?'

'That is a detail which I shall speedily supply.'

Lord St Simon shook his head. 'I am afraid that it will take wiser heads than yours or mine,' he remarked, and bowing in a stately, old-fashioned manner he departed.

'It is very good of Lord St Simon to honour my head by putting it on a level with his own,' said Sherlock Holmes, laughing. 'I think that

I shall have a whisky and soda and a cigar after all this cross-questioning. I had formed my conclusions as to the case before our client came into the room.'

'My dear Holmes!'

'I have notes of several similar cases, though none, as I remarked before, which were quite as prompt. My whole examination served to turn my conjecture into a certainty. Circumstantial evidence is occasionally very convincing, as when you find a trout in the milk, to quote Thoreau's example.'

'But I have heard all that you have heard.'

'Without, however, the knowledge of pre-existing cases which serves me so well. There was a parallel instance in Aberdeen some years back, and something on very much the same lines at Munich the year after the Franco-Prussian War. It is one of these cases – but, hallo, here is Lestrade! Good-afternoon, Lestrade! You will find an extra tumbler upon the sideboard, and there are cigars in the box.'

The official detective was attired in a pea-jacket and cravat, which gave him a decidedly nautical appearance, and he carried a black canvas bag in his hand. With a short greeting he seated himself and lit the cigar which had been offered to him.

'What's up, then?' asked Holmes with a twinkle in his eye. 'You look dissatisfied.'

'And I feel dissatisfied. It is this infernal St Simon marriage case. I can make neither head nor tail of the business.'

'Really! You surprise me.'

'Who ever heard of such a mixed affair? Every clue seems to slip through my fingers. I have been at work upon it all day.'

'And very wet it seems to have made you,' said Holmes laying his hand upon the arm of the pea-jacket.

'Yes, I have been dragging the Serpentine.'

'In heaven's name, what for?'

'In search of the body of Lady St Simon.'

Sherlock Holmes leaned back in his chair and laughed heartily.

'Have you dragged the basin of Trafalgar Square fountain?' he asked.

'Why? What do you mean?'

'Because you have just as good a chance of finding this lady in the one as in the other.'

Lestrade shot an angry glance at my companion. 'I suppose you know all about it,' he snarled.

'Well, I have only just heard the facts, but my mind is made up.'

'Oh, indeed! Then you think that the Serpentine plays no part in the matter?'

'I think it very unlikely.'

'Then perhaps you will kindly explain how it is that we found this in it?' He opened his bag as he spoke, and tumbled on to the floor a wedding-dress of watered silk, a pair of white satin shoes and a bride's wreath and veil, all discoloured and soaked in water. 'There,' said he, putting a new wedding-ring upon the top of the pile. 'There is a little nut for you to crack, Master Holmes.'

'Oh, indeed!' said my friend, blowing blue rings into the air. 'You dragged them from the Serpentine?'

'No. They were found floating near the margin by a park-keeper. They have been identified as her clothes, and it seemed to me that if the clothes were there the body would not be far off.'

'By the same brilliant reasoning, every man's body is to be found in the neighbourhood of his wardrobe. And pray what did you hope to arrive at through this?'

'At some evidence implicating Flora Millar in the disappearance.'

'I am afraid that you will find it difficult.'

'Are you, indeed, now?' cried Lestrade with some bitterness. 'I am afraid, Holmes, that you are not very practical with your deductions and your inferences. You have made two blunders in as many minutes. This dress does implicate Miss Flora Millar.'

'And how?'

'In the dress is a pocket. In the pocket is a card-case. In the card-case is a note. And here is the very note.' He slapped it down upon the table in front of him. 'Listen to this: "You will see me when all is ready. Come at once. F.H.M." Now my theory all along has been that Lady St Simon was decoyed away by Flora Millar, and that she, with confederates, no doubt, was responsible for her disappearance. Here, signed with her initials, is the very note which was no doubt quietly slipped into her hand at the door and which lured her within their reach.'

'Very good, Lestrade,' said Holmes, laughing. 'You really are very fine indeed. Let me see it.' He took up the paper in a listless way, but his attention instantly became riveted, and he gave a little cry of satisfaction. 'This is indeed important,' said he.

'Ha! you find it so?'

'Extremely so. I congratulate you warmly.'

Lestrade rose in his triumph and bent his head to look. 'Why,' he shrieked, 'you're looking at the wrong side!'

'On the contrary, this is the right side.'

'The right side? You're mad! Here is the note written in pencil over here.'

'And over here is what appears to be the fragment of a hotel bill, which interests me deeply.'

'There's nothing in it. I looked at it before,' said Lestrade. '"Oct. 4th, room 8s., breakfast 2s. 6d., cocktail 1s., lunch 2s. 6d., glass sherry, 8d." I see nothing in that.'

'Very likely not. It is most important, all the same. As to the note, it is important also, or at least the initials are, so I congratulate you again.'

'I've wasted time enough,' said Lestrade, rising. 'I believe in hard work and not in sitting by the fire spinning fine theories. Good-day, Mr Holmes, and we shall see which gets to the bottom of the matter first.' He gathered up the garments, thrust them into the bag, and made for the door.

'Just one hint to you, Lestrade,' drawled Holmes before his rival vanished; 'I will tell you the true solution of the matter. Lady St Simon is a myth. There is not, and there never has been, any such person.'

Lestrade looked sadly at my companion. Then he turned to me, tapped his forehead three times, shook his head solemnly and hurried away.

He had hardly shut the door behind him when Holmes rose to put on his overcoat. 'There is something in what the fellow says about outdoor work,' he remarked, 'so I think, Watson, that I must leave you to your papers for a little.'

It was after five o'clock when Sherlock Holmes left me, but I had no time to be lonely, for within an hour there arrived a confectioner's man with a very large flat box. This he unpacked with the help of a youth whom he had brought with him, and presently, to my very great astonishment, a quite epicurean little cold supper began to be laid out upon our humble lodging-house mahogany. There were a couple of brace of cold woodcock, a pheasant, a *p,tÉ de foie gras* pie with a group of ancient and cobwebby bottles. Having laid out all these luxuries, my two visitors vanished away, like the genii of the *Arabian Nights*, with no explanation save that the things had been paid for and were ordered to this address.

Just before nine o'clock Sherlock Holmes stepped briskly into the room. His features were gravely set, but there was a light in his eye which made me think that he had not been disappointed in his conclusions.

'They have laid the supper, then,' he said, rubbing his hands.

'You seem to expect company. They have laid for five.'

'Yes, I fancy we may have some company dropping in,' said he. 'I am surprised that Lord St Simon has not already arrived. Ha! I fancy that I hear his step now upon the stairs.'

It was indeed our visitor of the afternoon who came bustling in, dangling his glasses more vigorously than ever, and with a very perturbed expression upon his aristocratic features.

'My messenger reached you, then?' asked Holmes.

'Yes, and I confess that the contents startled me beyond measure. Have you good authority for what you say?'

'The best possible.'

Lord St Simon sank into a chair and passed his hand over his forehead.

'What will the duke say,' he murmured, 'when he hears that one of the family has been subjected to such humiliation?'

'It is the purest accident. I cannot allow that there is any humiliation.'

'Ah, you look on these things from another standpoint.'

'I fail to see that anyone is to blame. I can hardly see how the lady could have acted otherwise, though her abrupt method of doing it was undoubtedly to be regretted. Having no mother, she had no one to advise her at such a crisis.'

'It was a slight, sir, a public slight,' said Lord St Simon, tapping his fingers upon the table.

'You must make allowance for this poor girl, placed in so unprecedented a position.'

'I will make no allowance. I am very angry indeed, and I have been shamefully used.'

'I think that I heard a ring,' said Holmes. 'Yes, there are steps on the landing. If I cannot persuade you to take a lenient view of the matter, Lord St Simon, I have brought an advocate here who may be more successful.' He opened the door and ushered in a lady and gentleman. 'Lord St Simon,' said he, 'allow me to introduce you to Mr and Mrs Francis Hay Moulton. The lady, I think, you have already met.'

At the sight of these newcomers our client had sprung from his seat and stood very erect, with his eyes cast down and his hand thrust into the breast of his frock-coat, a picture of offended dignity. The lady had taken a quick step forward and had held out her hand to him, but he still refused to raise his eyes. It was as well for his resolution, perhaps, for her pleading face was one which it was hard to resist.

'You're angry, Robert,' said she. 'Well, I guess you have every cause to be.'

'Pray make no apology to me,' said Lord St Simon bitterly.

'Oh, yes, I know that I have treated you real bad and that I should have spoken to you before I went; but I was kind of rattled, and from the time when I saw Frank here again I just didn't know what I was doing or saying. I only wonder I didn't fall down and do a faint right there before the altar.'

'Perhaps, Mrs Moulton, you would like my friend and me to leave the room while you explain this matter?'

'If I may give an opinion,' remarked the strange gentleman, 'we've had just a little too much secrecy over this business already. For my part, I should like all Europe and America to hear the rights of it.' He was a small, wiry, sunburnt man, clean-shaven, with a sharp face and alert manner.

'Then I'll tell our story right away,' said the lady. 'Frank here and I met in 1884, in McQuire's camp, near the Rockies, where pa was working a claim. We were engaged to each other, Frank and I; but then one day father struck a rich pocket and made a pile, while poor Frank here had a claim that petered out and came to nothing. The richer pa grew the poorer was Frank; so at last pa wouldn't hear of our engagement lasting any longer, and he took me away to 'Frisco. Frank wouldn't throw up his hand, though; so he followed me there, and he saw me without pa knowing anything about it. It would only have made him mad to know, so we just fixed it all up for ourselves. Frank said that he would go and make his pile, too, and never come back to claim me until he had as much as pa. So then I promised to wait for him to the end of time and pledged myself not to marry anyone else while he lived. "Why shouldn't we be married right away, then," said he, "and then I will feel sure of you; and I won't claim to be your husband until I come back?" Well, we talked it over, and he had fixed it all up so nicely, with a clergyman all ready in waiting, that we just did it right there; and then Frank went off to seek his fortune, and I went back to pa.

'The next I heard of Frank was that he was in Montana, and then he went prospecting in Arizona, and then I heard of him from New Mexico. After that came a long newspaper story about how a miners' camp had been attacked by Apache Indians, and there was my Frank's name among the killed. I fainted dead away, and I was very sick for months after. Pa thought I had a decline and took me to half the doctors in 'Frisco. Not a word of news came for a year and more, so that I never doubted that Frank was really dead. Then Lord St Simon came to 'Frisco, and we came to London, and a marriage was arranged, and pa was very pleased, but I felt all the time that no man on this earth would ever take the place in my heart that had been given to my poor Frank.

'Still, if I had married Lord St Simon, of course I'd have done my duty by him. We can't command our love, but we can our actions. I went to the altar with him with the intention to make him just as good a wife as it was in me to be. But you may imagine what I felt when, just as I came to the altar rails, I glanced back and saw Frank standing and looking at me out of the first pew. I thought it was his ghost at first; but when I looked again there he was still, with a kind of question in his eyes, as if to ask me whether I were glad or sorry to see him. I wonder I didn't drop. I know that everything was turning round, and the words of the clergyman were just like the buzz of a bee in my ear. I didn't know what to do. Should I stop the service and make a scene in the church? I glanced at him again, and he seemed to know what I was thinking, for he raised his finger to his lips to tell me to be still. Then I saw him scribble on a piece of paper, and I knew that he was writing me a note. As I passed his pew on the way out I dropped my bouquet over to him, and he slipped the note into my hand when he returned me the flowers. It was only a line asking me to join him when he made the sign to me to do so. Of course I never doubted for a moment that my first duty was now to him, and I determined to do just whatever he might direct.

'When I got back I told my maid, who had known him in California, and had always been his friend. I ordered her to say nothing, but to get a few things packed and my ulster ready. I know I ought to have spoken to Lord St Simon, but it was dreadful hard before his mother and all those great people. I just made up my mind to run away and explain afterwards. I hadn't been at the table ten minutes before I saw Frank out of the window at the other side of the road. He beckoned to me and then began walking into the park. I slipped out, put on my things, and followed him. Some woman came talking something or other about Lord St Simon to me – seemed to me from the little I heard as if he had a little secret of his own before marriage also – but I managed to get away from her and soon overtook Frank. We got into a cab together, and away we drove to some lodgings he had taken in Gordon Square, and that was my true wedding after all those years of waiting. Frank had been a prisoner among the Apaches, had escaped, came on to 'Frisco, found that I had given him up for dead and had gone to England, followed me there, and had come upon me at last on the very morning of my second wedding.'

'I saw it in a paper,' explained the American. 'It gave the name and the church but not where the lady lived.'

'Then we had a talk as to what we should do, and Frank was all for openness, but I was so ashamed of it all that I felt as if I should like to vanish away and never see any of them again – just sending a line to pa, perhaps, to show him that I was alive. It was awful to me to think of all those lords and ladies sitting round that breakfast-table and waiting for me to come back. So Frank took my wedding-clothes and things and made a bundle of them, so that I should not be traced, and dropped them away somewhere where no one could find them. It is likely that we should have gone on to Paris tomorrow, only that this good gentleman, Mr Holmes, came round to us this evening, though how he found us is more than I can think, and he showed us very clearly and kindly that I was wrong and that Frank was right, and that we should be putting ourselves in the wrong if we were so secret. Then he offered to give us a chance of talking to Lord St Simon alone, and so we came right away round to his rooms at once. Now, Robert, you have heard it all, and I am very sorry if I have given you pain, and I hope that you do not think very meanly of me.'

Lord St Simon had by no means relaxed his rigid attitude, but had listened with a frowning brow and a compressed lip to this long narrative.

'Excuse me,' he said, 'but it is not my custom to discuss my most intimate personal affairs in this public manner.'

'Then you won't forgive me? You won't shake hands before I go?'

'Oh, certainly, if it would give you any pleasure.' He put out his hand and coldly grasped that which she extended to him.

'I had hoped,' suggested Holmes, 'that you would have joined us in a friendly supper.'

'I think that there you ask a little too much,' responded his lordship. 'I may be forced to acquiesce in these recent developments, but I can hardly be expected to make merry over them. I think that with your permission I will now wish you all a very good-night.' He included us all in a sweeping bow and stalked out of the room.

'Then I trust that you at least will honour me with your company,' said Sherlock Holmes. 'It is always a joy to meet an American, Mr Moulton, for I am one of those who believe that the folly of a monarch and the blundering of a minister in far-gone years will not prevent our children from being someday citizens of the same worldwide country under a flag which shall be a quartering of the Union Jack with the Stars and Stripes.'

'The case has been an interesting one,' remarked Holmes, when our visitors had left us, 'because it serves to show very clearly how simple the explanation may be of an affair which at first sight seems to be almost inexplicable. Nothing could be more natural than the sequence of events as narrated by this lady, and nothing stranger than the result when viewed, for instance, by Mr Lestrade of Scotland Yard.'

'You were not yourself at fault at all, then?'

'From the first, two facts were very obvious to me, the one that the lady had been quite willing to undergo the wedding ceremony, the other that she had repented of it within a few minutes of returning home. Obviously something had occurred during the morning, then, to cause her to change her mind. What could that something be? She could not have spoken to anyone when she was out, for she had been in the company of the bridegroom. Had she seen someone, then? If she had, it must be someone from America because she had spent so short a time in this country that she could hardly have allowed anyone to acquire so deep an influence over her that the mere sight of him would induce her to change her plans so completely. You see we have already arrived, by a process of exclusion, at the idea that she might have seen an American. Then who could this American be, and why should he possess so much influence over her? It might be a lover; it might be a husband. Her young womanhood had, I knew, been spent in rough scenes and under strange conditions. So far I had got before I ever heard Lord St Simon's narrative. When he told us of a man in a pew, of the change in the bride's manner, of so transparent a device for obtaining a note as the dropping of a bouquet, of her resort to her confidential maid, and of her very significant allusion to claim-jumping – which in miners' parlance means taking possession of that which another person has a prior claim to – the whole situation became absolutely clear. She had gone off with a man, and the man was either a lover or was a previous husband – the chances being in favour of the latter.'

'And how in the world did you find them?'

'It might have been difficult, but friend Lestrade held information in his hands the value of which he did not himself know. The initials were, of course, of the highest importance, but more valuable still was it to know that within a week he had settled his bill at one of the most select London hotels.'

'How did you deduce the select?'

'By the select prices. Eight shillings for a bed and eightpence for a glass of sherry pointed to one of the most expensive hotels. There are not many in London which charge at that rate. In the second one which I visited, in Northumberland Avenue, I learned by an inspection of the book that Francis H. Moulton, an American gentleman, had left only the day before, and on looking over the entries against him, I came upon the very items which I had seen in the duplicate bill. His letters were to be forwarded to 226 Gordon Square, so thither I travelled, and being fortunate enough to find the loving couple at home, I ventured to give them some paternal advice and to point out to them that it would be better in every way that they should make their position a little clearer both to the general public and to Lord St Simon in particular. I invited them to meet him here, and, as you see, I made him keep the appointment.'

'But with no very good result,' I remarked. 'His conduct was certainly not very gracious.'

'Ah, Watson,' said Holmes, smiling, 'perhaps you would not be very gracious either, if, after all the trouble of wooing and wedding, you found yourself deprived in an instant of wife and of fortune. I think that we may judge Lord St Simon very mercifully and thank our stars that we are never likely to find ourselves in the same position. Draw your chair up and hand me my violin, for the only problem we have still to solve is how to while away these bleak autumnal evenings.'

The Adventure of the Beryl Coronet

'Holmes,' said I, as I stood one morning in our bow-window looking down the street, 'here is a madman coming along. It seems rather sad that his relatives should allow him to come out alone.'

My friend rose lazily from his armchair and stood with his hands in the pockets of his dressing-gown, looking over my shoulder. It was a bright, crisp February morning, and the snow of the day before still lay deep upon the ground, shimmering brightly in the wintry sun. Down the centre of Baker Street it had been ploughed into a brown crumbly band by the traffic, but at either side and on the heaped-up edges of the footpaths it still lay as white as when it fell. The grey pavement had been cleaned and scraped, but was still dangerously slippery, so that there were fewer passengers than usual. Indeed, from the direction of the Metropolitan Line station no one was coming save the single gentleman whose eccentric conduct had drawn my attention.

He was a man of about fifty, tall, portly and imposing, with a massive, strongly marked face and a commanding figure. He was dressed in a sombre yet rich style, in black frock-coat, shining hat, neat brown gaiters and well-cut pearl-grey trousers. Yet his actions were in absurd contrast to the dignity of his dress and features, for he was running hard, with occasional little springs, such as a weary man gives who is little accustomed to set any tax upon his legs. As he ran he jerked his hands up and down, waggled his head, and writhed his face into the most extraordinary contortions.

'What on earth can be the matter with him?' I asked. 'He is looking up at the numbers of the houses.'

'I believe that he is coming here,' said Holmes, rubbing his hands.

'Here?'

'Yes; I rather think he is coming to consult me professionally. I think that I recognise the symptoms. Ha! did I not tell you?' As he spoke, the man, puffing and blowing, rushed at our door and pulled at our bell until the whole house resounded with the clanging.

A few moments later he was in our room, still puffing, still gesticulating, but with so fixed a look of grief and despair in his eyes that our smiles were turned in an instant to horror and pity. For a while he could not get his words out, but swayed his body and plucked at his hair like one who has been driven to the extreme limits of his reason. Then, suddenly springing to his feet, he beat his head against the wall with such force that we both rushed upon him and tore him away to the centre of the room. Sherlock Holmes pushed him down into the easy-chair and, sitting beside him, patted his hand and chatted with him in the easy, soothing tones which he knew so well how to employ.

'You have come to me to tell your story, have you not?' said he. 'You are fatigued with your haste. Pray wait until you have recovered yourself, and then I shall be most happy to look into any little problem which you may submit to me.'

The man sat for a minute or more with a heaving chest, fighting against his emotion. Then he passed his handkerchief over his brow, set his lips tight, and turned his face towards us.

'No doubt you think me mad?' said he.

'I see that you have had some great trouble,' responded Holmes.

'God knows I have! – a trouble which is enough to unseat my reason, so sudden and so terrible is it. Public disgrace I might have faced, although I am a man whose character has never yet borne a stain. Private affliction also is the lot of every man; but the two coming together, and in so frightful a form, have been enough to shake my very soul. Besides, it is not I alone. The very noblest in the land may suffer unless some way be found out of this horrible affair.'

'Pray compose yourself, sir,' said Holmes, 'and let me have a clear account of who you are and what it is that has befallen you.'

'My name,' answered our visitor, 'is probably familiar to your ears. I am Alexander Holder, of the banking firm of Holder & Stevenson, of Threadneedle Street.'

The name was indeed well known to us as belonging to the senior partner in the second largest private banking concern in the City of London. What could have happened, then, to bring one of the foremost citizens of London to this most pitiable pass? We waited, all curiosity, until with another effort he braced himself to tell his story.

'I feel that time is of value,' said he; 'that is why I hastened here when the police inspector suggested that I should secure your co-operation. I came to Baker Street by the Underground and hurried from there on foot, for the cabs go slowly through this snow. That is why I was so out of breath, for I am a man who takes very little exercise. I feel better now, and I will put the facts before you as shortly and yet as clearly as I can.

'It is, of course, well known to you that in a successful banking business as much depends upon our being able to find remunerative investments for our funds as upon our increasing our connection and the number of our depositors. One of our most lucrative means of laying out money is in the shape of loans, where the security is unimpeachable. We have done a good deal in this direction during the last few years, and there are many noble families to whom we have advanced large sums upon the security of their pictures, libraries or plate.

'Yesterday morning I was seated in my office at the bank when a card was brought in to me by one of the clerks. I started when I saw the name, for it was that of none other than – well, perhaps even to you I had better say no more than that it was a name which is a houschold word all over the earth – one of the highest, noblest, most exalted names in England. I was overwhelmed by the honour and attempted, when he entered, to say so, but he plunged at once into business with the air of a man who wishes to hurry quickly through a disagreeable task.

'"Mr Holder," said he, "I have been informed that you are in the habit of advancing money."

'"The firm does so when the security is good." I answered.

'"It is absolutely essential to me," said he, "that I should have £50,000 at once. I could, of course, borrow so trifling a sum ten times over from my friends, but I much prefer to make it a matter of business and to carry out that business myself. In my position you can readily understand that it is unwise to place oneself under obligations."

'"For how long, may I ask, do you want this sum?" I asked.

'"Next Monday I have a large sum due to me, and I shall then most certainly repay what you advance, with whatever interest you think it right to charge. But it is very essential to me that the money should be paid at once."

'"I should be happy to advance it without further parley from my own private purse," said I, "were it not that the strain would be rather more than it could bear. If, on the other hand, I am to do it in the name of the firm, then in justice to my partner I must insist that, even in your case, every businesslike precaution should be taken."

'"I should much prefer to have it so," said he, raising up a square black morocco case which he had laid beside his chair. "You have doubtless heard of the Beryl Coronet?"

'"One of the most precious public possessions of the empire," said I.

'"Precisely." He opened the case, and there, embedded in soft, flesh-coloured velvet, lay the magnificent piece of jewellery which he had named. "There are thirty-nine enormous beryls," said he, "and the price of the gold chasing is incalculable. The lowest estimate would put the worth of the coronet at double the sum which I have asked. I am prepared to leave it with you as my security."

'I took the precious case into my hands and looked in some perplexity from it to my illustrious client.

'"You doubt its value?" he asked.

'"Not at all. I only doubt –"

'"The propriety of my leaving it? You may set your mind at rest about that. I should not dream of doing so were it not absolutely certain that I should be able in four days to reclaim it. It is a pure matter of form. Is the security sufficient?"

'"Ample."

'"You understand, Mr Holder, that I am giving you a strong proof of the confidence which I have in you, founded upon all that I have heard of you. I rely upon you not only to be discreet and to refrain from all gossip upon the matter but, above all, to preserve this coronet with every possible precaution because I need not say that a great public scandal would be caused if any harm were to befall it. Any injury to it would be almost as serious as its complete loss, for there are no beryls in the world to match these, and it would be impossible to replace them. I leave it with you, however, with every confidence, and I shall call for it in person on Monday morning."

'Seeing that my client was anxious to leave, I said no more, but calling for my cashier, I ordered him to pay over fifty thousand-pound notes. When I was alone once more, however, with the precious case lying upon the table in front of me, I could not but think with some misgivings of the immense responsibility which it entailed upon me. There could be no doubt that, as it was a national possession, a horrible scandal would ensue if any misfortune should occur to it. I already regretted having ever consented to take charge of it. However, it was too late to alter the matter now, so I locked it up in my private safe and turned once more to my work.

'When evening came I felt that it would be an imprudence to leave so precious a thing in the office behind me. Bankers' safes had been forced before now, and why should not mine be? If so, how terrible would be the position in which I should find myself! I determined, therefore, that for the next few days I would always carry the case backwards and forwards with me, so that it might never be really out of my reach. With this intention, I called a cab and drove out to my house at Streatham, carrying the jewel with me. I did not breathe freely until I had taken it upstairs and locked it in the bureau of my dressing-room.

'And now a word as to my household, Mr Holmes, for I wish you thoroughly to understand the situation. My groom and my page sleep out of the house, and may be set aside altogether. I have three maid-servants who have been with me a number of years and whose absolute reliability is quite above suspicion. Another, Lucy Parr, the second waiting-maid, has only been in my service a few months. She came with an excellent character, however, and has always given me satisfaction. She is a very pretty girl and has attracted admirers who have occasionally hung about the place. That is the only drawback which we have found to her, but we believe her to be a thoroughly good girl in every way.

'So much for the servants. My family itself is so small that it will not take me long to describe it. I am a widower and have an only son, Arthur. He has been a disappointment to me, Mr Holmes – a grievous disappointment. I have no doubt that I am myself to blame. People tell me that I have spoiled him. Very likely I have. When my dear wife died I felt that he was all I had to love. I could not bear to see the smile fade even for a moment from his face. I have never denied him a wish. Perhaps it would have been better for both of us had I been sterner, but I meant it for the best.

'It was naturally my intention that he should succeed me in my business, but he was not of a business turn. He was wild, wayward and, to speak the truth, I could not trust him in the handling of large sums of money. When he was young, he became a member of an aristocratic club, and there, having charming manners, he was soon the intimate of a number of men with long purses and expensive habits. He learned to play heavily at cards and to squander money on the turf, until he had again and again to come to me and implore me to give him an advance upon his allowance, that he might settle his debts of honour. He tried more than once to break away from the dangerous company which he was keeping, but each time the influence of his friend, Sir George Burnwell, was enough to draw him back again.

'And, indeed, I could not wonder that such a man as Sir George Burnwell should gain an influence over him, for he has frequently brought him to my house, and I have found myself that I could hardly resist the fascination of his manner. He is older than Arthur, a man of the world to his fingertips, one who had been everywhere, seen everything, a brilliant talker and a man of great personal beauty. Yet when I think of him in cold blood, far away from the glamour of his presence, I am convinced from his cynical speech and the look which I have caught in his eyes that he is one who should be deeply distrusted. So I think, and so, too, thinks my little Mary, who has a woman's quick insight into character.

'And now there is only she to be described. She is my niece; but when my brother died five years ago and left her alone in the world I adopted her, and have looked upon her ever since as my daughter. She is a sunbeam in my house – sweet, loving, beautiful, a wonderful manager and housekeeper, yet as tender and quiet and gentle as a woman could be. She is my right hand. I do not know what I could do without her. In only one matter has she ever gone against my wishes. Twice my boy has asked her to marry him, for he loves her devotedly, but each time she has refused him. I think that if anyone could have drawn him into the right path it would have been she, and that his marriage might have changed his whole life; but now, alas! it is too late – for ever too late!

'Now, Mr Holmes, you know the people who live under my roof, and I shall continue with my miserable story.

'When we were taking coffee in the drawing-room that night after dinner, I told Arthur and Mary my experience, and of the precious treasure which we had under our roof, suppressing only the name of my client. Lucy Parr, who had brought in the coffee, had, I am sure, left the room; but I cannot swear that the door was closed. Mary and Arthur were much interested and wished to see the famous coronet, but I thought it better not to disturb it.

'"Where have you put it?" asked Arthur.

'"In my own bureau."

'"Well, I hope to goodness the house won't be burgled during the night." said he.

'"It is locked up," I answered.

'"Oh, any old key will fit that bureau. When I was a youngster I have opened it myself with the key of the box-room cupboard."

'He often had a wild way of talking, so that I thought little of what he said. He followed me to my room, however, that night with a very grave face.

'"Look here, dad," said he with his eyes cast down, "can you let me have two hundred pounds?"

'"No, I cannot!" I answered sharply. "I have been far too generous with you in money matters."

'"You have been very kind," said he, "but I must have this money, or else I can never show my face inside the club again."

'"And a very good thing, too!" I cried.

'"Yes, but you would not have me leave it a dishonoured man," said he. "I could not bear the disgrace. I must raise the money in some way, and if you will not let me have it, then I must try other means."

'I was very angry, for this was the third demand during the month. "You shall not have a farthing from me," I cried, on which he bowed and left the room without another word.

'When he was gone I unlocked my bureau, made sure that my treasure was safe, and locked it again. Then I started to go round the house to see that all was secure – a duty which I usually leave to Mary but which I thought it well to perform myself that night. As I came down the stairs I saw Mary herself at the side window of the hall, which she closed and fastened as I approached.

'"Tell me, uncle," said she, looking, I thought, a little disturbed, "did you give Lucy the maid leave to go out tonight?"

'"Certainly not."

'"She came in just now by the back door. I have no doubt that she has only been to the side gate to see someone, but I think that it is hardly safe and should be stopped."

'"You must speak to her in the morning – or I will, if you prefer it. Are you sure that everything is fastened?"

'"Quite sure, uncle."

'"Then, good-night." I kissed her and went up to my bedroom again, where I was soon asleep.

'I am endeavouring to tell you everything, Mr Holmes, which may have any bearing upon the case, but I beg that you will question me upon any point which I do not make clear.'

'On the contrary, your statement is singularly lucid.'

'I come to a part of my story now in which I should wish to be particularly so. I am not a very heavy sleeper, and the anxiety in my mind tended, no doubt, to make me even less so than usual. About two in the morning, then, I was awakened by some sound in the house. It had ceased ere I was wide awake, but it had left an impression behind it as though a window had gently closed somewhere. I lay listening with all my ears. Suddenly, to my horror, there was a distinct sound of footsteps moving softly in the next room. I slipped out of bed, all palpitating with fear, and peeped round the corner of my dressing-room door.

'"Arthur!" I screamed, "you villain! you thief! How dare you touch that coronet?"

'The gas was half up, as I had left it, and my unhappy boy, dressed only in his shirt and trousers, was standing beside the light, holding the coronet in his hands. He appeared to be wrenching at it, or bending it with all his strength. At my cry he dropped it from his grasp and turned as pale as death. I snatched it up and examined it. One of the gold corners, with three of the beryls in it, was missing.

'"You blackguard!" I shouted, beside myself with rage. "You have destroyed it! You have dishonoured me forever! Where are the jewels which you have stolen?"

'"Stolen!" he cried.

'"Yes, thief!" I roared, shaking him by the shoulder.

'"There are none missing. There cannot be any missing," said he.

'"There are three missing. And you know where they are. Must I call you a liar as well as a thief? Did I not see you trying to tear off another piece?"

'"You have called me names enough," said he; "I will not stand it any longer. I shall not say another word about this business, since you have chosen to insult me. I will leave your house in the morning and make my own way in the world."

'"You shall leave it in the hands of the police!" I cried half-mad with grief and rage. "I shall have this matter probed to the bottom."

'"You shall learn nothing from me," said he, with a passion such as I should not have thought was in his nature. "If you choose to call the police, let the police find what they can."

'By this time the whole house was astir, for I had raised my voice in my anger. Mary was the first to rush into my room, and, at the sight of the coronet and of Arthur's face, she read the whole story and, with a scream, fell down senseless on the ground. I sent the housemaid for the police and put the investigation into their hands at once. When the inspector and a constable entered the house, Arthur, who had stood sullenly with his arms folded, asked me whether it was my intention to charge him with theft. I answered that it had ceased to be a private matter, but had become a public one, since the ruined coronet was national property. I was determined that the law should have its way in everything.

'"At least," said he, "you will not have me arrested at once. It would be to your advantage as well as mine if I might leave the house for five minutes."

'"That you may get away, or perhaps that you may conceal what you have stolen," said I. And then, realising the dreadful position in which I was placed, I implored him to remember that not only my honour but that of one who was far greater than I was at stake; and that he threatened to raise a scandal which would convulse the nation. He might avert it all if he would but tell me what he had done with the three missing stones.

'"You may as well face the matter," said I; "you have been caught in the act, and no confession could make your guilt more heinous. If you but make such reparation as is in your power, by telling us where the beryls are, all shall be forgiven and forgotten."

'"Keep your forgiveness for those who ask for it," he answered, turning away from me with a sneer. I saw that he was too hardened for any words of mine to influence him. There was but one way for it. I called in the inspector and gave him into custody. A search was made at once not only of his person but of his room and of every portion of the house where he could possibly have concealed the gems; but no trace of them could be found, nor would the wretched boy open his mouth for all our persuasions and our threats. This morning he was removed to a cell, and I, after going through all the police formalities, have hurried round to you to implore you to use your skill in unravelling the matter. The police have openly confessed that they can at present make nothing of it. You may go to any expense which you think necessary. I have already offered a reward of a thousand pounds. My God, what shall I do! I have lost my honour, my gems and my son in one night. Oh, what shall I do!'

He put a hand on either side of his head and rocked himself to and fro, droning to himself like a child whose grief has got beyond words.

Sherlock Holmes sat silent for some few minutes, with his brows knitted and his eyes fixed upon the fire.

'Do you receive much company?' he asked.

'None save my partner with his family, and an occasional friend of Arthur's. Sir George Burnwell has been several times lately. No one else, I think.'

'Do you go out much in society?'

'Arthur does. Mary and I stay at home. We neither of us care for it.'

'That is unusual in a young girl.'

'She is of a quiet nature. Besides, she is not so very young. She is four-and-twenty.'

'This matter, from what you say, seems to have been a shock to her also.'

'Terrible! She is even more affected than I.'

'You have neither of you any doubt as to your son's guilt?'

'How can we have when I saw him with my own eyes with the coronet in his hands.'

'I hardly consider that a conclusive proof. Was the remainder of the coronet at all injured?'

'Yes, it was twisted.'

'Do you not think, then, that he might have been trying to straighten it?'

'God bless you! You are doing what you can for him and for me. But it is too heavy a task. What was he doing there at all? If his purpose were innocent, why did he not say so?'

'Precisely. And if it were guilty, why did he not invent a lie? His silence appears to me to cut both ways. There are several singular points about the case. What did the police think of the noise which awoke you from your sleep?'

'They considered that it might have been caused by Arthur's closing his bedroom door.'

'A likely story! As if a man bent on felony would slam his door so as to wake a household. What did they say, then, of the disappearance of these gems?'

'They are still sounding the planking and probing the furniture in the hope of finding them.'

'Have they thought of looking outside the house?'

'Yes, they have shown extraordinary energy. The whole garden has already been minutely examined.'

'Now, my dear sir,' said Holmes, 'is it not obvious to you now that this matter really strikes very much deeper than either you or the police were at first inclined to think? It appeared to you to be a simple case; to me it seems exceedingly complex. Consider what is involved by your theory. You suppose that your son came down from his bed, went, at great risk, to your dressing-room, opened your bureau, took out your coronet, broke off by main force a small portion of it, went off to some other place, concealed three gems out of the thirty-nine, with such skill that nobody can find them, and then returned with the other thirty-six into the room in which he exposed himself to the greatest danger of being discovered. I ask you now, is such a theory tenable?'

'But what other is there?' cried the banker with a gesture of despair. 'If his motives were innocent, why does he not explain them?'

'It is our task to find that out,' replied Holmes; 'so now, if you please, Mr Holder, we will set off for Streatham together and devote an hour to glancing a little more closely into details.'

My friend insisted upon my accompanying them on their expedition, which I was eager enough to do, for my curiosity and sympathy were deeply stirred by the story to which we had listened. I confess that the guilt of the banker's son appeared to me to be as obvious as it did to his unhappy father, but still I had such faith in Holmes's judgement that I felt that there must be some grounds for hope as long as he was dissatisfied with the accepted explanation. He hardly spoke a word the whole way out to the southern suburb, but sat with his chin upon his breast and his hat drawn over his eyes, sunk in the deepest thought. Our client appeared to have taken fresh heart at the little glimpse of hope which had been presented to him, and he even broke into a desultory chat with me over his business affairs. A short railway journey and a shorter walk brought us to Fairbank, the modest residence of the great financier.

Fairbank was a good-sized square house of white stone, standing back a little from the road. A double carriage-sweep, with a snow-clad lawn, stretched down in front to two large iron gates which closed the entrance. On the right side was a small wooden wicket, which led into a narrow path between two neat hedges stretching from the road to the kitchen door and forming the tradesmen's entrance. On the left ran a lane which led to the stables, and was not itself within the grounds at all, being a public, though little used, thoroughfare. Holmes left us standing at the door and walked slowly all round the house – across the front, down the tradesmen's path, and so round by the garden behind into the stable lane. So long was he that Mr Holder and I went into the dining-room and waited by the fire until he should return. We were sitting there in silence when the door opened and a young lady came in. She was rather above the middle height, slim, with dark hair and eyes, which seemed the darker against the absolute pallor of her skin. I do not think that I have ever seen such deadly paleness in a woman's face. Her lips, too, were bloodless, but her eyes were flushed with crying. As she swept silently into the room she impressed me with a greater sense of grief than the banker had done in the morning, and it was the more striking in her as she was evidently a woman of strong character, with immense capacity for self-restraint. Disregarding my presence, she went straight to her uncle and passed her hand over his head with a sweet womanly caress.

'You have given orders that Arthur should be liberated, have you not, uncle?' she asked.

'No, no, my girl, the matter must be probed to the bottom.'

'But I am so sure that he is innocent. You know what a woman's instincts are. I know that he has done no harm and that you will be sorry for having acted so harshly.'

'Why is he silent, then, if he is innocent?'

'Who knows? Perhaps because he was so angry that you should suspect him.'

'How could I help suspecting him, when I actually saw him with the coronet in his hand?'

'Oh, but he had only picked it up to look at it. Oh, do, do take my word for it that he is innocent. Let the matter drop and say no more. It is so dreadful to think of our dear Arthur in prison!'

'I shall never let it drop until the gems are found – never, Mary! Your affection for Arthur blinds you as to the awful consequences to me. Far from hushing the thing up, I have brought a gentleman down from London to enquire more deeply into it.'

'This gentleman?' she asked, facing round to me.

'No, his friend. He wished us to leave him alone. He is round in the stable lane now.'

'The stable lane?' She raised her dark eyebrows. 'What can he hope to find there? Ah! this, I suppose, is he. I trust, sir, that you will succeed in proving, what I feel sure is the truth, that my cousin Arthur is innocent of this crime.'

'I fully share your opinion, and I trust, with you, that we may prove it,' returned Holmes, going back to the mat to knock the snow from his shoes. 'I believe I have the honour of addressing Miss Mary Holder. Might I ask you a question or two?'

'Pray do, sir, if it may help to clear this horrible affair up.'

'You heard nothing yourself last night?'

'Nothing, until my uncle here began to speak loudly. I heard that, and I came down.'

'You shut up the windows and doors the night before. Did you fasten all the windows?'

'Yes.'

'Were they all fastened this morning?'

'Yes.'

'You have a maid who has a sweetheart? I think that you remarked to your uncle last night that she had been out to see him?'

'Yes, and she was the girl who waited in the drawing-room, and who may have heard uncle's remarks about the coronet.'

'I see. You infer that she may have gone out to tell her sweetheart, and that the two may have planned the robbery.'

'But what is the good of all these vague theories,' cried the banker impatiently, 'when I have told you that I saw Arthur with the coronet in his hands?'

'Wait a little, Mr Holder. We must come back to that. About this girl, Miss Holder. You saw her return by the kitchen door, I presume?'

'Yes; when I went to see if the door was fastened for the night I met her slipping in. I saw the man, too, in the gloom.'

'Do you know him?'

'Oh, yes! he is the greengrocer who brings our vegetables round. His name is Francis Prosper.'

'He stood,' said Holmes, 'to the left of the door – that is to say, farther up the path than is necessary to reach the door?'

'Yes, he did.'

'And he is a man with a wooden leg?'

Something like fear sprang up in the young lady's expressive black eyes. 'Why, you are like a magician,' said she. 'How do you know that?' She smiled, but there was no answering smile in Holmes's thin, eager face.

'I should be very glad now to go upstairs,' said he. 'I shall probably wish to go over the outside of the house again. Perhaps I had better take a look at the lower windows before I go up.'

He walked swiftly round from one to the other, pausing only at the large one which looked from the hall on to the stable lane. This he opened and made a very careful examination of the sill with his powerful magnifying lens. 'Now we shall go upstairs,' said he at last.

The banker's dressing-room was a plainly furnished little chamber, with a grey carpet, a large bureau and a long mirror. Holmes went to the bureau first and looked hard at the lock.

'Which key was used to open it?' he asked.

'That which my son himself indicated – that of the cupboard of the lumber-room.'

'Have you it here?'

'That is it on the dressing-table.'

Sherlock Holmes took it up and opened the bureau.

'It is a noiseless lock,' said he. 'It is no wonder that it did not wake you. This case, I presume, contains the coronet. We must have a look at it.' He opened the case, and taking out the diadem he laid it upon the table. It was a magnificent specimen of the jeweller's art, and the thirty-six stones were the finest that I have ever seen. At one side of the coronet was a cracked edge, where a corner holding three gems had been torn away.

'Now, Mr Holder,' said Holmes, 'here is the corner which corresponds to that which has been so unfortunately lost. Might I beg that you will break it off.'

The banker recoiled in horror. 'I should not dream of trying,' said he.

'Then I will.' Holmes suddenly bent his strength upon it, but without result. 'I feel it give a little,' said he; 'but, though I am exceptionally strong in the fingers, it would take me all my time to break it. An ordinary man could not do it. Now, what do you think would happen if I did break it, Mr Holder? There would be a noise like a pistol shot. Do you tell me that all this happened within a few yards of your bed and that you heard nothing of it?'

'I do not know what to think. It is all dark to me.'

'But perhaps it may grow lighter as we go. What do you think, Miss Holder?'

'I confess that I still share my uncle's perplexity.'

'Your son had no shoes or slippers on when you saw him?'

'He had nothing on save only his trousers and shirt.'

'Thank you. We have certainly been favoured with extraordinary luck during this inquiry, and it will be entirely our own fault if we do not succeed in clearing the matter up. With your permission, Mr Holder, I shall now continue my investigations outside.'

He went alone, at his own request, for he explained that any unnecessary footmarks might make his task more difficult. For an hour or more he was at work, returning at last with his feet heavy with snow and his features as inscrutable as ever.

'I think that I have seen now all that there is to see, Mr Holder,' said he; 'I can serve you best by returning to my rooms.'

'But the gems, Mr Holmes. Where are they?'

'I cannot tell.'

The banker wrung his hands. 'I shall never see them again!' he cried. 'And my son? You give me hopes?'

'My opinion is in no way altered.'

'Then, for God's sake, what was this dark business which was acted in my house last night?'

'If you can call upon me at my Baker Street rooms tomorrow morning between nine and ten I shall be happy to do what I can to make it clearer. I understand that you give me *carte blanche* to act for you, provided only that I get back the gems, and that you place no limit on the sum I may draw.'

'I would give my fortune to have them back.'

'Very good. I shall look into the matter between this and then. Goodbye; it is just possible that I may have to come over here again before evening.'

It was obvious to me that my companion's mind was now made up about the case, although what his conclusions were was more than I could even dimly imagine. Several times during our homeward journey I endeavoured to sound him upon the point, but he always glided away to some other topic, until at last I gave it over in despair. It was not yet three when we found ourselves in our rooms once more. He hurried to his chamber and was down again in a few minutes dressed as a common loafer. With his collar turned up, his shiny, seedy coat, his red cravat, and his worn boots, he was a perfect sample of the class.

'I think that this should do,' said he, glancing into the glass above the fireplace. 'I only wish that you could come with me, Watson, but I fear that it won't do. I may be on the trail in this matter, or I may be following a will-o'-the-wisp, but I shall soon know which it is. I hope that I may be back in a few hours.' He cut a slice of beef from the joint upon the sideboard, sandwiched it between two rounds of bread, and thrusting this rude meal into his pocket he started off upon his expedition.

I had just finished my tea when he returned, evidently in excellent spirits, swinging an old elastic-sided boot in his hand. He chucked it down into a corner and helped himself to a cup of tea.

'I only looked in as I passed,' said he. 'I am going right on.'

'Where to?'

'Oh, to the other side of the West End. It may be some time before I get back. Don't wait up for me in case I should be late.'

'How are you getting on?'

'Oh, so so. Nothing to complain of. I have been out to Streatham since I saw you last, but I did not call at the house. It is a very sweet little problem, and I would not have missed it for a good deal. However, I must not sit gossiping here, but must get these disreputable clothes off and return to my highly respectable self.'

I could see by his manner that he had stronger reasons for satisfaction than his words alone would imply. His eyes twinkled, and there was even a touch of colour upon his sallow cheeks. He hastened upstairs, and a few minutes later I heard the slam of the hall door, which told me that he was off once more upon his congenial hunt.

I waited until midnight, but there was no sign of his return, so I retired to my room. It was no uncommon thing for him to be away for days and nights on end when he was hot upon a scent, so that his lateness caused me no surprise. I do not know at what hour he came in, but when I came down to breakfast in the morning, there he was with a cup of coffee in one hand and the paper in the other, as fresh and trim as possible.

'You will excuse my beginning without you, Watson,' said he, 'but you remember that our client has rather an early appointment this morning.'

'Why, it is after nine now,' I answered. 'I should not be surprised if that were he. I thought I heard a ring.'

It was, indeed, our friend the financier. I was shocked by the change which had come over him, for his face, which was naturally of a broad and massive mould, was now pinched and fallen in, while his hair seemed to me at least a shade whiter. He entered with a weariness and lethargy which was even more painful than his violence of the morning before, and he dropped heavily into the armchair which I pushed forward for him.

'I do not know what I have done to be so severely tried,' said he. 'Only two days ago I was a happy and prosperous man, without a care in the world. Now I am left to a lonely and dishonoured age. One sorrow comes close upon the heels of another. My niece, Mary, has deserted me.'

'Deserted you?'

'Yes. Her bed this morning had not been slept in, her room was empty, and a note for me lay upon the hall table. I had said to her last night, in sorrow and not in anger, that if she had married my boy all might have been well with him. Perhaps it was thoughtless of me to say so. It is to that remark that she refers in this note:

> My dearest Uncle – I feel that I have brought trouble upon you, and that if I had acted differently this terrible misfortune might never have occurred. I cannot, with this thought in my mind, ever again be happy under your roof, and I feel that I must leave you for ever. Do not worry about my future, for that is provided for; and, above all, do not search for me, for it will be fruitless labour and an ill-service to me. In life or in death, I am ever your loving
>
> MARY.

'What could she mean by this note, Mr Holmes? Do you think it points to suicide?'

'No, no, nothing of the kind. It is perhaps the best possible solution. I trust, Mr Holder, that you are nearing the end of your troubles.'

'Ha! You say so! You have heard something, Mr Holmes? You have learned something? Where are the gems?'

'You would not think a thousand pounds apiece an excessive sum for them?'

'I would pay ten.'

'That would be unnecessary. Three thousand will cover the matter. And there is a little reward, I fancy. Have you your check-book? Here is a pen. Better make it out for four thousand pounds.'

With a dazed face the banker made out the required check. Holmes walked over to his desk, took out a little triangular piece of gold with three gems in it and threw it down upon the table.

With a shriek of joy our client clutched it up.

'You have it!' he gasped. 'I am saved! I am saved!'

The reaction of joy was as passionate as his grief had been, and he hugged his recovered gems to his bosom.

'There is one other thing you owe, Mr Holder,' said Sherlock Holmes rather sternly.

'Owe!' He caught up the pen. 'Name the sum, and I will pay it.'

'No, the debt is not to me. You owe a very humble apology to that noble lad, your son, who has carried himself in this matter as I should be proud to see my own son do, should I ever chance to have one.'

'Then it was not Arthur who took them?'

'I told you yesterday, and I repeat today, that it was not.'

'You are sure of it! Then let us hurry to him at once to let him know that the truth is known.'

'He knows it already. When I had cleared it all up I had an interview with him, and finding that he would not tell me the story, I told it to him, on which he had to confess that I was right and was able to add the very few details which were not yet quite clear to me. Your news of this morning, however, may open his lips.'

'For heaven's sake, tell me, then, what is this extraordinary mystery!'

'I will do so, and I will show you the steps by which I reached it. And let me say to you, first, that which it is hardest for me to say and for you to hear: there has been an understanding between Sir George Burnwell and your niece Mary. They have now fled together.'

'My Mary? Impossible!'

'It is unfortunately more than possible; it is certain. Neither you nor your son knew the true character of this man when you admitted him into your family circle. He is one of the most dangerous men in England – a ruined gambler, an absolutely desperate villain, a man without heart or conscience. Your niece knew nothing of such men. When he breathed his vows to her, as he had done to a hundred before her, she flattered herself that she alone had touched his heart. The devil knows best what he said, but at least she became his tool and was in the habit of seeing him nearly every evening.'

'I cannot, and I will not, believe it!' cried the banker with an ashen face.

'I will tell you, then, what occurred in your house last night. Your niece, when you had, as she thought, gone to your room, slipped down and talked to her lover through the window which leads into the stable lane. His footmarks had pressed right through the snow, so long had he stood there. She told him of the coronet. His wicked lust for gold kindled at the news, and he bent her to his will. I have no doubt that she loved you, but there are women in whom the love of a lover extinguishes all other loves, and I think that she must have been one. She had hardly listened to his instructions when she saw you coming downstairs, on which she closed the window rapidly, and told you about one of the servants' escapade with her wooden-legged lover, which was all perfectly true.

'Your boy, Arthur, went to bed after his interview with you, but he slept badly on account of his uneasiness about his club debts. In the middle of the night he heard a soft tread pass his door, so he rose and looking out was surprised to see his cousin walking very stealthily along the passage until she disappeared into your dressing-room. Petrified with astonishment, the lad slipped on some clothes and waited there in the dark to see what would come of this strange affair. Presently she emerged from the room again, and in the light of the passage-lamp your son saw that she carried the precious coronet in her hands. She passed down the stairs, and he, thrilling with horror, ran along and slipped behind the curtain near your door, whence he could see what passed in the hall beneath. He saw her stealthily open the window, hand out the coronet to someone in the gloom, and then closing it once more hurry back to her room, passing quite close to where he stood hid behind the curtain.

'As long as she was on the scene he could not take any action without a horrible exposure of the woman whom he loved. But the instant that she was gone, he realised how crushing a misfortune this would be for you, and how all-important it was to set it right. He rushed down, just as he was, in his bare feet, opened the window, sprang out into the snow, and ran down the lane, where he could see a dark figure in the moonlight. Sir George Burnwell tried to get away, but Arthur caught him, and there was a struggle between them, your lad tugging at one side of the coronet and his opponent at the other. In the scuffle, your son struck Sir George and cut him over the eye. Then something suddenly snapped, and your son, finding that he had the coronet in his hands, rushed back, closed the window, ascended to your room, and had just observed that the coronet had been twisted in the struggle, and was endeavouring to straighten it, when you appeared upon the scene.'

'Is it possible?' gasped the banker.

'You then roused his anger by calling him names at a moment when he felt that he had deserved your warmest thanks. He could not explain the true state of affairs without betraying one who certainly deserved little enough consideration at his hands. He took the more chivalrous view, however, and preserved her secret.'

'And that was why she shrieked and fainted when she saw the coronet,' cried Mr Holder. 'Oh, my God! what a blind fool I have been! And his asking to be allowed to go out for five minutes! The dear fellow wanted to see if the missing piece were at the scene of the struggle. How cruelly I have misjudged him!'

'When I arrived at the house,' continued Holmes, 'I at once went very carefully round it to observe if there were any traces in the snow which might help me. I knew that none had fallen since the evening before, and also that there had been a strong frost to preserve impressions. I passed along the tradesmen's path, but found it all trampled down and indistinguishable. Just beyond it, however, at the far side of the kitchen door, a woman had stood and talked with a man, whose round impression on one side showed that he had a wooden leg. I could even tell that they had been disturbed, for the woman had run back swiftly to the door, as was shown by her deep toe and light heel marks, while Wooden-leg had waited a little, and then had gone away. I thought at the time that this might be the maid and her sweetheart, of whom you had already spoken to me, and enquiry showed it was so. I passed round the garden without seeing anything more than random tracks, which I took to be the police; but when I got into the stable lane a very long and complex story was written in the snow in front of me.

'There was a double line of tracks of a booted man, and a second double line which I saw with delight belonged to a man with naked feet. I was at once convinced from what you had told me that the latter was your son. The first had walked both ways, but the other had run swiftly, and as his tread was marked in places over the depression of the boot, it was obvious that he had passed after the other. I followed them up and found they led to the hall window, where Boots had worn all the snow away while waiting. Then I walked to the other end, which was a hundred yards or more down the lane. I saw where Boots had faced round, where the snow was cut up as though there had been a struggle, and, finally, where a few drops of blood had fallen, to show me that I was not mistaken. Boots had then run down the lane, and another little smudge of blood showed that it was he who had been hurt. When he came to the high road at the other end, I found that the pavement had been cleared, so there was an end to that clue.

'On entering the house, however, I examined, as you remember, the sill and framework of the hall window with my lens, and I could at once see that someone had passed out. I could distinguish the outline of an instep where the wet foot had been placed in coming in. I was then beginning to be able to form an opinion as to what had occurred. A man had waited outside the window; someone had brought the gems; the deed had been overseen by your son; he had pursued the thief; had struggled with him; they had each tugged at the coronet, their united strength causing injuries which neither alone could have effected. He had returned with the prize, but had left a fragment in the grasp of his opponent. So far I was clear. The question now was, who was the man and who was it brought him the coronet?

'It is an old maxim of mine that when you have excluded the impossible, whatever remains, however improbable, must be the truth. Now, I knew that it was not you who had brought it down, so there only remained your niece and the maids. But if it were the maids, why should your son allow himself to be accused in their place? There could be no possible reason. As he loved his cousin, however, there was an excellent explanation why he should retain her secret – the more so as the secret was a disgraceful one. When I remembered that you had seen her at that window, and how she had fainted on seeing the coronet again, my conjecture became a certainty.

'And who could it be who was her confederate? A lover evidently, for who else could outweigh the love and gratitude which she must feel to you? I knew that you went out little, and that your circle of friends was a very limited one. But among them was Sir George Burnwell. I had heard of him before as being a man of evil reputation among women. It must have been he who wore those boots and retained the missing gems. Even though he knew that Arthur had discovered him, he might still flatter himself that he was safe, for the lad could not say a word without compromising his own family.

'Well, your own good sense will suggest what measures I took next. I went in the shape of a loafer to Sir George's house, managed to pick up an acquaintance with his valet, learned that his master had cut his head the night before and, finally, at the expense of six shillings, made all sure by buying a pair of his cast-off shoes. With these I journeyed down to Streatham and saw that they exactly fitted the tracks.'

'I saw an ill-dressed vagabond in the lane yesterday evening,' said Mr Holder.

'Precisely. It was I. I found that I had my man, so I came home and changed my clothes. It was a delicate part which I had to play then, for I saw that a prosecution must be avoided to avert scandal, and I knew that so astute a villain would see that our hands were tied in the matter. I went and saw him. At first, of course, he denied everything. But when I gave him every particular that had occurred, he tried to bluster and took down a life-preserver from the wall. I knew my man, however, and I clapped a pistol to his head before he could strike. Then he became a little more reasonable. I told him that we would give him a price for the stones he held – a thousand pounds apiece. That brought out the first signs of grief that he had shown. "Why, dash it all!" said he, "I've let them go at six hundred for the three!" I soon managed to get the address of the receiver who had them, on promising him that there would be no prosecution. Off I set to him, and after much chaffering I got our stones at a thousand pounds apiece. Then I looked in upon your son, told him that all was right, and eventually got to my bed about two o'clock, after what I may call a really hard day's work.'

'A day which has saved England from a great public scandal,' said the banker, rising. 'Sir, I cannot find words to thank you, but you shall not find me ungrateful for what you have done. Your skill has indeed exceeded all that I have heard of it. And now I must fly to my dear boy to apologise to him for the wrong which I have done him. As to what you tell me of poor Mary, it goes to my very heart. Not even your skill can inform me where she is now.'

'I think that we may safely say,' returned Holmes, 'that she is wherever Sir George Burnwell is. It is equally certain, too, that whatever her sins are, they will soon receive a more than sufficient punishment.'

The Adventure of the Copper Beaches

'To the man who loves art for its own sake,' remarked Sherlock Holmes, tossing aside the advertisement sheet of the *Daily Telegraph*, 'it is frequently in its least important and lowliest manifestations that the keenest pleasure is to be derived. It is pleasant to me to observe, Watson, that you have so far grasped this truth that in these little records of our cases which you have been good enough to draw up, and, I am bound to say, occasionally to embellish, you have given prominence not so much to the many *causes cÉl'bres* and sensational trials in which I have figured, but rather to those incidents which may have been trivial in themselves, but which have given room for those faculties of deduction and of logical synthesis which I have made my special province.'

'And yet,' said I, smiling, 'I cannot quite hold myself absolved from the charge of sensationalism which has been urged against my records.'

'You have erred, perhaps,' he observed, taking up a glowing cinder with the tongs and lighting with it the long cherry-wood pipe which was wont to replace his clay when he was in a disputatious rather than a meditative mood – 'you have erred perhaps in attempting to put colour and life into each of your statements instead of confining yourself to the task of placing upon record that severe reasoning from cause to effect which is really the only notable feature about the thing.'

'It seems to me that I have done you full justice in the matter,' I remarked with some coldness, for I was repelled by the egotism which I had more than once observed to be a strong factor in my friend's singular character.

'No, it is not selfishness or conceit,' said he, answering, as was his wont, my thoughts rather than my words. 'If I claim full justice for my art, it is because it is an impersonal thing – a thing beyond myself.

Crime is common. Logic is rare. Therefore it is upon the logic rather than upon the crime that you should dwell. You have degraded what should have been a course of lectures into a series of tales.'

It was a cold morning of the early spring, and we sat after break-fast on either side of a cheery fire in the old room at Baker Street. A thick fog rolled down between the lines of dun-coloured houses, and the opposing windows loomed like dark, shapeless blurs through the heavy yellow wreaths. Our gas was lit and shone on the white cloth and glimmer of china and metal, for the table had not been cleared yet. Sherlock Holmes had been silent all the morning, dipping continuously into the advertisement columns of a succession of papers until at last, having apparently given up his search, he had emerged in no very sweet temper to lecture me upon my literary shortcomings.

'At the same time,' he remarked after a pause, during which he had sat puffing at his long pipe and gazing down into the fire, 'you can hardly be open to a charge of sensationalism, for out of these cases which you have been so kind as to interest yourself in, a fair proportion do not treat of crime, in its legal sense, at all. The small matter in which I endeavoured to help the King of Bohemia, the singular experience of Miss Mary Sutherland, the problem connected with the man with the twisted lip and the incident of the noble bachelor were all matters which are outside the pale of the law. But in avoiding the sensational, I fear that you may have bordered on the trivial.'

'The end may have been so,' I answered, 'but the methods I hold to have been novel and of interest.'

'Pshaw, my dear fellow, what do the public, the great unobservant public, who could hardly tell a weaver by his tooth or a compositor by his left thumb, care about the finer shades of analysis and deduction! But, indeed, if you are trivial, I cannot blame you, for the days of the great cases are past. Man, or at least criminal man, has lost all enterprise and originality. As to my own little practice, it seems to be degenerating into an agency for recovering lost lead pencils and giving advice to young ladies from boarding-schools. I think that I have touched bottom at last, however. This note I had this morning marks my zero-point, I fancy. Read it!' He tossed a crumpled letter across to me.

It was dated from Montague Place upon the preceding evening, and ran thus:

Dear Mr Holmes – I am very anxious to consult you as to whether I should or should not accept a situation which has been offered to me as governess. I shall call at half-past ten tomorrow if I do not inconvenience you. Yours faithfully,

VIOLET HUNTER

'Do you know the young lady?' I asked.

'Not I.'

'It is half-past ten now.'

'Yes, and I have no doubt that is her ring.'

'It may turn out to be of more interest than you think. You remember that the affair of the blue carbuncle, which appeared to be a mere whim at first, developed into a serious investigation. It may be so in this case, also.'

'Well, let us hope so. But our doubts will very soon be solved, for here, unless I am much mistaken, is the person in question.'

As he spoke the door opened and a young lady entered the room. She was plainly but neatly dressed, with a bright, quick face, freckled like a plover's egg, and with the brisk manner of a woman who has had her own way to make in the world.

'You will excuse my troubling you, I am sure,' said she, as my companion rose to greet her, 'but I have had a very strange experience, and as I have no parents or relations of any sort from whom I could ask advice, I thought that perhaps you would be kind enough to tell me what I should do.'

'Pray take a seat, Miss Hunter. I shall be happy to do anything that I can to serve you.'

I could see that Holmes was favourably impressed by the manner and speech of his new client. He looked her over in his searching fashion, and then composed himself, with his lids drooping and his finger-tips together, to listen to her story.

'I have been a governess for five years,' said she, 'in the family of Colonel Spence Munro, but two months ago the colonel received an appointment at Halifax, in Nova Scotia, and took his children over to America with him, so that I found myself without a situation. I advertised, and I answered advertisements, but without success. At last the little money which I had saved began to run short, and I was at my wit's end as to what I should do.

'There is a well-known agency for governesses in the West End called Westaway's, and there I used to call about once a week in order to see whether anything had turned up which might suit me. Westaway was the name of the founder of the business, but it is really managed by Miss Stoper. She sits in her own little office, and the ladies who are seeking employment wait in an ante-room, and are then shown in one by one, when she consults her ledgers and sees whether she has anything which would suit them.

'Well, when I called last week I was shown into the little office as usual, but I found that Miss Stoper was not alone. A prodigiously stout man, with a very smiling face and a great heavy chin which rolled down in fold upon fold over his throat, sat at her elbow with a pair of glasses on his nose, looking very earnestly at the ladies who entered. As I came in he gave quite a jump in his chair and turned quickly to Miss Stoper. "That will do," said he; "I could not ask for anything better. Capital! Capital!" He seemed quite enthusiastic and rubbed his hands together in the most genial fashion. He was such a comfortable-looking man that it was quite a pleasure to look at him.

'"You are looking for a situation, miss?" he asked.

'"Yes, sir."

'"As governess?"

'"Yes, sir."

'"And what salary do you ask?"

'"I had four pounds a month in my last place with Colonel Spence Munro."

'"Oh, tut, tut! Sweating – rank sweating!" he cried, throwing his fat hands out into the air like a man who is in a boiling passion. "How could anyone offer so pitiful a sum to a lady with such attractions and accomplishments?"

'"My accomplishments, sir, may be less than you imagine," said I. "A little French, a little German, music and drawing –"

'"Tut, tut!" he cried. "This is all quite beside the question. The point is, have you or have you not the bearing and deportment of a lady? There it is in a nutshell. If you have not, you are not fitted for the rearing of a child who may someday play a considerable part in the history of the country. But if you have – why, then, how could any gentleman ask you to condescend to accept anything under the three figures? Your salary with me, madam, would commence at a hundred pounds a year."

'You may imagine, Mr Holmes, that to me, destitute as I was, such an offer seemed almost too good to be true. The gentleman, however, seeing perhaps the look of incredulity upon my face, opened a pocket-book and took out a note.

'"It is also my custom," said he, smiling in the most pleasant fashion until his eyes were just two little shining slits amid the white creases of his face, "to advance to my young ladies half their salary beforehand, so that they may meet any little expenses of their journey and their wardrobe."

'It seemed to me that I had never met so fascinating and so thoughtful a man. As I was already in debt to my tradesmen, the advance was a great convenience, and yet there was something unnatural about the whole transaction which made me wish to know a little more before I quite committed myself.

'"May I ask where you live, sir?" said I.

'"Hampshire. Charming rural place. The Copper Beeches, five miles on the far side of Winchester. It is the most lovely country, my dear young lady, and the dearest old country-house."

'"And my duties, sir? I should be glad to know what they would be."

'"One child – one dear little romper just six years old. Oh, if you could see him killing cockroaches with a slipper! Smack! smack!

smack! Three gone before you could wink!" He leaned back in his chair and laughed his eyes into his head again.

'I was a little startled at the nature of the child's amusement, but the father's laughter made me think that perhaps he was joking.

'"My sole duties, then," I asked, "are to take charge of a single child?"

'"No, no, not the sole, not the sole, my dear young lady," he cried. "Your duty would be, as I am sure your good sense would suggest, to obey any little commands my wife might give, provided always that they were such commands as a lady might with propriety obey. You see no difficulty, heh?"

'"I should be happy to make myself useful."

'"Quite so. In dress now, for example. We are faddy people, you know – faddy but kind-hearted. If you were asked to wear any dress which we might give you, you would not object to our little whim. Heh?"

'"No," said I, considerably astonished at his words.

'"Or to sit here, or sit there, that would not be offensive to you?"

'"Oh, no."

'"Or to cut your hair quite short before you come to us?"

'I could hardly believe my ears. As you may observe, Mr Holmes, my hair is somewhat luxuriant, and of a rather peculiar tint of chestnut. It has been considered artistic. I could not dream of sacrificing it in this offhand fashion.

'"I am afraid that that is quite impossible," said I. He had been watching me eagerly out of his small eyes, and I could see a shadow pass over his face as I spoke.

'"I am afraid that it is quite essential," said he. "It is a little fancy of my wife's, and ladies' fancies, you know, madam, ladies' fancies must be consulted. And so you won't cut your hair?"

'"No, sir, I really could not," I answered firmly.

'"Ah, very well; then that quite settles the matter. It is a pity, because in other respects you would really have done very nicely. In that case, Miss Stoper, I had best inspect a few more of your young ladies."

'The manageress had sat all this while busy with her papers without a word to either of us, but she glanced at me now with so much annoyance upon her face that I could not help suspecting that she had lost a handsome commission through my refusal.

'"Do you desire your name to be kept upon the books?" she asked.

'"If you please, Miss Stoper."

'"Well, really, it seems rather useless, since you refuse the most excellent offers in this fashion," said she sharply. "You can hardly expect us to exert ourselves to find another such opening for you. Good-day to you, Miss Hunter." She struck a gong upon the table, and I was shown out by the page.

'Well, Mr Holmes, when I got back to my lodgings and found little enough in the cupboard, and two or three bills upon the table. I began to ask myself whether I had not done a very foolish thing. After all, if these people had strange fads and expected obedience on the most extraordinary matters, they were at least ready to pay for their eccentricity. Very few governesses in England are getting a hundred pounds a year. Besides, what use was my hair to me? Many people are improved by wearing it short and perhaps I should be among the number. Next day I was inclined to think that I had made a mistake, and by the day after I was sure of it. I had almost overcome my pride so far as to go back to the agency and enquire whether the place was still open, when I received this letter from the gentleman himself.

'I have it here and I will read it to you:

> *The Copper Beeches, near Winchester*
> Dear Miss Hunter – Miss Stoper has very kindly given me your address, and I write from here to ask you whether you have reconsidered your decision. My wife is very anxious that you should come, for she has been much attracted by my description of you. We are willing to give thirty pounds a quarter, or a hundred and twenty a year, so as to recompense you for any little inconvenience which our fads may cause you. They are not very exacting, after all. My wife is fond of a particular shade of electric blue and would

like you to wear such a dress indoors in the morning. You need not, however, go to the expense of purchasing one, as we have one belonging to my dear daughter Alice (now in Philadelphia), which would, I should think, fit you very well. Then, as to sitting here or there, or amusing yourself in any manner indicated, that need cause you no inconvenience. As regards your hair, it is no doubt a pity, especially as I could not help remarking its beauty during our short interview, but I am afraid that I must remain firm upon this point, and I only hope that the increased salary may recompense you for the loss. Your duties, as far as the child is concerned, are very light. Now do try to come, and I shall meet you with the dog-cart at Winchester. Let me know your train.

Yours faithfully,

JEPHRO RUCASTLE.

'That is the letter which I have just received, Mr Holmes, and my mind is made up that I will accept it. I thought, however, that before taking the final step I should like to submit the whole matter to your consideration.'

'Well, Miss Hunter, if your mind is made up, that settles the question,' said Holmes, smiling.

'But you would not advise me to refuse?'

'I confess that it is not the situation which I should like to see a sister of mine apply for.'

'What is the meaning of it all, Mr Holmes?'

'Ah, I have no data. I cannot tell. Perhaps you have yourself formed some opinion?'

'Well, there seems to me to be only one possible solution. Mr Rucastle seemed to be a very kind, good-natured man. Is it not possible that his wife is a lunatic, that he desires to keep the matter quiet for fear she should be taken to an asylum, and that he humours her fancies in every way in order to prevent an outbreak?'

'That is a possible solution – in fact, as matters stand, it is the most probable one. But in any case it does not seem to be a nice household for a young lady.'

'But the money, Mr Holmes, the money!'

'Well, yes, of course the pay is good – too good. That is what makes me uneasy. Why should they give you a hundred and twenty a year, when they could have their pick for forty? There must be some strong reason behind it.'

'I thought that if I told you the circumstances you would under-stand afterwards if I wanted your help. I should feel so much stronger if I felt that you were at the back of me.'

'Oh, you may carry that feeling away with you. I assure you that your little problem promises to be the most interesting which has come my way for some months. There is something distinctly novel about some of the features. If you should find yourself in doubt or in danger –'

'Danger! What danger do you foresee?'

Holmes shook his head gravely. 'It would cease to be a danger if we could define it,' said he. 'But at any time, day or night, a telegram would bring me down to your help.'

'That is enough.' She rose briskly from her chair with the anxiety all swept from her face. 'I shall go down to Hampshire quite easy in my mind now. I shall write to Mr Rucastle at once, sacrifice my poor hair tonight, and start for Winchester tomorrow.' With a few grateful words to Holmes, she bade us both good-night and bustled off upon her way.

'At least,' said I, as we heard her quick firm steps descending the stairs, 'she seems to be a young lady who is very well able to take care of herself.'

'And she would need to be,' said Holmes gravely. 'I am much mis-taken if we do not hear from her before many days are past.'

It was not very long before my friend's prediction was fulfilled. A fortnight went by, during which I frequently found my thoughts turning in her direction and wondering what strange side-alley of human experience this lonely woman had strayed into. The unusual salary, the curious conditions, the light duties, all pointed to some-thing abnormal, though whether a fad or a plot, or whether the man were a philanthropist or a villain, it was quite beyond my powers to determine. As to Holmes, I observed that he sat frequently for half an hour on end, with knitted brows and an abstracted air, but he swept the matter away with a wave of his hand when I mentioned it. 'Data! data! data!' he cried impatiently. 'I can't make bricks without clay.' And yet he would always wind up by muttering that no sister of his should ever have accepted such a situation.

The telegram which we eventually received came late one night just as I was thinking of turning in and Holmes was settling down to one of those all-night chemical researches which he frequently indulged in, when I would leave him stooping over a retort and a test-tube at night and find him in the same position when I came down to breakfast in the morning. He opened the yellow envelope, and then, glancing at the message, threw it across to me.

'Just look up the trains in Bradshaw,' said he, and turned back to his chemical studies.

The summons was a brief and urgent one.

Please be at the Black Swan Hotel at Winchester at midday tomorrow [it said]. Do come! I am at my wit's end.

HUNTER

'Will you come with me?' asked Holmes, glancing up.

'I should wish to.'

'Just look it up, then.'

'There is a train at half-past nine,' said I, glancing over my Bradshaw. 'It is due at Winchester at 11:30.'

'That will do very nicely. Then perhaps I had better postpone my analysis of the acetones, as we may need to be at our best in the morning.'

By eleven o'clock the next day we were well upon our way to the old English capital. Holmes had been buried in the morning papers all the way down, but after we had passed the Hampshire border he threw them down and began to admire the scenery. It was an ideal spring day, a light blue sky, flecked with little fleecy white clouds drifting across from west to east. The sun was shining very brightly, and yet there was an exhilarating nip in the air, which set an edge to a man's energy. All over the countryside, away to the rolling hills around Aldershot, the little red and grey roofs of the farmsteadings peeped out from amid the light green of the new foliage.

'Are they not fresh and beautiful?' I cried with all the enthusiasm of a man fresh from the fogs of Baker Street.

But Holmes shook his head gravely.

'Do you know, Watson,' said he, 'that it is one of the curses of a mind with a turn like mine that I must look at everything with reference to my own special subject. You look at these scattered houses, and you are impressed by their beauty. I look at them, and the only thought which comes to me is a feeling of their isolation and of the impunity with which crime may be committed there.'

'Good heavens!' I cried. 'Who would associate crime with these dear old homesteads?'

'They always fill me with a certain horror. It is my belief, Watson, founded upon my experience, that the lowest and vilest alleys in London do not present a more dreadful record of sin than does the smiling and beautiful countryside.'

'You horrify me!'

'But the reason is very obvious. The pressure of public opinion can do in the town what the law cannot accomplish. There is no lane so vile that the scream of a tortured child or the thud of a drunkard's blow does not beget sympathy and indignation among the neighbours, and then the whole machinery of justice is ever so close that a word of complaint can set it going and there is but a step between the crime and the dock. But look at these lonely houses, each in its own fields, filled for the most part with poor ignorant folk who know little of the law. Think of the deeds of hellish cruelty, the hidden wickedness which may go on, year in, year out, in such places, and none the wiser. Had this lady who appeals to us for help gone to live in Winchester, I should never have had a fear for her. It is the five miles of country which makes the danger. Still, it is clear that she is not personally threatened.'

'No. If she can come to Winchester to meet us she can get away.'

'Quite so. She has her freedom.'

'What *can* be the matter, then? Can you suggest no explanation?'

'I have devised seven separate explanations, each of which would cover the facts as far as we know them. But which of these is correct can only be determined by the fresh information which we shall no doubt find waiting for us. Well, there is the tower of the cathedral, and we shall soon learn all that Miss Hunter has to tell.'

The Black Swan is an inn of repute in the High Street, at no distance from the station, and there we found the young lady waiting for us. She had engaged a sitting-room, and our lunch awaited us upon the table.

'I am so delighted that you have come,' she said earnestly. 'It is so very kind of you both; but indeed I do not know what I should do. Your advice will be altogether invaluable to me.'

'Pray tell us what has happened to you.'

'I will do so, and I must be quick, for I have promised Mr Rucastle to be back before three. I got his leave to come into town this morning, though he little knew for what purpose.'

'Let us have everything in its due order.' Holmes thrust his long thin legs out towards the fire and composed himself to listen.

'In the first place, I may say that I have met, on the whole, with no actual ill-treatment from Mr and Mrs Rucastle. It is only fair to them to say that. But I cannot understand them, and I am not easy in my mind about them.'

'What can you not understand?'

'Their reasons for their conduct. But you shall have it all just as it occurred. When I came down, Mr Rucastle met me here and drove me in his dogcart to The Copper Beeches. It is, as he said, beautifully situated, but it is not beautiful in itself, for it is a large square block of a house, whitewashed, but all stained and streaked with damp and bad weather. There are grounds round it, woods on three sides, and on the fourth a field which slopes down to the Southampton high road, which curves past about a hundred yards from the front door. This ground in front belongs to the house, but the woods all round are part of Lord Southerton's preserves. A clump of copper beeches immediately in front of the hall door has given the place its name.

'I was driven over by my employer, who was as amiable as ever, and was introduced by him that evening to his wife and the child. There was no truth, Mr Holmes, in the conjecture which seemed to us to be probable in your rooms at Baker Street. Mrs Rucastle is not mad. I found her to be a silent, pale-faced woman, much younger than her husband, not more than thirty, I should think, while he can hardly be less than forty-five. From their conversation I have gathered that they have been married about seven years, that he was a widower, and that his only child by the first wife was the daughter who has gone to Philadelphia. Mr Rucastle told me in private that the reason why she had left them was that she had an unreasoning aversion to her stepmother. As the daughter could not have been less than twenty, I can quite imagine that her position must have been uncomfortable with her father's young wife.

'Mrs Rucastle seemed to me to be colourless in mind as well as in feature. She impressed me neither favourably nor the reverse. She was a nonentity. It was easy to see that she was passionately devoted both to her husband and to her little son. Her light grey eyes wandered continually from one to the other, noting every little want and forestalling it if possible. He was kind to her also in his bluff, boisterous fashion, and on the whole they seemed to be a happy couple. And yet she had some secret sorrow, this woman. She would often be lost in deep thought, with the saddest look upon her face. More than once I have surprised her in tears. I have thought sometimes that it was the disposition of her child which weighed upon her mind, for I have never met so utterly spoiled and so ill-natured a little creature. He is small for his age, with a head which is quite disproportionately large. His whole life appears to be spent in an alternation between savage fits of passion and gloomy intervals of sulking. Giving pain to any creature weaker than himself seems to be his one idea of amusement, and he shows quite remarkable talent in planning the capture of mice, little birds and insects. But I would rather not talk about the creature, Mr Holmes, and, indeed, he has little to do with my story.'

'I am glad of all details,' remarked my friend, 'whether they seem to you to be relevant or not.'

'I shall try not to miss anything of importance. The one unpleasant thing about the house, which struck me at once, was the appearance and conduct of the servants. There are only two, a man and his wife. Toller, for that is his name, is a rough, uncouth man, with grizzled hair and whiskers and a perpetual smell of drink. Twice since I have been with them he has been quite drunk, and yet Mr Rucastle seemed to take no notice of it. His wife is a very tall and strong woman with a sour face, as silent as Mrs Rucastle and much less amiable. They are a most unpleasant couple, but fortunately I spend most of my time in the nursery and my own room, which are next to each other in one corner of the building.

'For two days after my arrival at The Copper Beeches my life was very quiet; on the third, Mrs Rucastle came down just after breakfast and whispered something to her husband.

'"Oh, yes," said he, turning to me, "we are very much obliged to you, Miss Hunter, for falling in with our whims so far as to cut your hair. I assure you that it has not detracted in the tiniest iota from your appearance. We shall now see how the electric-blue dress will become you. You will find it laid out upon the bed in your room, and if you would be so good as to put it on we should both be extremely obliged."

'The dress which I found waiting for me was of a peculiar shade of blue. It was of excellent material, a sort of beige, but it bore unmistakable signs of having been worn before. It could not have been a better fit if I had been measured for it. Both Mr and Mrs Rucastle expressed a delight at the look of it, which seemed quite exaggerated in its vehemence. They were waiting for me in the drawing-room, which is a very large room, stretching along the entire front of the house, with three long windows reaching down to the floor. A chair had been placed close to the central window, with its back turned towards it. In this I was asked to sit, and then Mr Rucastle, walking up and down on the other side of the room, began to tell me a series of the funniest stories that I have ever listened to. You cannot imagine how comical he was, and I laughed until I was quite weary. Mrs Rucastle, however, who has evidently no sense of humour, never so much as smiled, but sat with her hands in her lap, and a sad, anxious look upon her face. After an hour or so, Mr Rucastle suddenly remarked that it was time to commence the duties of the day, and that I might change my dress and go to little Edward in the nursery.

'Two days later this same performance was gone through under exactly similar circumstances. Again I changed my dress, again I sat in the window, and again I laughed very heartily at the funny stories of which my employer had an immense repertoire, and which he told inimitably. Then he handed me a yellow-backed novel, and moving my chair a little sideways, that my own shadow might not fall upon the page, he begged me to read aloud to him. I read for about ten minutes, beginning in the heart of a chapter, and then suddenly, in the middle of a sentence, he ordered me to cease and to change my dress.

'You can easily imagine, Mr Holmes, how curious I became as to what the meaning of this extraordinary performance could possibly be. They were always very careful, I observed, to turn my face away from the window, so that I became consumed with the desire to see what was going on behind my back. At first it seemed to be impossible, but I soon devised a means. My hand-mirror had been broken, so a happy thought seized me, and I concealed a piece of the glass in my handkerchief. On the next occasion, in the midst of my laughter, I put my handkerchief up to my eyes, and was able with a little management to see all that there was behind me. I confess that I was disappointed. There was nothing. At least that was my first impression. At the second glance, however, I perceived that there was a man standing in the Southampton Road, a small bearded man in a grey suit, who seemed to be looking in my direction. The road is an important highway, and there are usually people there. This man, however, was leaning against the railings which bordered our field and was looking earnestly up. I lowered my handkerchief and glanced at Mrs Rucastle to find her eyes fixed upon me with a most searching gaze. She said nothing, but I am convinced that she had divined that I had a mirror in my hand and had seen what was behind me. She rose at once.

'"Jephro," said she, "there is an impertinent fellow upon the road there who stares up at Miss Hunter."

'"No friend of yours, Miss Hunter?" he asked.

'"No, I know no one in these parts."

'"Dear me! How very impertinent! Kindly turn round and motion to him to go away."

'"Surely it would be better to take no notice."

'"No, no, we should have him loitering here always. Kindly turn round and wave him away like that."

'I did as I was told, and at the same instant Mrs Rucastle drew down the blind. That was a week ago, and from that time I have not sat again in the window, nor have I worn the blue dress, nor seen the man in the road.'

'Pray continue,' said Holmes. 'Your narrative promises to be a most interesting one.'

'You will find it rather disconnected, I fear, and there may prove to be little relation between the different incidents of which I speak. On the very first day that I was at The Copper Beeches, Mr Rucastle took me to a small outhouse which stands near the kitchen door. As we approached it, I heard the sharp rattling of a chain and the sound as of a large animal moving about.

'"Look in here!" said Mr Rucastle, showing me a slit between two planks. "Is he not a beauty?"

'I looked through and was conscious of two glowing eyes, and of a vague figure huddled up in the darkness.

'Don't be frightened," said my employer, laughing at the start which I had given. "It's only Carlo, my mastiff. I call him mine, but really old Toller, my groom, is the only man who can do anything with him. We feed him once a day, and not too much then, so that he is always as keen as mustard. Toller lets him loose every night, and God help the trespasser whom he lays his fangs upon. For goodness' sake don't you ever on any pretext set your foot over the threshold at night, for it's as much as your life is worth."

'The warning was no idle one, for two nights later I happened to look out of my bedroom window about two o'clock in the morning. It was a beautiful moonlight night, and the lawn in front of the house was silvered over and almost as bright as day. I was standing, rapt in the peaceful beauty of the scene, when I was aware that something was moving under the shadow of the copper beeches. As it emerged into the moonshine I saw what it was. It was a giant dog, as large as a calf, tawny tinted, with hanging jowl, black muzzle and huge projecting bones. It walked slowly across the lawn and vanished into the shadow upon the other side. That dreadful sentinel sent a chill to my heart which I do not think any burglar could have done.

'And now I have a very strange experience to tell you. I had, as you know, cut off my hair in London, and I had placed it in a great coil at the bottom of my trunk. One evening, after the child was in bed, I began to amuse myself by examining the furniture of my room and by rearranging my own little things. There was an old chest of drawers in the room, the two upper ones empty and open, the lower one locked. I had filled the first two with my linen, and as I had still much to pack away I was naturally annoyed at not having the use of the third drawer. It struck me that it might have been fastened by a mere oversight, so I took out my bunch of keys and tried to open it. The very first key fitted to perfection, and I drew the drawer open. There was only one thing in it, but I am sure that you would never guess what it was. It was my coil of hair.

'I took it up and examined it. It was of the same peculiar tint, and the same thickness. But then the impossibility of the thing obtruded itself upon me. How could my hair have been locked in the drawer? With trembling hands I undid my trunk, turned out the contents, and drew from the bottom my own hair. I laid the two tresses together, and

I assure you that they were identical. Was it not extraordinary? Puzzle as I would, I could make nothing at all of what it meant. I returned the strange hair to the drawer, and I said nothing of the matter to the Rucastles as I felt that I had put myself in the wrong by opening a drawer which they had locked.

'I am naturally observant, as you may have remarked, Mr Holmes, and I soon had a pretty good plan of the whole house in my head. There was one wing, however, which appeared not to be inhabited at all. A door which faced that which led into the quarters of the Tollers opened into this suite, but it was invariably locked. One day, however, as I ascended the stair, I met Mr Rucastle coming out through this door, his keys in his hand and a look on his face which made him a very different person to the round, jovial man to whom I was accustomed. His cheeks were red, his brow was all crinkled with anger and the veins stood out at his temples with passion. He locked the door and hurried past me without a word or a look.

'This aroused my curiosity, so when I went out for a walk in the grounds with my charge, I strolled round to the side from which I could see the windows of this part of the house. There were four of them in a row, three of which were simply dirty, while the fourth was shuttered up. They were evidently all deserted. As I strolled up and down, glancing at them occasionally, Mr Rucastle came out to me, looking as merry and jovial as ever.

'"Ah!" said he, "you must not think me rude if I passed you without a word, my dear young lady. I was preoccupied with business matters."

'I assured him that I was not offended. "By the way," said I, "you seem to have quite a suite of spare rooms up there, and one of them has the shutters up."

'He looked surprised and, as it seemed to me, a little startled at my remark.

'"Photography is one of my hobbies," said he. "I have made my dark room up there. But, dear me! what an observant young lady we have come upon. Who would have believed it? Who would have ever believed it?" He spoke in a jesting tone, but there was no jest in his eyes as he looked at me. I read suspicion there and annoyance, but no jest.

'Well, Mr Holmes, from the moment I understood there was something about that suite of rooms which I was not to know, I was all on fire to go over them. It was not mere curiosity, though I have my share of that. It was more a feeling of duty – a feeling that some good might come from my penetrating to this place. They talk of woman's instinct; perhaps it was woman's instinct which gave me that feeling. At any rate, it was there, and I was keenly on the lookout for any chance to pass the forbidden door.

'It was only yesterday that the chance came. I may tell you that, besides Mr Rucastle, both Toller and his wife find something to do in these deserted rooms, and I once saw him carrying a large black linen bag with him through the door. Recently he has been drinking hard, and yesterday evening he was very drunk; and when I came upstairs there was the key in the door. I have no doubt at all that he had left it there. Mr and Mrs Rucastle were both downstairs, and the child was with them, so that I had an admirable opportunity. I turned the key gently in the lock, opened the door, and slipped through.

'There was a little passage in front of me, unpapered and uncarpeted, which turned at a right angle at the farther end. Round this corner were three doors in a line, the first and third of which were open. They each led into an empty room, dusty and cheerless, with two windows in the one and one in the other, so thick with dirt that the evening light glimmered only dimly through them. The centre door was closed, and across the outside of it had been fastened one of the broad bars of an iron bed, padlocked at one end to a ring in the wall, and fastened at the other with stout cord. The door itself was locked as well, and the key was not there. This barricaded door corresponded clearly with the shuttered window outside, and yet I could see by the glimmer from beneath it that the room was not in darkness. Evidently there was a skylight which let in light from above. As I stood in the passage gazing at the sinister door and wondering what secret it might veil, I suddenly heard the sound of steps within the room and saw a shadow pass backwards and forwards against the little slit of dim light which shone out from under the door. A mad, unreasoning terror rose up in me at the sight, Mr Holmes. My overstrung nerves failed me suddenly and I turned and ran – ran as though some dreadful hand were behind me, clutching at the skirt of my dress. I rushed down the passage, through the door, and straight into the arms of Mr Rucastle, who was waiting outside.

'"So," said he, smiling, "it was you, then. I thought that it must be when I saw the door open."

'"Oh, I am so frightened!" I panted.

'"My dear young lady! my dear young lady!" – you cannot think how caressing and soothing his manner was – "and what has frightened you, my dear young lady?"

'But his voice was just a little too coaxing. He overdid it. I was keenly on my guard against him.

'"I was foolish enough to go into the empty wing," I answered. "But it is so lonely and eerie in this dim light that I was frightened and ran out again. Oh, it is so dreadfully still in there!"

'"Only that?" said he, looking at me keenly.

'"Why, what did you think?" I asked.

'"Why do you think that I lock this door?"

'"I am sure that I do not know."

'"It is to keep people out who have no business there. Do you see?" He was still smiling in the most amiable manner.

'"I am sure if I had known –"

'"Well, then, you know now. And if you ever put your foot over that threshold again" – here in an instant the smile hardened into a grin of rage, and he glared down at me with the face of a demon – "I'll throw you to the mastiff."

'I was so terrified that I do not know what I did. I suppose that I must have rushed past him into my room. I remember nothing until I found myself lying on my bed trembling all over. Then I thought of you, Mr Holmes. I could not live there longer without some advice. I was frightened of the house, of the man, of the woman, of the servants, even of the child. They were all horrible to me. If I could only bring you down, all would be well. Of course I might have fled from the house, but my curiosity was almost as strong as my fears. My mind was soon made up. I would send you a wire. I put on my hat and cloak, went down to the office, which is about half a mile from the house, and then returned, feeling very much easier. A horrible doubt came into my mind as I approached the door lest the dog might be loose, but I remembered that Toller had drunk himself into a state of insensibility that evening, and I knew that he was the only one in the household who had any influence with the savage creature, or who would venture to set him free. I slipped in in safety and lay awake half the night in my joy at the thought of seeing you. I had no difficulty in getting leave to come into Winchester this morning, but I must be back before three o'clock, for Mr and Mrs Rucastle are going on a visit and will be away all the evening, so that I must look after the child. Now I have told you all my adventures, Mr Holmes, and I should be very glad if you could tell me what it all means, and above all, what I should do.'

Holmes and I had listened spellbound to this extraordinary story. My friend rose now and paced up and down the room, his hands in his pockets and an expression of the most profound gravity upon his face.

'Is Toller still drunk?' he asked.

'Yes. I heard his wife tell Mrs Rucastle that she could do nothing with him.'

'That is well. And the Rucastles go out tonight?'

'Yes.'

'Is there a cellar with a good strong lock?'

'Yes, the wine-cellar.'

'You seem to me to have acted all through this matter like a very brave and sensible girl, Miss Hunter. Do you think that you could perform one more feat? I should not ask it of you if I did not think you a quite exceptional woman.'

'I will try. What is it?'

'We shall be at The Copper Beeches by seven o'clock, my friend and I. The Rucastles will be gone by that time, and Toller will, we hope, be incapable. There only remains Mrs Toller, who might give the alarm. If you could send her into the cellar on some errand, and then turn the key upon her, you would facilitate matters immensely.'

'I will do it.'

'Excellent! We shall then look thoroughly into the affair. Of course there is only one feasible explanation. You have been brought there to personate someone, and the real person is imprisoned in this chamber. That is obvious. As to who this prisoner is, I have no doubt that it is the daughter, Miss Alice Rucastle, if I remember right, who was said to have gone to America. You were chosen, doubtless, as resembling her in height, figure and the colour of your hair. Hers had been cut off, very possibly in some illness through which she has passed, and so, of course, yours had to be sacrificed also. By a curious chance you came upon her tresses. The man in the road was undoubtedly some friend of hers – possibly her fiancÉ – and no doubt, as you wore the girl's dress and were so like her, he was convinced from your laughter, whenever he saw you, and afterwards from your gesture, that Miss Rucastle was perfectly happy, and that she no longer desired his attentions. The dog is let loose at night to prevent him from endeavouring to communicate with her. So much is fairly clear. The most serious point in the case is the disposition of the child.'

'What on earth has that to do with it?' I ejaculated.

'My dear Watson, you as a medical man are continually gaining light as to the tendencies of a child by the study of the parents. Don't you see that the converse is equally valid. I have frequently gained my first real insight into the character of parents by studying their children. This child's disposition is abnormally cruel, merely for cruelty's sake, and whether he derives this from his smiling father, as I should suspect, or from his mother, it bodes evil for the poor girl who is in their power.'

'I am sure that you are right, Mr Holmes,' cried our client. 'A thousand things come back to me which make me certain that you have hit it. Oh, let us lose not an instant in bringing help to this poor creature.'

'We must be circumspect, for we are dealing with a very cunning man. We can do nothing until seven o'clock. At that hour we shall be with you, and it will not be long before we solve the mystery.'

We were as good as our word, for it was just seven when we reached The Copper Beeches, having put up our trap at a wayside public-house. The group of trees, with their dark leaves shining like burnished metal in the light of the setting sun, were sufficient to mark the house even had Miss Hunter not been standing smiling on the doorstep.

'Have you managed it?' asked Holmes.

A loud thudding noise came from somewhere downstairs. 'That is Mrs Toller in the cellar,' said she. 'Her husband lies snoring on the kitchen rug. Here are his keys, which are the duplicates of Mr Rucastle's.'

'You have done well indeed!' cried Holmes with enthusiasm. 'Now lead the way, and we shall soon see the end of this black business.'

We passed up the stair, unlocked the door, followed on down a passage, and found ourselves in front of the barricade which Miss Hunter had described. Holmes cut the cord and removed the transverse bar. Then he tried the various keys in the lock, but without success. No sound came from within, and at the silence Holmes's face clouded over.

'I trust that we are not too late,' said he. 'I think, Miss Hunter, that we had better go in without you. Now, Watson, put your shoulder to it, and we shall see whether we cannot make our way in.'

It was an old rickety door and gave at once before our united strength. Together we rushed into the room. It was empty. There was no furniture save a little pallet bed, a small table and a basketful of linen. The skylight above was open, and the prisoner gone.

'There has been some villainy here,' said Holmes; 'this beauty has guessed Miss Hunter's intentions and has carried his victim off.'

'But how?'

'Through the skylight. We shall soon see how he managed it.' He swung himself up on to the roof. 'Ah, yes,' he cried, 'here's the end of a long light ladder against the eaves. That is how he did it.'

'But it is impossible,' said Miss Hunter; 'the ladder was not there when the Rucastles went away.'

'He has come back and done it. I tell you that he is a clever and dangerous man. I should not be very much surprised if this were he whose step I hear now upon the stair. I think, Watson, that it would be as well for you to have your pistol ready.'

The words were hardly out of his mouth before a man appeared at the door of the room, a very fat and burly man, with a heavy stick in his hand. Miss Hunter screamed and shrank against the wall at the sight of him, but Sherlock Holmes sprang forward and confronted him.

'You villain!' said he, 'where's your daughter?'

The fat man cast his eyes round, and then up at the open skylight.

'It is for me to ask you that,' he shrieked, 'you thieves! Spies and thieves! I have caught you, have I? You are in my power. I'll serve you!' He turned and clattered down the stairs as hard as he could go.

'He's gone for the dog!' cried Miss Hunter.

'I have my revolver,' said I.

'Better close the front door,' cried Holmes, and we all rushed down the stairs together. We had hardly reached the hall when we heard the baying of a hound, and then a scream of agony, with a horrible worrying sound which it was dreadful to listen to. An elderly man with a red face and shaking limbs came staggering out of a side door.

'My God!' he cried. 'Someone has loosed the dog. It's not been fed for two days. Quick, quick, or it'll be too late!'

Holmes and I rushed out and round the angle of the house, with Toller hurrying behind us. There was the huge famished brute, its black muzzle buried in Rucastle's throat, while he writhed and screamed upon the ground. Running up, I blew its brains out, and it fell over with its keen white teeth still meeting in the great creases of his neck. With much labour we separated them and carried him, living but horribly mangled, into the house. We laid him upon the drawing-room sofa, and having dispatched the sobered Toller to bear the news to his wife, I did what I could to relieve his pain. We were all assembled round him when the door opened, and a tall, gaunt woman entered the room.

'Mrs Toller!' cried Miss Hunter.

'Yes, miss. Mr Rucastle let me out when he came back before he went up to you. Ah, miss, it is a pity you didn't let me know what you were planning, for I would have told you that your pains were wasted.'

'Ha!' said Holmes, looking keenly at her. 'It is clear that Mrs Toller knows more about this matter than anyone else.'

'Yes, sir, I do, and I am ready enough to tell what I know.'

'Then, pray, sit down, and let us hear it, for there are several points on which I must confess that I am still in the dark.'

'I will soon make it clear to you,' said she; 'and I'd have done so before now if I could ha' got out from the cellar. If there's police-court business over this, you'll remember that I was the one that stood your friend, and that I was Miss Alice's friend too.

'She was never happy at home, Miss Alice wasn't, from the time that her father married again. She was slighted like and had no say in anything, but it never really became bad for her until after she met Mr Fowler at a friend's house. As well as I could learn, Miss Alice had rights of her own by will, but she was so quiet and patient, she was, that she never said a word about them but just left everything in Mr Rucastle's hands. He knew he was safe with her; but when there was a chance of a husband coming forward, who would ask for all that the law would give him, then her father thought it time to put a stop on it. He wanted her to sign a paper, so that whether she married or not, he could use her money. When she wouldn't do it, he kept on worrying her until she got brain-fever, and for six weeks was at death's door. Then she got better at last, all worn to a shadow, and with her beautiful hair cut off; but that didn't make no change in her young man, and he stuck to her as true as man could be.'

'Ah,' said Holmes, 'I think that what you have been good enough to tell us makes the matter fairly clear, and that I can deduce all that remains. Mr Rucastle then, I presume, took to this system of imprisonment?'

'Yes, sir.'

'And brought Miss Hunter down from London in order to get rid of the disagreeable persistence of Mr Fowler.'

'That was it, sir.'

'But Mr Fowler, being a persevering man, as a good seaman should be, blockaded the house, and having met you, succeeded by certain arguments, metallic or otherwise, in convincing you that your interests were the same as his.'

'Mr Fowler was a very kind-spoken, free-handed gentleman,' said Mrs Toller serenely.

'And in this way he managed that your good man should have no want of drink, and that a ladder should be ready at the moment when your master had gone out.'

'You have it, sir, just as it happened.'

'I am sure we owe you an apology, Mrs Toller,' said Holmes, 'for you have certainly cleared up everything which puzzled us. And here comes the country surgeon and Mrs Rucastle, so I think, Watson, that we had best escort Miss Hunter back to Winchester, as it seems to me that our *locus standi* now is rather a questionable one.'

And thus was solved the mystery of the sinister house with the copper beeches in front of the door. Mr Rucastle survived, but was always a broken man, kept alive solely through the care of his devoted wife. They still live with their old servants, who probably know so much of Rucastle's past life that he finds it difficult to part from them. Mr Fowler and Miss Rucastle were married, by special licence, in Southampton the day after their flight, and he is now the holder of a government appointment on the island of Mauritius. As to Miss Violet Hunter, my friend Holmes, rather to my disappointment, manifested no further interest in her when once she had ceased to be the centre of one of his problems, and she is now the head of a private school in Walsall, where I believe that she has met with considerable success.

Stories from
The Memoirs of
Sherlock Holmes

The Adventure of the Yellow Face

In publishing these short sketches based upon the numerous cases in which my companion's singular gifts have made us the listeners to, and eventually the actors in, some strange drama, it is only natural that I should dwell rather upon his successes than upon his failures. And this not so much for the sake of his reputation – for, indeed, it was when he was at his wits' end that his energy and his versatility were most admirable – but because where he failed it happened too often that no one else succeeded, and that the tale was left for ever without a conclusion. Now and again, however, it chanced that even when he erred, the truth was still discovered. I have notes of some half-dozen cases of the kind of which the affair of the second stain and that which I am about to recount are the two which present the strongest features of interest.

Sherlock Holmes was a man who seldom took exercise for exercise's sake. Few men were capable of greater muscular effort, and he was undoubtedly one of the finest boxers of his weight that I have ever seen; but he looked upon aimless bodily exertion as a waste of energy, and he seldom bestirred himself save when there was some professional object to be served. Then he was absolutely untiring and indefatigable. That he should have kept himself in training under such circumstances is remarkable, but his diet was usually of the sparest, and his habits were simple to the verge of austerity. Save for the occasional use of cocaine, he had no vices, and he only turned to the drug as a protest against the monotony of existence when cases were scanty and the papers uninteresting.

One day in early spring he had so far relaxed as to go for a walk with me in the Park, where the first faint shoots of green were breaking out upon the elms, and the sticky spearheads of the chestnuts were just beginning to burst into their fivefold leaves. For two hours we rambled about together, in silence for the most part, as befits two men who know each other intimately. It was nearly five before we were back in Baker Street once more.

'Beg pardon, sir,' said our pageboy, as he opened the door. 'There's been a gentleman here asking for you, sir.'

Holmes glanced reproachfully at me. 'So much for afternoon walks!' said he. 'Has this gentleman gone, then?'

'Yes, sir.'

'Didn't you ask him in?'

'Yes, sir; he came in.'

'How long did he wait?'

'Half an hour, sir. He was a very restless gentleman, sir, a-walkin' and a-stampin' all the time he was here. I was waitin' outside the door, sir, and I could hear him. At last he goes out into the passage, and he cries, "Is that man never goin' to come?" Those were his very words, sir. "You'll only need to wait a little longer," says I. "Then I'll wait in the open air, for I feel half choked," says he. "I'll be back before long." And with that he ups and he outs, and all I could say wouldn't hold him back.'

'Well, well, you did your best,' said Holmes, as we walked into our room. 'It's very annoying, though, Watson. I was badly in need of a case, and this looks, from the man's impatience, as if it were of importance. Hullo! That's not your pipe on the table. He must have left his behind him. A nice old brier with a good long stem of what the tobacconists call amber. I wonder how many real amber mouthpieces there are in London? Some people think that a fly in it is a sign. Well, he must have been disturbed in his mind to leave a pipe behind him which he evidently values highly.'

'How do you know that he values it highly?' I asked.

'Well, I should put the original cost of the pipe at seven and sixpence. Now it has, you see, been twice mended, once in the wooden stem and once in the amber. Each of these mends, done, as you observe, with silver bands, must have cost more than the pipe did originally. The man must value the pipe highly when he prefers to patch it up rather than buy a new one with the same money.'

'Anything else?' I asked, for Holmes was turning the pipe about in his hand, and staring at it in his peculiar pensive way.

He held it up and tapped on it with his long, thin forefinger, as a professor might who was lecturing on a bone.

'Pipes are occasionally of extraordinary interest,' said he. 'Nothing has more individuality, save perhaps watches and bootlaces. The indications here, however, are neither very marked nor very important. The owner is obviously a muscular man, left-handed, with an excellent set of teeth, careless in his habits, and with no need to practise economy.'

My friend threw out the information in a very offhand way, but I saw that he cocked his eye at me to see if I had followed his reasoning.

'You think a man must be well-to-do if he smokes a seven-shilling pipe,' said I.

'This is Grosvenor mixture at eightpence an ounce,' Holmes answered, knocking a little out on his palm. 'As he might get an excellent smoke for half the price, he has no need to practise economy.'

'And the other points?'

'He has been in the habit of lighting his pipe at lamps and gasjets. You can see that it is quite charred all down one side. Of course a match could not have done that. Why should a man hold a match to the side of his pipe? But you cannot light it at a lamp without getting the bowl charred. And it is all on the right side of the pipe. From that I gather that he is a left-handed man. You hold your own pipe to the lamp, and see how naturally you, being right-handed, hold the left side to the flame. You might do it once the other way, but not as a constancy. This has always been held so. Then he has bitten through his amber. It takes a muscular, energetic fellow, and one with a good set of teeth, to do that. But if I am not mistaken I hear him upon the stair, so we shall have something more interesting than his pipe to study.'

An instant later our door opened, and a tall young man entered the room. He was well but quietly dressed in a dark-grey suit, and carried a brown wide-awake in his hand. I should have put him at about thirty, though he was really some years older.

'I beg your pardon,' said he, with some embarrassment; 'I suppose I should have knocked. Yes, of course I should have knocked. The fact is that I am a little upset, and you must put it all down to that.' He passed his hand over his forehead like a man who is half dazed, and then fell rather than sat down upon a chair.

'I can see that you have not slept for a night or two,' said Holmes, in his easy, genial way. 'That tries a man's nerves more than work, and more even than pleasure. May I ask how I can help you?'

'I wanted your advice, sir. I don't know what to do and my whole life seems to have gone to pieces.'

'You wish to employ me as a consulting detective?'

'Not that only. I want your opinion as a judicious man – as a man of the world. I want to know what I ought to do next. I hope to God you'll be able to tell me.'

He spoke in little, sharp, jerky outbursts, and it seemed to me that to speak at all was very painful to him, and that his will all through was overriding his inclinations.

'It's a very delicate thing,' said he. 'One does not like to speak of one's domestic affairs to strangers. It seems dreadful to discuss the conduct of one's wife with two men whom I have never seen before. It's horrible to have to do it. But I've got to the end of my tether, and I must have advice.'

'My dear Mr Grant Munro –' began Holmes.

Our visitor sprang from his chair. 'What!' he cried, 'you know my name?'

'If you wish to preserve your incognito,' said Holmes, smiling, 'I would suggest that you cease to write your name upon the lining of your hat, or else that you turn the crown towards the person whom you are addressing. I was about to say that my friend and I have listened to a good many strange secrets in this room, and that we have had the good fortune to bring peace to many troubled souls. I trust that we may do as much for you. Might I beg you, as time may prove to be of importance, to furnish me with the facts of your case without further delay?'

Our visitor again passed his hand over his forehead, as if he found it bitterly hard. From every gesture and expression I could see that he was a reserved, self-contained man, with a dash of pride in his nature, more likely to hide his wounds than to expose them. Then suddenly, with a fierce gesture of his closed hand, like one who throws reserve to the winds, he began.

'The facts are these, Mr Holmes,' said he. 'I am a married man, and have been so for three years. During that time my wife and I have loved each other as fondly and lived as happily as any two that ever were joined. We have not had a difference, not one, in thought or word or deed. And now, since last Monday, there has suddenly sprung up a barrier between us, and I find that there is something in her life and in her thoughts of which I know as little as if she were the woman who brushes by me in the street. We are estranged, and I want to know why.

'Now there is one thing that I want to impress upon you before I go any further, Mr Holmes. Effie loves me. Don't let there be any mistake about that. She loves me with her whole heart and soul, and never more than now. I know it. I feel it. I don't want to argue about that. A man can tell easily enough when a woman loves him. But there's this secret between us, and we can never be the same until it is cleared.'

'Kindly let me have the facts, Mr Munro,' said Holmes, with some impatience.

'I'll tell you what I know about Effie's history. She was a widow when I met her first, though quite young – only twenty-five. Her name then was Mrs Hebron. She went out to America when she was young, and lived in the town of Atlanta, where she married this Hebron, who was a lawyer with a good practice. They had one child, but the yellow fever broke out badly in the place, and both husband and child died of it. I have seen his death certificate. This sickened her of America, and she came back to live with a maiden aunt at Pinner, in Middlesex.

I may mention that her husband had left her comfortably off, and that she had a capital of about four thousand five hundred pounds, which had been so well invested by him that it returned an average of seven per cent. She had only been six months at Pinner when I met her; we fell in love with each other, and we married a few weeks afterwards.

'I am a hop merchant myself, and as I have an income of seven or eight hundred, we found ourselves comfortably off, and took a nice eighty-pound-a-year villa at Norbury. Our little place was very countrified, considering that it is so close to town. We had an inn and two houses a little above us, and a single cottage at the other side of the field which faces us, and except those there were no houses until you got halfway to the station. My business took me into town at certain seasons, but in summer I had less to do, and then in our country home my wife and I were just as happy as could be wished. I tell you that there never was a shadow between us until this accursed affair began.

'There's one thing I ought to tell you before I go further. When we married, my wife made over all her property to me – rather against my will, for I saw how awkward it would be if my business affairs went wrong. However, she would have it so, and it was done. Well, about six weeks ago she came to me.

'"Jack," said she, "when you took my money you said that if ever I wanted any I was to ask you for it."

'"Certainly," said I. "It's all your own."

'"Well," said she, "I want a hundred pounds."

'I was a bit staggered at this, for I had imagined it was simply a new dress or something of the kind that she was after.

'"What on earth for?" I asked.

'"Oh," said she, in her playful way, "you said that you were only my banker, and bankers never ask questions, you know."

'"If you really mean it, of course you shall have the money," said I.

'"Oh, yes, I really mean it."

'"And you won't tell me what you want it for?"

'"Someday, perhaps, but not just at present, Jack."

'So I had to be content with that, though it was the first time that there had ever been any secret between us. I gave her a cheque, and I never thought any more of the matter. It may have nothing to do with what came afterwards, but I thought it only right to mention it.

'Well, I told you just now that there is a cottage not far from our house. There is just a field between us, but to reach it you have to go along the road and then turn down a lane. Just beyond it is a nice little grove of Scotch firs, and I used to be very fond of strolling down there, for trees are always neighbourly kinds of things. The cottage had been standing empty this eight months, and it was a pity, for it was a pretty two-storeyed place, with an old-fashioned porch and honeysuckle about it. I have stood many a time and thought what a neat little homestead it would make.

'Well, last Monday evening I was taking a stroll down that way, when I met an empty van coming up the lane, and saw a pile of carpets and things lying about on the grass-plot beside the porch. It was clear that the cottage had at last been let. I walked past it, and wondered what sort of folk they were who had come to live so near us. And as I looked I suddenly became aware that a face was watching me out of one of the upper windows.

'I don't know what there was about that face, Mr Holmes, but it seemed to send a chill right down my back. I was some little way off, so that I could not make out the features, but there was something unnatural and inhuman about the face. That was the impression that I had, and I moved quickly forwards to get a nearer view of the person who was watching me. But as I did so the face suddenly disappeared, so suddenly that it seemed to have been plucked away into the darkness of the room. I stood for five minutes thinking the business over, and trying to analyse my impressions. I could not tell if the face were that of a man or a woman. It had been too far from me for that. But its colour was what had impressed me most. It was of a livid chalky white, and with something set and rigid about it which was shockingly unnatural. So disturbed was I that I determined to see a little more of the new inmates of the cottage. I approached and knocked at the door, which was instantly opened by a tall, gaunt woman with a harsh, forbidding face.

'"What may you be wantin'?" she asked, in a Northern accent.

'"I am your neighbour over yonder," said I, nodding towards my house. "I see that you have only just moved in, so I thought that if I could be of any help to you in any – "

'"Ay, we'll just ask ye when we want ye," said she, and shut the door in my face. Annoyed at the churlish rebuff, I turned my back and walked home. All evening, though I tried to think of other things, my mind would still turn to the apparition at the window and the rudeness of the woman. I determined to say nothing about the former to my wife, for she is a nervous, highly strung woman, and I had no wish that she should share the unpleasant impression which had been produced upon myself. I remarked to her, however, before I fell asleep, that the cottage was now occupied, to which she returned no reply.

'I am usually an extremely sound sleeper. It has been a standing jest in the family that nothing could ever wake me during the night. And yet somehow on that particular night, whether it may have been the slight excitement produced by my little adventure or not I know not, but I slept much more lightly than usual. Half in my dreams I was dimly conscious that something was going on in the room, and gradually became aware that my wife had dressed herself and was slipping on her mantle and her bonnet. My lips were parted to murmur out some sleepy words of surprise or remonstrance at this untimely preparation, when suddenly my half-opened eyes fell upon her face, illuminated by the candlelight, and astonishment held me dumb. She wore an expression such as I had never seen before – such as I should have thought her incapable of assuming. She was deadly pale and breathing fast, glancing furtively towards the bed as she fastened her mantle, to see if she had disturbed me. Then, thinking that I was still asleep, she slipped noiselessly from the room, and an instant later I heard a sharp creaking which could only come from the hinges of the front door. I sat up in bed and rapped my knuckles against the rail to make certain that I was truly awake. Then I took my watch from under the pillow. It was three in the morning. What on this earth could my wife be doing out on the country road at three in the morning?

'I had sat for about twenty minutes turning the thing over in my mind and trying to find some possible explanation. The more I thought, the more extraordinary and inexplicable did it appear. I was still puzzling over it when I heard the door gently close again, and her footsteps coming up the stairs.

'"Where in the world have you been, Effie?" I asked as she entered.

'She gave a violent start and a kind of gasping cry when I spoke, and that cry and start troubled me more than all the rest, for there was something indescribably guilty about them. My wife had always been a woman of a frank, open nature, and it gave me a chill to see her slinking into her own room, and crying out and wincing when her own husband spoke to her.

'"You awake, Jack?" she cried, with a nervous laugh. "Why, I thought that nothing could awake you."

'"Where have you been?" I asked, more sternly.

'"I don't wonder that you are surprised," said she, and I could see that her fingers were trembling as she undid the fastenings of her mantle. "Why, I never remember having done such a thing in my life before. The fact is that I felt as though I were choking, and had a perfect longing for a breath of fresh air. I really think that I should have fainted if I had not gone out. I stood at the door for a few minutes, and now I am quite myself again."

'All the time that she was telling me this story she never once looked in my direction, and her voice was quite unlike her usual tones. It was evident to me that she was saying what was false. I said nothing in reply, but turned my face to the wall, sick at heart, with my mind filled with a thousand venomous doubts and suspicions. What was it that my wife was concealing from me? Where had she been during that strange expedition? I felt that I should have no peace until I knew, and yet I shrank from asking her again after once she had told me what was false. All the rest of the night I tossed and tumbled, framing theory after theory, each more unlikely than the last.

'I should have gone to the City that day, but I was too disturbed in my mind to be able to pay attention to business matters. My wife seemed to be as upset as myself, and I could see from the little questioning glances which she kept shooting at me that she understood that I disbelieved her statement, and that she was at her wits' end what to do. We hardly exchanged a word during breakfast, and immediately afterwards I went out for a walk, that I might think the matter out in the fresh morning air.

'I went as far as the Crystal Palace, spent an hour in the grounds, and was back in Norbury by one o'clock. It happened that my way took me past the cottage, and I stopped for an instant to look at the windows, and to see if I could catch a glimpse of the strange face which had looked out at me on the day before. As I stood there, imagine my surprise, Mr Holmes, when the door suddenly opened and my wife walked out.

'I was struck dumb with astonishment at the sight of her; but my emotions were nothing to those which showed themselves upon her face when our eyes met. She seemed for an instant to wish to shrink back inside the house again; and then, seeing how useless all concealment must be, she came forward, with a very white face and frightened eyes which belied the smile upon her lips.

'"Ah, Jack," she said, "I have just been in to see if I can be of any assistance to our new neighbours. Why do you look at me like that, Jack? You are not angry with me?"

'"So," said I, "this is where you went during the night."

'"What do you mean?" she cried.

'"You came here. I am sure of it. Who are these people, that you should visit them at such an hour?"

'"I have not been here before."

'"How can you tell me what you know is false?" I cried. "Your very voice changes as you speak. When have I ever had a secret from you? I shall enter that cottage, and I shall probe the matter to the bottom."

'"No, no, Jack, for God's sake!" she gasped, in uncontrollable emotion. Then, as I approached the door, she seized my sleeve and pulled me back with convulsive strength.

'"I implore you not to do this, Jack," she cried. "I swear that I will tell you everything some day, but nothing but misery can come of it if you enter that cottage." Then, as I tried to shake her off, she clung to me in a frenzy of entreaty.

'"Trust me, Jack!" she cried. "Trust me only this once. You will never have cause to regret it. You know that I would not have a secret from you if it were not for your own sake. Our whole lives are at stake in this. If you come home with me, all will be well. If you force your way into that cottage, all is over between us."

'There was such earnestness, such despair, in her manner that her words arrested me, and I stood irresolute before the door.

'"I will trust you on one condition, and on one condition only," said I at last. "It is that this mystery comes to an end from now. You are at liberty to preserve your secret, but you must promise me that there shall be no more nightly visits, no more doings which are kept from my knowledge. I am willing to forget those which are passed if you will promise that there shall be no more in the future."

'"I was sure that you would trust me," she cried, with a great sigh of relief. "It shall be just as you wish. Come away – oh, come away up to the house."

'Still pulling at my sleeve, she led me away from the cottage. As we went I glanced back, and there was that yellow livid face watching us out of the upper window. What link could there be between that creature and my wife? Or how could the coarse, rough woman whom I had seen the day before be connected with her? It was a strange puzzle, and yet I knew that my mind could never know ease again until I had solved it.

'For two days after this I stayed at home, and my wife appeared to abide loyally by our engagement, for, as far as I know, she never stirred out of the house. On the third day, however, I had ample evidence that her solemn promise was not enough to hold her back from this secret influence which drew her away from her husband and her duty.

'I had gone into town on that day, but I returned by the 2.40 instead of the 3.36, which is my usual train. As I entered the house the maid ran into the hall with a startled face.

THE ADVENTURE OF THE YELLOW FACE 🌱 🌿 🌱

'"Where is your mistress?" I asked.

'"I think that she has gone out for a walk," she answered.

'My mind was instantly filled with suspicion. I rushed upstairs to make sure that she was not in the house. As I did so I happened to glance out of one of the upper windows, and saw the maid with whom I had just been speaking running across the field in the direction of the cottage. Then of course I saw exactly what it all meant. My wife had gone over there, and had asked the servant to call her if I should return. Tingling with anger, I rushed down and hurried across, determined to end the matter once and for ever. I saw my wife and the maid hurrying back along the lane, but I did not stop to speak with them. In the cottage lay the secret which was casting a shadow over my life. I vowed that, come what might, it should be a secret no longer. I did not even knock when I reached it, but turned the handle and rushed into the passage.

'It was all still and quiet upon the ground floor. In the kitchen a kettle was singing on the fire, and a large black cat lay coiled up in the basket; but there was no sign of the woman whom I had seen before. I ran into the other room, but it was equally deserted. Then I rushed up the stairs, only to find two other rooms empty and deserted at the top. There was no one at all in the whole house. The furniture and pictures were of the most common and vulgar description, save in the one chamber at the window of which I had seen the strange face. That was comfortable and elegant, and all my suspicions rose into a fierce bitter flame when I saw that on the mantelpiece stood a copy of a full-length photograph of my wife, which had been taken at my request only three months ago.

'I stayed long enough to make certain that the house was absolutely empty. Then I left it, feeling a weight at my heart such as I had never had before. My wife came out into the hall as I entered my house; but I was too hurt and angry to speak with her, and pushing past her, I made my way into my study. She followed me, however, before I could close the door.

'"I am sorry that I broke my promise, Jack," said she; "but if you knew all the circumstances I am sure that you would forgive me."

'"Tell me everything, then," said I.

'"I cannot, Jack, I cannot," she cried.

'"Until you tell me who it is that has been living in that cottage, and who it is to whom you have given that photograph, there can never be any confidence between us," said I, and breaking away from her, I left the house. That was yesterday, Mr Holmes, and I have not seen her since, nor do I know anything more about this strange business. It is the first shadow that has come between us, and it has so shaken me that I do not know what I should do for the best. Suddenly this morning it occurred to me that you were the man to advise me, so I have hurried to you now, and I place myself unreservedly in your hands. If there is any point which I have not made clear, pray question me about it. But, above all, tell me quickly what I am to do, for this misery is more than I can bear.'

Holmes and I had listened with the utmost interest to this extraordinary statement, which had been delivered in the jerky, broken fashion of a man who is under the influence of extreme emotions. My companion sat silent for some time, with his chin upon his hand, lost in thought.

'Tell me,' said he at last, 'could you swear that this was a man's face which you saw at the window?'

'Each time that I saw it I was some distance away from it, so that it is impossible for me to say.'

'You appear, however, to have been disagreeably impressed by it.'

'It seemed to be of an unnatural colour, and to have a strange rigidity about the features. When I approached, it vanished with a jerk.'

'How long is it since your wife asked you for a hundred pounds?'

'Nearly two months.'

'Have you ever seen a photograph of her first husband?'

'No; there was a great fire at Atlanta very shortly after his death, and all her papers were destroyed.'

'And yet she had a certificate of death. You say that you saw it.'

'Yes; she got a duplicate after the fire.'

'Did you ever meet anyone who knew her in America?'

'No.'

'Did she ever talk of revisiting the place?'

'No.'

'Or get letters from it?'

'No.'

'Thank you. I should like to think over the matter a little now. If the cottage is now permanently deserted we may have some difficulty. If, on the other hand, as I fancy is more likely, the inmates were warned of you coming, and left before you entered yesterday, then they may be back now, and we should clear it all up easily. Let me advise you, then, to return to Norbury, and to examine the windows of the cottage again. If you have reason to believe that it is inhabited, do not force your way in, but send a wire to my friend and me. We shall be with you within an hour of receiving it, and we shall then very soon get to the bottom of the business.'

'And if it is still empty?'

'In that case I shall come out tomorrow and talk it over with you. Goodbye; and, above all, do not fret until you know that you really have a cause for it.'

'I am afraid that this is a bad business, Watson,' said my companion, as he returned after accompanying Mr Grant Munro to the door. 'What do you make of it?'

'It had an ugly sound,' I answered.

'Yes. There's blackmail in it, or I am much mistaken.'

'And who is the blackmailer?'

'Well, it must be the creature who lives in the only comfortable room in the place, and has her photograph above his fireplace. Upon my word, Watson, there is something very attractive about that livid face at the window, and I would not have missed the case for worlds.'

'You have a theory?'

'Yes, a provisional one. But I shall be surprised if it does not turn out to be correct. This woman's first husband is in that cottage.'

'Why do you think so?'

'How else can we explain her frenzied anxiety that her second one should not enter it? The facts, as I read them, are something like this: This woman was married in America. Her husband developed some hateful qualities; or shall we say that he contracted some loathsome disease, and became a leper or an imbecile? She flies from him at last, returns to England, changes her name, and starts her life, as she thinks, afresh. She has been married three years, and believes that her position is quite secure, having shown her husband the death certificate of some man whose name she has assumed, when suddenly her whereabouts was discovered by her first husband; or, we may suppose, by some unscrupulous woman who has attached herself to the invalid. They write to the wife, and threaten to come and expose her. She asks for a hundred pounds, and endeavours to buy them off. They come in spite of it, and when the husband mentions casually to the wife that there are newcomers in the cottage, she knows in some way that they are her pursuers. She waits until her husband is asleep, and then she rushes down to endeavour to persuade them to leave her in peace. Having no success, she goes again next morning, and her husband meets her, as he has told us, as she comes out. She promises him then not to go there again, but two days afterwards the hope of getting rid of those dreadful neighbours was too strong for her, and she made another attempt, taking down with her the photograph which had probably been demanded from her. In the midst of this interview the maid rushed in to say that the master had come home, on which the wife, knowing that he would come straight down to the cottage, hurried the inmates out at the back door, into the grove of fir-trees, probably, which was mentioned as standing near. In this way he found the place deserted. I shall be very much surprised, however, if it is still so when he reconnoitres it this evening. What do you think of my theory?'

'It is all surmise.'

'But at least it covers all the facts. When new facts come to our knowledge which cannot be covered by it, it will be time enough to reconsider it. We can do nothing more until we have a message from our friend at Norbury.'

But we had not a very long time to wait for that. It came just as we had finished our tea. 'The cottage is still tenanted,' it said. 'Have seen the face again at the window. Will meet the seven o'clock train, and will take no steps until you arrive.'

He was waiting on the platform when we stepped out, and we could see in the light of the station lamps that he was very pale, and quivering with agitation.

'They are still there, Mr Holmes,' said he, laying his hand hard upon my friend's sleeve. 'I saw lights in the cottage as I came down. We shall settle it now once and for all.'

'What is your plan, then?' asked Holmes, as he walked down the dark, tree-lined road.

'I am going to force my way in and see for myself who is in the house. I wish you both to be there as witnesses.'

'You are quite determined to do this, in spite of your wife's warning that it is better that you should not solve the mystery?'

'Yes, I am determined.'

'Well, I think that you are in the right. Any truth is better than indefinite doubt. We had better go up at once. Of course, legally, we are putting ourselves hopelessly in the wrong; but I think that it is worth it.'

It was a very dark night, and a thin rain began to fall as we turned from the high road into a narrow lane, deeply rutted, with hedges on either side. Mr Grant Munro pushed impatiently forward, however, and we stumbled after him as best we could.

'There are the lights of my house,' he murmured, pointing to a glimmer among the trees. 'And here is the cottage which I am going to enter.'

We turned a corner in the lane as he spoke, and there was the building close beside us. A yellow bar falling across the black foreground showed that the door was not quite closed, and one window in the upper storey was brightly illuminated. As we looked, we saw a dark blur moving across the blind.

'There is that creature!' cried Grant Munro. 'You can see for yourselves that someone is there. Now follow me, and we shall soon know all.'

We approached the door; but suddenly a woman appeared out of the shadow and stood in the golden track of the lamplight. I could not see her face in the darkness, but her arms were thrown out in an attitude of entreaty.

'For God's sake, don't, Jack!' she cried. 'I had a presentiment that you would come this evening. Think better of it, dear! Trust me again, and you will never have cause to regret it.'

'I have trusted you too long, Effie,' he cried, sternly. 'Leave go of me! I must pass you. My friends and I are going to settle this matter once and for ever!' He pushed her to one side, and we followed closely after him. As he threw the door open an old woman ran out in front of him and tried to bar his passage, but he thrust her back, and an instant afterwards we were all upon the stairs. Grant Munro rushed into the lighted room at the top, and we entered it at his heels.

It was a cosy, well-furnished apartment, with two candles burning upon the table and two upon the mantelpiece. In the corner, stooping over a desk, there sat what appeared to be a little girl. Her face was turned away as we entered, but we could see that she was dressed in a red frock, and that she had long white gloves on. As she whisked round to us, I gave a cry of surprise and horror. The face which she turned towards us was of the strangest livid tint, and the features were absolutely devoid of any expression. An instant later the mystery was explained. Holmes, with a laugh, passed his hand behind the child's ear, a mask peeled off from her countenance, and there was a little coal-black negress, with all her white teeth flashing in amusement at our amazed faces. I burst out laughing, out of sympathy with her merriment; but Grant Munro stood staring, with his hand clutching his throat.

'My God!' he cried. 'What can be the meaning of this?'

'I will tell you the meaning of it,' cried the lady, sweeping into the room with a proud, set face. 'You have forced me, against my own judgment, to tell you, and now we must both make the best of it. My husband died at Atlanta. My child survived.'

'Your child?'

She drew a large silver locket from her bosom. 'You have never seen this open.'

'I understood that it did not open.'

She touched a spring, and the front hinged back. There was a portrait within of a man strikingly handsome and intelligent-looking, but bearing unmistakable signs upon his features of his African descent.

'That is John Hebron, of Atlanta,' said the lady, 'and a nobler man never walked the earth. I cut myself off from my race in order to wed him, but never once while he lived did I for an instant regret it. It was our misfortune that our only child took after his people rather than mine. It is often so in such matches, and little Lucy is darker far than ever her father was. But dark or fair, she is my own dear little girlie, and her mother's pet.' The little creature ran across at the words and nestled up against the lady's dress. 'When I left her in America,' she continued, 'it was only because her health was weak, and the change might have done her harm. She was given to the care of a faithful Scotch woman who had once been our servant. Never for an instant did I dream of disowning her as my child. But when chance threw you in my way, Jack, and I learned to love you, I feared to tell you about my child. God forgive me, I feared that I should lose you, and I had not the courage to tell you. I had to choose between you, and in my weakness I turned away from my own little girl. For three years I have kept her existence a secret from you, but I heard from the nurse, and I knew that all was well with her. At last, however, there came an overwhelming desire to see the child once more. I struggled against it, but in vain. Though I knew the danger, I determined to have the child over, if it were but for a few weeks. I sent a hundred pounds to the nurse, and I gave her instructions about this cottage, so that she might come as a neighbour, without my appearing to be in any way connected with her. I pushed my precautions so far as to order her to keep the child in the house during the daytime, and to cover up her little face and hands so that even those who might see her at the window should not gossip about there being a black child in the neighbourhood. If I had been less cautious I might have been more wise, but I was half crazy with fear that you should learn the truth.

'It was you who told me first that the cottage was occupied. I should have waited for the morning, but I could not sleep for excitement, and so at last I slipped out, knowing how difficult it is to awake you. But you saw me go, and that was the beginning of my troubles. Next day you had my secret at your mercy, but you nobly refrained from pursuing your advantage. Three days later, however, the nurse and child only just escaped from the back door as you rushed in at the front one. And now tonight you at last know all, and I ask you what is to become of us, my child and me?' She clasped her hands and waited for an answer.

It was a long ten minutes before Grant Munro broke the silence, and when his answer came it was one of which I love to think. He lifted the little child, kissed her, and then, still carrying her, he held his other hand out to his wife and turned towards the door.

'We can talk it over more comfortably at home,' said he. 'I am not a very good man, Effie, but I think that I am a better one than you have given me credit for being.'

Holmes and I followed them down the lane, and my friend plucked at my sleeve as we came out.

'I think,' said he, 'that we shall be of more use in London than in Norbury.'

Not another word did he say of the case until late that night, when he was turning away, with his lighted candle, for his bedroom.

'Watson,' said he, 'if it should ever strike you that I am getting a little over-confident in my powers, or giving less pains to a case than it deserves, kindly whisper "Norbury" in my ear, and I shall be infinitely obliged to you.'

The Adventure of
the Stockbroker's Clerk

Shortly after my marriage I had bought a connection in the Paddington district. Old Mr Farquhar, from whom I purchased it, had at one time an excellent general practice; but his age, and an affliction of the nature of St Vitus's dance from which he suffered, had very much thinned it. The public not unnaturally goes on the principle that he who would heal others must himself be whole, and looks askance at the curative powers of the man whose own case is beyond the reach of his drugs. Thus, as my predecessor weakened his practice declined, until when I purchased it from him it had sunk from twelve hundred to little more than three hundred a year. I had confidence, however, in my own youth and energy, and was convinced that in a very few years the concern would be as flourishing as ever.

For three months after taking over the practice I was kept very closely at work, and saw little of my friend Sherlock Holmes, for I was too busy to visit Baker Street, and he seldom went anywhere himself save upon professional business. I was surprised, therefore, when, one morning in June, as I sat reading the *British Medical Journal* after breakfast, I heard a ring at the bell, followed by the high, somewhat strident tones of my old companion's voice.

'Ah, my dear Watson,' said he, striding into the room, 'I am very delighted to see you! I trust that Mrs Watson has entirely recovered from all the little excitements connected with our adventure of the Sign of Four.'

'Thank you, we are both very well,' said I, shaking him warmly by the hand.

'And I hope, also,' he continued, sitting down in the rocking-chair, 'that the cares of medical practice have not entirely obliterated the interest which you used to take in our little deductive problems.'

'On the contrary,' I answered, 'it was only last night that I was looking over my old notes, and classifying some of our past results.'

'I trust that you don't consider your collection closed.'

'Not at all. I should wish nothing better than to have some more of such experiences.'

'Today, for example?'

'Yes, today, if you like.'

'And as far off as Birmingham?'

'Certainly, if you wish it.'

'And the practice?'

'I do my neighbour's when he goes. He is always ready to work off the debt.'

'Ha! Nothing could be better,' said Holmes, leaning back in his chair and looking keenly at me from under his half-closed lids. 'I perceive that you have been unwell lately. Summer colds are always a little trying.'

'I was confined to the house by a severe chill for three days last week. I thought, however, that I had cast off every trace of it.'

'So you have. You look remarkably robust.'

'How, then, did you know of it?'

'My dear fellow, you know my methods.'

'You deduced it, then?'

'Certainly.'

'And from what?'

'From your slippers.'

I glanced down at the new patent leathers which I was wearing. 'How on earth –' I began, but Holmes answered my question before it was asked.

'Your slippers are new,' he said. 'You could not have had them more than a few weeks. The soles which you are at this moment presenting to me are slightly scorched. For a moment I thought they might have got wet and been burned in the drying. But near the instep there is a small circular wafer of paper with the shopman's hieroglyphics upon it. Damp would of course have removed this. You had, then, been sitting with your feet outstretched to the fire, which a man would hardly do even in so wet a June as this if he were in his full health.'

Like all Holmes's reasoning the thing seemed simplicity itself when it was once explained. He read the thought upon my features, and his smile had a tinge of bitterness.

'I am afraid that I rather give myself away when I explain,' said he. 'Results without causes are much more impressive. You are ready to come to Birmingham, then?'

'Certainly. What is the case?'

'You shall hear it all in the train. My client is outside in a four-wheeler. Can you come at once?'

'In an instant.' I scribbled a note to my neighbour, rushed upstairs to explain the matter to my wife, and joined Holmes upon the doorstep.

'Your neighbour is a doctor,' said he, nodding at the brass plate.

'Yes; he bought a practice, as I did.'

'An old-established one?'

'Just the same as mine. Both have been ever since the houses were built.'

'Ah! Then you got hold of the better of the two.'

'I think I did. But how do you know?'

'By the steps, my boy. Yours are worn three inches deeper than his. But this gentleman in the cab is my client, Mr Hall Pycroft. Allow me to introduce you to him. Whip your horse up, cabby, for we have only just time to catch our train.'

The man whom I found myself facing was a well-built, fresh-complexioned young fellow, with a frank, honest face and a slight, crisp, yellow moustache. He wore a very shiny top hat and a neat suit of sober black, which made him look what he was – a smart young City man, of the class who have been labelled cockneys, but who give us our crack volunteer regiments, and who turn out more fine athletes and sportsmen than any body of men in these islands. His round, ruddy face was naturally full of cheeriness, but the corners of his mouth seemed to me to be pulled down in a half-comical distress. It was not, however, until we were all in a first-class carriage and well started upon our journey to Birmingham that I was able to learn what the trouble was which had driven him to Sherlock Holmes.

'We have a clear run here of seventy minutes,' Holmes remarked. 'I want you, Mr Hall Pycroft, to tell my friend your very interesting experience exactly as you have told it to me, or with more detail if possible. It will be of use to me to hear the succession of events again. It is a case, Watson, which may prove to have something in it, or may prove to have nothing, but which, at least, presents those unusual and *outré* features which are as dear to you as they are to me. Now, Mr Pycroft, I shall not interrupt you again.'

Our young companion looked at me with a twinkle in his eye.

'The worst of the story is,' said he, 'that I show myself up as such a confounded fool. Of course it may work out all right, and I don't see that I could have done otherwise; but if I have lost my crib and get nothing in exchange I shall feel what a soft Johnnie I have been. I'm not very good at telling a story, Dr Watson, but it is like this with me.

'I used to have a billet at Coxon & Woodhouse's, of Drapers' Gardens, but they were let in early in the spring through the Venezuelan loan, as no doubt you remember, and came a nasty cropper. I had been with them five years, and old Coxon gave me a ripping good testimonial when the smash came, but of course we clerks were all turned adrift, the twenty-seven of us. I tried here and tried there, but there were lots of other chaps on the same lay as myself, and it was a perfect frost for a long time. I had been taking three pounds a week at Coxon's, and I had saved about seventy of them, but I soon worked my way through that and out at the other end. I was fairly at the end of my tether at last, and could hardly find the stamps to answer the advertisements or the envelopes to stick them to. I had worn out my boots padding up office stairs, and I seemed just as far from getting a billet as ever.

'At last I saw a vacancy at Mawson & Williams's, the great stock-broking firm in Lombard Street. I dare say E.C. is not much in your line, but I can tell you that this is about the richest house in London. The advertisement was to be answered by letter only. I sent in my testimonial and application, but without the least hope of getting it. Back came an answer by return, saying that if I would appear next Monday I might take over my new duties at once, provided that my appearance was satisfactory. No one knows how these things are worked. Some people say that the manager just plunges his hand into the heap and takes the first that comes. Anyhow it was my innings that time, and I don't ever wish to feel better pleased. The screw was a pound a week rise, and the duties just about the same as at Coxon's.

'And now I come to the queer part of the business. I was in diggings out Hampstead way, 17 Potter's Terrace. Well, I was sitting doing a smoke that very evening after I had been promised the appointment, when up came my landlady with a card which had "Arthur Pinner, Financial Agent" printed upon it. I had never heard the name before and could not imagine what he wanted with me; but, of course, I asked her to show him up. In he walked, a middle-sized, dark-haired, dark-eyed, black-bearded man, with a touch of the Sheeny about his nose. He had a brisk kind of way with him and spoke sharply, like a man who knew the value of time.

'"Mr Hall Pycroft, I believe?" said he.

'"Yes, sir," I answered, pushing a chair towards him.

'"Lately engaged at Coxon & Woodhouse's?"

'"Yes, sir."

'"And now on the staff of Mawson's."

'"Quite so."

'"Well," said he, "the fact is that I have heard some really extraordinary stories about your financial ability. You remember Parker, who used to be Coxon's manager? He can never say enough about it."

'Of course, I was pleased to hear this. I had always been pretty sharp in the office, but I had never dreamed that I was talked about in the City in this fashion.

'"You have a good memory?" said he.

'"Pretty fair," I answered, modestly.

'"Have you kept in touch with the market while you have been out of work?" he asked.

'"Yes. I read the stock exchange list every morning."

'"Now that shows real application!" he cried. "That is the way to prosper! You won't mind my testing you, will you? Let me see. How are Ayrshires?"

'"A hundred and six and a quarter to a hundred and five and seven-eighths."

'"And New Zealand consolidated?"

'"A hundred and four."

'"And British Broken Hills?"

'"Seven to seven-and-six."

'"Wonderful!" he cried, with his hands up. "This quite fits in with all that I had heard. My boy, my boy, you are very much too good to be a clerk at Mawson's!"

'This outburst rather astonished me, as you can think. "Well," said I, "other people don't think quite so much of me as you seem to do, Mr Pinner. I had a hard enough fight to get this berth, and I am very glad to have it."

'"Pooh, man; you should soar above it. You are not in your true sphere. Now, I'll tell you how it stands with me. What I have to offer is little enough when measured by your ability, but when compared with Mawson's, it's light to dark. Let me see. When do you go to Mawson's?"

'"On Monday."

'"Ha, ha! I think I would risk a little sporting flutter that you don't go there at all."

'"Not go to Mawson's?"

'"No, sir. By that day you will be the business manager of the Franco-Midland Hardware Company, Limited, with a hundred and thirty-four branches in the towns and villages of France, not counting one in Brussels and one in San Remo."

'This took my breath away. "I never heard of it," said I.

'"Very likely not. It has been kept very quiet, for the capital was all privately subscribed, and it's too good a thing to let the public into. My brother, Harry Pinner, is promoter, and joins the board after allotment as managing director. He knew I was in the swim down here, and asked me to pick up a good man cheap. A young, pushing man with plenty of snap about him. Parker spoke of you, and that brought me here tonight. We can only offer you a beggarly five hundred to start with."

'"Five hundred a year!" I shouted.

'"Only that at the beginning; but you are to have an overriding commission of one per cent on all business done by your agents, and you may take my word for it that this will come to more than your salary."

'"But I know nothing about hardware."

'"Tut, my boy; you know about figures."

'My head buzzed, and I could hardly sit still in my chair. But suddenly a little chill of doubt came upon me.

'"I must be frank with you," said I. "Mawson only gives me two hundred, but Mawson is safe. Now, really, I know so little about your company that – "

'"Ah, smart, smart!" he cried, in a kind of ecstasy of delight. "You are the very man for us. You are not to be talked over, and quite right, too. Now, here's a note for a hundred pounds, and if you think that we can do business you may just slip it into your pocket as an advance upon your salary."

'"That is very handsome," said I. "When should I take over my new duties?"

'"Be in Birmingham tomorrow at one," said he. "I have a note in my pocket here which you will take to my brother. You will find him at 126b Corporation Street, where the temporary offices of the company are situated. Of course he must confirm your engagement, but between ourselves it will be all right."

'"Really, I hardly know how to express my gratitude, Mr Pinner," said I.

'"Not at all, my boy. You have only got your desserts. There are one or two small things – mere formalities – which I must arrange with you. You have a bit of paper beside you there. Kindly write upon it 'I am perfectly willing to act as business manager to the Franco-Midland Hardware Company, Limited, at a minimum salary of £500.'"

'I did as he asked, and he put the paper in his pocket.

'"There is one other detail," said he. "What do you intend to do about Mawson's?"

'I had forgotten all about Mawson's in my joy. "I'll write and resign," said I.

'"Precisely what I don't want you to do. I had a row over you with Mawson's manager. I had gone up to ask him about you, and he was very offensive; accused me of coaxing you away from the service of the firm, and that sort of thing. At last I fairly lost my temper. 'If you want good men you should pay them a good price,' said I. 'He would rather have our small price than your big one,' said he. 'I'll lay you a fiver,' said I, 'that when he has my offer you'll never so much as hear from him again.' 'Done!' said he. 'We picked him out of the gutter, and he won't leave us so easily.' Those were his very words."

'"The impudent scoundrel!" I cried. "I've never so much as seen him in my life. Why should I consider him in any way? I shall certainly not write if you would rather I didn't."

'"Good! That's a promise," said he, rising from his chair. 'Well, I'm delighted to have got so good a man for my brother. Here's your advance of a hundred pounds, and here is the letter. Make a note of the address, 126b Corporation Street, and remember that one o'clock tomorrow is your appointment. Good-night; and may you have all the fortune that you deserve!"

'That's just about all that passed between us, as near as I can remember. You can imagine, Dr Watson, how pleased I was at such an extraordinary bit of good fortune. I sat up half the night hugging myself over it, and next day I was off to Birmingham in a train that would take me in plenty of time for my appointment. I took my things to a hotel in New Street, and then I made my way to the address which had been given me.

'It was a quarter of an hour before my time, but I thought that would make no difference. 126b was a passage between two large shops, which led to a winding stone stair, from which there were many flats, let as offices to companies or professional men. The names of the occupants were painted at the bottom on the wall, but there was no such name as the Franco-Midland Hardware Company, Limited. I stood for a few minutes with my heart in my boots, wondering whether the whole thing was an elaborate hoax or not, when up came a man and addressed me. He was very like the chap I had seen the night before, the same figure and voice, but he was clean shaven and his hair was lighter.

'"Are you Mr Hall Pycroft?" he asked.

'"Yes," said I.

'"Oh! I was expecting you, but you are a trifle before your time. I had a note from my brother this morning in which he sang your praises very loudly."

'"I was just looking for the offices when you came."

'We have not got our name up yet, for we only secured these temporary premises last week. Come up with me, and we will talk the matter over.

'I followed him to the top of a very lofty stair, and there, right under the slates, were a couple of empty, dusty little rooms, uncarpeted and uncurtained, into which he led me. I had thought of a great office with shining tables and rows of clerks, such as I was used to, and I dare say I stared rather straight at the two deal chairs and one little table, which, with a ledger and a waste paper basket, made up the whole furniture.

'"Don't be disheartened, Mr Pycroft," said my new acquaintance, seeing the length of my face. "Rome was not built in a day, and we have lots of money at our backs, though we don't cut much dash yet in offices. Pray sit down, and let me have your letter."

'I gave it to him, and her read it over very carefully.

'"You seem to have made a vast impression upon my brother Arthur," said he; "and I know that he is a pretty shrewd judge. He swears by London, you know; and I by Birmingham; but this time I shall follow his advice. Pray consider yourself definitely engaged."

'"What are my duties?" I asked.

'"You will eventually manage the great depot in Paris, which will pour a flood of English crockery into the shops of a hundred and thirty-four agents in France. The purchase will be completed in a week, and meanwhile you will remain in Birmingham and make yourself useful."

'"How?"'

'For answer, he took a big red book out of a drawer.

'"This is a directory of Paris," said he, "with the trades after the names of the people. I want you to take it home with you, and to mark off all the hardware sellers, with their addresses. It would be of the greatest use to me to have them."

'"Surely there are classified lists?" I suggested.

'"Not reliable ones. Their system is different from ours. Stick at it, and let me have the lists by Monday, at twelve. Good-day, Mr Pycroft. If you continue to show zeal and intelligence you will find the company a good master."

'I went back to the hotel with the big book under my arm, and with very conflicting feelings in my breast. On the one hand, I was definitely engaged and had a hundred pounds in my pocket; on the other, the look of the offices, the absence of name on the wall, and other of the points which would strike a businessman had left a bad impression as to the position of my employers. However, come what might, I had my money, so I settled down to my task. All Sunday I was kept hard at work, and yet by Monday I had only got as far as H. I went round to my employer, found him in the same dismantled kind of room, and was told to keep at it until Wednesday, and then come again. On Wednesday it was still unfinished, so I hammered away until Friday – that is, yesterday. Then I brought it round to Mr Harry Pinner.

'"Thank you very much," said he; "I fear that I underrated the difficulty of the task. This list will be of very material assistance to me."

'"It took some time," said I.

'"And now," said he,"I want you to make a list of the furniture shops, for they all sell crockery."

'"Very good."

'"And you can come up tomorrow evening, at seven, and let me know how you are getting on. Don't overwork yourself. A couple of hours at Day's Music Hall in the evening would do you no harm after your labours." He laughed as he spoke, and I saw with a thrill that his second tooth upon the left-hand side had been very badly stuffed with gold.'

Sherlock Holmes rubbed his hands with delight, and I stared with astonishment at our client.

'You may well look surprised, Dr Watson; but it is this way,' said he: 'When I was speaking to the other chap in London, at the time that he laughed at my not going to Mawson's, I happened to notice that his tooth was stuffed in this very identical fashion. The glint of the gold in each case caught my eye, you see. When I put that with the voice and figure being the same, and only those things altered which might be changed by a razor or a wig, I could not doubt that it was the same man. Of course you expect two brothers to be alike, but not that they should have the same tooth stuffed in the same way. He bowed me out, and I found myself in the street, hardly knowing whether I was on my head or my heels. Back I went to my hotel, put my head in a basin of cold water, and tried to think it out. Why had he sent me from London to Birmingham? Why had he got there before me? And why had he written a letter from himself to himself? It was altogether too much for me, and I could make no sense of it. And then suddenly it struck me that what was dark to me might be very light to Mr Sherlock Holmes. I had just time to get up to town by the night train to see him this morning, and to bring you both back with me to Birmingham.'

There was a pause after the stockbroker's clerk had concluded his surprising experience. Then Sherlock Holmes cocked his eye at me, leaning back on the cushions with a pleased and yet critical face, like a connoisseur who has just taken his first sip of a comet vintage.

'Rather fine, Watson, is it not?' said he. 'There are points in it which please me. I think that you will agree with me that an interview with Mr Arthur Harry Pinner in the temporary offices of the Franco-Midland Hardware Company, Limited, would be a rather interesting experience for both of us.'

'But how can we do it?' I asked.

'Oh, easily enough,' said Hall Pycroft, cheerily. 'You are two friends of mine who are in want of a billet, and what could be more natural than that I should bring you both round to the managing director?'

'Quite so, of course,' said Holmes. 'I should like to have a look at the gentleman, and see if I can make anything of his little game. What qualities have you, my friend, which would make your services so valuable? or is it possible that –' He began biting his nails and staring blankly out of the window, and we hardly drew another word from him until we were in New Street.

At seven o'clock that evening we were walking, the three of us, down Corporation Street to the company's offices.

'It is no use our being at all before our time,' said our client. 'He only comes there to see me, apparently, for the place is deserted up to the very hour he names.'

'That is suggestive,' remarked Holmes.

'By Jove, I told you so!' cried the clerk. 'That's he walking ahead of us there.'

He pointed to a smallish, dark, well-dressed man who was bustling along the other side of the road. As we watched him he looked across at a boy who was bawling out the latest edition of the evening paper, and running over among the cabs and buses, he bought one from him. Then, clutching it in his hand, he vanished through a doorway.

'There he goes!' cried Hall Pycroft. 'These are the company's offices into which he has gone. Come with me, and I'll fix it up as easily as possible.'

Following his lead, we ascended five storeys, until we found ourselves outside a half-opened door, at which our client tapped. A voice within bade us enter, and we entered a bare, unfurnished room such as Hall Pycroft had described. At the single table sat the man whom we had seen in the street, with his evening paper spread out in front of him, and as he looked up at us it seemed to me that I had never looked upon a face which bore such marks of grief, and of something beyond grief – of a horror such as comes to few men in a lifetime. His brow glistened with perspiration, his cheeks were of the dull, dead white of a fish's belly, and his eyes were wild and staring. He looked at his clerk as though he failed to recognise him, and I could see by the astonishment depicted upon our conductor's face that this was by no means the usual appearance of his employer.

'You look ill, Mr Pinner!' he exclaimed.

'Yes, I am not very well,' answered the other, making obvious efforts to pull himself together, and licking his dry lips before he spoke. 'Who are these gentlemen whom you have brought with you?'

'One is Mr Harris, of Bermondsey, and the other is Mr Price, of this town,' said our clerk, glibly. 'They are friends of mine and gentlemen of experience, but they have been out of a place for some little time, and they hoped that perhaps you might find an opening for them in the company's employment.'

'Very possibly! Very possibly!' cried Mr Pinner with a ghastly smile. 'Yes, I have no doubt that we shall be able to do something for you. What is your particular line, Mr Harris?'

'I am an accountant,' said Holmes.

'Ah yes, we shall want something of the sort. And you, Mr Price?'

'A clerk,' said I.

'I have every hope that the company may accommodate you. I will let you know about it as soon as we come to any conclusion. And now I beg that you will go. For God's sake leave me to myself!'

These last words were shot out of him, as though the constraint which he was evidently setting upon himself had suddenly and utterly burst asunder. Holmes and I glanced at each other, and Hall Pycroft took a step towards the table.

'You forget, Mr Pinner, that I am here by appointment to receive some directions from you,' said he.

'Certainly, Mr Pycroft, certainly,' the other resumed in a calmer tone. 'You may wait here a moment; and there is no reason why your friends should not wait with you. I will be entirely at your service in three minutes, if I might trespass upon your patience so far.' He rose with a very courteous air, and, bowing to us, he passed out through a door at the farther end of the room, which he closed behind him.

'What now?' whispered Holmes. 'Is he giving us the slip?'

'Impossible,' answered Pycroft.

'Why so?'

'That door leads into an inner room.'

'There is no exit?'

'None.'

'Is it furnished?'

'It was empty yesterday.'

'Then what on earth can he be doing? There is something which I don't understand in his manner. If ever a man was three parts mad with terror, that man's name is Pinner. What can have put the shivers on him?'

'He suspects that we are detectives,' I suggested.

'That's it,' cried Pycroft.

Holmes shook his head. 'He did not turn pale. He was pale when we entered the room,' said he. 'It is just possible that –'

His words were interrupted by a sharp rat-tat from the direction of the inner door.

'What the deuce is he knocking at his own door for?' cried the clerk.

Again and much louder came the rat-tat-tat. We all gazed expectantly at the closed door. Glancing at Holmes, I saw his face turn rigid, and he leaned forward in intense excitement. Then suddenly came a low gurgling, gargling sound, and a brisk drumming upon woodwork. Holmes sprang frantically across the room and pushed at the door. It was fastened on the inner side. Following his example, we threw ourselves upon it with all our weight. One hinge snapped, then the other, and down came the door with a crash. Rushing over it, we found ourselves in the inner room. It was empty.

But it was only for a moment that we were at fault. At one corner, the corner nearest the room which we had left, there was a second door. Holmes sprang to it and pulled it open. A coat and waistcoat were lying on the floor, and from a hook behind the door, with his own braces round his neck, was hanging the managing director of the Franco-Midland Hardware Company. His knees were drawn up, his head hung at a dreadful angle to his body, and the clatter of his heels against the door made the noise which had broken in upon our conversation. In an instant I had caught him round the waist, and held him up while Holmes and Pycroft untied the elastic bands which had disappeared between the livid creases of skin. Then we carried him into the other room, where he lay with a clay-coloured face, puffing his purple lips in and out with every breath – a dreadful wreck of all that he had been but five minutes before.

'What do you think of him, Watson?' asked Holmes.

I stooped over him and examined him. His pulse was feeble and intermittent, but his breathing grew longer, and there was a little shivering of his eyelids, which showed a thin white slit of ball beneath.

'It has been touch and go with him,' said I, 'but he'll live now. Just open that window, and hand me the water carafe.' I undid his collar, poured the cold water over his face, and raised and sank his arms until he drew a long, natural breath. 'It's only a question of time now,' said I, as I turned away from him.

Holmes stood by the table, with his hands deep in his trouser pockets and his chin upon his breast.

'I suppose we ought to call the police in now,' said he. 'And yet I confess that I'd like to give them a complete case when they come.'

'It's a blessed mystery to me,' cried Pycroft, scratching his head. 'Whatever they wanted to bring me all the way up here for, and then –'

'Pooh! All that is clear enough,' said Holmes impatiently. 'It is this last sudden move.'

'You understand the rest, then?'

'I think that it is fairly obvious. What do you say, Watson?'

I shrugged my shoulders. 'I must confess that I am out of my depths,' said I.

'Oh surely if you consider the events at first they can only point to one conclusion.'

'What do you make of them?'

'Well, the whole thing hinges upon two points. The first is the making of Pycroft write a declaration by which he entered the service of this preposterous company. Do you not see how very suggestive that is?'

'I am afraid I miss the point.'

'Well, why did they want him to do it? Not as a business matter, for these arrangements are usually verbal, and there was no earthly business reason why this should be an exception. Don't you see, my young friend, that they were very anxious to obtain a specimen of your handwriting, and had no other way of doing it?'

'And why?'

'Quite so. Why? When we answer that we have made some progress with our little problem. Why? There can be only one adequate reason. Someone wanted to learn to imitate your writing, and had to procure a specimen of it first. And now if we pass on to the second point we find that each throws light upon the other. That point is the request made by Pinner that you should not resign your place, but should leave the manager of this important business in the full expectation that a Mr Hall Pycroft, whom he had never seen, was about to enter the office upon the Monday morning.'

'My God!' cried our client, 'what a blind beetle I have been!'

'Now you see the point about the handwriting. Suppose that someone turned up in your place who wrote a completely different hand from that in which you had applied for the vacancy, of course the game would have been up. But in the interval the rogue had learned to imitate you, and his position was therefore secure, as I presume that nobody in the office had ever set eyes upon you.'

'Not a soul,' groaned Hall Pycroft.

'Very good. Of course it was of the utmost importance to prevent you from thinking better of it, and also to keep you from coming into contact with anyone who might tell you that your double was at work in Mawson's office. Therefore they gave you a handsome advance on your salary, and ran you off to the Midlands, where they gave you enough work to do to prevent your going to London, where you might have burst their little game up. That is all plain enough.'

'But why should this man pretend to be his own brother?'

'Well, that is pretty clear also. There are evidently only two of them in it. The other is impersonating you at the office. This one acted as your engager, and then found that he could not find you an employer without admitting a third person into his plot. That he was most unwilling to do. He changed his appearance as far as he could, and trusted that the likeness, which you could not fail to observe, would be put down to a family resemblance. But for the happy chance of the gold stuffing, your suspicions would probably never have been aroused.'

Hall Pycroft shook his clenched hands in the air. 'Good Lord!' he cried, 'while I have been fooled in this way, what has this other Hall Pycroft been doing at Mawson's? What should we do, Mr Holmes? Tell me what to do.'

'We must wire to Mawson's.'

'They shut at twelve on Saturdays.'

'Never mind. There may be some doorkeeper or attendant –'

'Ah yes, they keep a permanent guard there on account of the value of the securities that they hold. I remember hearing it talked of in the City.'

'Very good; we shall wire to him, and see if all is well, and if a clerk of your name is working there. That is clear enough; but what is not so clear is why at sight of us one of the rogues should instantly walk out of the room and hang himself.'

'The paper!' croaked a voice behind us. The man was sitting up, blanched and ghastly, with returning reason in his eyes, and hands which rubbed nervously at the broad red band which still encircled his throat.

'The paper! Of course!' yelled Holmes, in a paroxysm of excitement. 'Idiot that I was! I thought so much of our visit that the paper never entered my head for an instant. To be sure, the secret must be there.' He flattened it out upon the table, and a cry of triumph burst from his lips. 'Look at this, Watson,' he cried. 'It is a London paper, an early edition of the *Evening Standard*. Here is what we want. Look at the headlines: "Crime in the City. Murder at Mawson & Williams's. Gigantic attempted Robbery. Capture of the Criminal." Here, Watson, we are all equally anxious to hear it, so kindly read it aloud to us.'

It appeared from its position in the paper to have been the one event of importance in town, and the account of it ran in this way:

'A desperate attempt at robbery, culminating in the death of one man and the capture of the criminal, occurred this afternoon in the City. For some time back Mawson & Williams, the famous financial house, have been the guardians of securities which amount in the aggregate to a sum of considerably over a million sterling. So conscious was the manager of the responsibility which devolved upon him in consequence of the great interests at stake that safes of the very latest construction have been employed, and an armed watchman has been left day and night in the building. It appears that last week a new clerk named Hall Pycroft was engaged by the firm. This person appears to have been none other than Beddington, the famous forger and cracksman, who, with his brother, had only recently emerged from a five years' spell of penal servitude. By some means, which are not yet clear, he succeeded in winning, under a false name, this official position in the office, which he utilised in order to obtain mouldings of various locks, and a thorough knowledge of the position of the strong-room and the safes.

'It is customary at Mawson's for the clerks to leave at midday on Saturday. Sergeant Tuson, of the City Police, was somewhat surprised, therefore, to see a gentleman with a carpet bag come down the steps at twenty minutes past one. His suspicions being aroused, the sergeant followed the man, and with the aid of Constable Pollock succeeded, after a most desperate resistance, in arresting him. It was at once clear that a daring and gigantic robbery had been committed. Nearly a hundred thousand pounds' worth of American railway bonds, with a large amount of scrip in mines and other companies, was discovered in the bag. On examining the premises the body of the unfortunate watchman was found doubled up and thrust into the largest of the safes, where it would not have been discovered until Monday morning had it not been for the prompt action of Sergeant Tuson. The man's skull had been shattered by a blow from a poker delivered from behind. There could be no doubt that Beddington had obtained entrance by pretending that he had left something behind him, and having murdered the watchman, rapidly rifled the large safe, and then made off with his booty. His brother, who usually works with him, has not appeared in this job as far as can at present be ascertained, although the police are making energetic enquiries as to his whereabouts.'

'Well, we may save the police some little trouble in that direction,' said Holmes, glancing at the haggard figure huddled up by the window. 'Human nature is a strange mixture, Watson. You see that even a villain and murderer can inspire such affection that his brother turns to suicide when he learns that his neck is forfeited. However, we have no choice as to our action. The doctor and I will remain on guard, Mr Pycroft, if you will have the kindness to step out for the police.'

The Adventure of
the *Gloria Scott*

'I have some papers here,' said my friend Sherlock Holmes, as we sat one winter's night on either side of the fire, 'which I really think, Watson, that it would be worth your while to glance over. These are the documents in the extraordinary case of the *Gloria Scott*, and this is the message which struck Justice of the Peace Trevor dead with horror when he read it.'

He had picked from a drawer a little tarnished cylinder, and, undoing the tape, he handed me a short note scrawled upon a half-sheet of slate-grey paper.

'The supply of game for London is going steadily up,' it ran. 'Head-keeper Hudson, we believe, has been now told to receive all orders for flypaper and for preservation of your hen-pheasant's life.'

As I glanced up from reading this enigmatical message, I saw Holmes chuckling at the expression upon my face.

'You look a little bewildered,' said he.

'I cannot see how such a message as this could inspire horror. It seems to me to be rather grotesque than otherwise.'

'Very likely. Yet the fact remains that the reader, who was a fine, robust old man, was knocked clean down by it as if it had been the butt end of a pistol.'

'You arouse my curiosity,' said I. 'But why did you say just now that there were very particular reasons why I should study this case?'

'Because it was the first in which I was ever engaged.'

I had often endeavoured to elicit from my companion what had first turned his mind in the direction of criminal research, but had never caught him before in a communicative humour. Now he sat forward in his armchair and spread out the documents upon his knees. Then he lit his pipe and sat for some time smoking and turn-ing them over.

'You never heard me talk of Victor Trevor?' he asked. 'He was the only friend I made during the two years I was at college. I was never a very sociable fellow, Watson, always rather fond of moping in my rooms and working out my own little methods of thought, so that I never mixed much with the men of my year. Bar fencing and boxing I had few athletic tastes, and then my line of study was quite distinct from that of the other fellows, so that we had no points of contact at all. Trevor was the only man I knew, and that only through the accident of his bull terrier freezing on to my ankle one morning as I went down to chapel.

'It was a prosaic way of forming a friendship, but it was effec-tive. I was laid by the heels for ten days, but Trevor used to come in to enquire after me. At first it was only a minute's chat, but soon his visits lengthened, and before the end of the term we were close friends. He was a hearty, full-blooded fellow, full of spirit and energy, the very opposite to me in most respects, but we had some subjects in common, and it was a bond of union when I found that he was as friendless as I. Finally, he invited me down to his father's place at Donnithorpe, in Norfolk, and I accepted his hospitality for a month of the long vacation.

'Old Trevor was evidently a man of some wealth and considera-tion, a J.P., and a landed proprietor. Donnithorpe is a little hamlet just to the north of Langmere, in the country of the Broads. The house was an old-fashioned, widespread, oak-beamed brick building, with a fine lime-lined avenue leading up to it. There was excellent wild-duck shooting in the fens, remarkably good fishing, a small but select library, taken over, as I understood, from a former occupant, and a tolerable cook, so that he would be a fastidious man who could not put in a pleasant month there.

'Trevor senior was a widower, and my friend his only son. There had been a daughter, I heard, but she had died of diphtheria while on a visit to Birmingham. The father interested me extremely. He was a man of little culture, but with a considerable amount of rude strength, both physically and mentally. He knew hardly any books, but he had travelled far, had seen much of the world. And had remembered all that he had learned. In person he was a thick-set, burly man with a shock of grizzled hair, a brown, weather-beaten face, and blue eyes which were keen to the verge of fierceness. Yet he had a reputation for kindness and charity on the countryside, and was noted for the leniency of his sentences from the bench.

'One evening, shortly after my arrival, we were sitting over a glass of port after dinner, when young Trevor began to talk about those habits of observation and inference which I had already formed into a system, although I had not yet appreciated the part which they were to play in my life. The old man evidently thought that his son was exaggerating in his description of one or two trivial feats which I had performed.

'"Come, now, Mr Holmes," said he, laughing good-humouredly. "I'm an excellent subject, if you can deduce anything from me."

'"I fear there is not very much," I answered; "I might suggest that you have gone about in fear of some personal attack within the last twelve months."

'The laugh faded from his lips, and he stared at me in great surprise.

'"Well, that's true enough," said he. "You know, Victor," turning to his son, "when we broke up that poaching gang they swore to knife us, and Sir Edward Holby has actually been attacked. I've always been on my guard since then, though I have no idea how you know it."

'"You have a very handsome stick," I answered. "By the inscription I observed that you had not had it more than a year. But you have taken some pains to bore the head of it and pour melted lead into the hole so as to make it a formidable weapon. I argued that you would not take such precautions unless you had some danger to fear."

'"Anything else?" he asked, smiling.

'"You have boxed a good deal in your youth."

'"Right again. How did you know it? Is my nose knocked a little out of the straight?"

'"No," said I. "It is your ears. They have the peculiar flattening and thickening which marks the boxing man."

'"Anything else?"

'"You have done a good deal of digging, by your callosities."

'"Made all my money at the gold fields."

'"You have been in New Zealand."

'"Right again."

'"You have visited Japan."

'"Quite true."

'"And you have been most intimately associated with someone whose initials were J. A., and whom you afterwards were eager to entirely forget."

'Mr Trevor stood slowly up, fixed his large blue eyes upon me with a strange wild stare, and then pitched forward, with his face among the nutshells which strewed the cloth, in a dead faint.

'You can imagine, Watson, how shocked both his son and I were. His attack did not last long, however, for when we undid his collar, and sprinkled the water from one of the finger-glasses over his face, he gave a gasp or two and sat up.

'"Ah, boys," said he, forcing a smile, "I hope I haven't frightened you. Strong as I look, there is a weak place in my heart, and it does not take much to knock me over. I don't know how you manage this, Mr Holmes, but it seems to me that all the detectives of fact and of fancy would be children in your hands. That's your line of life, sir, and you may take the word of a man who has seen something of the world."

'And that recommendation, with the exaggerated estimate of my ability with which he prefaced it, was, if you will believe me, Watson, the very first thing which ever made me feel that a profession might be made out of what had up to that time been the merest hobby. At the moment, however, I was too much concerned at the sudden illness of my host to think of anything else.

'"I hope that I have said nothing to pain you?" said I.

'"Well, you certainly touched upon rather a tender point. Might I ask how you know, and how much you know?" He spoke now in a half-jesting fashion, but a look of terror still lurked at the back of his eyes.

'"It is simplicity itself," said I. "When you bared your arm to draw that fish into the boat I saw that 'J. A.' had been tattooed in the bend of the elbow. The letters were still legible, but it was perfectly clear from their blurred appearance, and from the staining of the skin round them, that efforts had been made to obliterate them. It was obvious, then, that those initials had once been very familiar to you, and that you had afterwards wished to forget them."

'"What an eye you have!" he cried, with a sigh of relief. "It is just as you say. But we won't talk of it. Of all ghosts the ghosts of our old lovers are the worst. Come into the billiard-room and have a quiet cigar."

'From that day, amid all his cordiality, there was always a touch of suspicion in Mr Trevor's manner towards me. Even his son remarked it. "You've given the governor such a turn," said he, "that he'll never be sure again of what you know and what you don't know." He did not mean to show it, I am sure, but it was so strongly in his mind that it peeped out at every action. At last I became so convinced that I was causing him uneasiness that I drew my visit to a close. On the very day, however, before I left, an incident occurred which proved in the sequel to be of importance.

'We were sitting out upon the lawn on garden chairs, the three of us, basking in the sun and admiring the view across the Broads, when a maid came out to say that there was a man at the door who wanted to see Mr Trevor.

'"What is his name?" asked my host.

'"He would not give any."

'"What does he want, then?"

'"He says that you know him, and that he only wants a moment's conversation."

'"Show him round here." An instant afterwards there appeared a little wizened fellow with a cringing manner and a shambling style of walking. He wore an open jacket, with a splotch of tar on the sleeve, a red-and-black check shirt, dungaree trousers, and heavy boots badly worn. His face was thin and brown and crafty, with a perpetual smile upon it, which showed an irregular line of yellow teeth, and his crinkled hands were half closed in a way that is distinctive of sailors. As he came slouching across the lawn I heard Mr Trevor make a sort of hiccoughing noise in his throat, and jumping out of his chair, he ran into the house. He was back in a moment, and I smelt a strong reek of brandy as he passed me.

'"Well, my man," said he. "What can I do for you?"

'The sailor stood looking at him with puckered eyes, and with the same loose-lipped smile upon his face.

'"You don't know me?" he asked.

'"Why, dear me, it is surely Hudson," said Mr Trevor in a tone of surprise.

'"Hudson it is, sir," said the seaman. "Why, it's thirty year and more since I saw you last. Here you are in your house, and me still picking my salt meat out of the harness cask."

'"Tut, you will find that I have not forgotten old times," cried Mr Trevor, and, walking towards the sailor, he said something in a low voice. "Go into the kitchen," he continued out loud, "and you will get food and drink. I have no doubt that I shall find you a situation."

'"Thank you, sir," said the seaman, touching his forelock. "I'm just off a two-yearer in an eight-knot tramp, short-handed at that, and I wants a rest. I thought I'd get it either with Mr Beddoes or with you."

'"Ah!" cried Trevor. "You know where Mr Beddoes is?"

'"Bless you, sir, I know where all my old friends are," said the fellow with a sinister smile, and he slouched off after the maid to the kitchen. Mr Trevor mumbled something to us about having been shipmate with the man when he was going back to the diggings, and then, leaving us on the lawn, he went indoors. An hour later, when we entered the house, we found him stretched dead drunk upon the dining-room sofa. The whole incident left a most ugly impression upon my mind, and I was not sorry next day to leave Donnithorpe behind me, for I felt that my presence must be a source of embarrassment to my friend.

'All this occurred during the first month of the long vacation. I went up to my London rooms, where I spent seven weeks working out a few experiments in organic chemistry. On day, however, when the autumn was far advanced and the vacation drawing to a close, I received a telegram from my friend imploring me to return to Donnithorpe, and saying that he was in great need of my advice and assistance. Of course I dropped everything and set out for the North once more.

'He met me with the dog-cart at the station, and I saw at a glance that the last two months had been very trying ones for him. He had grown thin and careworn, and had lost the loud, cheery manner for which he had been remarkable.

'"The governor is dying," were the first words he said.

'"Impossible!" I cried. "What is the matter?"

'"Apoplexy. Nervous shock. He's been on the verge all day. I doubt if we shall find him alive."

'I was, as you may think, Watson, horrified at this unexpected news.

'"What has caused it?" I asked.

'"Ah, that is the point. Jump in and we can talk it over while we drive. You remember that fellow who came upon the evening before you left us?"

'"Perfectly."

'"Do you know who it was that we let into the house that day?"

'"I have no idea."

'"It was the devil, Holmes," he cried.

'I stared at him in astonishment.

'"Yes, it was the devil himself. We have not had a peaceful hour since – not one. The governor has never held up his head from that evening, and now the life has been crushed out of him and his heart broken, all through this accursed Hudson.'

'"What power had he, then?"

'"Ah, that is what I would give so much to know. The kindly, charitable, good old governor – how could he have fallen into the clutches of such a ruffian! But I am so glad that you have come, Holmes. I trust very much to your judgment and discretion, and I know that you will advise me for the best.'

'We were dashing along the smooth white country road, with the long stretch of the Broads in front of us glimmering in the red light of the setting sun. From a grove upon our left I could already see the high chimneys and the flagstaff which marked the squire's dwelling.

'"My father made the fellow gardener," said my companion, "and then, as that did not satisfy him, he was promoted to be butler. The house seemed to be at his mercy, and he wandered about and did what he chose in it. The maids complained of his drunken habits and his vile language. The dad raised their wages all round to recompense them for the annoyance. The fellow would take the boat and my father's best gun and treat himself to little shooting trips. And all this with such a sneering, leering, insolent face that I would have knocked him down twenty times over if he had been a man of my own age. I tell you, Holmes, I have had to keep a tight hold upon myself all this time; and now I am asking myself whether, if I had let myself go a little more, I might not have been a wiser man.

'"Well, matters went from bad to worse with us, and this animal Hudson became more and more intrusive, until at last, on making some insolent reply to my father in my presence one day, I took him by the shoulders and turned him out of the room. He slunk away with a livid face and two venomous eyes which uttered more threats than his tongue could do. I don't know what passed between the poor dad and him after that, but the dad came to me next day and asked me whether I would mind apologising to Hudson. I refused, as you can imagine, and asked my father how he could allow such a wretch to take such liberties with himself and his household.

'"'Ah, my boy,' said he, 'it is all very well to talk, but you don't know how I am placed. But you shall know, Victor. I'll see that you shall know, come what may. You wouldn't believe harm of your poor old father, would you, lad?' He was very much moved, and shut himself up in the study all day, where I could see through the window that he was writing busily.

STORIES FROM *THE MEMOIRS OF SHERLOCK HOLMES*

'"That evening there came what seemed to me to be a grand release, for Hudson told us that he was going to leave us. He walked into the dining-room as we sat after dinner, and announced his intention in the thick voice of a half-drunken man.

'"'I've had enough of Norfolk,' said he. 'I'll run down to Mr Beddoes in Hampshire. He'll be as glad to see me as you were, I dare say.'

'"'You're not going away in any kind of spirit, Hudson, I hope,' said my father, with a tameness which made my blood boil.

'"'I've not had my 'pology,' said he sulkily, glancing in my direction.

'"'Victor, you will acknowledge that you have used this worthy fellow rather roughly,' said the dad, turning to me.

'"'On the contrary, I think that we have both shown extraordinary patience towards him,' I answered.

'"'Oh, you do, do you?' he snarls. 'Very good, mate. We'll see about that!'

'"He slouched out of the room, and half an hour afterwards left the house, leaving my father in a state of pitiable nervousness. Night after night I heard him pacing his room, and it was just as he was recovering his confidence that the blow did at last fall."

'"And how?" I asked eagerly.

'"In a most extraordinary fashion. A letter arrived for my father yesterday evening, bearing the Fordingbridge postmark. My father read it, clapped both his hands to his head, and began running round the room in little circles like a man who has been driven out of his senses. When I at last drew him down on to the sofa, his mouth and eyelids were all puckered on one side, and I saw that he had a stroke. Dr Fordham came over at once. We put him to bed; but the paralysis has spread, he has shown no sign of returning consciousness, and I think that we shall hardly find him alive."

'"You horrify me, Trevor!" I cried. "What then could have been in this letter to cause so dreadful a result?"

'"Nothing. There lies the inexplicable part of it. The message was absurd and trivial. Ah, my God, it is as I feared!"

'As he spoke we came round the curve of the avenue, and saw in the fading light that every blind in the house had been drawn down. As we dashed up to the door, my friend's face convulsed with grief, a gentleman in black emerged from it.

'"When did it happen, doctor?" asked Trevor.

'"Almost immediately after you left."

'"Did he recover consciousness?"

'"For an instant before the end."

'"Any message for me?"

'"Only that the papers were in the back drawer of the Japanese cabinet."

'My friend ascended with the doctor to the chamber of death, while I remained in the study, turning the whole matter over and over in my head, and feeling as sombre as ever I had done in my life. What was the past of this Trevor, pugilist, traveller, and gold-digger, and how had he placed himself in the power of this acid-faced seaman? Why, too, should he faint at an allusion to the half-effaced initials upon his arm, and die of fright when he had a letter from Fordingham? Then I remembered that Fordingham was in Hampshire, and that this Mr Beddoes, whom the seaman had gone to visit and presumably to blackmail, had also been mentioned as living in Hampshire. The letter, then, might either come from Hudson, the seaman, saying that he had betrayed the guilty secret which appeared to exist, or it might come from Beddoes, warning an old confederate that such a betrayal was imminent. So far it seemed clear enough. But then how could this letter be trivial and grotesque, as described by the son? He must have misread it. If so, it must have been one of those ingenious secret codes which mean one thing while they seem to mean another. I must see this letter. If there were a hidden meaning in it, I was confident that I could pluck it forth. For an hour I sat pondering over it in the gloom, until at last a weeping maid brought in a lamp, and close at her heels came my friend Trevor, pale but composed, with these very papers which lie upon my knee held in his grasp. He sat down opposite to me, drew the lamp to the edge of the table, and handed me a short note scribbled, as you see, upon a single sheet of grey paper. "The supply of game for London is going steadily up," it ran. "Head-keeper Hudson, we believe, has been now told to receive all orders for flypaper and for preservation of your hen-pheasant's life."

'I dare say my face looked as bewildered as yours did just now when first I read this message. Then I reread it very carefully. It was evidently as I had thought, and some secret meaning must lie buried in this strange combination of words. Or could it be that there was a prearranged significance to such phrases as "flypaper" and "hen-pheasant"? Such a meaning would be arbitrary and could not be deduced in any way. And yet I was loath to believe that this was the case, and the presence of the word Hudson seemed to show that the subject of the message was as I had guessed, and that it was from Beddoes rather than the sailor. I tried it backwards, but the combination "life pheasant's hen" was not encouraging. Then I tried alternate words, but neither "the of for" nor "supply game London" promised to throw any light upon it.

'And then in an instant the key of the riddle was in my hands, and I saw that every third word, beginning with the first, would give a message which might well drive old Trevor to despair.

'It was short and terse, the warning, as I now read it to my companion:

'"The game is up. Hudson has told all. Fly for your life."

'Victor Trevor sank his face into his shaking hands. "It must be that, I suppose," said he. "This is worse than death, for it means disgrace as well. But what is the meaning of these 'head-keepers' and 'hen-pheasants'?"

'"It means nothing to the message, but it might mean a good deal to us if we had no other means of discovering the sender. You see that he has begun by writing 'The . . . game . . . is,' and so on. Afterwards he had, to fulfil the prearranged cipher, to fill in any two words in each space. He would naturally use the first words which came to his mind, and if there were so many which referred to sport among them, you may be tolerably sure that he is either an ardent shot or interested in breeding. Do you know anything of this Beddoes?"

'"Why, now that you mention it," said he, "I remember that my poor father used to have an invitation from him to shoot over his preserves every autumn."

'"Then it is undoubtedly from him that the note comes," said I. "It only remains for us to find out what this secret was which the sailor Hudson seems to have held over the heads of these two wealthy and respected men."

'"Alas, Holmes, I fear that it is one of sin and shame!" cried my friend. "But from you I shall have no secrets. Here is the statement which was drawn up by my father when he knew that the danger from Hudson had become imminent. I found it in the Japanese cabinet, as he told the doctor. Take it and read it to me, for I have neither the strength nor the courage to do it myself."

'These are the very papers, Watson, which he handed to me, and I will read them to you, as I read them in the old study that night to him. They are endorsed outside, as you see, "Some particulars of the voyage of the bark *Gloria Scott*, from her leaving Falmouth on the 8th October, 1855, to her destruction in N. Lat. 15° 20', W. Long. 25° 14' on November 6th.' It is in the form of a letter, and runs in this way:

'"My dear, dear son, now that approaching disgrace begins to darken the closing years of my life, I can write with all truth and honesty that it is not the terror of the law, it is not the loss of my position in the county, nor is it my fall in the eyes of all who have known me, which cuts me to the heart; but it is the thought that you should come to blush for me – you who love me and who have seldom, I hope, had reason to do other than respect me. But if the blow falls which is for ever hanging over me, then I should wish you to read this, that you may know straight from me how far I have been to blame. On the other hand, if all should go well (which may kind God Almighty grant!), then if by any chance this paper should be still undestroyed and should fall into your hands, I conjure you, by all you hold sacred, by the memory of your dear mother, and by the love which had been between us, to hurl it into the fire and to never give one thought to it again.

"'If then your eye goes on to read this line, I know that I shall already have been exposed and dragged from my home, or as is more likely, for you know that my heart is weak, by lying with my tongue sealed for ever in death. In either case the time for suppression is past, and every word which I tell you is the naked truth, and this I swear as I hope for mercy.

"'My name, dear lad, is not Trevor. I was James Armitage in my younger days, and you can understand now the shock that it was to me a few weeks ago when your college friend addressed me in words which seemed to imply that he had surprised my secret. As Armitage it was that I entered a London banking-house, and as Armitage I was convicted of breaking my country's laws, and was sentenced to transportation. Do not think very harshly of me, laddie. It was a debt of honour, so called, which I had to pay, and I used money which was not my own to do it, in the certainty that I could replace it before there could be any possibility of its being missed. But the most dreadful ill-luck pursued me. The money which I had reckoned upon never came to hand, and a premature examination of accounts exposed my deficit. The case might have been dealt leniently with, but the laws were more harshly administered thirty years ago than now, and on my twenty-third birthday I found myself chained as a felon with thirty-seven other convicts in the 'tween-decks of the bark *Gloria Scott*, bound for Australia.

"'It was the year 1855, when the Crimean war was at its height, and the old convict ships had been largely used as transports in the Black Sea. The government was compelled, therefore, to use smaller and less suitable vessels for sending out their prisoners. The *Gloria Scott* had been in the Chinese tea-trade, but she was an old-fashioned, heavy-bowed, broad-beamed craft, and the new clippers had cut her out. She was a five-hundred-ton boat; and besides her thirty-eight gaolbirds, she carried twenty-six of a crew, eighteen soldiers, a captain, three mates, a doctor, a chaplain, and four warders. Nearly a hundred souls were in her, all told, when we set sail from Falmouth.

"'The partitions between the cells of the convicts, instead of being of thick oak, as is usual in convict-ships, were quite thin and frail. The man next to me, upon the aft side, was one whom I had particularly noticed when we were led down the quay. He was a young man with a clear, hairless face, a long, thin nose, and rather nutcracker jaws. He carried his head very jauntily in the air, had a swaggering style of walking, and was, above all else, remarkable for his extraordinary height. I don't think any of our heads would have come up to his shoulder, and I am sure that he could not have measured less than six and a half feet. It was strange among so many sad and weary faces to see one which was full of energy and resolution. The sight of it was to me like a fire in a snowstorm. I was glad, then, to find that he was my neighbour, and gladder still when, in the dead of the night, I heard a whisper close to my ear, and found that he had managed to cut an opening in the board which separated us.

"'"Hullo, chummy!' said he, 'what's your name, and what are you here for?'

"'I answered him, and asked in turn who I was talking with.

"'"I'm Jack Prendergast,' said he, 'and by God! You'll learn to bless my name before you've done with me.'

"'I remembered hearing of his case, for it was one which had made an immense sensation throughout the country some time before my own arrest. He was a man of good family and of great ability, but of incurably vicious habits, who had, by an ingenious system of fraud, obtained huge sums of money from the leading London merchants.

"'"Ha, ha! You remember my case!' said he proudly.

"'"Very well indeed.'

"'"Then maybe you remember something queer about it?'

"'"What was that, then?'

"'"I'd had nearly a quarter of a million, hadn't I?'

"'"So it was said.'

'"'But none was recovered, eh?'

'"'No.'

'"'Well, where d'ye suppose the balance is?' he asked.

'"'I have no idea,' said I.

'"'Right between my finger and thumb,' he cried. 'By God! I've got more pounds to my name than you've hairs on your head. And if you've money, my son, and know how to handle it and spread it, you can do anything. Now, you don't think it likely that a man who could do anything is going to wear his breeches out sitting in the stinking hold of a rat-gutted, beetle-ridden, mouldy old coffin of a China coaster? No, sir, such a man will look after himself and will look after his chums. You may lay to that! You hold on to him, and you may kiss the Book that he'll haul you through.'

'"That was his style of talk, and at first I thought it meant nothing; but after a while, when he had tested me and sworn me in with all possible solemnity, he let me understand that there really was a plot to gain command of the vessel. A dozen of the prisoners had hatched it before they came aboard, Prendergast was the leader, and his money was the motive power.

'"'I'd a partner,' said he, 'a rare good man, as true as a stock to a barrel. He's got the dibbs, he has, and where do you think he is at this moment? Why, he's the chaplain of this ship – the chaplain, no less! He came aboard with a black coat, and his papers right, and money enough in his box to buy the thing right up from keel to main-truck. The crew are his, body and soul. He could buy 'em at so much a gross with a cash discount, and he did it before ever they signed on. He's got two of the warders and Mercer, the second mate, and he'd get the captain himself, if he thought him worth it.'

'"'What are we to do, then?' I asked.

'"'What do you think?' said he. 'We'll make the coats of some of these soldiers redder than ever the tailor did.'

'"'But they are armed,' said I.

'"'And so shall we be, my boy. There's a brace of pistols for every mother's son of us, and if we can't carry this ship, with the crew at our back, it's time we were all sent to a young misses' boarding-school. You speak to your mate upon the left tonight, and see if he is to be trusted.'

'"I did so, and found my other neighbour to be a young fellow in much the same position as myself, whose crime had been forgery. His name was Evans, but he afterwards changed it, like myself, and he is now a rich and prosperous man in the south of England. He was ready enough to join the conspiracy, as the only means of saving ourselves, and before we had crossed the Bay there were only two of the prisoners who were not in the secret. One of these was of weak mind, and we did not dare to trust him, and the other was suffering from jaundice, and could not be of any use to us.

'"From the beginning there was really nothing to prevent us from taking possession of the ship. The crew were a set of ruffians, specially picked for the job. The sham chaplain came into our cells to exhort us, carrying a black bag, supposed to be full of tracts, and so often did he come that by the third day we had each stowed away at the foot of our beds a file, a brace of pistols, a pound of powder, and twenty slugs. Two of the warders were agents of Prendergast, and the second mate was his right-hand man. The captain, the two mates, two warders, Lieutenant Martin, his eighteen soldiers, and the doctor were all that we had against us. Yet, safe as it was, we determined to neglect no precaution, and to make our attack suddenly by night. It came, however, more quickly than we expected, and in this way.

'"One evening, about the third week after our start, the doctor had come down to see one of the prisoners who was ill, and putting his hand down on the bottom of his bunk he felt the outline of the pistols. If he had been silent he might have blown the whole thing, but he was a nervous little chap, so he gave a cry of surprise and turned so pale that the man knew what was up in an instant and seized him. He was gagged before he could give the alarm, and tied down upon the bed. He had unlocked the door that led to the deck, and we were through it in a rush. The two sentries were shot down, and so was a corporal who came running to see what was the matter. There were two more soldiers at the door of the stateroom, and their muskets seemed not to be loaded, for they never fired upon us, and they were shot while trying to fix their bayonets. Then we rushed on into the captain's cabin, but as we pushed open the door there was an explosion from within, and there he lay with his brains smeared over the chart of the Atlantic which was pinned upon the table, while the chaplain stood with a smoking pistol in his hand at his elbow. The two mates had both been seized by the crew, and the whole business seemed to be settled.

'"The stateroom was next the cabin, and we flocked in there and flopped down on the settees, all speaking together, for we were just mad with the feeling that we were free once more. There were lockers all round, and Wilson, the sham chaplain, knocked one of them in, and pulled out a dozen of brown sherry. We cracked off the necks of the bottles, poured the stuff out into tumblers, and were just tossing them off, when in an instant without warning there came the roar of muskets in our ears, and the saloon was so full of smoke that we could not see across the table. When it cleared again the place was a shambles. Wilson and eight others were wriggling on the top of each other on the floor, and the blood and the brown sherry on that table turn me sick now when I think of it. We were so cowed by the sight that I think we should have given the job up if it had not been for Prendergast. He bellowed like a bull and rushed for the door with all that were left alive at his heels. Out we ran, and there on the poop were the lieutenant and ten of his men. The swing skylights above the saloon table had been a bit open, and they had fired on us through the slit. We got on them before they could load, and they stood to it like men; but we had the upper hand of them, and in five minutes it was all over. My God! Was there ever a slaughterhouse like that ship! Prendergast was like a raging devil, and he picked the soldiers up as if they had been children and threw them overboard alive or dead. There was one sergeant that was horribly wounded and yet kept on swimming for a surprising time, until someone in mercy blew out his brains. When the fighting was over there was no one left of our enemies except just the warders, the mates, and the doctor.

'"It was over them that the great quarrel arose. There were many of us who were glad enough to win back our freedom, and yet who had no wish to have murder on our souls. It was one thing to knock the soldiers over with their muskets in their hands, and it was another to stand by while men were being killed in cold blood. Eight of us, five convicts and three sailors, said that we would not see it done. But there was no moving Prendergast and those who were with him. Our only chance of safety lay in making a clean job of it, said he, and he would not leave a tongue with power to wag in a witness-box. It nearly came to our sharing the fate of the prisoners, but at last he said that if we wished we might take a boat and go. We jumped at the offer, for we were already sick of these bloodthirsty doings, and we saw that there would be worse before it was done. We were given a suit of sailor togs each, a barrel of water, two casks, one of junk and one of biscuits, and a compass. Prendergast threw us over a chart, told us that we were ship-wrecked mariners whose ship had foundered in lat. 15° N. and long. 25° W., and then cut the painter and let us go.

'"And now I come to the most surprising part of my story, my dear son. The seamen had hauled the fore-yard aback during the rising, but now as we left them they brought it square again, and as there was a light wind from the north and east the bark began to draw slowly away from us. Our boat lay, rising and falling, upon the long, smooth roll-ers, and Evans and I, who were the most educated of the party, were sitting in the sheets working out our position and planning what coast we should make for. It was a nice question, for the Cape de Verds was about five hundred miles to the north of us, and the African coast about seven hundred to the east. On the whole, as the wind was coming round to the north, we thought that Sierra Leone might be best, and turned our head in that direction, the bark being at that time nearly hull down on our starboard quarter. Suddenly as we looked at her we saw a dense black cloud of smoke shoot up from her, which hung like a monstrous tree upon the skyline. A few seconds later a roar like thunder burst upon our ears, and as the smoke thinned away there was no sign left of the *Gloria Scott*. In an instant we swept the boat's head round again and pulled with all our strength for the place where the haze still trailing over the water marked the scene of this catastrophe.

'"It was a long hour before we reached it, and at first we feared that we had come too late to save anyone. A splintered boat and a number of crates and fragments of spars rising and falling on the waves showed us where the vessel had foundered; but there was no sign of life, and we had turned away in despair when we heard a cry for help, and saw at some distance a piece of wreckage with a man lying stretched across it. When we pulled him aboard the boat he proved to be a young seaman of the name of Hudson, who was so burned and exhausted that he could give us no account of what had happened until the following morning.

'"It seemed that after we had left, Prendergast and his gang had proceeded to put to death the five remaining prisoners. The two warders had been shot and thrown overboard, and so also had the third mate. Prendergast then descended into the 'tween-decks and with his own hands cut the throat of the unfortunate surgeon. There only remained the first mate, who was a bold and active man. When he saw the convict approaching him with the bloody knife in his hand he kicked off his bonds, which he had somehow contrived to loosen, and rushing down the deck he plunged into the after-hold. A dozen convicts, who descended with their pistols in search of him, found him with a matchbox in his hand seated beside an open powder-barrel, which was one of a hundred carried on board, and swearing that he would blow all hands up if he were in any way molested. An instant later the explosion occurred, though Hudson thought it was caused by the misdirected bullet of one of the convicts rather than the mate's match. Be the cause what it may, it was the end of the *Gloria Scott* and of the rabble who held command of her.

'"Such, in a few words, my dear boy, is the history of this terrible business in which I was involved. Next day we were picked up by the brig *Hotspur*, bound for Australia, whose captain found no difficulty in believing that we were the survivors of a passenger ship which had foundered. The transport ship *Gloria Scott* was set down by the Admiralty as being lost at sea, and no word has ever leaked out as to her true fate. After an excellent voyage the *Hotspur* landed us at Sydney, where Evans and I changed our names and made our way to the diggings, where, among the crowds who were gathered from all nations, we had no difficulty in losing our former identities.

'"The rest I need not relate. We prospered, we travelled, we came back as rich colonials to England, and we bought country estates. For more than twenty years we have led peaceful and useful lives, and we hoped that our past was for ever buried. Imagine, then, my feelings when in the seaman who came to us I recognised instantly the man who had been picked off the wreck. He had tracked us down somehow, and had set himself to live upon our fears. You will understand now how it was that I strove to keep the peace with him, and you will in some measure sympathise with me in the fears which fill me, now that he has gone from me to his other victim with threats upon his tongue."

'Underneath is written in a hand so shaky as to be hardly legible, "Beddoes writes in cipher to say H. has told all. Sweet Lord, have mercy on our souls!"

'That was the narrative which I read that night to young Trevor, and I think, Watson, that under the circumstances it was a dramatic one. The good fellow was heartbroken at it, and went out to the Terai tea planting, where I hear that he is doing well. As to the sailor and Beddoes, neither of them was ever heard of again after that day on which the letter of warning was written. They both disappeared utterly and completely. No complaint had been lodged with the police, so that Beddoes had mistaken a threat for a deed. Hudson had been seen lurking about, and it was believed by the police that he had done away with Beddoes and had fled. For myself I believe that the truth was exactly the opposite. I think that it is most probable that Beddoes, pushed to desperation and believing himself to have been already betrayed, had revenged himself upon Hudson, and had fled from the country with as much money as he could lay his hands on. Those are the facts of the case, doctor, and if they are of any use to your collection, I am sure that they are very heartily at your service.'